## THE TURNING POINT:
## FROM MALPRACTICE TO MURDER

The deep guttural sound of a wide-open carburetor sucking air and the whine of an engine at high RPM was totally out of place on the quiet rural road. Jonathan was jogging, and instinct told him to move and move fast. Yet the fear of imminent danger seemed to numb and immobilize his body as he, as if in slow motion, stepped—then dove—for the side of the road. No sooner had he begun his leap when he felt a painful blow shoot deep into his right thigh and throw him helplessly, rolling over and over into the roadside dirt and weeds. . . .

All the nagging doubts were gone. For the first time since he had been retained by Ruth Feinerman he knew the truth about Aaron's death. Aaron had been murdered and *he* was to be the killer's next victim.

## A QUESTION OF JUDGMENT

# A QUESTION OF JUDGMENT

## TERENCE MIX
### AND
## VICTOR J. ROSEN

BANTAM BOOKS
TORONTO • NEW YORK • LONDON • SYDNEY • AUCKLAND

A QUESTION OF JUDGMENT

*A Bantam Book / November 1985*

ISBN 0-553-25249-6

*Published simultaneously in the United States and Canada*

---

*Bantam Books are published by Bantam Books, Inc. Its*
*trademark, consisting of the words "Bantam Books" and the*
*portrayal of a rooster, is Registered in U.S. Patent and*
*Trademark Office and in other countries. Marca Registrada.*
*Bantam Books, Inc., 666 Fifth Avenue, New York, New York*
*10103.*

---

PRINTED IN THE UNITED STATES OF AMERICA

O    0 9 8 7 6 5 4 3 2 1

# Acknowledgments

Special thanks to my former law partner, Steven Hall, without whose counseling, contributions, and encouragement this first novel would never have been completed.

I would also like to express my deepest appreciation to my wife, Janet, for her continued love, patience and understanding throughout this literary effort.

—Terence Mix

# Chapter I

Wednesday, June 13, 1979

The old man stepped into the damp night air, then turned and locked the double glass doors behind him. Inside, the lights of the lobby were turned low and gave a glow to the recently waxed terrazzo floor. For a moment he allowed himself a prideful smile. A job worth doing was worth doing well. The work ethic had never left him. Maybe everything else, but not that.

He tugged at the handle a couple of times to ensure that the deadbolt was securely in place, then turned again and pulled up the frayed collar of his worn, stained overcoat. A heavy, drifting fog seemed to swallow the stairs below.

Suddenly he was overcome by a chill that penetrated to the depths of his soul. It came without warning and almost took his breath away. With trembling hands he clumsily fastened the top button of his coat.

The gravity of his decision had finally come home.

No one knew. No one could possibly know. He had used the utmost care. The risks had been kept to a minimum. There was absolutely nothing to fear. The reassurances kept racing through his mind.

But the peace he sought eluded him. Once he had pulled open the file drawer, the commitment had been made. There was no turning back. At the very moment he had seen the name, he had intruded on sacred ground, and sooner or later knowledge of his violation would surface. Once, he might have been able to conceal his guilt, but not now. His emotional control had been reduced to a thread.

With a quivering hand he fumbled into his pocket for the pint of courage he carried there, and promptly emptied it by a quarter. As always, it gave him the crutch he craved. He capped and returned the bottle to his pocket and wiped the

1

residue from his lips with a sweep of his sleeve. Now was the time. If it were going to be done, it had to be now.

The old man descended the seven concrete steps to the damp sidewalk. He walked with a pronounced limp, favoring the artificial joint in his left hip and grimacing from the pain. Twelve years ago he had fallen down another flight of stairs in a drunken stupor and had shattered his hip.

Times had been better then in spite of his recent divorce. After all, he'd still been a salesman for one of the largest life-insurance companies in the country. He'd been one of their best salesmen on the East Coast. As long as a man had a good job, he could deal with any contingency. Above all else, he had to provide. That was the man's role.

But it was this very conviction that had led to the erosion of his marriage—and had made him a stranger to his daughters. He had been a provider, and a good one, but not a husband and father.

It was not long after their departure that he'd begun to appreciate the loss. That's when the drinking had started.

His staggering gait quickened as he thought of the warmth and security of his apartment only three blocks away. By the time he had reached the first corner and turned he was winded. Anxiety was draining his energy.

He heard a dog's bark but could not determine where it came from. Instinctively he looked back, only to be startled by something he thought he saw. Had he really seen it? He swallowed more cheap bourbon and returned the bottle to his pocket.

Why would anyone bother with him, a tired old janitor with a buried past? Obviously, his imagination was running away. He had to regain control now.

He pushed on at an even faster pace. The pain in his hip was sharper, driving deeper, causing him to drag the tip of his shoe. His breathing quickened.

How would the doctor react to the phone call? The old man would be asking for money. But after all, he would also be selling information that could save the doctor's life. Why would he be hostile? He should be thankful that someone was willing to take the risk to warn him—even if it *was* expensive. And if he refused to pay? What the hell, he'd probably tell him anyway.

The apartment seemed so far away. Had he made his turn

after one block or two? Was he on the right street? Was he . . . was he hearing footsteps?

He stopped and listened, leaning against the wall of a brownstone. There was no sound other than that of his heavy breathing. There was absolutely nothing to fear. As far as anyone knew, he had just finished his job and was walking back to his room exactly as he had been doing six nights a week for the past three and a half years.

Except . . . to his right there seemed to be something standing tall and erect, almost defiantly, in the fog. He stepped cautiously in its direction, not knowing what to expect. His breathing had now almost stopped. He leaned forward, ready to react.

Almost magically, the fog lifted and revealed a familiar sight—a telephone booth. He rushed forward and embraced it like a long-lost friend, leaning his face against the cold wet glass. Its familiarity offered him a sense of security, a temporary sanctuary from his plight—real or imagined. Stumbling inside, he collapsed onto the small bench seat and slammed the door. All he needed now was a few minutes to recapture his breath—and time to regain his sanity.

Panting and rubbing his hip, his glance drifted up to the black telephone receiver. If destiny had provided this shelter, it had also supplied him with a telephone. Maybe the time had arrived for placing the call. Maybe it was never meant that he use his own phone. Maybe his own telephone had been tapped.

The old man nodded. He knew what he had to do and that it had to be now. How should he identify himself? He obviously could not give the doctor his correct name. But then how would he maintain any credibility?

He pulled a piece of paper from his overcoat and unfolded it. He looked at the name and tried to imagine the face it belonged to. He wondered how such a man would react to a strange telephone call in the middle of the night. Could he make the man realize the danger he was facing?

The old man dropped a dime in the slot and listened to it activate the dial tone; then dialed the long-distance number.

Suddenly the door behind him exploded open. Instinctively he turned in its direction. Something hard slammed into his face with a numbing thud. Stunned, he dropped to his knees. He stared at the concrete floor. This couldn't possibly be real. It was too terrifying to be anything other than a nightmare. The strange but unmistakable taste of blood filled his mouth and his hand rose to investigate the burning sensation on his lip, but was intercepted and pulled down and then up behind his back with one sweeping motion. A searing pain tore through his shoulder, impelling him to scream out, only to be silenced by a muscular arm thrust up under his chin from behind. Gagging, he was pulled helplessly into the cold damp air. With his free hand he pulled at the arm locked like a vise around his neck, but to no avail. He was in the grip of a professional. Out of desperation he reached up, not knowing what he could grab—an eye, a nose, a mouth—anything vital. His effort was rewarded with a handful of heavy, damp hair, which he promptly yanked with all his remaining strength.

"Bastard!" screamed the assailant, in a slight but discernible accent. The old man's easy mark had actually inflicted pain; the assailant retaliated by thrusting the old man's arm even higher up his back, until he heard the sharp snap of a joint being dislocated.

The old man's eyes flooded with tears and his legs collapsed beneath him like those of a rag doll. A wave of nausea threatened to make him regurgitate the roast-beef sandwich he had eaten two hours earlier. He was beyond fighting now. His arm and head hung limply as his body was dragged across the sidewalk to the curb, where assailant and victim came to a stop.

The old man began to drift into unconsciousness, but the remaining glimmer of his will to live would not allow it to happen. His survival might depend on his awareness now. He instinctively knew that once he went under, that would be the end.

In the distance he heard the labored moan of something mechanical. His eyes fluttered open. Behind him, his attacker stood silently, holding him in an iron grip.

Now he could see two fuzzy circles of light accompanying the sound of a large vehicle.

Suddenly the old janitor realized what was to happen. His face twisted in horror as he attempted his final plea.

"O merciful heaven, no! God, man, please! I know nothing! I swear! Please, for God's sake, don't—"

His body was thrust forward into the path of the

municipal bus completing its final run of the evening. Defensively he reached out with his uninjured arm, only to be struck by the headlight and knocked from his feet like a solitary pin in a bowling alley. The right front tire of the bus hit his foot and climbed up his leg and over his chest, flattening the cavity to one-fourth its normal size.

The bus driver attempted to apply his brakes but was unable to do so before the rear tires passed over the old man. Fifty feet farther down the street the bus came to a stop.

The panicked driver found the crumpled body of the janitor at the curb. Only the odor from a shattered bottle of bourbon offered a mute explanation for the tragedy.

In the shadow of a nearby alley, a powerfully built man flicked a cigarette lighter and held it up near a small piece of paper. On it was a scribbled phone number and the name Aaron Feinerman, M.D. Raising the flame to the bottom of the paper, he watched it burn.

A man who found pleasure in his work, his normally stoic features relaxed in a momentary grin. It had been a clean and efficient job.

# Chapter II

*Friday, June 15, 1979*

Jonathan Rand sat on the edge of his bed looking at the clock on the nightstand. It was 6:07, and the darkness in the apartment was just beginning to dissipate. Weakly he reached over and pushed in the alarm plunger. As usual, he had awakened thirty minutes before the clock growled out its scheduled 6:30 reminder. Jonathan yawned and ran his fingers through his blond hair. His eyes burned from lack of sleep. Even when he retired late, he still woke at the blasted hour of 6:00.

With a sigh of disgust, he closed his eyes and began to ponder the day ahead. His mind groped through the myriad of legal matters he had been working on that week. A nine-o'clock motion in front of Judge Brandish. The Steinberg case. A motion for summary judgment—that was it.

Jonathan yawned again, stretched, thought of the notes he still had to review, and silently cursed.

Mustering the necessary energy, he struggled up and looked back at the form nestled under the sheet on the other side of the king-sized bed. It caught him by surprise and for a moment he forgot who she was. Then he remembered. Rachel Hennessy, from Rabin, Stein, and Burroughs. The cute little legal secretary. His mind flashed back to the activities of the preceding evening. How could he possibly have forgotten last night?

Shaking his head, Jonathan continued into the bathroom, where he splashed cold water onto his face. A one-day growth of dark stubble covered his face. A few traces of red branched around his otherwise clear blue eyes.

*Got to get glasses,* he thought, noticing the fine red lines. Seven years of college and law school and ten years of practice had finally taken their toll. He thought about making an appointment with an ophthalmologist next week, but couldn't convince himself. Maybe it would help if he started getting more sleep. He was certainly disciplined enough to do it.

Jonathan Rand met every goal with a determination that bordered on compulsiveness, a trait that was largely responsible for pulling him through the ordeal of law school. But, along with his ability to commit to a goal, Jonathan had an unyielding streak of stubbornness. And that meant he would probably be walking into walls before he bought glasses.

This very same character flaw had been responsible for drawing Jonathan into a number of altercations with certain judges and opposing counsel. "Wisdom should not only tell you how to use your mouth, Counsel, but also when to keep it shut," he had once been told by a red-faced judge. "I heard your argument and I don't agree with it. So zip it shut and sit down."

However, while it frustrated and angered members of the judiciary and bar, Jonathan's persistence was the cornerstone of his success in the courtroom. Representing a client demanded nothing less than total commitment; *can't* and *impossible* were words that seldom found their way into his vocabulary and the more difficult cases seemed to draw out the best of his talents.

Reared on a farm in Kansas, Jonathan was not gifted with

eloquence and polish. But, with his aggressive street-fighter style of going after an opponent, he had acquired an amazingly large number of scalps on his victory belt. While others used finesse, Jonathan fought his way right to the core of a point and hammered it home. And although this frequently stimulated the ire of an adversary, it just as often brought favor from juries. His firebrand way of going after a witness came across as nothing more than a "dang" and "darn" type of farm-boy honesty, and juries saw his methods as open, honest, and sincere—as well as colorful and entertaining.

Jonathan wiped a few drops of water from the mirror, neatly folded the towel, and returned it to the rack, centering it exactly in the middle. He then slipped into his sweatsuit, then made his way back to the bedroom. Rachel had changed position but was still sound asleep. *Should I . . . ? No. Let her be. I'll wake her when I get back.*

Five minutes later Jonathan's 1975 Cadillac Coupe de Ville slowed to a stop alongside a rural two-lane stretch of road outside Stratford, Connecticut. The misty road was tree lined, cutting across a number of heavily wooded low-lying hills.

It was a new course, longer and more demanding: 4.8 miles of torturous ups and downs, concluding with a quarter-mile four-percent grade cresting back at the point of origin. This was Jonathan's third attempt to meet his newest challenge. The first two times, he had failed halfway up the final grade, winded, his legs near collapse. But this time it was going to be different.

He began his morning ritual by stretching, pulling, twisting, limbering up his relaxed muscles. Then, with the efficiency of a machine, he sat down and teetered back and forth through fifty sit-ups, then a like number of push-ups.

Ready to run, he began striding out at a six-minute-mile pace, arms bent at the elbows, rhythmically rocking with his smooth powerful stride, hands loosely clenched.

Jonathan was strikingly handsome in a rugged way, with a determined-looking square jaw and a slight bump on his nose, which had been broken while he was playing defensive halfback in high school. He stood six-foot-one and weighed 180 pounds. He had the lean, sculptured body of an athlete. His forearms were very muscular, the result of years of loading hay bales.

It had not been an easy decision to leave his home in

Lawrence, Kansas, seventeen years earlier. The University of
Kansas had offered him a full football scholarship, which meant
that he could spend most weekends at home, working with his
father on the farm he would one day own.

But Penn State, the perennial powerhouse of the East
Coast, had also sought the services of Jonathan Rand. Jack
Teelman, a part-time scout for the Nittany Lions, had seen him
play and decided to take a chance. "A diamond in the rough,"
he had called Jonathan. "All you need is a little polishing. A
couple of years with the coaching staff back at University Park
and you'll be a consensus All-American."

For an eighteen-year-old high-school graduate who had
never traveled more than a hundred miles from home, it was
the opportunity of a lifetime.

It didn't take much to paint a tempting picture for the
wide-eyed youth. All-American could mean a lucrative contract with a professional football team. But, just as important, a
move to Pennsylvania meant a new life in a different part of the
country; a change, a chance to live in the city . . . and maybe
his only opportunity ever to get out of Lawrence.

Jonathan dreaded telling his father. Hiram Rand had
worked his farm twelve hours a day, six days a week, for
twenty-three years. He had toiled hard and proud over his
land and soon would own it outright. His dream was to be in
partnership with his only child. Jonathan would marry some
pretty little thing from school and put up his own farm on the
south sixty acres, probably next to the lean-to near Blackstone
Creek.

As Jonathan ran, the aroma of frying bacon through an
open window triggered the painful memory of his last day at
home. That last conversation with his father would forever
plague him.

"Pa, I've finally made up my mind about the football
scholarship."

Hiram's face looked hard. His skin had the baked and
weathered appearance of a man who had spent his entire life
outdoors; his wrinkles were deeply etched. He knew about
this Teelman fellow and had a nagging worry about what he
was about to hear. But, as always, he displayed no emotion.

"What's that, son?"

Jonathan looked down at the worn linoleum floor of the
kitchen. "I want you to know this hasn't been easy for

me. . . . I know what this farm means to you and . . . my being here. . . ." Jonathan still couldn't look up.

Anger began to boil inside as Hiram for the first time came face to face with his son's choice.

"Well, what is it? Spit it out, boy," he snapped.

Jonathan took a deep breath, exhaled, and looked his father straight in the eye.

"I'm going to Pennsylvania, Pa."

The words hit hard and Hiram's chest heaved. He was a quiet man and seldom angered, but when he did the roof would blow.

"So that's it, huh," he shouted. "I work my ass off for twenty-three years, and my son sticks up his nose. For twenty-three years I sweat so that one day I can give him this farm . . . this dream . . . and what does he do, this son of mine? He turns his back on me, that's what. Some glib-tongued back-alley carpetbagger comes into town, makes some silver promises, and my son can't wait to turn his back on his family."

Jonathan's mother, peeling potatoes at the sink, tried to intercede. "Please, Hiram, he's got every right to—"

"Stay out of this, Mildred. This is between me and the boy." Hiram's nostrils flared and the veins in his neck stood out like ridges.

Jonathan set his jaw and looked at his father with his typical determined glare. "That's the problem, Pa. You still see me as a *boy*. But you're wrong. I'm not a boy anymore, and I've got to make my own way."

"You want to make it on your own? That's fine with me. But you won't do it here. Not under my roof," he shouted. "I expect to see you out of here by tomorrow morning." Storming out of the kitchen, Hiram slammed the screen door and disappeared into the barn.

That was the last time Jonathan Rand had seen his father.

Moisture accumulated in Jonathan's eyes as the vision of his father faded into the long road ahead, but he passed it off as residue from the morning mist. Damned if he would ever cry about *him*. His father didn't want a son, so that's the way it would be.

Rachel blinked her eyes several times, then looked around the unfamiliar room. Where was she? Wasn't this a workday? Jonathan Rand. She remembered meeting him at Hagan's for cocktails, and it all came back. A mischievous smile creased her face, but disappeared when she turned her head to the right and saw the empty bed, the sheet thrown back. She looked at the clock; it was 7:10. Still plenty of time to get to work.

Rising to her elbows, she called out softly, "Jon?" There was no response.

She sat upright, holding the sheet around her neck. "Jon?" she called again, slightly louder. Still nothing.

Realizing that he was gone, she let the sheet fall from her nude body and rose from the bed. She had always been somewhat adventurous, but never before had she done anything like this. Meet a man at a bar and follow him home to spend the night in his bed. Shame on her. A proper girl from New Haven just didn't do something like that. Again she smiled at herself.

Rachel returned to the bedroom, stood in front of the large mirror over the dresser, and stared at her reflection. She had straight, raven-black hair that shone of cleanliness and hung halfway down her back. Her eyes were large and chocolate brown and, along with her upturned nose, cast a misleading aura of innocence. Although not promiscuous, she loved sex for the pure thrill and excitement of it. No pretense, no facade of purity. Just a "pure, unadulterated love of fucking," she admitted. But Rachel had one saving grace that appeased the conscience that lingered from her strict Catholic upbringing: she was highly selective about the men she slept with. Unless a man met her demanding standards, she had an absolute "hands off" policy. To her disappointment, this conviction had resulted in a ten-month celibacy—until she had met "Mister Gorgeous" on Tuesday.

Rachel's eyes lowered to her curvaceous torso. Her breasts were not large, but against her five-foot-one-inch frame they were conspicuous and frequently drew stares from the men at her office. This pleased and impelled her to tease and provoke by conveniently leaning over, stretching, arching just at the right moment. Flirting was always fun when it was safe.

She slowly drew her hands down over her breasts, depressing them and then watching them rise, the nipples standing out, tingling. Her hands moved lower, over her navel . . . and lower, trying to recapture the ecstasy of the night before. The hands were not hers. They were bigger and stronger. They were Jonathan's as they explored her delicate anatomy, preliminary to that moment for which she had waited ten long months. She closed her eyes and swallowed. Why wasn't he here now? Why had he left so damn early? Rachel reached even lower. Her mind flashed to Jonathan lying beneath her gyrating body. Again she swallowed, then took a deep breath that quivered when she exhaled. Maybe he would come back. Maybe she'd give him a call and they could see each other again tonight.

Rachel opened her eyes and the sight of her manipulating hand immediately drew her back to reality. She stopped, inhaled, slowly closed and opened her eyes, and thought of taking a shower—a cold one.

Jonathan's chest pounded. Perspiration flowed freely through his pores and cascaded down his forehead, his cheeks, his neck. He had almost reached his goal now. His car was waiting only a quarter mile away, as he began his ascent up the last grade, the final 1,320 feet of challenge. He was about to close the grueling rectangular course for the first time.

The sun had already climbed over the trees to the east and was casting its warmth onto his face. A large bead of sweat found its way into a corner of his right eye. Without breaking his pace, he eased the sleeve of his forearm up, mopped his eye, his brow. Just over a thousand feet now.

In April he had turned thirty-five, but he was damned if he'd concede that he was no longer the man he was when he had stepped onto a football field in the final game of his career. It had all happened so fast. An interception, a twelve-yard return, a spearing head-on tackle into his right knee, a sickening crack heard all over the stadium, a stretcher, surgery. Some torn ligaments and a fractured patella, they told him. "The ligaments should be no problem," the surgeon said. "But the patella—that's a different matter. If you continue to play football, you're almost certain to need a patellectomy—complete removal of your kneecap." Why was he thinking about that now? Something he had fought so hard to put behind him.

His pace now dropped to eight minutes per mile. The large quadricep muscles in the fronts of his thighs began to tighten, and his legs felt as if he were wearing ten-pound shoes. A grating pain from within his right knee also found its way into his thoughts, and at once he knew why the black memories of 1964 were haunting him again. *No dammit, no. Not now. Only 750 feet more.*

Just beyond the rise he could see the tail section of his de Ville, five hundred feet away. The pain was getting sharper, burning, begging him to stop. His lungs were starved for air, his mouth open, sucking; his head swayed from side to side. Unwilling to look at the distance ahead, he directed his stare at the ground. One step at a time—first the driveway, then the tree, then the mailbox, then the large rock with the address painted in red—he was determined, refusing to quit.

The pain was intense, causing him to grimace each time he pounded onto his injured leg, but still he would not stop. He concentrated on the pain. The more it hurt, the greater the test of his determination. Nothing would stop him this time.

Three hundred feet; two hundred; one hundred; fifty. Finally, mercifully, he reached the top, took a few additional steps with a pronounced limp until he was next to his car, stopped, bent over at the waist, and with his hands on his hips drew in a deep breath—then another. The pain in his knee surged in waves. A dizziness swept over him and he caught the fender with his right hand. He had proven himself—but at what price? He reached down and felt his swollen, tender knee through the sweat-soaked leg of his sweatsuit. *Now* what had he done? Dammit, he should have stopped. Dammit. *Always have to prove yourself, don't you, stupid?*

Curious about her host, Rachel, wearing Jonathan's bathrobe, walked through the apartment. In the kitchen, the dishes, silverware, pots, and pans were neatly arranged. Everything was organized, polished, and sparkling clean. Not one item in the entire apartment was out-of-place.

Just then she heard the sound of a key entering a lock, and the door swung open suddenly, startling her. Jonathan stood in the doorway, in his burgundy sweatsuit spotted with sweat. His hair was saturated and hung into his face.

"Sorry," he said. "Thought you'd still be sleeping." He continued into the room, squinting from pain, favoring his leg.

"I thought you had gone. When I woke up I couldn't find you and . . . Is anything wrong?"

"Nothing serious. Just an old war wound. Got it on

Guadalcanal in forty-three. Acts up on me every so often, but nothing to be concerned about."

Rachel frowned. He couldn't possibly be that old! That would make him at least . . .

Jonathan grinned, flashing his white teeth, chuckled, then limped into the bathroom. Rachel followed.

"You wouldn't tease a naïve little girl from New Haven, would you?" Rachel smiled, hanging on to the doorjamb.

"Wouldn't think of it," he replied, then twisted a chrome valve, leaned over the sink, and threw some cold water onto his face. "Tell me," he continued, "what's a naïve little girl from New Haven doing getting involved with an old lecher like me anyway?"

"You're not so old," she said, "and maybe I'm not so naïve."

Jonathan caught a flirting glint from her eyes, nodded, and said, "Yes, I'm inclined to agree with you." He grabbed a towel, blotted the water from his face, noted its dampness from Rachel's shower, and tossed it into the hamper against the wall. Then he pulled off his sweats and likewise deposited them into the receptacle, grimacing slightly as he glanced down at his swollen knee.

"What happened to your knee?"

"I hurt it playing football in college, but it hasn't bothered me in a couple of years—at least nothing like this."

"It looks pretty bad. Maybe you should see a doctor."

Jonathan felt his knee again, winced, and said, "Yeah. *Dammit!*" Then he reached in and turned on the shower. As the steam began rising from behind the sliding glass door, he stepped in and yelled out at Rachel, "I'll be through here in just a few minutes."

Rachel closed the bathroom door behind her. "That's all right," she said, approaching the shower. The mirror was fogged now and the room began to fill with steam. She wet her lips with her tongue, dropped the robe onto the floor, slid back the shower door, stepped in, and slid the door closed.

Rachel put her hands on his shoulders and stood on her toes to kiss him. "I thought you might enjoy the company."

In Jonathan's office in Bridgeport, Sally Romberg had just finished putting the morning mail on his desk when she heard him close the front door to the one-office suite.

"Morning, Sally." Jonathan smiled as he limped past her in the secretarial bay.

"Good morning, Mr. Rand." Sally followed him and stood at the library door. "How did the Steinberg motion go?" she asked cautiously.

"Won it," he said while reading a book with his index finger. Suddenly he slammed it shut. "I *knew* it! I *knew* that bastard was misciting the Rowback case." Jonathan broke into a grin of pride. His two days of boring research had paid off and he had caught that cagey old Bernie Porter in a misstatement of the law. At least he had convinced Judge Brandish of it, based on his vague recollection of reading the case.

Sally stepped aside as Jonathan picked up his briefcase and started for his office. He stopped next to her and stared down into her eyes, deadly serious.

"There was never the slightest doubt in my mind, you understand."

Sally looked up and nodded.

Finally he grinned and she reciprocated. Jonathan continued into his office, smiling to himself.

Sally was not an attractive girl. She was thin, with a small bustline and hips that had barely enough substance to sit on. She had a long straight nose and wore square metal-framed glasses with quarter-inch-thick lenses that magnified her dark green eyes. Her brunette hair was thin, never holding a curl and was usually hanging in stringy strands by the end of the day. However, what Sally lacked in beauty she more than made up for in efficiency and devotion. At twenty-two she had the knowledge and sophistication of a legal secretary ten years her senior. To Jonathan she was a valuable aid and one that was not likely to be lost to marriage or pregnancy, a problem he had faced with his last two secretaries.

As he sorted through his mail, his knee began to throb. The morning activities had taken his mind off the pain, but now it was back—fiercely.

He looked at the phone. Hell, he might as well make an appointment now. Waiting wasn't going to make it any better. Wasn't Aaron an orthopedic surgeon? Yeah, he was sure of it. Aaron, down at the Yacht Club. Aaron . . . Aaron *Feinerman*, that was it. Aaron Feinerman. As a matter of fact, he was sure he had his card. Jonathan pulled open the bottom drawer to his desk, withdrew a small metal box, and began thumbing through the three-by-five index cards, each with a business card pasted to it and each in alphabetical order. . . . There it was: Aaron Feinerman, Orthopedic Surgery.

Jonathan dialed the number. A soft, cheerful voice answered, "Good morning, Dr. Feinerman's office."

"This is Jonathan Rand. I'd like to see Dr. Feinerman this afternoon, if that's possible. I'm a friend of his from the Yacht Club."

"I'm sorry, Mr. Rand, Dr. Feinerman is not taking any appointments. He's having some minor surgery and will be out of the office for at least three weeks. Would you like me to refer you to another doctor?"

"Yes, please."

"All right. Call Dr. Howard Jacobs, at 555-2976. He's in our building and a *very* good doctor."

"Thank you, Miss . . . Miss . . . ?"

"Brennan. Danielle Brennan."

# Chapter III

The soft clang of metal tray covers from the breakfast service greeted Jason Reed as he left the elevator for the sixth-floor nursing station to complete his morning rounds. He had just finished with the intensive-care unit and was trying to overcome the impact of losing one of his patients, an emotional reaction he had never been able to master after thirty-two years in medicine. The surgical repair of the aneurysm had been performed with his usual skill, but at seventy-three the patient had been unable to survive the shock of major surgery. He had died shortly after leaving the operating room, and Reed had just finished breaking the news to the man's wife.

It was not remorse for the patient that so upset him. Death was a day-to-day reality that Reed had learned to deal with many years earlier, and one reason why he never allowed himself to get too close to any patient. He left that to the primary-care physicians, the family practitioners, the GPs.

The role of physician's physician—a referral doctor—suited him fine. It allowed him the luxury of maintaining a professional detachment from those whose lives were literally in his hands.

No, it was the ugly reminder of his own imperfection that was so troublesome. The difficulty of accepting the fact that his best was not always good enough.

By the time he was halfway to the nursing station, Reed had captured the attention of Janice Litchfield, the ward clerk, as well as a number of other nurses and orderlies in the general vicinity. His presence seemed to be felt even before his arrival.

"Good morning, Dr. Reed," said Miss Litchfield.

Reed stopped at the counter and stared at the floor, deep in thought, one hand in a pocket of his white hospital coat, the other tapping the counter.

"Oh! Morning, Litchfield." Reed ran his hand over his head, the top of which was bald, bordered by a closely trimmed bush of frosty gray hair.

"Let me see the charts on McCutchin, Leventhal, and Feinerman," he said in a somewhat sharp tone.

"Yes, Doctor," she replied, sensing he was upset, and turned to retrieve the records.

Physically, Jason Reed was as imposing as his explosive personality, a portly two hundred pounds with a round face and double chin. He had a thick nose that turned up with a rounded end and added a combative appearance to match his usual disposition. His dark eyebrows complemented piercing green eyes that could frighten any nurse into blind obedience. No one crossed Jason Reed—not if he wanted to keep his job. In the last two and a half years, an RN, a nurse's aide, and two orderlies had lost their jobs directly as a result of altercations with Dr. Reed. Behind his back the nursing staff referred to him as obnoxious, hostile, and egomaniacal, but grudgingly conceded that he was the finest surgeon ever to operate at Rivergarden Community Hospital.

Litchfield handed the charts to Reed, who accepted them without comment. Carefully he reviewed the lab studies, the vitals, and the nurses' notes on the McCutchin chart, then began persuing similar records on Leventhal.

Finally Reed began throwing pages back on the clipboard as if he had lost something. His bald head began to radiate red—a danger signal.

"Where are the blood gases on Leventhal?" he growled. "I ordered them completed and returned by ten, and it is now ten twenty-five," he said, nodding at the clock on the wall.

"I don't know, Doctor. If it was back from lab, it would be in there."

Audrey Norris, the head nurse on the day shift, reluctantly approached. "Is there anything wrong, Dr. Reed?"

"You're damn right there is," he retorted. "It's written right here in the physician's orders. 'Blood gases by ten A.M.'" Reed again glanced up at the clock. "Ten A.M. was exactly twenty-six minutes ago," he emphasized. "And anyone who has worked here for over a week knows that when I say ten o'clock, I don't mean ten-thirty or eleven o'clock. I mean *ten*— at the latest."

"I'm sorry, Doctor," said Norris. "But I'm positive that the blood was drawn and sent to the lab some time ago. If there is any holdup, it's at their end—not here."

"I don't want to hear any buck-passing, Norris. It's *your* responsibility to see that these orders are carried out. I'm going to duck in and see Dr. Feinerman. If those lab reports are not in the chart by the time I get back, all hell is going to break loose."

With that, Reed stormed off down the hall.

Norris bit her lower lip. She didn't have to take that crap; she didn't care *who* he was. Seeing Litchfield rushing to the phone at the other end of the counter, Norris gave a fleeting glance in either direction, then put her thumb up against her puckered nose and began wiggling her fingers at Reed's back.

Just then the young neurosurgical chief resident stepped up behind her and said, "Do you wave good-bye to all the physicians or is this something reserved for only Dr. Reed?"

Norris slapped down her hand and spun around. "Oh, Dr. Thomas. I . . . didn't know you were standing there. I'm—"

"That's quite obvious," he said sternly.

"I'm sorry, Doctor. I don't know what came over me."

"Not exactly what I would call professional conduct, is it, Norris?"

"No, Doctor. You're not going to mention this to anyone, are you?"

Thomas rubbed his chin contemplatively. "Well . . . on one condition," he said.

"What's that, Doctor?"

Thomas grinned. "On the condition that you promise to say nothing the next time you catch me doing the same thing."

Norris smiled and extended her hand. "Deal," she said.

"Deal," he repeated, pumping her hand.


Aaron lay comfortably gazing out the window of his private room. His gray eyes were troubled. Had he really done the right thing? The answer had been eluding him for the past two weeks. Maybe he would never know.

What the hell . . . he was being foolish. Nothing had happened yet. No threats; nothing even suspicious. Certainly by now—fourteen days—you'd think something would have happened. Unless perhaps it was being dropped and forgotten. Still, the scheduled surgery had the specter of finality about it.

"I wish you'd talk about it," urged Ruth.

Aaron looked up at his wife standing next to his bed. Forcing his usual comforting smile, he squeezed her hand and said, "Don't concern yourself, babe. Just a little preoccupied with the surgery."

"I've never seen you like this. For the past couple of weeks you've been so . . . so edgy."

Aaron stared at her for a moment. Even after eleven years he still admired her classic beauty: the short and neatly coiffed brunette hair; the high cheekbones and elegantly chiseled features; her tall, slender, expensively dressed figure—a page right out of *Harper's Bazaar*. But it was her deeply set pale blue eyes that were her most striking feature. They had a peaceful, serene, almost distant appearance, and together with her warm and quiet personality seemed to cast a mystique about her. Many times they had calmed Aaron in his most troubled moments—but not today.

"You're still as beautiful as the day I met you," he said, trying to change the subject.

"And you're avoiding the question. Something's troubling you and it's more than the surgery."

Why was she always so damned perceptive? No, this was one time she would not find out. He had to convince her she was wrong.

"Really, babe, it's only the surgery. For years I've been operating on patients; running them through hospitals like a conveyor belt. At the time, they're real people, personalities, patients with names and problems." Aaron shook his head. "But after a while you look back and they're all . . . well, nothing more than a bunch of numbers—statistics—another laminectomy, another meniscectomy, a tendon repair. Now all of a sudden, for the first time, *I'm* one of those statistics for someone else. I guess it's because I know exactly what will be done and what kind of things can go wrong. . . . I know I'm being foolish. Reed is the best general surgeon in the state and it's a relatively simple operation, but it's the first damn time in my life that I've been a surgical patient—unless you want to count a tonsillectomy when I was six—and I'm having a difficult time adjusting to the role."

Ruth took Aaron's hand and looked deep into his eyes. "You're being absolutely straight with me?"

"I'd never lie to you about anything like this." As long as he was alive, she would never know. She had to be shielded. And if something happened . . . well, she'd understand and forgive him.

Suddenly Jason Reed walked through the open door. His temper under control again, he managed a slight grin and said, "Good morning. How are my two favorite people this fine day?"

"Hi," said Ruth.

"Morning, Jason," said Aaron. "I was just telling Ruth how you were going to run through this herniorrhaphy using only your left hand—just to put to rest any possible doubts about your unequaled talents with a scalpel."

Reed stepped to the side of the bed and picked up Aaron's arm to take his pulse. His demeanor was somber. "You mean you didn't tell her about the blindfold?" he asked, as he began to time the pulse from his watch. Even when he joked with colleagues his expression was stern.

*What a wonderful bedside manner,* Ruth thought sarcastically.

"Well, I didn't want her to get *too* worried," said Aaron. "I was going to save that surprise until after the surgery."

"It'll be a piece of cake," Reed said to Ruth, as he stuck a thermometer in Aaron's mouth and began listening to his chest. He next tapped the chest and sternum, then had Aaron roll to his side and repeated the same procedure on his back.

Ruth stood quietly watching the standard exam she had seen a thousand times before. It was as a young registered nurse that she had met Aaron at this very hospital. A recent graduate from nursing school, she had been idealistic and eager for a life devoted to caring for the sick, the lame, the helpless. A Florence Nightingale incarnate. She had even considered going on to medical school. But from the day she met Aaron Feinerman, her whole life was dramatically turned upside down. In every romantic sense of the phrase, she had been "swept off her feet."

Aaron was completing his third year of residency in orthopedic surgery. He was eight years her senior and, to her, a man of the world. He was handsome, well traveled, and a medical fountain of knowledge. But it was his vibrant, charismatic personality that overwhelmed her—the charm, the soft laughter, the engaging smile, the irrepressible wit. Like every other young nurse in the hospital, she was hooked from the moment she saw him. Within six months they were married.

Reed removed the thermometer, took a reading, scribbled some notes in the hospital chart, and began depressing different areas of Aaron's lower abdomen. Finally Aaron winced.

Reed looked up at him and said, "Still quite tender, but I don't see any evidence of incarceration. Just a simple inguinal hernia. Shouldn't be more than an hour in OR, and I'd bet you'll be on your feet by the following day."

"I know you're right, Jason, but you see things from a whole different perspective down here. An inguinal hernia it might be, but a *simple* inguinal hernia it'll never be. Not when it's your own groin that someone is cutting. This entire thing has been quite an education for me."

Reed smiled again and nodded. "You're absolutely right," he said. "And we all need to be reminded about it—yours truly no exception."

Reed turned to leave, then stopped and faced Aaron again. For a brief moment his expression was personal, even pleasant. "You know, it's been a very long time since I operated on anyone I . . . well, cared for. I guess this is something of an achievement for me."

Aaron's eyes communicated an understanding of the reference. "I know," he said.

Reed took a breath. "I'm glad I'll be able to help you, Aaron. You've been a good friend. . . . Well, I'll see you tomorrow morning."

Ruth waited until Reed was out of the room, then said, "I'll never understand that man. I *want* to like him—and heaven knows I've tried—but I can't stand him. The only time he smiles is when he's around you. I bet he doesn't have another friend in the world."

"Don't be hard on him, babe. He's a complicated man and a product of his past, as we all are."

"But he doesn't even make an effort to get along. It's like he's in a self-imposed exile."

"You're closer to the truth than you may realize."

"What do you mean?"

"Oh, it's something that happened a long time ago . . . a very unfortunate event that he's lived with for most of his professional life. I can't say it justifies his conduct, but it certainly has helped me to understand it."

"What happened?"

"I wish I could tell you. But I promised Jason I would never repeat it. You understand, don't you?"

Ruth nodded, then smiled. Lines were beginning to form around Aaron's eyes, as well as across his forehead, and his black wavy hair was now peppered with gray. But with his bronzed complexion from the weekends on the yacht, he was more attractive than ever. He certainly didn't look like a hospital patient. "You're very special, you know," she said.

"I don't know about that, but I'm sure I've got the prettiest gal in town."

Ruth leaned over and kissed him. As she began to pull back, Aaron put his arms around her and held her next to his cheek. "I love you, babe," he whispered. "I haven't said it very often, but I don't want you to forget it."

Ruth pulled back and looked at him curiously. "Are you sure there's nothing else bothering you?"

"What's the matter? A man can't tell his wife he loves her? There's nothing wrong, so quit concerning yourself about it."

"All right," she said, straightening her skirt and blouse. "Well, I've got some running around to do. I'll see you back here about dinnertime. Anything you want me to pick up for you?"

"How about smuggling in a fifth of Chivas?"

"And destroy that magnificent image—never. I can just see you being wheeled down to the OR reeking of Scotch."

"Oh, there *is* one thing, babe." Aaron pulled his gold

wedding band from his finger and handed it to Ruth. "You'd better hang on to this until I get out of here. I'm sure they'll make me get rid of it during surgery."

Ruth looked at the ring. Except for its size, it was a perfect match with her own. Inside it was inscribed "Together Forever."

"All right," she said. "But this doesn't mean you can play around, you know."

Aaron laughed, promised he'd behave himself, and said good-bye.


The pathology conference room was the coolest and most elegant room in the hospital and no one could understand how the pathologists had managed such a feat. Rather than being relegated to a basement alcove, the room was immediately above the beautifully cantilevered entrance waiting room and had a sweeping view of the small brook that coursed through the hospital property. It was this brook and the surrounding trees that had inspired its name and established Rivergarden as "the hospital in the park."

In the conference room, charts had been arranged for review at the tissue-committee meeting and the luncheon buffet was being set up. The tissue-audit slips for all the hysterectomies of the past six months were arranged in neat stacks by each doctor's desk. Surgeons were coded rather than named and all the material was reviewed anonymously until trends were noted on the monthly follow-up charts.

Jason Reed was one of the first surgeons to enter. This had not been one of his better days. His hair was disheveled; his silk tie was pulled loose from the folds of his thick neck, red and moistened with perspiration; the collar of his yellow dress shirt was soiled.

Reed began inspecting the trays of food on the buffet table. Meat loaf. *Dammit, that horrible meat loaf again. Can't anything go right today?*

As he began to focus on the tossed salad, Bill Nicholas approached him and extended his hand. In it he held a recently completed pathology report.

"Glad I could reach you. Bad news on Schneider. I tried to call you in ICU this morning, but you had already left."

Reed took the report from the young pathologist and

began reading without comment. As he neared the end he began shaking his head.

"No," he said. "This can't be correct. I saw the tissue myself. I felt it. It was nothing more than a gastric ulcer. That was my opinion then and it still is."

"There's no error, Jason. I looked at it myself. I admit it was a difficult read, but it's an adenocarcinoma. I certainly wouldn't take a chance that it isn't. I'm afraid you were wrong this time."

Reed glared at Nicholas. "I don't make mistakes," he snapped. "If I don't know, I don't venture an opinion. But *this* I'm sure of." Reed thought for a moment, then said, "Bill, I'd like you to have Hoefsteader take a look at this."

His pride injured, Nicholas said, "It's been a while since you questioned one of my readings, Jason. . . . All right, you're entitled to a second opinion. I'll have Ray get on this right away. Be back in fifteen minutes to start the meeting."

With that, Nicholas abruptly turned and left.

Reed shrugged and turned his attention back to the salad. Not much they could do to ruin that.

*Saturday, June 16, 1979*

The small Nembutal capsule had knocked Aaron out. Even at six-thirty the following morning he felt a lingering grogginess from the nighttime sedative.

Aaron blinked and looked over at the window, trying to get a fix on the time of day. He was about to reach over and pick up his watch from the small table next to his bed when Lois Collins, the medication nurse, entered with the morning hypo.

"Good morning, Dr. Feinerman," she said cheerfully.

Unable to clear the cobwebs, Aaron could only smile.

"Wha' ya usin'?" Aaron's words were slurred.

"Oh, a little Phenergan with Valium along with a quarter grain of morphine. You should float to the operating room, Doctor."

Aaron detested drugs. Normally he wouldn't even take aspirin, let alone resort to the wide assortment of barbiturates and analgesics he had easy access to. However, he had promised himself to follow all orders and hospital procedures. He would not play doctor for himself. And by now he had been swept up in the preop routine and was beyond voicing any disagreement or resentment of anything.

Aaron winced as he felt the needle enter the subcutaneous fat of his right arm. "There," said Collins as she removed the needle. "Most people just love this trip. You should be no exception."

He wanted to express his disagreement but had neither the strength nor the motivation. No sooner had he leaned back in his bed than an orderly entered, changed him into a gown, and placed one of the silly bouffant operating-room caps over his head.

Except for a brief awareness of Ruth coming in to wish him well, the next forty-five minutes were a blur. At seven-twenty, ever-faithful Jack Hennings, the surgical orderly, helped Aaron onto his bedside gurney and wheeled him down the corridor to the elevators, then descended to the basement operating pavilion. The friendly greetings from the nurses, orderlies, aides, and technicians on the way to the operating room, plus the "trip" induced by the medication, produced a comfortable, warm glow in Aaron as he was wheeled to OR number four.

The pale blue-gray tiles, the terrazzo floor, the overhead light, the X-ray view box, and the gowned figures all looked so different from the patient's point of view. For the moment, Aaron was no longer a surgeon.

"You should feel a slight prick in your right arm, Aaron," said Jack Osborne, the anesthesiologist, as he deftly placed a number-fifteen needle into Aaron's antecubital vein and started the IV.

Aaron had no recollection of the spinal anesthetic or anything else when he awoke two hours later in the recovery room. Susan Wethersby reminded him who he was, where he was, and why he was there. By noon he was feeling better and the grogginess was beginning to fade. Sensation was returning to his legs and there was no significant operative pain. Back in his room, he was surrounded by flowers, boxes of candy, and the contrived cheerfulness that greets the returning surgical patient. Sips of ginger ale relieved the dry, cottony feeling in his mouth, and a brief face wash and hair combing made him presentable again.

By four o'clock he was dictating reports, reviewing old charts, and scanning the latest orthopedic journal as though nothing had happened. Quietly reflecting, he thought how silly he had been to be so fearful over such a trivial procedure. *Nothing had happened.* He was alive, he was awake, and there had been no complications. He had been in his most vulnerable state, and he had come out alive.

Maybe the whole incident was going to be forgotten.

Ruth had spent the entire day at the hospital, first in the waiting room adjacent to the operating pavilion, then outside the recovery room—once sneaking inside for five minutes—and then finally in Aaron's private room after his return at one o'clock.

It hadn't been easy for her. She had talked with Jason and knew the surgery had gone as expected, but still she could not shrug off the uneasy feeling that all was not right. In the eleven and a half years she had known him, she had never seen Aaron worry about anything. No matter what the occasion—financial problems early in their marriage, a difficult and dangerous surgery, speaking engagements—Aaron never seemed fazed. But now, she knew, something had shaken him.

In mid-afternoon she impulsively picked up Aaron's hospital chart and began to read it. Aaron reminded her that it was against hospital rules, but she ignored his suggestion and read in detail each entry and lab report. A short time later she snapped at a licensed vocational nurse and two aides as they attempted to rotate Aaron in his bed. Finally, he told her that she was behaving like an old Jewish mother doting on her son and that it would be better if she sat down, relaxed, and watched television. Reluctantly, she obliged.

After dinner she departed, leaving instructions that there should be no visitors that evening, so that Aaron could rest, and that well-wishers should leave messages at the nurses' station. Finally, the evening medication took over, and after sipping some warm chicken broth Aaron fell into a deep, worry-free sleep.

*Sunday, June 17, 1979*

Something was wrong. The feeling of icy cold rapidly built into a crescendo of massive shaking chills. A wave of severe nausea and a sense of impending doom swept over Aaron. He groped for his watch. Where had the afternoon and evening gone? It was almost 3:00 A.M. The chill extended to all parts of his body, as did an overwhelming weakness. With considerable difficulty he managed to ring the nurse's buzzer. Miss Henderson, the team leader on the eleven-to-seven shift, was there within seconds.

"Something's wrong, Nurse," whispered Aaron, barely able to summon the strength to make his problem known. "I think you'd better call Reed."

Henderson quickly left the room and returned with a thermometer. She placed it in Aaron's mouth and left the room again. A tightness developed across his chest as he broke into a heavy sweat. His hospital gown was soaked. An uncontrollable panic began to develop, as he tried to grasp what was happening to him.

Aaron fought, but he couldn't quite hold on to consciousness. He felt himself slipping back and forth between a semi-awareness of where he was and a total loss of reality.

Henderson returned, took his pulse, his respiration, read his temperature, then left again.

Jason Reed lay on his back, moaning. Pleasurable moans that had started with a few quiet grunts and now were becoming louder and more emotional. The time was getting close. He could feel it inside as he began to arch his back to meet his partner above him. The rhythmic rocking of the bed generated a repeated squeak from the box springs.

He had lasted much longer tonight. Perhaps it was the five bourbon-and-Sevens that had dulled his senses, but still he was proud of himself. It had been years since he had felt so masculine. His partner was also approaching orgasm, as she bent her head back, tossing it from side to side. Harder and harder she thrust herself, causing the headboard now to start tapping the wall. "Yes . . . yes . . . oh yes!" she cried.

Suddenly the moment was there. Reed's body went into a trembling spasm and he pulled her close, holding her tight to prolong the ecstasy. Uncontrollably his fingers dug into her buttocks.

Then vaguely, through his euphoria, he thought he heard something. At first he didn't recognize it and the noise stopped. Then he heard it again. *Dammit, the phone*, he thought. *Not now. Goddammit, not now.* They were still tightly holding each other, savoring the waning pleasure of the climax. Again it rang; and again. Finally, in disgust, he reached over to the nightstand and picked up the receiver.

"Hello! Who in the hell is this?"

"Dr. Reed, I'm terribly sorry to bother you at this hour, but this is Nurse Henderson at the hospital. We may be having a problem with Dr. Feinerman; he asked me to give you a call."

"What kind of a problem? What time is it?"

"It's ten after three, Doctor. Dr. Feinerman has started to experience some shaking chills and is perspiring profusely."

"What are his vitals?"

"Respiration is thirty; his pulse is a hundred and ten; and his temperature is one hundred three point six, up from ninety-nine point eight at midnight."

Reed's partner began kissing his neck, then made her way up to his earlobe. As her moist tongue entered his ear, a chill ran down his spine. It was uncanny. Although he was completely drained, she was getting him aroused again. Reed tried to focus his attention on the phone call, but he had difficulty grasping the significance of the vitals. They seemed no more than meaningless numbers.

"Get a chest plate done, if the X-ray technician is available, and have Dr. Feinerman blow up a rubber glove to expand his lungs. It's probably only a little atelectasis, so don't bother me unless something really gets serious. I'll be there by seven this morning."

"Okay, Doctor. Good night."

Henderson returned to Aaron's room. "Dr. Reed says it's probably only some atelectasis from the anesthesia. He said he would be here first thing in the morning and that there was nothing to worry about." Henderson handed him a rubber surgical glove. "Here, Doctor. Blow on this a while and I'll be back in a few minutes, if you need any help." Without hesitation, she turned and left to report the turn of events to her supervisor.

No! No, Reed was wrong. It wasn't atelectasis. It parroted the symptoms, but it was too . . . too severe. This was serious. He knew it, but he was totally helpless. *Oh, my God,* they've done it. *Something has finally happened. I've been . . . been . . .* Aaron's mind reeled. Reality slowly slipped away. A terrible weariness enveloped him and for the second time that night he fell into unconsciousness.

Fifteen minutes later he was awake again. This time, however, he felt warm. The chilly sensations were gone, although he was still shaking.

The nursing staff began cooling measures. Alcohol packs were wrung out and placed over Aaron's arms and legs. An electric fan was set up by the bedside table. Trying to communicate his fear, he found the words would not come out of his mouth. His breathing was labored and it was all he could do to inhale. Again Henderson left.

A few minutes later she returned with Joyce Montgomery, the night supervisor. Now Aaron was markedly cyanotic. A bluish discoloration under his fingernails was becoming quite pronounced from the lack of oxygen in his blood.

"We'd better maintain fifteen-minute vital signs, Joan," said Montgomery. "I don't like the looks of this."

His temperature was now spiking to 105 degrees. His pulse was 140 per minute and his respiratory rate was 40. His blood pressure was recorded at 100/60. Another call to Dr. Reed failed to get even an answer.

At 5:30 A.M. a code-blue alert was given and the entire emergency-room staff converged on Aaron Feinerman's room. Aaron was now hanging desperately to a thin thread of consciousness. The faces of the emergency-room crew working above him were unrecognizable blurs, as they started cutdowns and administered pressor amines to elevate his blood pressure. As his lungs rapidly expanded and contracted at the rate of fifty cycles per minute, a feeling of suffocation overwhelmed him. Not even the plastic tube feeding oxygen down his airway appeared to help, as he frantically gasped for air. Aaron's heart was pounding so fast and hard that his whole body seemed to be shaking. Total weakness overcame him like a paralysis.

"Pulse?" shouted Dr. Raider, who had been called up from the emergency room.

"One hundred sixty, Doctor," replied Nurse Henderson.

"Blood pressure?"

"Sixty over forty."

As Aaron slipped again into unconsciousness, he heard the word *forty* echo and linger, as if in a narrow tile hallway, and then fade into a loud buzz before blacking out.

"We're losing him. He's going into shock," called Raider.

"Forty over twenty, Doctor."

Aaron's heart started beating out of rhythm and then suddenly stopped.

"Cardiac arrest," shouted Raider, as he began performing

cardiopulmonary resuscitation. With each evenly timed thrust into Aaron's chest, Raider kept repeated to himself, "C'mon Aaron . . . c'mon Aaron . . . c'mon Aaron." Giving up on the CPR, he reached for the electrodes to the defibrillator. Three jolts of electricity brought no response on the monitor that Aaron had been hooked up to. Finally Raider stopped. There was anguish and resignation in his eyes as, perspiration soaked, he stood, breathing heavily.

Aaron lay motionless, his eyes closed. His skin had a gray pallor and beads of perspiration still covered his forehead. It was 6:20 A.M., forty minutes before Jason Reed was to begin his rounds, and Aaron Feinerman was dead.

At 7:10 A.M., the phone rang at the Feinerman residence. Ruth had not slept well that night and was awake almost immediately. Sensing that something was wrong, she hesitated, then picked up the receiver.

"Hello," she said reluctantly, hoping it was the wrong number.

"Ruth, this is Jason. . . . I'm down here at the hospital."

Out of the corner of her eye, Ruth saw Aaron's wedding band next to the base of the telephone.

"I don't know how to tell you this, Ruth, but apparently Aaron had some kind of pulmonary problem—probably a massive viral pneumonia—and he passed away about an hour ago."

Ruth's head suddenly went numb as the shock hit her. For a moment it was as if she were experiencing a nightmare. No, this wasn't really happening.

"I know how this must hit you now, Ruth, but it's true," he said quietly, firmly.

As the reality began to sink in, Ruth could see Aaron's face, his head against the pilllow, as he told her to go home and get some rest. "Oh no!" she cried as tears flushed her eyes.

Reed waited a couple of minutes, then continued. "I wish there were something I could say. . . . Maybe, if you feel up to it, you could have someone bring you down here to the hospital to sign the necessary papers. I don't think an autopsy will be necessary, as I think I know what we are dealing with. . . . Again, Ruth, I'm terribly sorry."

Slowly Reed hung up the telephone receiver at the nurses' station. He covered his eyes with his hand. The cruelty of life, the agonizing twists of fate, had again fallen heavily on him. It had taken so long to forget, to bury the past, and now this. If he could only have last night back. But life had taught him that there was no turning back. This, too, he would have to learn to live with.

A red-eyed but amazingly composed and well-groomed Ruth Feinerman appeared at the nurses' station to collect her husband's personal effects, after spending more than half an hour sitting with Aaron. An air of unreality persisted.

"I want an autopsy, Jason," Ruth declared.

Reed looked at her, surprised at her demand. "It's not necessary," he said. "This is pretty typical of viral pneumonia. I really can't see any purpose in putting you through that."

"I want to know exactly what happened," she said with a determined glare. "When I left last night he looked like he was ready to come home. Twelve hours later you . . . you call me to say that he's . . . gone." Ruth fought to control her emotions. "I want to know what happened to my husband. And where were *you* when this was going on?"

"Ruth, this all happened very suddenly. He was doing perfectly well until around three this morning . . . and I was at home sleeping at the time."

"I don't believe this. Didn't anyone call you?"

"Yes. I got a call, Ruth, but at the time Aaron's problem appeared to be nothing more than some atelectasis from the surgery." Guilt ridden, Reed was unable to meet her eyes. He stared at the floor. Nervously he rubbed the back of his neck. "Often, when a patient is having his breathing controlled while on a general anesthetic, mucus will begin plugging the little air sacs inside the lungs. This causes the patient to breathe harder and generally produces an increase in his temperature and other vital signs. Because this frequently occurs . . . well, it was my immediate thought when I received the call. That's why, when I was told of the symptoms, I ordered a chest X-ray and had him blow on a rubber glove to expand his lungs and break up the mucus."

"Jason, he was your friend. How could you even take a chance? How could you? I want an autopsy," she demanded. Ruth turned to the counter at the nurses' station and requested an autopsy form. After signing, without saying another word, she picked up Aaron's personal effects and headed for the elevator.

# Chapter IV

The cool northeast wind gusting against his face felt refreshing as Jonathan sat at the tiller of his twenty-six-foot sloop, *Dreamboat*. It was June and it was sunny, but the breeze was a constant reminder that summer had not yet arrived. Still, the smell of the fresh salt air, along with the taut full sails, as he cut a northwest tack across the Sound, was the best tonic that Jonathan could have ordered for himself.

Friday afternoon he had seen Dr. Jacobs, who had X-rayed and then aspirated his knee. "Stay off your feet as much as possible for at least two weeks," he had been told. "The inside of your kneecap looks like the surface of the moon. And the more you jog on it, the more you will irritate it. My best advice is to stop jogging altogether. If you don't, we'll probably end up removing the kneecap within a year."

For most of Saturday he had sat around, moody, contemplating the prospect of dropping his favorite exercise. It was not a pleasant thought. He had always enjoyed running. As a child, over the fields and dirt roads to school; on the track teams in high school; and the jogging in later years.

He had quit once before. Finally, one day—his thirtieth birthday—he'd stared into the mirror at the paunch rising prominently over the top of his belt and vowed to put himself back into shape. He was disgusted with himself. And, as with all his previous goals and challenges, he embarked on his exercise program with religious—almost fanatical—devotion. Soon he was again "running with the wind" like he had as a youth. And now *this*.

Despondently, Jonathan watched the wake from his bow crest and then fade into the brownish green water of Long Island Sound. The invigorating morning air, the sight of the beautiful green countryside, and the vitality of strong, powerful legs beneath him would soon be only memories.

The fluttering of the sails hanging loose in the wind

brought Jonathan back to the present. As he sat daydreaming about his misfortune, he had come about too far north and was heading almost directly into the wind. Quickly he pulled the tiller to the right. As the boat picked up its original course, the sails caught the air, forcing the boat back into its lean to the port and sending it charging forward.

"Hey, what's going on up there?" Rachel shouted from below. "I almost spilled everything all over the place."

"Quiet," said an embarrassed Jonathan. "If I hear any more insubordination, I'll have you hung from the yardarm."

"Well, if you can't hold this boat on an even course," she retorted, emerging from below carrying a Bloody Mary in each hand, "you're going to have a mutiny on your hands." She lifted the glasses. "Surprise," she said with a smile. "I thought you could use a pick-me-up. You've been looking a little depressed all morning."

"Well, thanks, Rachel," he said with a note of surprise.

Rachel handed Jonathan his drink, then joined him in a ballasting lean on the starboard bench seat. Jonathan brought the glass to his lips, sipped, and enjoyed the bite of Tabasco sauce as it warmed his throat.

"How is it?" she asked.

"Perfect." He smiled. "You must be psychic. It's exactly as I like it. The Tabasco, the lime, everything."

Rachel angled her head back and scanned the nylon mainsail above, bowing from the aggressive wind. From below it looked immense.

"Do you go sailing often?" she asked.

"Not as often as I'd like. My practice takes up too much of my time."

She closed her eyes while taking a deep, pleasurable breath and said, "I don't know how you could stay away. If I had something like this, I'd be out here every weekend."

"Days like this I feel the same way. But my practice . . . it's like a hobby to me. You might even call it my mistress." Jonathan thought for a minute. "Yes, I guess I *love* my work—at least most of it. I could spend seven days a week at it without a second thought—and have, on many occasions."

Rachel softly laughed. "I can see you have a different view of work than I do. At five o'clock I turn it off and tune it out. If I had to take it home, I'd go bananas. To me it's just a job."

"How is it working for Rabin? Is he as charming as he is in the courtroom?"

"Charming? . . . I guess that's one way of looking at him. I know he's a great lawyer, but there are some things about him that . . . Well, I really shouldn't be talking about it."

Jonathan took another sip from his glass. "What do you mean?"

"I've really said too much already. You have some cases against our office and I honestly shouldn't be talking to you about it."

Momentarily uncomfortable, Jonathan shook his head. "No, I'd never ask you to disclose something about one of my cases. That's definitely out-of-bounds. Forget I even asked."

Rachel was impulsively baiting him. Her job gave her a unique advantage over any other woman whom Jonathan might be dating, and she wasn't going to hesitate to use it.

"Actually, it has nothing to do with your cases at all. It's more about Mr. Rabin himself. But I shouldn't. . . ."

Jonathan already knew about Arnold Rabin and wasn't about to play Rachel's game. Casually he tilted his glass and took another swallow.

"It would be better if you kept it to yourself, Rachel. If anyone found out that you had talked to me about the office, they'd fire you on the spot—not that they'd learn it from me, you understand."

Damn! It wasn't working. How could he be so indifferent about it? She could tell him things about Rabin that would be invaluable. Didn't he have the sense to realize it?"

"You *do* have a trial coming up with him, don't you?"

"Yes, in three months. But don't worry. With me, Arnold Rabin will not get away with a thing." Jonathan's voice exuded confidence.

"But you don't know what he can do, what he gets away with."

"I know everything about him. We've locked horns before and I have the scars to prove it. I know he's a master of trickery and deceit, and I know he's got the personality to get away with it."

Rachel was stunned. "You know!"

"Of course I do. I know *everything* about my opponent before I go to trial with him." Jonathan again noted the luffing of his sail and pulled at the tiller, forcing the bow leeward to recapture the northeast wind. "I also know how to beat him," he added.

"How do you plan to do that?"

"That, Rachel my dear, is *my* secret." Jonathan punctuated his claim by tapping his chest with his index finger.

Yes, he knew how to beat Rabin. He had studied him like a map. Last summer he had even sat in on two of his trials. He had seen Rabin's subtle way of slipping prejudicial and inadmissible facts to a jury while his opponent sat writing notes. He had even heard of Rabin improperly talking to jurors outside the courtroom. Yes, Jonathan knew all his tricks—at least he thought he did. But even if he didn't, it wouldn't matter. He knew exactly what it would take. Anticipation was the key. Every minute, every second, of the trial he would be on his toes. Whenever Rabin opened his mouth, Jonathan would be on top of him like a cat.

"This case is pretty important to you, isn't it?"

"Yes, it is. My client has a severe fracture of his leg, leaving him with a permanent limp. The case has a few problems, but I think I can ring the bell on it. If I do, the verdict should be well over a hundred thousand dollars—not to mention knocking off the noted Arnold Rabin. Yes, you might say it's important to me."

"You mentioned having scars. Is there something personal in this?"

"Not really. Rabin is only a stepping-stone to building a reputation. If I bury him, and especially with a six-figure verdict, every lawyer in town will hear about it."

"But you already have quite a reputation. I've heard people talking about you at the office."

It was pleasing to hear. Jonathan had an insatiable appetite for compliments. A trait, he had reconciled, that was typical of most trial lawyers. Compliments were confidence builders. "You heard this at the office?"

"Yes, I did. As a matter of fact, it was because of your reputation that Rabin was assigned to your case. So why the big need for a rep builder?"

Jonathan stared out over the Sound. "Because I want to be known as a heavy hitter. In a courtroom I'm as good as *any* lawyer. I have the experience—ten years—and have tried every kind of case imaginable—criminal, domestic, commercial, everything. But if I want to join the ranks of the elite—Bill Colson, Jake Fuchsberg, Mo Levine, Bruck Walkup, Ned Good—I need something big: the right case, a blockbuster."

"You wouldn't call your case against Rabin a blockbuster, would you?"

"No. But it could bring one in. The bigger the bait, the bigger the fish." He smiled. "See? I'm just on a big ego trip."

Stratford Point, three miles distant, suddenly came gliding into view across the starboard bow, drawing Jonathan's attention away from his companion. His smile quickly vanished and he barked, "Get ready to come about. Hard alee," he said.

"So much for the practice of law," Rachel offered after they were back on course. "What are you doing for dinner tonight? I thought you might like to come by my place tonight. I have this great casserole recipe you'd be wild about."

"Well, I'm not sure." Jonathan had the time, but he was not prepared to make a commitment. They'd been together Thursday night; then a movie, cocktails, and dinner Saturday, after which Rachel had stayed overnight with him; and now they were out sailing Sunday morning. Enough was enough. He could feel the noose tightening.

"No . . . no, it wouldn't be possible, Rachel. I have an appellate brief due on Tuesday. I just can't spare the time right now." A lie, but Jonathan was sensitive to her feelings. How could she understand that he wanted no ties with *any* woman? He needed freedom to do what he wanted, when he wanted.

With the saddened eyes of a puppy, she asked, "How about Tuesday night? You'll have the brief filed and should be ready for a special treat by then." Rachel gave it a double meaning as she drew her hand up over the inside of his left thigh.

Jonathan caught and softly held her hand, while shifting in his seat for a more comfortable distance. "I really couldn't say right now, Rachel. My week is going to be quite busy. Let me check my office calendar. If I can break free, I'll give you a buzz. I'm certain I've got the time, but right now I don't want to make any promises."

She sensed it was time to back off. "Okay. Just an idea I had. Give me a call if you find yourself with a little free time." She tried to convey indifference, but her eyes betrayed a longing that added to Jonathan's uneasiness.

"I'm . . . uh . . . sure you'll be hearing from me, Rachel. It's just this brief. You know what time they take. And I've never been the one to sail through legal research. Then there's a number of other things that have been piling up at the office. But certainly by the end of the week . . . certainly by then you'll be hearing from me."

# Chapter V

At 10:30 A.M. Bill Nicholas was enjoying his Sunday breakfast, when he was reached by the hospital operator. Nicholas and his senior associate, Ray Hoefsteader, alternated weekends on call and, when necessary, performed the autopsies that came in on Sundays, rather than hold them over until the next day. The operator did not mention the name of the patient, but informed him that a chart was in the pathology office with a valid signed consent and that the autopsy assistant would meet him at the hospital at 11:15.

Nicholas's wife had grown used to such morbid interruptions on the weekends; they never meant more than two or three hours away from the family. Still she voiced her usual complaint, which was Joan's way to ensure that her husband would return promptly.

The association with Dr. Hoefsteader extended back almost three years, during which time Nicholas had slowly improved his relationship with the surgeons at Rivergarden. Gradually they had gained more and more confidence in the young pathologist, who had early learned the difficulty of establishing credibility with skeptical and opinionated doctors. "What does Hoefsteader think of it?" was the question that most would ask during the first months of his association with the chief of pathology.

Nicholas's features misrepresented his thirty-three years. He looked more like a high-school student than a well-trained pathologist in his third year of private practice. He was short, with a soft, round face and the blanched complexion of a man who seldom saw the light of day. His hair was the color of bleached hay.

But his perseverance had paid off and he had found himself not only respected but frequently sought after, even by surgeons from other hospitals. He was considered an excellent pathologist with "good eyes." Even Jason Reed would now allow him the "privilege" of interpreting a frozen section from one of his patients. Still, the second-guessing by Reed on Friday had been quite unsettling. It had been some time since it had last happened.

Nicholas pulled into the Rivergarden parking lot and eased to a stop in front of the pathology office. Eager to get back to the Sunday paper at home, he jumped out of his car and quickly made his way to the private entrance. He entered the office, closed the door, turned, and saw Jason Reed sitting on a couch holding a medical chart. His face was a mask of sadness, his eyes reddened and tormented.

"Hi, Jas. What are you doing here?"

"Morning, Bill." Reed's voice was subdued as he rose from the couch and approached Nicholas.

"I told them not to tell you who the patient was over the phone. I . . . didn't want you to be upset on your way in."

"What are you talking about?" Nicholas looked through the open door leading to the autopsy pavilion. "What patient?"

"Aaron Feinerman died this morning."

"What! This can't be true."

"I wish it weren't."

"But he was only in for a herniorrhaphy. What happened?"

"A nightmare, Bill. The whole thing is a nightmare." Reed ran his hand over his bald head. "I've tried to piece it together and the only answer I can get is viral pneumonia. Apparently, Aaron had a viral pneumonia that was masked when he entered the hospital. We certainly didn't pick it up during the admittance exam or any of the preop testing. Then, about three o'clock this morning—probably because of weakness from the surgery—it hit him like a freight train. When I was first called he was having respiratory difficulties and my first thought was atelectasis. But before I learned it was more serious than that, he went into cardiac arrest and died. It happened too fast for anyone to do anything."

Nicholas slumped down into the secretary's chair, at a loss

for words. Like most of the physicians at Rivergarden, he had always considered Aaron a friend. It was Aaron who had helped him during his first year in the pathology lab when the patronizing and second-guessing had finally gotten to him. Now they wanted an autopsy on him.

Reed handed the chart to Nicholas. "I'm sure you'll want to look this over," he said. "Everything's completed. Progress record, nurses' notes, lab reports . . . everything." Nicholas stared blankly at the chart resting in his lap, while Reed walked to the door. Before leaving he turned and said, "Look, Bill, this whole thing is pretty clear-cut. It's viral pneumonia. Raider was with him when he died, and he concurs. I'm quite confident you'll agree with us after the postmortem. In fact, I'm *positive* you will."

"I'm sorry, I didn't follow."

"Everything here is being . . . well, dumped in your lap, in a manner of speaking. I'm only suggesting that you consider your position with the hospital before making your final diagnosis. Make some reckless finding, ignore the obvious, and you could stir up a hornet's nest." For a moment their eyes caught each other's, as if communicating telepathically. "Anyway, give it some thought," Reed continued. "I'll be back in an hour and a half to review the organs."

Nicholas continued to stare at the door as if Reed were still standing there. He had to think this out, although one thing was certain. Viral pneumonia would be perfect: difficult to diagnose under the circumstances and almost impossible to treat in its advanced stages. *Viral pneumonia means Reed walks away clean*. But what would he do if the results were incriminating? Reed was a powerful man—and vindictive. Nicholas's whole career could be affected. *Well, he's probably right anyway, so why worry about it?*

Steeling himself for what he considered a grim ordeal, Nicholas finished reading the chart, changed into a scrub suit, then put on his shoe covers and proceeded to the autopsy pavilion fifty feet down the hall.

Johnny Wilson, the diener, had already prepared Aaron's body for the examination, had recorded height and weight, and had mapped out scars, incisions, needle puncture marks, and skin lesions. He had also placed a towel over Aaron's face, which helped to depersonalize the situation.

Wilson, old, crusty, and emotionless, especially at work,

had assisted in more than a thousand autopsies and had seen it all.

"Doc, I think you ought to take a look at this red patch here." Wilson pointed to a red egg-shaped area over Aaron's left hip just behind the greater trochanter.

"It looks quite inflamed," Nicholas said. "It may be a small area of cellulitis. Perhaps there was some local reaction to his preoperative or pain medication."

The lesion measured three inches by two and a half and was located in an area that was a common site for intramuscular injections. The implication was unsettling: a contaminated injection.

"Get me a sterile syringe, needle, and culture tube, Johnny. I want to pull a culture out of this lesion. We might have a little infection here."

Wilson lit the Bunsen burner on the side worktable and skillfully handed Nicholas the necessary equipment. A small amount of tissue fluid was withdrawn in the needle, inoculated into a transfer medium, and readied for the trip to bacteriology for culture. The fluid had a puslike appearance, which added to Nicholas's concern that he was dealing with a localized infection.

"It's situations like this that can cloud one's objectivity," he muttered, not wanting to believe the infection had anything to do with Aaron's death.

Over the next hour and a half, Nicholas proceeded to describe his examination of each organ and its weight and measurement into the tape-recorder's microphone that hung over the table, then returned the organs to the body cavity. From each organ, he took a slice of tissue and placed it on a glass slide, to review microscopically later.

The incision looked clean. Small petechial hemorrhages were noted over the sclerae of the eyes and several were also seen over Aaron's chest. Probably hypoxia, Nicholas thought; consistent with Aaron's restricted oxygen intake. Jason was probably right. However, such small pinpoint hemorrhages also occurred with septicemia, and the possibility of a blood infection kept nagging at him as he continued his review of the organs.

There was little else to note, as most of the tissue reflected a healthful life-style and good heredity. Arteriosclerosis was at a surprising minimum for a man in his forties, and no hidden malignancies were uncovered. The only striking features were the weight and texture of the lungs. While normal lungs averaged between 300 and 400 grams apiece, the left lung weighed 800 grams and the right 920 grams. Both were airless, wet, dark red to blue in color, and had the appearance of any number of processes from atelectasis and congestion to viral pneumonia and a few rare forms of pneumonitis. But another bothersome piece of the puzzle also fell into place: the appearance was also consistent with *shock lung*, a condition that was the terminal event of a fatal septicemia.

*I'm sure Jason was right,* Nicholas reassured himself. *Everything fits with it being a viral pneumonia: the clinical picture; the condition of the lungs; everything.* He would need the microscopics to confirm it, but he was certain that he was right.

At 12:45 P.M., Reed strolled into the autopsy room, this time in better control of his emotions. As if he were part of the autopsy team, he picked up a pair of surgical gloves, pulled them on with some assistance from Wilson, and approached the open body of Aaron Feinerman.

"About finished, Bill?"

Nicholas nodded, while taking a section from the disembodied liver. "Yeah. A few more sections and I'll wrap it up."

Reed reached into the chest cavity and withdrew a lung. Carefully he turned it over in both of his hands, squeezed it for texture, and held it to the light. "Just as I suspected. A clear case of viral pneumonia."

Nicholas offered no comment.

"What did the lungs weigh? This one feels quite heavy."

"Eight hundred on the left and nine twenty for the right." Nicholas kept working without looking at Reed.

"Classic," Reed said. "Haven't seen a clearer case of viral pneumonia since I interned."

Nicholas placed the completed liver slides into a specially constructed box and turned to Reed, unwilling to look at his antagonist. He started to tell him of the hip lesion, but caught himself. *Why create a problem now? It's probably unrelated, and if it isn't . . . well, it would be easier to have Reed see it in the report than to tell him to his face. Damn! Why couldn't this have been Ray's weekend?*

Nicholas began pulling off his gloves. "I'm sure you're right, Jason. But we'll have to review the slides to get a final on this."

Reed didn't like the uncertainty in Nicholas's voice. "Sure, Bill. That's standard protocol." Quickly he placed the lung back into Aaron's chest and removed his gloves. "You're not harboring any doubt about this, are you?"

"No. I think I have enough for you to sign it out as viral pneumonia. I just want to confirm it with the slides. If I come up with anything new, I'll just do a supplement for the death certificate. But for now I've got enough to buy pneumonia."

Nicholas started for the door. He had never been more eager to be at home with Joan and the kids. "Finish up in here, will you, Johnny?"

"Sure, Doc. See you tomorrow. Oh, what about the blood I drew for the cultures—wanna run 'em?"

Another uneasy glance at Reed. "No. Forget it. I've got all I need."

Reed followed Nicholas and put his arm around the shorter doctor. "This has been pretty tough on you, Bill. On *both* of us."

Nicholas nodded.

"You know, Bill, over the past three years you've really built quite a reputation around here. And I know it hasn't been easy—putting up with demanding and second-guessing surgeons like myself. In fact, I would think you'd be a prime candidate for chief of pathology when Ray retires next year."

Nicholas could see it coming. Reed had never been known for his subtlety.

"Of course, you understand that a good part of your future depends on how this autopsy comes out. A poorly considered opinion could hurt a lot of people. And I needn't tell you what they could do. Even Ruth could be hurt. The last thing she needs is to have someone pointing an accusing finger, stirring up a big mess for years to come. The best therapy for her would be to put this whole tragedy in a box and bury it with Aaron. The sooner she forgets this, the sooner she can get her life straightened out."

The two of them stopped in the parking lot before separating. "I'll give it a lot of thought, Jason."

"I know you will." Reed's comment was almost an instruction. Confidently he patted Nicholas on the back, said good-bye, and headed for his Rolls-Royce Silver Cloud.

Nicholas watched Reed get into his car and drive away, then cursed out loud.

* * *

Jason Reed stopped his Silver Cloud at the top of the circular drive in front of his home. As with everything that he owned, the house was large, majestic, and expensive. The shrubs and flowers had been professionally trimmed, the lawn closely mowed and raked.

For a moment he just sat in the car staring into space, his hands still holding the steering wheel. His heart carried the double burden of grief and concern. . . . Nicholas. What could be expected of Nicholas? His actions at the hospital worried Reed. He had never really thought much of him before. He was always so small and . . . weak; so easily intimidated. How he had enjoyed watching him nervously stammer during those early days. Even now Nicholas lacked conviction in his readings. No, he shouldn't be a problem.

Reed entered the house, and immediately went to the study. This was *his* room, his sanctuary. The rest of the house was Patricia's domain, but the study was his. The room was paneled in dark walnut and had a completely stocked wet bar. One entire wall was paved with diplomas, certificates, photographs, and documents attesting to his surgical prowess. The custom-designed African mahogany desk with the tooled leather top, the fine French bronze inkstand, and the antique Ushak carpet affirmed his expertise in matters other than surgery. The bookcases were filled with medical texts, periodicals, and a choice selection of novels.

Reed poured himself a bourbon-and-Seven and crossed to the sumptuous leather chair behind his desk, where he promptly collapsed. With three gulps he dispatched the drink.

The whole weekend had been a nightmare. From the moment she had knocked at the door last night until . . . No. That part had not been unpleasant at all. It had been wild, exciting, reckless—a fantasy. In the farthest reaches of his imagination he had never dreamed of an affair like last night.

And in his mind he deserved every minute of it.

For years his marriage with Patricia had been deteriorating. They shared the same household, the same dinner table, even the same bedroom, but they led separate lives. Reed had his practice and County Medical Association activities, while Patricia had her bridge club and her charity work. Their lives together had become stale and routine. What little sex they still engaged in had been reduced to a weekly ritual. Every Wednesday evening at eleven o'clock Patricia would return from her bridge-club meeting, glowing from her customary three glasses of Galliano on the rocks. Reed would already be relaxing in bed with the latest medical journal, waiting to fulfill his weekly obligations. Within ten minutes they would be through and would roll over, drifting off to sleep without a word being spoken.

So what was wrong with taking advantage of the opportunity? He had never been attractive to anyone before, not even to Patricia. She'd had an unhappy home life with her parents and obviously had taken the opportunity to get out and at the same time marry a doctor. He had always secretly believed that scenario, even though he had never expressed it before. Why bring up something unpleasant that she would only deny? Anyway, he was overweight and accepted it as a fact of life. No, not overweight—he was *fat*. Portly, pleasingly plump, heavy, obese—no matter how you sliced it, it still came out as fat. Worse than that, he was homely. His nose was shaped funny or his eyes were too far apart or some such thing. Once, back in medical school, a nurse who had slept with almost every other student in his class had called him repulsive. Yes, he had received his share of insults and rejections. *More* than his share.

Then along comes a young, beautiful woman who, for some exotic reason known only to herself, finds him attractive. For one blessed night in his whole damn life he had actually captivated the interest of a gorgeous, sensual woman. For one night he was Gable and Redford. The heroine was starving for *his* body. This had been his fantasy and he had lived it to the fullest.

For a moment the activities flashed through his mind. The liquor, the induced high, the preliminaries, the raw, uninhibited sex.

Then, just as quickly, the gray lifeless body of Aaron Feinerman appeared. *Oh God, I'm so sorry, Aaron,* he thought. *Of all people, why did it have to be you? The only man who ever understood me, helped me. One harmless indiscretion and I take away your life. It isn't fair. It just isn't fair—neither to you or me. I should be entitled to make one mistake without paying such a penalty. Just one damn mistake in thirty-two years of medicine. I'm entitled. . . . No, two mistakes. But Lord knows what I've done to make amends for the last one. There isn't a better general surgeon in this state. . . . And the hours, the commitment . . . I've paid the price to become the best.*

Reed's thoughts shifted again—this time to the autopsy room and Bill Nicholas. The uncertainty in his eyes, that's what was nagging him. *What if that little mouse puts down the wrong cause of death? That would please everyone, wouldn't it? All of them. They've all been waiting for him to make a mistake. For years they've been waiting, the whole incompetent lot of them. Anything to satisfy their envy, to degrade him behind his back. And to leave this in the hands of a weak little kid.* That was the greatest injustice of all. Well, he had made his point at the hospital, and whatever qualities Bill Nicholas lacked as a pathologist, he certainly wasn't stupid. No, Bill shouldn't be a problem.

Fifteen minutes later, Reed was still holding the empty glass in his hand when he heard the front door open, followed by muffled voices as Patricia paid the cabdriver who had brought in her luggage and placed it in the foyer. A few minutes later he heard the door close.

"I'm home," she announced while hanging her coat in the entrance closet.

Reed didn't respond.

Patricia straightened her rumpled dress suit and rubbed at her lower back, which was still aching from the flight from Los Angeles. Soon it would be relieved by the hot bath that she had been thinking about since landing at Kennedy Airport.

As she made her way to the stairs to her bedroom, Patricia passed the open door to the study and caught a glimpse of Reed.

"Oh, I didn't know you were down here," she said.

Reed stared blankly at her. "How was the flight?" he asked mechanically.

"A little bumpy over the Rockies, but otherwise nothing to complain about."

"And your mother?"

"She'll never change. Still complaining about everything from the weather to the way I wear my hair. She's even worse than she was last year. But at eighty-three I guess it's to be expected. Maybe she's getting a little senile."

"Maybe so."

"Well, I'm going upstairs and slip into a hot bath. I'd appreciate it if you could bring up the luggage."

Reed nodded.

Patricia momentarily hesitated. It had been at least a couple of years since they had last greeted each other with the slightest indication of affection.

Thirty minutes later she returned. Reed was still seated in the same slumped position with the same empty glass in his hand. Slowly his eyes rose and met hers.

"Something's wrong, isn't it?" she asked.

Reed stared, then nodded.

Patricia took a couple of steps into the room. "What is it? Something at the hospital?"

Silence. Then, "It's Aaron," he finally said. "Aaron Feinerman."

"What about Aaron? I hope it's nothing serious. We were planning on having them over in a couple—"

"Aaron is *dead*," he interrupted, not wanting to hear about the dinner they had planned for the end of Aaron's recuperation. "He died at six-twenty this morning."

"Oh my God. But . . . I don't understand. You were going to perform . . . I don't understand. What happened?"

"I *did* perform surgery on him." Reed set his glass on the desk and straightened in the chair, trying to regain his professional composure. "He died of viral pneumonia. It was totally unrelated to the hernia or the surgery. He probably had it when he was admitted to the hospital, but unfortunately it wasn't picked up in any of the preop testing. These things happen; it's rare, but they happen."

"Poor Ruth. Has she been told?"

Reed rose from the chair and walked to the bar. "Yes. I told her myself this morning. She's taking it pretty well under the circumstances. . . . Care for a drink?" he asked, while pouring himself another.

"No. Nothing . . . Poor Ruth. She loved that man so much. And her all alone in that big house. I should go over and see her. She really needs someone right now."

"They *do* have a maid. I'm sure she'll be all right."

"It's Sunday. The maid's day off."

After taking a swallow he said, "Well, Ruth's a strong woman. It'll be tough on her for a while, but she'll make it all right."

"You don't understand. She needs somebody *now*—today—a shoulder to cry on. Men are so insensitive to these things. I should go over and see her. They have no relatives around here."

Reed tipped the glass again. "Well, if you feel she really needs the company, why don't you go?"

"I shouldn't be more than a couple of hours. If I'm going to be longer, I'll give you a call." Patricia started to leave the room, then stopped. "I'm sorry. How thoughtless of me. I never bothered to ask how *you* were doing. This must have been a tremendous blow to you, too. I know how much Aaron meant to you as a friend. Will you be all right here alone?"

Reed pondered the two ice cubes floating in his glass as if peering into a crystal ball. "I'm a doctor, Patricia. I've had patients die on me before and I'm sure I will again. It's an inescapable reality of practicing medicine. To most people, something like this might be devastating. But a doctor learns to deal with it. He has to, or he would lose his objective approach to the practice of medicine."

"But this was Aaron, your best friend."

Reed looked up at her and said firmly, "He was a patient, Patricia, and I'm not going to lose sight of that fact. I won't let myself."

*Wednesday, June 20, 1979*

Three days had passed since Aaron's death, and he was due to be buried that afternoon. Bill Nicholas sat at his desk in the pathology office staring at the wall. He had just finished his review of the slides taken during Sunday's autopsy. It seemed right that he should be finished before Aaron went into the ground. So, that morning he made a point to arrive early to review and analyze all seventy-three sections.

What he found confirmed what he had feared all along. Although it was a close question, the slides clearly disclosed a shock-lung condition, not viral pneumonia. The large collection of leukocytes and neutrophils in the organs also strongly suggested that Aaron had died from a shock-lung condition produced by septicemia. It was textbook medicine. Whenever a bacterial infection has entered the bloodstream, the body's natural response is to generate an increase in the white cells to fight the invading microorganisms. Thus, the residual clusters of white cells in Aaron's lungs, stomach, pancreas, and other organs indicated that he had been battling bacteria throughout his cardiovascular system in the last hours of his life.

Uncertain at first, Nicholas kept going over the slides. But as he grew more convinced of the diagnosis, the fear that he had dismissed so lightly when he saw the lesion on Sunday had grown to a life-sized reality. Aaron had died as a result of a contaminated injection into his left hip, which had rapidly evolved into a full-blown septicemia. Without antibiotics, he had died swiftly and helplessly.

"No, dammit," Nicholas said out loud, though no one was there to hear him. "It's a mistake. It's *got* to be."

Carefully he looked again at the section taken from the hip lesion. Under the microscope there was no mistake: the material clearly was pus, with the same accumulation of leukocytes and neutrophils that he had found in the other organs.

"Dammit!" he said again. Grabbing a pencil, he flung it across the room, striking the wall. "Dammit! Some stupid fuckin' nurse. All of this because of a lazy bitch who didn't have the intelligence to use a lousy alcohol pad. Dammit!"

His anger was a confused mixture of remorse over the unnecessary death of a friend and resentment of the fact that he was being forced to make a diagnosis that could affect his career. Why him—and why now? In five years his opinion would be accepted without question. But now—only three years into private practice—he would surely be second-guessed. It was a setback he could ill afford. No one would want to believe that Aaron's death was any more than an unavoidable tragedy; especially with the invincible, the perfect, Jason Reed as attending physician. Why couldn't they have dropped this on Hoefsteader?

Cursing the fates, however, would not help. The autopsy report had to be prepared. With a considerable amount of misgiving and anxiety Nicholas held the microphone to his mouth to begin dictation. Then he hesitated. Recalling that the culture taken from the lesion might be ready, he placed a call to bacteriology.

"Yes, it's ready, Doctor," said the lab technician. "It cultured out as beta hemolytic streptococcus. Do you want the sensitivity study?"

"No, this is a postmortem," Nicholas replied. "Thank you."

Again he held up the mike. Of course, he could always ask Hoefsteader to confirm his diagnosis. *No. Ray wouldn't touch this with the proverbial ten-foot pole*. However good he was as a pathologist, Ray was also a pragmatist. He would be retiring next year and wouldn't want to go out with a tarnished record. "Call it as you see it," he would say. "There comes a time when you have to stand on your own two feet, and this is the time." But then, why not go along with Reed? If Ray could be pragmatic in his approach to medicine, why shouldn't Nicholas? If he called it viral pneumonia, who would be there to say he was wrong? Certainly no one on the staff of Rivergarden. And with Reed as an ally, he'd be virtually assured of becoming chief of pathology next year. The idea was repugnant to every standard he tried to live by. But, after all, he had Joan and the kids to think about, and there was nothing that could be done to help Aaron now. Ruth? Reed was absolutely right. The best thing for Ruth would be to forget this whole tragic mess.

Nicholas glanced at his wristwatch. Eleven-fifteen. No need to finish the report now. He could leave early, have a relaxed lunch, and finish his dictation after the funeral. It would be easier after Aaron had been buried.

No one could have picked a better location for Aaron Feinerman's final resting place. Windward Cemetery was situated only a mile and a half from Long Island Sound and had the sharp smell of salt air. The invigorating winds rushing off the Sound seemed to help cleanse the sorrow as the throng stood listening to the final words over Aaron's grave. Above the pastor's voice and the rustling of the trees, one could hear an occasional sob.

Ruth Feinerman, still controlling her emotions, sat on a folding chair next to the casket, along with a few of Aaron's immediate relatives who had driven up from New York.

Bill Nicholas stood looking intently at the casket. The funeral had been much more difficult to endure than he had anticipated. Dealing with death on a daily basis was much easier when he could ignore its effects on those who were left behind.

Earlier at the mortuary Nicholas had looked into the casket at Aaron's quiet and motionless face. Aaron's eyes were delicately closed and, except for the heavy makeup and ruffled silk lining of the casket, imparted the impression that he had only fallen into a deep, restful sleep. Nicholas had reached in to feel the cold lifeless hands to reassure himself that it was the same body on which he had performed an autopsy on Sunday. At that very moment he had felt a bond with the deceased that no one else in attendance shared, including Ruth. It wasn't the fact that he and he alone had inspected every organ in Aaron's body—even microscopically. It went deeper than that. Bill Nicholas suddenly realized that he might be the only one who knew exactly how Aaron had died. For five long minutes he continued to stare at Aaron, almost hoping to see him open his eyes and say, "Go ahead, Bill, I'll understand. Do what you have to do."

After a few consoling words to Ruth, he began making his way through the crowd to his car. Then from behind he heard a familiar voice.

"Bill! Nicholas!"

Nicholas stopped and waited for Reed without looking back at him.

"I wasn't sure if I'd see you here," said Reed, as he stepped alongside. "You had mentioned you might not be able to make it."

They continued walking across the grass toward the cars, a hundred yards away.

Nicholas pulled out a cigarette and tapped it against the side of the pack. He had cut down to five a day, but the time had never seemed more appropriate. "I changed my mind," he said. "Everyone else was going, so I figured, what the hell."

"I arrived a little late, but caught most of the service. Aaron would be quite happy if he saw the number of his friends who are here to see him."

"Friends! You think all these people are friends? Take a look around. Half the people here hardly knew him."

"Why else would they be here? Don't you think they have better things to do than attend funerals?"

Nicholas pulled a lighter from his pocket, cupped his hands, and lit the cigarette. "It's all a show—an act. They're here because it's expected of them. Name me one staff member who would dare show his face at the hospital after missing this funeral without some reasonable excuse."

"Well, he *was* chief of staff. I don't think it's so surprising that everyone would want to pay their last respect—even those who may not have known him that well."

Nicholas took a long, satisfying draw on his cigarette. It was his first of the day. "That's my point. Last respects for whose benefit? Certainly not for Aaron. Do you think his spirit is sitting up in a tree watching this? Aaron is dead and gone. And if he had the great fortune to check in up above, I'm sure he has more important things to do than count the number of people that show up at his funeral. . . . No, I think this is all a bunch of bullshit."

Reed's bald head began to redden. "I noticed *you* showed up for this . . . bullshit, as you put it. Why are you so different from everyone else?"

Another puff on the cigarette and a contemplative look at a nearby grave marker. "My motives are different. Not any more commendable, but different."

"How?"

"I'd prefer not to go into it at this time."

"I think you owe me an explanation," Reed snapped. "If I'm a hypocrite, why aren't you?"

"Maybe you're right," Nicholas conceded. "I hadn't fully understood why I was out here, myself—that is, until I started talking with you. I detest funerals. But I had some questions I had to answer. Questions about myself. I guess I had to come out here and see Aaron to get the answers." Nicholas took another drag.

"What kind of questions? I don't follow you."

"As I was finishing the autopsy report this morning, I began to realize I was at a crossroads in my life. Was I going to do what was expected of me—take the safe and secure road— or was I finally going to stand up and be counted? Telling the truth is not always easy in this business. . . . Aaron had helped me over a stumbling block once before in my life. How ironic that he should be the one to give me direction once again—and after his death, at that."

Reed ran a hand over his glistening head. "It sounds as though you've already made your choice."

"I guess I have."

"You know, truth is not necessarily inconsistent with safety and security."

"It is *this* time."

A strong hand shot out, grabbing Nicholas by the arm.

"You'd better explain yourself, Nicholas," Reed growled. "If you've got something to say that reflects on my medical care, I want to hear it and I want to hear it *now*."

Nicholas looked up at Reed for the first time. His fat glaring face—indignant, intimidating—personified all that Nicholas had hated about his practice over the past three years. "All right. You want to hear it?" he shouted back. "Well, here it is. Aaron died of septicemia, not viral pneumonia. You hear that, Dr. Perfect? While you were sleeping in your comfortable bed, Aaron lay dying of an infection that any number of antibiotics could have knocked out in a matter of hours. To put it succinctly, you *blew* it. He died because you wouldn't get off your lazy ass and go down to the hospital."

Like Reed's, Nicholas's face was flushed with anger. Mourners who had been walking toward their cars began to stare at the two yelling doctors. For a moment there was silence as Reed noticed the attention they were drawing. His lower lip quivered.

"You're through, Nicholas. Your career as a pathologist is over. By the time I'm finished with you, there won't be a doctor in this town who will have a thing to do with you. Your opinion in this case will brand you once and for all as an incompetent."

Nicholas angrily threw his cigarette to the ground. "My opinion will withstand the scrutiny of any reputable pathologist you can name," he snapped. "Attack my competence just once and I'll sue you for slander."

Patricia, who had been left at the grave site, finally reached her husband and took his arm to lead him away. "C'mon," she said. "People are staring."

Ignoring her, Reed said, "You really think everyone will back you up? You're a bigger fool than I thought. The only convincing test for septicemia is a *blood culture*, and you told Wilson not to run them—or did you forget? Go ahead and sue me, you ass. Without cultures there isn't a doctor in town who would dare agree with you."

Patricia was finally able to pull Reed away, while Nicholas, stunned, continued to look on. Reed was right. Without cultures to analyze the organisms in Aaron's blood, there would always be room for doubt. Any honest pathologist would privately agree that septicemia was the likely cause of death. But officially, Nicholas was in for a problem—and he knew it.

No one would ever implicate Reed or the hospital as long as there was any room for disagreement.

Ray Thomas stepped up beside Nicholas. He had been walking a short distance behind and had caught most of the shouting match. "I will say this, Bill," he offered. "You've sure got balls. Boy, do you ever. I didn't know you had it in you."

"Neither did I. Unfortunately, I have a sneaking suspicion that Reed will shortly be cutting them off."

# Chapter VI

*Monday, July 23, 1979*

Rachel Hennessy's usual effervescence had waned to a look of uncertainty and apprehension as she slid into the booth at Hagan's. Rigidly she sat searching the face across the table for some sign of reassurance.

"Hi. You're looking well," she said.

Uncomfortable at the reason for their meeting, Jonathan fidgeted in his seat. In his hand he held a necessary crutch: Tanqueray on the rocks bathing a large green olive.

"You're as pretty as ever, yourself, Rachel," he lied. The luster was gone from her hair, and redness framed her eyes. Not even the artistic application of makeup could hide the fact that she recently had been crying.

After what seemed a long silence she said, "I called your office several times last week. Don't you ever return phone calls?"

"I've been busy. Sometimes the most important calls go unanswered—at least for a while. . . . How are things at your office?"

Rachel lowered her eyes and shook her head. "I didn't go in today. As a matter of fact, I didn't go in on Friday, either."

"Why not? Aren't you feeling well?"

Her eyes widened and fluttered in an effort to hold back the tears. The last thing she wanted to do was create a scene. She wanted no sympathy. "I . . . I'm fine. I've just been a little emotional the past couple of days. You know how women can get at times."

Jonathan stared into his drink. "Yes . . . yes, I understand."

There had been a sense of finality in his voice when he had called her early that morning—a cool uneasiness. The conversation had been short; a simple invitation to lunch "to talk over a few things." But Rachel had known why he wanted to see her. They hadn't dated in over a week and he wasn't even returning her calls. Initially she pretended that he only wanted to establish some ground rules for their relationship, but finally she admitted to herself that their short-lived affair was coming to an end. Still, she grabbed at the disappearing hope that she was wrong.

Rachel reached into her beige leather purse, withdrew a handkerchief, and softly blotted at the accumulating moisture in her eyes. "I still don't understand why we have to see each other only once a week," she said. "We had so much fun earlier. I know that if you gave it half a chance, you would see what a perfect match we are for each other. We have so many things in common: we're both from small towns, we both love sailing, our careers are in law. We even read the same—"

"Rachel, it's not going to work," he interrupted.

"But . . . but it's got to. You're wrong. You haven't even—"

Just then the waiter arrived and handed them the menus. *What timing,* Jonathan thought. Noting his drink, the waiter turned to Rachel and said, "Could I get you a cocktail while you're looking at the menu?"

"Yes, I'd like a Bloody Mary. No, make that a Cutty and soda—a double."

After the waiter had left, Jonathan said, "Are you sure? You know how fast liquor hits you."

"I'm sure."

"Look, Rachel, I've been doing some thinking over the past week . . . about us . . . our relationship. I hope you understand this is not easy for me."

Rachel stared at him with glassy eyes.

"I've been a loner all my life," he continued. "It's this big defect in my personality. I can't seem to establish any kind of meaningful relationship with anyone. I'm thirty-five years old and I've never been engaged. I haven't even gone steady. Oh, there have been women that I dated for a while—but never exclusively. I just don't want to be tied down."

"I understand how you feel, Jon. Really I do. You want your freedom. All I'm asking is that you give it a chance to work. If what you want is once a week, okay, then it'll be once a week. I can accept it. I wish I could see you more, but I can accept it." A tear rolled down Rachel's cheek. She was beginning to lose control. "But please, Jon, please don't break it off."

"Rachel, I've *got* to. We'd be prolonging the inevitable. It wouldn't be fair to either of us."

Rachel bit down on her lower lip. "You don't care for me, do you?"

"That's not true, Rachel. I *do* care. It's only that . . ."

"At least you could be up front with me. If you cared, you wouldn't be doing this."

"If I didn't care," he said firmly, "I wouldn't be sitting here right now. I would have called and told you over the phone. Do you think I'm enjoying this?"

"Then why won't you try?"

The waiter appeared and deposited Rachel's drink in front of her. Embarrassed at her tears, she turned away.

"Have you decided yet?" asked the waiter, who seemed oblivious to the untimeliness of his arrival.

"Give us another ten or fifteen minutes," Jonathan said.

"If you're being honest and truly care for me, why can't we continue to see each other? *What are you afraid of?*" she persisted.

"Look, Rachel. Nothing is going to be gained by going into this. Why don't we—"

"You owe it to me, Jon."

"It's . . . it's just that whenever a relationship starts becoming serious—more intimate—I become like a caged animal, like I'm suffocating. I need my freedom, without commitment. It's the only way I'm happy."

"If you felt this way, why didn't you tell me up front?"

"I made no promises."

"You made no promises, but there are ways of leading a girl on. . . . Don't you understand? I've fallen in *love* with you." Her tears began rolling uncontrollably. Eagerly she finished the second half of her drink. "*Now* what do I do? All I can think about all day is you. My work is suffering. I don't sleep well. . . . It's just not fair."

Ridden with guilt, he said softly, "I'm so sorry, Rachel. I never wanted to hurt you. You're a very special woman and the last one in the world that I would purposely mislead." Jonathan lifted his drink for the first time since her arrival and took a sip. Up to this point the word *love* had not been used by either of them and it seemed to bring home the depth of Rachel's anguish.

"You're never going to be close to *anyone*, Jon," she said, "unless you give it a chance. You're fighting it. I really understand you now. It's something I can deal with, so why don't we try?"

He shook his head, rejecting the idea. "Because . . . because I'm not in love with you, Rachel. I care. I care deeply. But I'm not in love. Maybe someday I'll change, but right now the best thing is for both of us to go our separate ways. It's the way I want it."

Rachel inhaled deeply to gain strength, and looked around at the sea of strangers. It would be hard, but she was going to leave with dignity.

"Well, I'd just as soon pass on lunch," she said. "I hope you understand."

"I understand," he said, looking up. "I'm sure we'll be seeing each other around. I hope we can remain friends."

She gazed into his eyes for a moment, then turned and left. She would have to give it some thought.

# Chapter VII

Most of life is spent following a series of routines. That's the way Jonathan saw it and the way he always wanted it. In an existence full of pitfalls and uncertainty, it offered security. Familiarity was the key. Without a family to fall back on during moments of need, the routines of daily living gave him strength. In a way that only he understood, Jonathan's law practice had become his family.

It was five minutes after two when he reached the door to

his suite. He had walked through that door at least a couple of thousand times since he had first leased the offices four years earlier. The routine was always the same: the rapid clatter of the typewriter sounding much like a ticker tape; the journey through the secretarial bay while depositing his coat on the twenty-year-old coat rack he had picked up at a garage sale; the quick salute to Sally as he was loosening his tie; her responding nod and smile without breaking stride on the keyboard. This was the way it had always been.

Thus, the silence from within hit him like an explosion as he opened the door. Through the open window between the reception room and the bay he could see Sally. She was pacing back and forth, working on a slowly disappearing fingernail.

As the door snapped shut, Sally caught Jonathan's presence and started toward him, almost stumbling over herself in the process.

"Oh, Mr. Rand. Thank God you're here."

"What is it, Sally? Has something happened?"

"It's Mrs. Feinerman. Dr. Feinerman's widow." She spoke with almost reverent excitement, her voice just above a whisper. "She's here," she said, pointing with her left hand and cupping her mouth with the other. "Right here in your library. She called after you'd left for lunch and wanted to see you this afternoon. I tried to put her off until you got in, but she wanted an appointment immediately. She said it was extremely important, so I set it up for one-thirty. You're *always* back by one-thirty, so I didn't think there would be any problem."

"I went for a drive after leaving Hagan's."

"I hope I did right, Mr. Rand. This has to be the biggest case to hit this town in two years. I didn't want to take a chance on her going to another lawyer."

"What are you talking about?"

"Malpractice! Haven't you heard the rumor? It's all over town. A girl friend of mine told me. She's a nurse's aide at Rivergarden. There was a big blowup about it at Dr. Feinerman's funeral. Did I do right, Mr. Rand?"

"You did right, Sally. Why is she in the library?"

"After she had waited for thirty minutes, I thought it would be better if she was in the library. That way I could talk with you before you saw her."

"Good thinking. See if you can locate Rusty Murdoch," he

said, stepping toward the closed library door. "If he's still on the wagon, I may need him to do some work for me."

"Hi," said Jonathan as he swung open the door. "I'm sorry I was late. I had to stop by the courthouse on my way back from lunch." Falsehoods were always justified when away from the office on personal matters.

Ruth sat calmly at the far end of the conference table clasping her hands. "That's quite all right, Mr. Rand. I was just admiring your library. I kind of sprung this on you, anyway."

"No problem," he assured her. "I've got nothing pressing this afternoon. Why don't we step into my office? Oh, and please call me Jon. I hate formality."

As Jonathan followed her through the door, he took note of her graceful movements. As befitted her bereavement, she wore a dark blue skirt and matching blouse. A short baby-blue scarf was tied around her neck and added just enough brightness to her attire to be tastefully stylish.

They had met once before, at the Yacht Club. Over the ensuing months they had waved and said hi but had never really talked.

After helping Ruth into the client chair and easing into his own behind the desk, Jonathan said, "You look like you're holding up well. I imagine this past month has not been easy."

"No, it hasn't. But I'm doing much better now. Look, I know I kind of pushed myself in here this afternoon, but I just had to talk to you."

"I hope I can help you, Ruth. Take whatever time you need." Jonathan sensed what she was leading up to, and it was all he could do to hide his exuberance. Slowly he leaned back in his chair, trying to look relaxed.

"You, of course, know what happened with . . . Aaron. Well, for the past couple of weeks I'd been calling for the autopsy report. Calling and waiting. First it was in dictation and hadn't been transcribed. Then the pathologist wasn't around to review and sign it." Ruth stiffened in her chair as she reached into her purse and withdrew a folded paper. "Well, today . . ." she said, her voice breaking with emotion, "today it finally came. It was delivered in the morning mail." Ruth closed her eyes and swallowed. "After I read it, I just sat in total shock. I couldn't believe it. I read it again and I . . . I became angry." Ruth handed over the report. "Aaron didn't die of viral pneumonia as I had been told. He died of septicemia. *Septicemia,* an infection of the blood. He also had an infected area on his left hip, right where he would have received intramuscular injections. The implication is obvious. Some incompetent RN injected him with a dirty needle, and they just sat around and watched him die without once giving an antibiotic." Ruth's voice shook with vengeance.

Regaining her composure, she said, "Aaron once mentioned to me that you occasionally took on a malpractice case, so I called a few lawyer friends of mine. They all said that you were the best. . . . Jon, I want you to represent me. I don't care what it costs and I don't care who this falls on. I want to come down on someone and I want it to hurt. Will you do it?"

He wanted to say yes without further thought. He was flushed with excitement. The thought of benefiting from another's tragedy was personally repugnant, but still he found it impossible to suppress his enthusiasm: with Aaron's likely income, Ruth's wrongful-death case was worth at least two or three million dollars, maybe more. But he directed his attention to the autopsy report. "Let me take a look at this," he said, trying to maintain his professional detachment. "It sounds like you might have a hell of a case, but I'd like to review this report for a moment."

He carefully read the five-page report, referring several times to the *Dorland's Medical Dictionary* on the credenza behind his chair. Although he did not understand some of the medical terms, his experience on other personal-injury cases had provided him with sufficient medical knowledge to pick out a few significant points.

"I see they never did a blood culture," he observed.

"I know. But Bill Nicholas feels it was septicemia, and that's good enough for me."

"Maybe so. But I'd still like to have a good pathologist look at the slides. I've used Wesley Lundgren up in New Haven on a couple of cases. He's an excellent man and is not easily intimidated."

"That's fine with me, Jon. Whatever it takes. Just tell me you'll take the case."

Jonathan's restraint surprised even himself. He was on the verge of signing a case that not only could make him wealthy but possibly could establish him as one of the top personal-injury lawyers on the East Coast. Yet, he was as calm and patient as if he were signing a ten-thousand-dollar whiplash.

Again he looked at the report. "There's another loose end. Dr. Nicholas does not draw any connection between the infection on the hip and the septicemia. He only reports its existence without—"

"It's connected," she snapped. "I *know* it. I was a nurse for ten years. How else would the bacteria get into Aaron's blood? It doesn't just show up one day. There had to be some means of it entering the bloodstream, and the autopsy report has no other explanation."

"Ruth, I hope you understand that I'm only trying to cover some potential problem areas. My questions should not in any way be interpreted as lack of interest in your case."

Ruth shook her head. "I'm sorry, Jon. You're right. Absolutely right. We should have these things thoroughly evaluated."

"Look, Ruth, if you want me to represent you, we can sign a retainer right now. My fee is forty percent of the gross recovery."

"I don't care about the fee. You can have all of it for all I care. I just want to hit back in the only way I know how."

"Well, the State Bar might frown a bit if I took *all* of it. Forty percent will be just fine. I'll also need twenty-five hundred dollars as an advance toward costs."

Ruth immediately opened her purse and scribbled out a check. "If you need more," she said, "just give me a call."

Accepting the check, he said, "This will be fine for now, Ruth," then switched on his intercom. "Sally, draw up a forty-percent retainer for Mrs. Feinerman and bring in some medical authorization forms."

Jonathan sat back in his chair. "Now, I want to explain a little bit about what you're letting yourself in for. The closer your relationship with Aaron, the bigger your loss. This equates to a large award. Conversely, a poor marriage means fewer dollars. So, once we file suit, your entire marital relationship with Aaron will be open game. Everything from your most intimate moments to your most vocal arguments will be the subject of inquiry. The questions will be deep, probing, and sometimes quite embarrassing. At the slightest indication of any—how should I put it—indiscretion, by either you or Aaron—even unsubstantiated—there will be insinuation, innuendo, and possibly outright accusation of running around. You won't believe the dirt that will be thrown if there is the slightest opening. Aaron's income will also be subject to scrutiny. His books will be reviewed in detail. In short, once this suit is filed, very little will be private in your life anymore."

Ruth was unaffected by the bleak picture Jonathan painted. She would willingly give up her privacy to bring Reed to his knees. And she also wanted to shake Rivergarden to its very foundation. "It makes no difference, Jon. It'll be a small price."

"There's more," he cautioned. "This is a malpractice suit. Your whole life has centered around medicine and Rivergarden Hospital. You may lose a lot of friends over this. There may even be threats; it's happened before." The admonition was his standard one. Now Jonathan began to regret his compulsive need for routine. The last thing he wanted to do was talk her out of the suit.

"Aaron and I had something special," she said, "and it didn't come easy. At one point we even talked about divorce. But about a year and a half ago a number of things happened and turned it all around. Aaron became my friend. He was also my partner and lover. We were virtually inseparable. We actually *enjoyed* being with each other. It might sound trite, but we had the kind of marriage I dreamed about as a child." Ruth's normally serene eyes were afire with conviction. "I don't give a damn about my privacy, I don't give a damn about Rivergarden, and most of all I don't give a damn about any so-called *friends* that I might lose by filing this suit."

"Then that's exactly what we'll do. But while we're waiting for Sally, maybe you could tell me a little bit about you and Aaron. I'm especially interested in why you contemplated divorce and exactly what happened to change your mind."

"I guess things really started happening in Aaron's career about seven years ago—only a few years after we were married. He'd already finished his residency in orthopedic surgery and had passed his boards. Anyway, he had this special patient that he had been treating for an incurable arthritic condition. Nora Hamilton was her name. She was the sweetest old lady and had won Aaron over more than I'd ever seen before or since. We even had her out to our home for dinner once. Her problem was getting quite severe and there was absolutely no hope for relief through any kind of surgery that was known at the time. It was tragic. This wonderful woman was faced with the prospect of either going through her few remaining years with near-intolerable pain or loading up on addictive pain medication.

"Well, Aaron was seldom without an answer for anything. He'd read about a physician in West Germany who had had considerable success with hypnotherapy. Aaron reviewed all of his articles and even called and spoke with him a couple of times. When he was satisfied that he knew what he was doing, he began using the German's technique on Mrs. Hamilton. He worked with her for over six months, gradually developing his own methods. Gradually her pain began to subside and then finally disappeared.

"You should have seen him, Jon. He was like a child. His excitement . . . You would have thought he had discovered the fountain of youth. About a year later he submitted an article describing his technique that was published in the *New England Journal of Medicine*. As you might guess, following the publication came a large number of patient referrals from other physicians along the eastern seaboard. During the next three or four years he published an additional twenty-three articles and one textbook. Eventually he was seeing patients from all over the United States and even an occasional patient from England and Europe.

"I guess that's when things started turning bad for us. As Aaron's prestige and popularity grew, so did the size of his practice. In spite of opening his own clinic and taking on two young physicians to assist him, most of his patients still had to wait as long as a month to undergo his treatments. And the years of long hours were taking their toll. I lost patience and began to rebel. Arguments became more frequent, fueled by Aaron's continued refusal to have children. 'It would be unfair to our kids,' he would say. 'Wait until I have the clinic running on its own, when I can spend more time with my family. Just a few more months,' he promised. But the months had turned into years and I was thirty-two years old.

"Then, about a year and a half ago, something wonderful happened. They say that money can't buy happiness. Don't believe them. Aaron inherited almost two million dollars from his grandfather. One day we're killing ourselves to enjoy a little luxury and build a nest egg for the future, the next we're sitting with it all in our laps. All the excuses were suddenly gone. Finally we were given cause to sit back and reflect on our life-style and what was happening to us. I still remember lying in bed, talking straight through the night. It was wonderful. When the sun came up the next morning, we were two different people. Since that night, almost without fail, we spent every Saturday and Sunday together. And that's when we decided to buy the boat.

"Aaron was badly in need of a weekend escape from his practice, so we took a portion of his inheritance and purchased our fifteen-year-old Trumpy. You may recall how badly it needed painting and varnishing and general repair. Aaron was almost as excited about doing the work as buying the boat itself. Working on the yacht was exactly what the doctor ordered, and we'd spend all our weekends dressed in old clothes, knee deep in paint and sandpaper. That's when we named her *The Prescription*.

"From then on our life together was like a fantasy, right up until Aaron went into the hospital. . . . Well, almost, anyway. I . . . Oh, never mind."

"Is there anything else?" Jonathan asked. "You seem a little uncertain about something."

Ruth looked down at the floor, perplexed, wondering if she should bring it up. "Well, I don't think it's really important, but . . ."

"Why don't you go ahead and tell me," he insisted. "Maybe it isn't, but I should know everything. Let *me* make the decision."

"Well, about two weeks before he was admitted to the hospital, Aaron attended a meeting of the Orthopedic Surgeons Advisory Committee at the Food and Drug Administration in Rockville. As usual, I was at Sikorsky Airport to meet and drive him home. I had seen him tired and irritable before, when he'd gotten off an airplane. But on this particular afternoon he was . . . it's kind of hard to describe . . . he was nervous—no, he looked more like he was frightened.

"Now, I knew he had been a little upset about the surgery," she continued, "but this was different, so I asked him about it. But he just passed it off as concern over the operation and I let it drop. I asked him again the night before his surgery and got the same reply. Since his death, however, I've thought more and more about the timing of this, although I can't really see how the two could be tied together."

"Was he a member of the committee or just a witness?" Jonathan asked.

"He was a regular member of the committee. In fact, he'd attended about six or seven other meetings over the previous year."

"What did they discuss at these meetings?"

"Well, I asked," she replied, "because it seemed like six or seven meetings over a year for an FDA committee would be more than I'd expect. Although I really don't know that much about it. But Aaron said they were only reviewing testimony and studies about Chymopapain injections."

"Chymopapain! Are you talking about that papaya-juice stuff they inject into herniated discs?"

"Yes. Apparently it's supposed to dissolve the disc so that they can avoid the necessity of surgery. And Aaron was quite interested in it, because he was always looking for alternate methods to surgery. But he told me they were getting unsatisfactory reports."

"I think I recall reading about it," Jonathan offered. "Weren't there some deaths associated with its use?"

"Yes, there were. It was a very controversial drug. . . . Why? Do you think that it has something to do with all of this?"

"I doubt it," Jonathan said. "But let me ask you. Do you know whether Aaron had ever used it?"

"No, he hadn't. At least he denied it to me."

Jonathan sat a minute pondering her story. "Well, I'm sure that all this is totally irrelevant—as we lawyers always say. So I wouldn't worry about it. You've got a good case against Reed and possibly against the hospital. That's where the evidence points, anyway. Let's not confuse matters by dwelling on something that might have bothered Aaron a couple of weeks earlier."

"Okay, Jon. You're the boss."

"Right now I want to get a few details from you about what happened at the hospital. Six months or a year from now, you may have forgotten a lot of points, many of which may turn out to be important. I know it might be a little painful now, but . . ."

Jonathan took the next hour to complete the written statement from Ruth. Nothing was left unexplored. Every detail, every conversation, her thoughts at the time, Aaron's prior medical history, everything she knew about Jason Reed—all were committed to paper. Jonathan always took pride in his thoroughness and this case above all was to be no exception. Months down the line, things that seemed unimportant now might turn out to be critical to the outcome of the case. Ruth would also be able to use the notes to refresh her memory just before the trial, when her memory would surely be dimmed. By the time he had finished, Ruth was emotionally exhausted and eager to leave.

"Is that it?" She sighed.

"One more thing. We only touched on Aaron's earnings. Do you recall how much he made last year? That would be for 1978."

"Somewhere around three hundred and twenty-five thousand dollars. The books are still in his office. If you want, I could have them run over to you."

"I'll be near there next week. I'd prefer to stop in and pick them up myself. Will there be anyone in his office? I'd like to talk to some of Aaron's staff."

"Well, the office is closed now. His two associates have left and formed a partnership. But Dani now works down the hall in Dr. Jacobs's office and could let you in. I'm also sure she'd be glad to talk to you."

"Dani?"

"Danielle Brennan. She was Aaron's receptionist and medical assistant."

"Oh, yes. I recall talking to her on the phone."

"If you want, I'll give her a call and tell her to expect you."

"That'll be fine." Jonathan stood up. "And as soon as I've had Aaron's medical records reviewed, I'll give you a call. Shouldn't be over two or three weeks."

Ruth thought of Jason Reed sitting on a witness stand, squirming under heated cross-examination, and for the first time in a month she smiled. Finally, she was doing something positive to release her anger.

As Ruth closed the door to the office, Jonathan slammed his fist into his open hand and smiled. The case of a lifetime. A dream come true.

Pacing restlessly around his office, Jonathan waited a couple of minutes for Ruth to leave the suite, then opened the door to begin barking out instructions. Sally stood at attention with a pen poised over a notepad. Like Jonathan's, her face beamed with enthusiasm.

"All right, here it is. Run—don't mail—these authorizations over to the copy service and have them photocopy all of Aaron's records at Rivergarden. Super rush. When they're in, shoot them over to Dr. Simpson in Hartford. I need an evaluation of the standard of care at Rivergarden, *as well* as of Dr. Reed. At the same time, have Rusty stop in and get another authorization. He'll have to pick up the autopsy slides and run them, along with the report, up to Dr. Lundgren at Yale. When he gets back, I'll have some investigative work for him to do. Oh, and one other thing."

"What's that, Mr. Rand?"

"If you have any pressing need for medical attention, get it done in the next week and a half. After we file this suit, there won't be a doctor in town who'll even talk to us."

# Chapter VIII

*Thursday, August 2, 1979*

Ray Hoefsteader's jaws churned at a long green Havana cigar as he nervously geared up for a distasteful task.

Through the large bay window of the doctors' lounge he watched the usual variety of patients and visitors entering and leaving the hospital. Along the walkway the marigolds and pansies blossomed in radiant colors. The brook splashed through the square under the wooden bridge leading to the public parking lot. It was a familiar sight and one that Hoefsteader had never tired of looking at in the seventeen years he had been at the hospital.

In one corner of the room sat George Stein and Harold Wasserman, young interns on their afternoon break. One was intently taking notes from a textbook on gynecological oncology, while the other browsed through a six-month-old issue of *Playboy*. The room was scattered with other magazines, dirty ashtrays, empty Coke bottles, and coffee-stained paper cups. The cleaning crew was not due until three-thirty, shortly after the end of the day shift.

When Bill Nicholas pushed his way through the door, he

already had a good idea of what he was about to encounter. Since yesterday, Rivergarden had been alive with a rumor that the hospital was being sued for the death of Aaron Feinerman. Speculation on the amount of the suit ranged from one to fifteen million dollars. Furtive glances had greeted him all morning. Everyone from staff physicians down to the orderlies seemed to know about the lawsuit and who was responsible for it.

Hoefsteader's long, gangly figure was silhouetted against the window. Smoke billowed up from his cigar.

"You wanted to see me, Ray?"

Hoefsteader continued looking out the window, rolling the cigar over in his fingers. "Yes, I did, Bill. Come on in and have a seat."

Guardedly, Nicholas made his way across the room and stopped behind his mentor of three years. "If it's all the same to you, Ray, I'd prefer to remain standing."

Hoefsteader pulled the cigar from his mouth and slowly turned. The air was tense, and Stein did not waste any time gathering his notes and book and promptly leaving; Wasserman dropped his magazine on the table and followed.

"This is somewhat of a private matter, Bill. Maybe we should use my office."

Nicholas scanned the empty room. "No need. I'm sure this'll be fine for whatever you have to say."

Hoefsteader again gnawed at the end of his cigar. His eyes hung sadly on his long and wrinkled face. He looked ten years older than his true age of sixty and was looking forward to retirement at the end of March, next year. Reluctantly he pulled a legal document from his pocket and handed it to Nicholas.

"The hospital was served with this yesterday morning. It's a lawsuit. . . . I think you already know what it's all about. As you can see, Jason Reed was also sued."

Nicholas slowly turned the pages, mentally extracting some of the legal phraseology: ". . . so negligently and carelessly diagnosed, medicated, cared for and treated decedent AARON S. FEINERMAN, so as to proximately cause the death of said decedent, and the damages to plaintiff as hereinafter alleged . . . as a proximate result of said negligence and carelessness of said defendants, and each of them, plaintiff has suffered loss of support, society, companionship and affection in the total sum of five million dollars ($5,000,000) . . ." Only five million! To hear everyone talk, you would have thought the suit equaled the national debt.

"Yes, I heard about it," said Nicholas, handing the papers back to Hoefsteader. "It's unfortunate, but I guess it was more or less inevitable."

"Unfortunate, yes. But inevitable?" He shrugged. "There are a few who would disagree with you."

"Tell me, Ray, are you one of those few?"

"That's rather unimportant at this point," said Hoefsteader.

"Not to *me* it isn't. For days I agonized over this before signing out that goddamn autopsy report. In the process, I took on Jason Reed and had such a violent fight with my wife that she almost took the kids and moved out on me. Since then I have been ignored, humiliated, chastised, and treated like a freak in a sideshow. Half the staff thinks I'm Benedict Arnold and the other half is convinced I'm a fuckin' incompetent who couldn't tell a pathology slide from the bottom of a Coke bottle. Now it looks like I'm about to lose my job. But I'd do it all again, because I believe that what I was doing was *right*. I'm . . . I'm standing all alone, Ray. And I guess I want some assurance from a man I have always looked up to that there are still principles to be followed in this dollars-and-cents world."

Hoefsteader turned to the scene outside the window. "If my opinion was so important, why didn't you consult with me before finishing your report?"

"Oh, I was tempted. But I didn't because . . . because I respect you too much." Nicholas groped for a cigarette, found one in his near-empty pack, lit it, then collapsed onto a nearby couch. "I didn't ask for this assignment, Ray, but I wasn't going to dump a hornet's nest into your lap too. I also didn't want to be influenced by what you might have to say. Then I'd have an excuse to compromise my opinion. The only way I could prove my integrity was to call it alone. Besides, I was convinced that you wouldn't want to get involved."

Hoefsteader carefully selected his words. "This morning I spent a very uncomfortable two hours with the Medical Executive Committee. They were all there. Smith, Sanderson, Kline—all of them. We first talked about the lawsuit. As you might guess, everyone was quite upset. They wanted to know why you chose to ignore all the clinical evidence of viral pneumonia when you had no cultures to verify a septicemia."

"Sounds like someone's been talking to them. Was he there?"

"You have to ask?" said Hoefsteader. "He was *also* served with the suit yesterday. It doesn't take much imagination to see what Reed has at stake here."

"I guess not. But he's wrong."

"Do you really think that makes a difference? If you do, you're a fool. That's a policy-making group up there. They've got one foot in medicine, but the other is in business. What's happened here may have a substantial impact on the hospital, and that means loss of prestige and income. They've already been told that the hospital's insurance premiums are going up. Kline even suggested that you went off half-cocked in some reckless effort to retaliate against Reed."

"What! Where in the hell did they get that idea?"

"Reed told them. Where do you think? Didn't you have some kind of a run-in with him a day or two before Aaron's surgery?"

"A run-in? I wouldn't call it a run-in. I got a little upset because he started second-guessing me again. It was no big thing. You mean he's using that as a . . . ?" Nicholas sat stunned. He couldn't believe what he was hearing. "And they're actually *believing* all this shit?"

"Wake up, Bill. You know what kind of influence Reed has on the MEC. His reputation as a surgeon brings a lot of money to this hospital."

"But I never thought they'd *sleep* together."

"What do you think they're doing up there right now? They're forming their game plan on the lawsuit, that's what."

Nicholas took a long drag on his cigarette and helplessly looked up. "What's the bottom line?" he asked with resignation.

Before Hoefsteader could reply, the PA blared. "Dr. Nicholas. Please call Admitting. Dr. Nicholas. Please call Admitting." The voice sounded more like a recording than a live page.

"I'd better catch this," Nicholas said, as he rose and walked to the hospital phone next to the door. After getting his message, he hung up and returned. "Nothing urgent . . . Well, you might as well get it over with, Ray."

Again, silence. Hoefsteader thought of the MEC. He

hated them for their power and what they were putting him through at this moment. "Did you know I was one of the founding directors here? Even Chief of Staff the first year."

Nicholas nodded.

"Oh, yeah, I forgot I told you. I also helped lay out the pathology conference room. They wanted to shove it down in the basement someplace, but I overruled them. Funny how they tend to typecast the pathologists. . . . I really love this place, Bill. But I want you to believe this: in spite of it, I wouldn't be doing this if I had even the slightest choice in this matter. But I don't. I'm under pressure that I . . . They're not going to renew our contract, Bill. That is, if you're still a member of the partnership. I tried to talk them out of it, but they wouldn't listen."

"Did they ask what *you* thought of the slides?"

"Yes, they did. I told them I hadn't reviewed them— which was true. I hadn't. But I told them our doctors had a right to their own opinions, and that if I happened to see it any differently it wouldn't change the final diagnosis on the autopsy report, nor the fact that the hospital had been sued."

"It might change their minds about my competence."

"Don't you see, Bill? They don't *want* to hear you were right. The fact that you came up with an opinion that dropped a lawsuit on them is all they're thinking about. If it hadn't been a close question, that would have been an entirely different matter. But the way they see it, you had room to reach a conclusion that would not have implicated the hospital. When you didn't . . . well, it amounted to a disavowal of your allegiance to Rivergarden."

Nicholas's lips curled into a scornful smile. "Allegiance, huh—I thought my allegiance was to the truth. Rather archaic of me, isn't it? . . . I guess that brings us back to the same question, Ray. Did I do the right thing?"

"There are five other pathologists in our group—each with a family. My wife and I are alone, but we just bought a farm down in Virginia for my retirement. We all rely on our contracts for Rivergarden's pathology work. And it has paid well. Next March I'll be retiring, and without one blemish or controversy in almost forty years of medicine." Hoefsteader stared down at the floor, uncomfortable with what he was saying. "If it had been me, I'm somewhat ashamed to say, I probably would have gone along with them. On the other hand, if I were you, at your age and with my whole career ahead of me, I would have called it as I had seen it. I want to believe I would, anyway. That's about the best answer I can give you."

"Thanks for your honesty, Ray. You'll have my resignation in the morning." Nicholas walked proudly to the door. He had never felt so tall, so confident.

"One more thing I'd like you to know," Hoefsteader called out.

Holding the door open, Nicholas looked back. "What's that?"

"After my meeting with the MEC, I pulled out the Feinerman slides. I'm not really sure why. Maybe to appease my conscience—maybe my curiosity—I don't know. I spent a good hour reviewing them. I didn't want you leaving here without knowing. I totally agree with your conclusion on the cause of death. I'm proud of your work, and I envy your integrity."

Nicholas took one last look, nodded, then let the door close on the first chapter of his professional life.

If visual impressions meant anything, Rusty Murdoch was an intimidating, pugnacious man unwilling to accept anything less than what he was after. He was built like a fireplug, with the wide, strong jaws of a bulldog. His head was afire with curly orange-red hair, the source of his nickname and a suggestion that he might explode if denied immediate acquiescence to his demands.

In truth, his manner was mild and courteous, although his vocation as a private investigator, as well as twelve years with the Hartford Police Department, had taught him that directness was the best approach.

After talking with the admitting clerk who had paged him, Nicholas walked into the hospital lobby, where Murdoch was waiting and introduced himself.

Nicholas expected a crushing injury to his right hand, but instead was pleased to feel only a firm squeeze. "I understand you wanted to speak to me." Nicholas immediately noted the reddened pug nose laced with small broken vessels, the earmark of a heavy drinker.

"Yes, sir." Murdoch handed the doctor his business card. "I've been retained to represent the interests of Ruth Feinerman, the widow of Dr. Feinerman. I understand, sir, that you did the autopsy?"

"Yes, I did. But that would be privileged information."

"Oh, yes. Here's an authorization signed by Mrs. Feinerman," Murdoch said, handing Nicholas the paper.

"How can I help you, Mr. Murdoch?"

"Well, sir, if we could step out into the garden area here, I'd like to ask you about a few of your opinions concerning the cause of death. I'm particularly curious about how the bacteria got into the doctor's bloodstream. Perhaps you might have some comments on that. I'd also be interested in knowing what you thought about the conduct of Dr. Reed in this entire matter."

Nicholas looked up as if he could see through to the third-floor doctors' lounge, then started for the glass doors leading to the square. "Mr. Murdoch, you couldn't have caught me at a better time. I'd be glad to talk to you. So, if you have one of those recording devices, or however you do this sort of thing, you'd better turn it on. A week from now I might not feel as candid."

# Chapter IX

*Friday, August 3, 1979*

Jonathan sat thumbing through a seven-month-old issue of *Newsweek*. Outside, the temperature had soared to the low nineties, and it was refreshing to feel the chill of an air-conditioned office. He had spent the entire morning driving out to see Dr. Simpson in Hartford, only to find on arrival that he had been called away for emergency surgery. Then the long trip back—all without the use of his car's air-conditioner; the damn thing never worked when the weather got hot. Now he sat in Dr. Jacobs's reception room, waiting to see Aaron's medical assistant, vowing to unload the Cadillac the first day he could break free.

"You must be the lawyer. Anyway, you seem to be the only

one foolish enough to wear a vest in this godforsaken heat wave."

Startled, Jonathan dropped the magazine into his lap and looked up in the direction of the voice. He was about to hurl back a witty rebuke, but the words froze in his throat. The striking beauty above him left Jonathan speechless.

Her soft, moist lips curled up ever so slightly in an amused, playful smile. Her hazel eyes seemed to sparkle.

"You *are* Jonathan Rand, aren't you?" She stood almost defiantly with her arms crossed beneath her large full breasts, which strained against her white uniform.

"Uh . . . I'm not quite sure at the moment. But give me a couple of minutes. I usually come up with an answer to that one."

Jonathan managed to struggle to his feet to take a better look. Her long auburn hair hung below her shoulders, gleaming as if it had just been shampooed, and framed a satin-textured olive complexion that seemed without blemish. Her delicate nose rose with a gradual curve.

Mesmerized, Jonathan slowly extended his hand.

"Yes. Yes, I'm Jonathan Rand. And I assume you're Dani . . . Or Danielle, is it?"

"Dani is fine. You wanted to take Dr. Feinerman's books, I understand?"

"Yes. Ruth told me you had a key. I would also like to talk with you about Dr. Feinerman, if you have a few moments."

"I'll take you down the hall and get the books, but we're quite busy right now. Maybe we could save our talk for another time."

The thought of seeing her again was quite pleasing. "Sure. Another time would be fine. Perfect." Not since Sally Reidecker back in high school had he been so taken by the sight of a pretty girl. Had he known in advance, had he been prepared, he would have been in command. His disdain for involvement had equipped him well to handle most attractive women with indifference. But he had been thrown off balance by the unexpected confrontation.

"Come on," she suggested. "I'll show you the office."

Jonathan stepped beside her as they walked down the hall. "You *are* right, you know."

"That's nice to hear. About what?"

"It is rather foolish to be wearing a vest on a day like this."

"Well, you've got an image to maintain."

"It's not that. . . . Well, maybe it is. I had to see a doctor today—professionally, that is. He's a little on the stuffy side. So"—Jonathan pulled back his coat to display his matching vest—"today I look like a lawyer."

Danielle inserted the key, unlocked the door, and smiled. "As I said, you've got an image to maintain."

She flipped on the lights as they entered the reception room. Every bit of furnishing—chairs, tables, lamps, pictures—had been removed. A number of cardboard boxes were scattered around in disorganized stacks. A dolly stood in the middle of the open doorway to the interior offices, partially blocking their path.

"Damn moving crew! They were supposed to be here this morning to finish their job. Probably at a beach someplace. We sold all the furniture and medical equipment to a young doctor fresh into practice and *he* hired the crew. Got a couple of college kids working on their summer vacation. Bargain rate, you understand."

"You get what you pay for, my pa would always say."

Danielle rolled the dolly to the side and proceeded through the doorway and down the hall. Jonathan followed. "Your pa was absolutely right," she said. "And this time it has screwed up everything. We had some cleaners scheduled for this afternoon. *That* had to be postponed. Then on Monday a new tenant was to be moving in. And because the cleaners won't be in today, *that* had to be postponed. Which all means that Mrs. Feinerman will be stuck with several more days of extra rent. A big screwed-up mess."

Jonathan had a natural curiosity about the remainder of the office suite. It was all that was left of the business practice of the man whose life would be the focus of Jonathan's attention for months and maybe years to come. Still, he could not take his eyes off Danielle as she entered an office at the end of the long hall.

"Kind of like the domino theory," he said, trying to be witty.

Aaron's office had not yet been touched by the movers, except for two stacks of six cardboard boxes neatly pushed off in a corner. Otherwise, the exquisitely decorated room appeared ready for immediate use. Even Aaron's degrees, certificates, and plaques still hung on the wall behind the desk.

Danielle turned and faced him, again with her arms crossed. "Domino theory! Very good," she said, as if patronizing a six-year-old child. "You lawyers are amazing, how you throw out these little analogies."

"I see you don't care much for lawyers."

"Let's just say I tolerate them."

"We're not *all* that bad, you know. Some of us have actually done some good in society."

Danielle sighed. "I'm sorry. I've just had my fill of attorneys. My brilliant divorce lawyer was so effective last year, he couldn't even get me alimony. Then this morning— that was the topper. This imbecilic tenant—who didn't hesitate to remind me that *he* was a lawyer—threatens to sue because he won't be able to move in on Monday. He also says that if we don't have the suite ready by Wednesday, he's going to cancel the lease. Which isn't a lease at all but a sublease, because Aar . . . Dr. Feinerman had two more years to go on his lease with the owner. All of this, mind you, because of two unreliable college kids—who I'm sure are planning to go on to law school." With a flick of her hand, Danielle tossed her hair back over her shoulder. "As I say, I've had my fill of lawyers."

Jonathan's discerning ear picked up the near-personal reference to Aaron, and a parade of illicit possibilities flashed through his mind. Consciously he tried to shove them aside. It was something he did not want to believe, for a number of reasons. But it also had a sobering effect on him.

"Don't worry about the lease with the owner," he said firmly. "If it doesn't work out with the tenant, I'll get you out of it."

"No, you don't understand. This was a written lease signed by Dr. Feinerman. It has another two years on a five-year term."

"I understand. As I said, I'll get you out of it."

"Just like that?"

"Just like that. Talk to Ruth about it. If you want, I'll call the owner on Monday and terminate the lease. I'll only need his name and phone number and a copy of the agreement."

"But it's a written contract. How can you possibly—"

Jonathan's face transformed into mock astonishment. "How! You stand talking to the finest lawyer in Connecticut and have to ask *how*? Why, I work little miracles like that several times a week without giving it a second thought." A flash of white teeth as Jonathan began to amuse himself. "Seriously, it's only a little something called impossibility of performance. Any first-year law student would know about it. Dr. Feinerman's unforeseeable death has made it impossible to perform the terms of the lease. It's totally unenforceable."

"Are you sure?"

"Positive."

"Here I thought all along—"

"You should have consulted a lawyer. I'll also call your new imbecilic tenant and put him in *his* place, if you wish. Just all part of the service."

Danielle looked up at Jonathan with the awakening realization that he was not the bumbling schoolboy she'd first thought. He was taking charge, a trait that she had always found attractive in men. He was also downright handsome.

Danielle picked up a pen from Aaron's desk. "All right. Give me your phone number. I'll talk to Mrs. Feinerman and give you a call on Monday."

"Better yet, take my card," he said, handing one to her.

She held it up as if inspecting an important document. "So you're going to sue Dr. Reed, I understand."

"I already have. Rivergarden, too. I served both of them with the papers yesterday."

Danielle ran the end of the pen over the bottom row of her teeth. "Funny. I never thought I would willingly talk to a malpractice lawyer. You hear some pretty nasty things about them around a doctor's office. But somehow you . . . you're different. . . . Well, I'd better get back to the office before they start pulling their hair out." She pulled back a few flaps from one of the cardboard boxes and withdrew three black ledgers. "Here they are," she said. "Income and expenses for the last three years. The accountants have the tax forms and they'll be mailed to you next week."

Jonathan accepted the ledgers. "Thank you," he said, then looked at her quizzically. Danielle's devotion seemed to exceed that of the average employee. "Something I don't quite understand."

"What's that?"

"Are you still on salary with the office? You seem to have taken on some added responsibility since Dr. Feinerman's death."

"Just doing a favor. After a year and a half with the doctor,

I was familiar with his practice, and Mrs. Feinerman needed help. He had always treated me with fairness and understanding, and this was a small way of paying him back. So if you're looking for hidden motives, Mr. Rand, you're going to be disappointed."

"Don't take me wrong, Dani. I have a natural curiosity about *everything*. It's an affliction of my profession." Jonathan *was* looking for hidden motives, and Danielle's perception made him uncomfortable. "Look, I know you've got to get back, but there is a lot I want to ask you about Dr. Feinerman. Maybe we could meet for dinner tonight? I know a great restaurant not far from here that serves an excellent veal Oskar."

"I'm sorry. Tonight is out. Perhaps some other time."

"Then I've got a better idea. I have a small sloop at Connecticut Marina—where Dr. Feinerman kept his yacht. We could meet down there tomorrow morning—say about nine—and get in a little sailing out on the Sound. We could relax, get some relief from the heat, and have a little chat about Dr. Feinerman. More important, you'll get to see that I'm not the arrogant vest-wearing lawyer that you think I am."

Danielle had plans for Saturday, but Jonathan's idea sounded appealing. For a moment she thought of how she could rearrange the weekend, then again displayed her provocative smile. "Why, Mr. Rand, you're asking me out for a date. I thought it was customary to keep business separated from pleasure."

"I detest being customary," he said.

Again she pondered. "All right. I'll meet you down there at nine. What do I bring?"

*Just your beautiful body*, Jonathan thought, but said, "Dress for the weather and bring along a bathing suit, a towel, and rubber-soled shoes. Everything else you'll need I have on board. Let me tell you how to get there."

"That's unnecessary, Mr. Rand. I've been there before."

### Saturday, August 4, 1979

The summer heat and its accompanying humidity created an alliance of discomfort as pervasive as any in recent memory. The loudest sound along the Connecticut coast seemed to be the hum of air-conditioners straining to give relief from the thick, moist air. Long Island Sound had the appearance of a turnpike for boats.

For Jonathan, the day offered more than a temporary escape from the oppressive weather. This day would be a test for him. He would be seeing Danielle again, but this time on his own terrain and under his own conditions. He also knew what to expect and would be well armed. This time he would be in total command.

By six-thirty Saturday morning, Jonathan had shaved, showered, dressed, gathered everything he needed for a day of boating, and was on his way to the marina. He was anxious. And because he was anxious, he was confused. He knew it didn't make sense; *no* woman was going to have that kind of an effect on him.

At the marina he washed down the boat, dried it with a chamois, then spent an hour cleaning below decks and putting everything in its proper place. By eight-thirty he had finished his preparation. Although it was early, every five minutes he looked up toward the landing to see if perhaps she was as eager to begin the day as he was. Slowly the time ticked away.

As the clock reached nine thirty-five, Jonathan was beside himself. He was certain that he had been stood up. Fuck her. If she was so indifferent about the two of them sharing a day together, then so was he. He wouldn't wait any longer, nor would he call to find out why she hadn't come. He would not give her that pleasure. If she came late, she would find nothing but an empty slip. Wouldn't it be wonderful to see her face, Jonathan thought, as he started the outboard engine and prepared to shove off. He wanted to scan the landing one more time as he untied the line from the bow, but fought the urge. It would be much easier if he just dropped the lines and got under way.

Jonathan had reached over to remove the stern line from the chromed cleat on the starboard deck when he felt the presence of someone standing behind him.

"There you are!" said Danielle. "You weren't going to leave without me, were you?"

"I didn't think you were coming."

Out of her white uniform, and displaying her long tan legs, Danielle wore a pair of snug-fitting white shorts with a yellow cotton blouse tied in a knot at the midriff and strategically buttoned to expose her abundant cleavage. Under one arm she clutched a rolled-up towel; with the other she held a bag of groceries.

"I wanted to pick up a few things for sandwiches, so I stopped at a local market. You wouldn't believe the line. Everybody and their brother seemed to be buying beer and Cokes. That and bags of ice. Besides, how did you expect me to find you without a vest on?"

Jonathan laughed, partly at himself, then took the towel and groceries and stepped on board. A delay of thirty-five minutes was not unreasonable under the circumstances. Why had he gotten so upset about it?

"I knew I felt kind of naked running around here," he said. "I must have forgotten to put it on this morning. And me with this image to maintain."

Still smiling, he reached and took her hand to help her on board. Danielle stepped up, then leaned forward to step from the deck into the cockpit. Jonathan's eyes were immediately drawn to the perfection of her breasts. With the close proximity, he detected a slight scent of an enticing perfume, and it was all he could do to take his hands from her as she finally stepped down before him.

"I must apologize, Dani. Yesterday you didn't seem to have much use for lawyers, and when it got to be nine-thirty— I just thought you'd found something better to do."

Again the provocative smile. "You needn't apologize, Jon. I was late. You had every right to expect I wasn't going to show up."

"Well, I should have been more patient. Anyway, you're here and I'm glad you came. Let me stow this stuff and show you around down below. You may also want to put on your bathing suit. It looks like it's going to be another scorcher."

The mainsail of *Dreamboat* hung limp from the mast. Enjoying the salt air and the occasional spray of water slapping against the sides, Danielle and Jonathan lay on the bench seats in the cockpit of the sailboat, indifferent to their location and direction. Despite the slight breeze, the temperature was still in the low eighties, and the heat of the late-morning sun sapped the last vestige of energy from their bodies.

"You mentioned a divorce yesterday," said Jonathan. "How long had you been married?"

"Six long and agonizing months. The attraction was there, but we just couldn't live together. I doubt that a day went by when we weren't at each other about something. The only thing pleasant about the whole marriage was the divorce."

"I take it there were no children."

"Thank God for that. He had two from an earlier marriage. Brats, both of them. Two boys, ten and twelve. We had them every other weekend, which I guess was one of the reasons we argued so much. I made up my mind early that we'd have none of our own. *That* didn't make him happy either."

"Children can be a burden. I swore off a long time ago, myself. I don't think I could stand the restriction. I guess I enjoy my freedom too much."

This was a pleasant surprise. Every man she had ever been interested in had raved about having children—an attitude she considered selfish and inconsiderate. Of course, it was great for them: they would come home in the evening to bounce the precious little things on their knees, shake rattles, make silly faces, then dash off the following morning leaving her with the crying, the dirty diapers, and ten loads of laundry. No, that wasn't the life for her. Not now. Maybe never. That Jonathan would share her attitude about children made him even more attractive.

Jonathan lay still with his eyes closed. A pair of sunglasses sat propped on his nose. "Don't get me wrong," he said. "Children are great. Just as long as they're owned by someone else."

"Well, I'm going down for a refill," Danielle said, rising. "Could I get you another beer?"

"Love it," he said. "Anything to impede the dehydration process."

Danielle scanned the water surrounding the boat. Except for a few white specks on the horizon, they were alone. After another look at Jonathan, she disappeared below.

Up on the deck, Jonathan reached for the railing of the cockpit and pulled himself to an upright position.

"You worked with Dr. Feinerman for a year and a half, I recall," Jonathan called to her, wiping his brow with his forearm. "What did you do before that?"

Below, Danielle was groping through a number of drawers for the suntan lotion. She was sure she had seen Jonathan put it in one of them. "Oh, the usual thing," she called out. "Secretarial, bookkeeping . . . even was a waitress for a while. *That* didn't take long. A month of dodging passes was about all I could take."

"Waitress, hurry up with that beer," he urged. "I'm at the mercy of the sun out here."

"Be up in a second," she responded. Inside, warm excitement began racing through her. She reached behind and gave a tug at the bow holding up the top of her two-piece bathing suit. Feeling it loosen, she shrugged her shoulders forward and let it drop to the floor. Never had she done anything like this before. But then she had always enjoyed doing the unexpected. The heat, the isolation, Jonathan's overt masculinity—whatever it was, it had control over her and she responded.

Grabbing her glass of wine in one hand and a beer and plastic glass for Jonathan in the other, she headed topside.

As she emerged through the open cabin door, her seminudity did not immediately catch Jonathan's attention. His head was tilted back, his eyes closed.

"Here's your order, sir. One ice-cold beer."

"Wonderful." Jonathan extended his right hand toward Danielle as he opened his eyes. For a moment he just stared, trying to adjust to what he was seeing. It must be the damn sun. . . . Bewildered, he pulled off his sunglasses and looked again. His mouth was half-open.

"I hope you don't mind," she said, stepping through the doorway. "I've wanted an all-over tan for years, and this is the best opportunity I have ever had. Nothing you haven't seen before, I'm sure."

Jonathan's eyes were riveted to her breasts. "I . . . I'm not so sure about that," he said uneasily.

No. Not again. Dammit, this time it would be different. Jonathan replaced his sunglasses and cleared his throat. "But . . . uh . . . be my guest. We *are* alone, and we're both adults." Again he leaned back and took a long swallow of the chilled beer. Maybe that would help.

Danielle returned to her seat opposite Jonathan, sipped her wine, and began to apply the lotion to her breasts. Jonathan's face was now flushed and his desires were becoming quite apparent.

"Would you care to help me?" she asked. She wanted

him. Propriety, morality, and what he would think of her were suddenly meaningless considerations.

Unable to muster a verbal response, Jonathan slightly nodded his head, removed his glasses, then stepped to the other side of the boat. As he sat next to her, Danielle returned to her original prone position.

She handed him the lotion. "Here," she said. "Don't miss anything. I don't want to burn." Her eyes no longer teased but demanded.

With a gentle but deliberate motion, Jonathan plied her abdomen with the liquid, methodically rubbing her skin with an up-and-down movement. With each forward thrust he progressively inched closer to her full breasts. Gradually her nipples began to harden, standing, tingling. Gathering more of the white liquid, he began to massage with both hands. Danielle was losing control. Her eyes closed tightly.

Mercifully, he engulfed her firm bosom, his fingers kneading, fondling. His lubricated hands rubbed tenderly over her nipples. Losing all restraint, she grabbed the back of Jonathan's head and pulled him to her open mouth.

Within moments their bathing suits had been thrown aside and their two writhing bodies had merged into one. Jonathan could not remember ever making love with such abandon or finding more satisfaction in the act of sex.

He could not immediately comprehend why he had awakened. How much time had passed? An hour? An hour and a half? The sun was now much farther west. My God, had he actually slept that long? He felt the sense of something imminent, maybe even dangerous, but he could not understand why.

His eyes widened as he made an effort to gain his bearings. The sky was a deep, clear blue. Not even a trace of clouds could be seen. The wind was gusting more and the sail was flapping. Maybe that was it. If he didn't pull in the mainsail, who knows where they might be blown to.

Beside him, still on her back, Danielle lay soundly sleeping, displaying her femininity for the world to see. Jonathan looked down at himself. A pinkish cast had begun to color the area below his waist, which had never before been exposed to the sun.

No. It wasn't the sails that had bothered him. It was

something else, something he could hear. A churning. Something immense was nearby. Maybe a boat. A large one. Jonathan now heard the hum of massive engines casually torquing over a large propeller. *Oh, my God, a ship!*

At the moment of his horrifying realization, Jonathan heard someone whistle, followed by laughter.

"Dani!" he shouted. "Dani, wake up! Hurry!" Frantically he shook her as he crouched and grabbed for his towel on the opposite bench seat.

One hundred yards astern was a large freighter, maybe four hundred feet long, heading toward the open Atlantic. Though riding low with a full load, its hull rose sixty feet above the waterline. Its faded blue siding was corroded and badly in need of paint. A crowd of ten to fifteen crewmen had accumulated, laughing, whistling, shouting catcalls. Three or four of them seemed to be fighting over a pair of binoculars.

Responding to the commotion and to Jonathan's shaking, Danielle sat up and rubbed her eyes, which brought on an even louder barrage of whistling and yelling.

"What's going on?" Danielle's eyes widened in shock at the same time that Jonathan threw a towel over her.

"Down below!" he shouted. "I've got to get the boat around or we'll be swamped by the wake."

Not needing a second command, Danielle dashed below as Jonathan threw on the start switch and desperately tugged at the rope of the outboard.

Having safely passed the small sloop, the freighter began to pull away. Rusted white letters across the stern read: *SAN CARLO, SANTOS.*" The crew had now shifted to the rear for their final look at what would be the subject of their storytelling and jokes for years to come.

Luck was with the young couple as the small engine sputtered on with the fifth yank. Without wasting a moment, Jonathan pushed the tiller to port and gunned the throttle. No sooner had he swung into the oncoming three-foot wake than it arrived, shoving the bow up and then down like a bobbing cork. As the boat continued to teeter, he angrily spun around to bid the *San Carlo* and its crew a final farewell. Jonathan thrust his right arm high into the air, his middle finger pointing toward the heavens. "Fuck you!" he screamed.

Jonathan went down below to confront Danielle. Had it not been for the sunburn on his face, the flush of his embarrassment would have been evident. Danielle sat on a bunk, again wearing her white shorts and yellow blouse, while Jonathan stood halfway down the steps, holding the towel in one hand. He was looking at her, fishing for the right words. He was as compulsive about boating safety as he was about everything he took on. What was happening to him?

Danielle's lips were squeezed tight in apparent anger, then gradually relaxed, transforming to a warm smile, then to laughter. Jonathan reacted with equal amusement. The vision of their nude bodies making a desperate run for cover brought on even louder laughter. Tears ran from their eyes.

The Connecticut Yacht Club was a two-story structure that sat only twenty-five feet back from the top of the gangplank that bridged from its private slips. The front of the building faced the Housatonic, with floor-to-ceiling windows on both levels providing a panoramic view of the marina and the river.

As they entered the foyer, the chill was almost breathtaking. Danielle closed her eyes and delicately wiped her brow.

"How marvelous. I never want to leave," she said, sighing.

"We'll set up camp at the end of the bar," Jonathan said.

Rudy Varone, the maître d', approached them wearing an expression of pronounced disappointment. "Oh, Mr. Rand, I'm so sorry. It's two-fifteen. I held your table as long as I could, but when you didn't show up for your one o'clock, I thought you had made other plans for today."

Jonathan smiled. "No problem, Rudy. Out on the Sound a little longer than expected today. Grabbed some sandwiches on board." Jonathan led Danielle into the cocktail lounge, waved to Sam the bartender, found an open booth, and ordered drinks.

"Here's to a day I won't soon forget," Danielle said, holding up her drink.

Jonathan raised his glass. "An unusual one, to say the least."

They drank their toast, then looked at each other for a moment.

"You're quite an interesting man," she said, breaking the silence. "I enjoyed today, but I'm hoping you don't think this is the way I normally spend my Saturdays."

"Things happen. What went on today we had no more control over than . . . No explanations are necessary, Dani."

It was what she wanted to hear, so he had said it. Her true motives, however, were something Jonathan was trying to understand. The possibility of a personal relationship between Danielle and Aaron still nagged at him. She was beautiful. Enough incentive to draw some men away from even a happy marriage, let alone one that had been strained for a number of years. Some women find great satisfaction in seducing men away from their wives. Maybe Danielle was one of them. But Ruth had been so convincing about the closeness of her relationship with Aaron. And Jonathan's overpowering attraction to Danielle only added to his confusion.

"So you're a hot-dog malpractice lawyer," she said, wanting to move to a more comfortable subject. "Tell me a little about your practice."

Until now, Jonathan had carefully avoided the subject of law. The day had been too enjoyable, and lawyers seemed to be a source of irritation to her. But since she had opened the subject . . .

"Malpractice lawyer! No, not really. I try to *emphasize* personal injury, which can include malpractice. PI we call it. But Bridgeport is too small to concentrate on malpractice as a specialty—or even PI for that matter. I pretty much take anything that walks in the door. Divorces, probate, criminal, corporate. You name it and I've probably done it."

"And if you had a choice?"

"If I had a choice . . . no contest. I love PI. It's my first and only affair with the law."

"Why PI? What's so great about chasing after ambulances?" The question was teasing, rather than ridiculing.

"It's many things. The mixture of medicine and law, the courtroom drama, being able to help people who have been tragically disabled . . . I love it. To me, there's nothing more challenging than to take on in court a doctor who has been called by the defense to testify against my client. You're on his turf now. He's the expert. He went to medical school and he knows it all. At least he wants everyone to believe he does. You've jumped into his waters and he's just waiting for the opportunity to eat you alive. And many of them are like sharks, believe me. But instead of taking him head on, you duck, you parry, you jab. You've done your homework. You know the medical records inside and out, whereas he has only scanned them. You've reviewed medical texts for hours that he hasn't seen in years. You know all the medical principles that support your position and you force him to admit them. He's being paid by the other side to deprive your client of a reasonable verdict, and you're going to stick it to him. There are some doctors I have turned totally around—right on the witness stand. When I finished, they had actually conceded the merits of my client's injury. There was even one case—"

Jonathan stopped. Danielle was staring intently into his eyes, her hands cradling her chin. On her face was the same amused smile he had seen when he first met her in Dr. Jacobs's office. "See what you started," he said, laughing at himself.

"Yes. You *do* love PI."

"I'm a mongrel wanting to be a thoroughbred."

"Then why don't you leave Bridgeport and go to a larger city?"

"It's the country boy still in me. I can't take the city. I tried it once. Manhattan, no less. Took the New York bar exam and everything. I lasted about fifteen months. It's a jungle down there. Came back to Bridgeport with my tail between my legs . . . No, the real answer is my reputation. If I ever make the big hit, bring in the verdict that everyone will read about, then I can start getting referrals from other cities—even other states. I could live my quiet life here but pick and choose the cases I wanted to try in other cities. But I need the right case. Something big, maybe even controversial."

"The Feinerman case?"

Jonathan nodded slowly. "That's it. I've been waiting ten years for it. I've trained, I've worked, I've hoped—and now it's finally here. My ticket to the kind of practice I've dreamed about."

"Well, I hope you're able to help Mrs. Feinerman. I don't know how good a case you have, but this has all hit her very hard."

The case. Mrs. Feinerman. The perfect opening to ask Danielle a few questions.

For the next forty minutes they discussed Aaron's medical practice—the volume of patients he saw, where they came from, his hours, his relationship with his two associates and how they were paid—everything. Gradually he led up to a question he felt was sensitive.

"You worked with Dr. Feinerman for a year and a half. I would imagine you got to know him pretty well—from an employer-employee standpoint, of course."

"I guess as well as anyone could get to know her boss over that length of time. Dr. Feinerman had a very congenial personality. He seemed to be friendly with everyone."

"Did he ever talk to you about . . . personal matters?"

"Yes," she said, slowly and cautiously. "Occasionally. Why?"

"This is strictly routine, Dani. I hope you understand that." She gave no response, which made Jonathan uncomfortable. "Did he . . . did he ever mention how he was getting along with Ruth?"

"Is all this necessary?"

"Unfortunately, yes. The defense will be digging for every piece of dirt they can find. If there's a skeleton somewhere, I'd better know about it first."

"We never talked about things *that* personal, Jon. But he seemed to care for her very much. He mentioned her quite often, if that's any help."

"What did he talk about?"

"Oh, just small things. What they were going to be doing, where they had been, what they did on the boat. As I said, small things."

"Nothing that suggested they weren't getting along?"

"No, never."

"Was there anything unusual about Dr. Feinerman the last couple of weeks before he died? Anything he did, something he said, his behavior—anything." Jonathan purposely avoided making reference to Ruth's observation, not wanting to influence Danielle. Why had Aaron been so worried, so fearful? He had speculated over that since the interview with Ruth. Common sense told him there had to be a logical explanation for it.

Dani looked away, bit down on a thumbnail, then found his eyes again.

"Is this important?"

"It may be. I'm not certain."

"I made a promise."

Promises. Nothing as simple as a promise should stand in his way of learning the truth. "Sometimes they have to be broken. We've *all* broken promises at one time or another."

"I don't feel right about breaking promises, especially to people I respect."

"Was this to Dr. Feinerman?"

"Yes."

"He's gone. Maybe he'd want you to say something now."

Again the thumbnail to the mouth. "It's as if he knew he was going to die—like he foresaw it."

"What do you mean? I'm not following you."

"He had this hernia, this inguinal hernia. And it had been causing him a lot of pain. So we started canceling appointments, transferring as many as we could to his two associates. A few he sent down the hall to Dr. Jacobs. One day—a couple of days before his surgery, as I recall—I took it upon myself to start rescheduling some of the less urgent matters for about three weeks after the operation. Well, on this particular day he was really irritable—nothing like his usual self—and he saw me writing out a new appointment. And he . . . he exploded. He grabbed the appointment book and asked me what the hell I was doing. I told him, and he shouted that he wanted no more appointments set up. 'There won't be any *need*,' he said. Those were his exact words. 'There won't be any *need*.' Fifteen minutes later he called me into his office, apologized, and told me to go ahead and set them up. He also asked me not to mention the incident to anyone. Is this important?"

"Important? No, I don't think so. At least I hope not. I certainly hope not."

Two women, apparently independently of each other, shared a feeling that Aaron had been terrified about something shortly before his death. Maybe even resigned to it.

What did it mean? If it had anything to do with the reason for Aaron's death, it could add a substantial complication to the lawsuit. He knew he should let it alone. The facts surrounding Aaron's death were pretty much out in the open and the case would probably be won or lost on the issue of whether he died of septicemia or of viral pneumonia. Certainly the other side wouldn't be exploring the case beyond that question. The wisest thing to do would be to drop the whole matter.

But Jonathan knew he'd never be satisfied without an answer.

# Chapter X

Jonathan was drying himself off after his evening shower when he heard the phone ring in the living room. It had been four days since he had last seen Danielle and for a moment he hoped it might be she. After their drinks at the club, he had asked her out to dinner. She was busy and declined. Persisting, he had asked her for Sunday. Again, she had something to do. When he had started to ask for a third time, he stopped himself. Maybe she was embarrassed about what had happened aboard *Dreamboat*. Maybe she needed time. One thing was certain: he was damned if he was going to chase after her like a lovesick bull. Yet, not a day had gone by without his reliving their first and only date together, and the painful sunburn below his waist did little to let him forget.

By the third ring, Jonathan had dashed out of the bathroom and picked up the receiver, still clutching the towel in his hand. To his disappointment, the voice was masculine. It was also unfamiliar.

"Mr. Rand?"

"Yes, this is Jonathan Rand."

"Mr. Rand, this is Dr. Lundgren. I hope you don't mind my calling you at home."

"No, Doctor. Not at all. I've been very anxious to hear from you."

Jonathan had been eagerly awaiting Lundgren's call for over two weeks. His opinion tying the hip lesion to Aaron's death was the last thing he needed to put the case into a neat, complete package. With the statement from Dr. Nicholas that Rusty had given him on Monday, it was the last link in nailing down the hospital, *as well* as Reed.

"I'm sorry I wasn't able to get back to you sooner, Mr. Rand, but I had a few extra things that I wanted to do before I talked to you."

"No problem. Have you reached any conclusion?"

"I finished my workup on this only about a half an hour ago. There are conclusions . . . and there are opinions. I've got some opinions. How conclusive they are . . ." Lundgren hesitated, seeming uncertain, even troubled. "I really should talk to you in person. As soon as possible. That's the reason I called you tonight rather than wait until tomorrow."

"I don't understand. Didn't Dr. Feinerman die of septicemia?"

"Yes. That I'm certain about. An overwhelming septicemia, as a matter of fact. But it's more involved than that. *Much* more involved."

The words made Jonathan uneasy. *Involved!* A complication. An obstacle. This was a multimillion-dollar lawsuit. Why did it have to be *involved*?

"Doctor, you're going to have to be a little more explicit. Are you in need of more records? Didn't you get all the autopsy slides?"

"No, it's nothing like that. I've received everything I need. I've finished my review. But it's imperative that I see you here at the lab."

Just then the intercom buzzer sounded. Someone was outside at the entrance to the security-locked building.

"Excuse me for a moment, Doctor. Someone's at my front door."

"Who is it?" Jonathan asked while pressing the "talk" switch.

"It's Dani! A friend bearing gifts."

Danielle's face flashed before him. The eyes, the nose . . . the haunting smile. Excitedly he pressed the button that electrically released the lock at the front door, opened his apartment door, then returned to the phone, wrapping the towel around his waist in the process.

Jonathan picked up the receiver. Distracted, he began to search his memory for where they had left off. Dr. Lundgren; the Feinerman case; the slides; a complication. "Sorry for the interruption."

Silence.

"Doctor, are you there?"

"Look, you've got company . . . and I'd prefer not to talk about this on the phone. Can we set up a meeting?"

"How about Monday or Tuesday? I'll have my secretary call you tomorrow morning and set up a time."

"Mr. Rand, you're not sensing the urgency of this. Could I see you tomorrow? The earlier the better."

Danielle entered the apartment. Seeing Jonathan standing at the phone, she softly closed the door. She wore close-fitting slacks that flared at the bottom and accentuated her long legs and small waist. Her matching blouse was unbuttoned down to an enticing level. She mouthed a "hi" and walked over to him. In front of her she held a small paper bag.

"Tomorrow would be impossible. I'm going to Washington and I'll be there most of the day. We'll have to make it some other time."

"Then Friday. I *really* should see you before the weekend."

"Friday . . . Yes, I think that's all right. What time did you have in mind?"

Danielle, now standing beside Jonathan, impulsively flicked at a corner of the towel that had been tucked in over his buttocks. In the blink of an eye it was gone and Jonathan stood exhibiting his punishment from the merciless sun of Saturday.

"Nine o'clock would work out best. I'm usually in at eight-thirty and could have everything ready by the time you arrive. Can you get here that early?"

"What the—! Uh . . . nine. Nine A.M. Sure, that'll be fine."

Danielle's hand rose to her open mouth as she saw the sunburn. She began to laugh.

"Good-bye, Doctor."

Feigning anger, Jonathan slowly hung up the receiver. Something witty seemed appropriate, but all he could think to do was shake his head.

Danielle continued to laugh. "Poor little fella. I had no idea. I'm a little sore myself, but nothing like that."

"Us fair-haired farm boys are not accustomed to running around in the buff," he finally managed to say.

"I figured you might be suffering a little bit, so I thought I'd play doctor and bring along a little relief." Danielle reached into her bag and pulled out a can of Solarcaine. "I would help you put some on, but . . . no sense in getting something started you obviously could never finish."

"Don't be so sure. I lean toward masochism."

"Well, my whip and spurs are at home, and I've got to be on my way."

"On your way! You just got here."

"I'm driving over to see a friend, and I'm late now. I was in the neighborhood, thought about you, and decided to drop in. I remember you weren't getting around too well Saturday afternoon, so I stopped at a drugstore and picked up the Solarcaine. Wear it well," she said, starting for the door.

Jonathan picked up the towel and replaced it around his waist. He wasn't going to plead. Besides, he had important things to do. He had brought home Aaron's medical records and was going to spend some quiet hours reviewing them after dinner. And he wasn't going to ask who the "friend" was.

"Well, I wish you could stay for a few minutes and talk. But if you're late for a date . . ."

She didn't correct him. Maybe it really *was* a date.

With indecision he took her hands and began searching for an affectionate reaction. Finding amusement in his dilemma, Danielle looked curiously into his eyes, her face chiseled in stone. Not easily deterred, Jonathan tilted his head and kissed her unresponsive lips; he felt as if he were kissing a mannequin.

Again she was toying with him. But this time he wouldn't take the bait. This time *she* would be the one who was off balance. Accepting the challenge, Jonathan suddenly dropped his hands to the small of her back and drew her up to his hips. His aggressive mouth smoothly worked its way from her lips to the nape of her neck. Danielle closed her eyes, willingly submitting to her growing passion. Her previously unoccupied hands found themselves tightly clutching the back of Jonathan's head.

*Now* who was losing control, he thought. The fox was being chased by the chicken. How satisfying. The tables had been turned.

Suddenly Danielle pushed him away. "You're tempting me, but I really have to go," she said. "I'm already fifteen minutes late."

He fought his compulsion to grab her again. "You are absolutely right," he said, surprising even himself. "It would be unfair for me to even *suggest* that you stay."

"I'm tempted. But if I stay another five minutes, I might *never* leave," she said.

The thought brought on a sudden tingling in Jonathan's groin. "In another five minutes I might not *want* you to."

Had he actually said it? Jonathan couldn't believe his words. Give up his freedom, his independence? No, never.

Danielle reached up, took his face between her hands, and planted a soft kiss on Jonathan's lips. But before he could react, she had backed away. "Give me a call on Friday," she whispered, and opened the door. Jonathan then nodded mechanically, his eyes peering deeply into hers. "All right. Friday. I'll call you Friday afternoon."

*Thursday, August 9, 1979*

The cabdriver cursed, almost inaudibly, as the faded blue VW Bug suddenly pulled into the lane in front of him, then came to an abrupt stop to avoid hitting the traffic slowing for the stoplight ahead. The cabdriver slammed on his brakes and decelerated at a rate just short of screeching his tires, coming to a stop only a couple of feet behind the rear bumper of the VW.

Inside the Volkswagen sat a young man, not over twenty, with a kinky Afro hairdo and a short, thin beard.

Probably another goddamned hippie spaced out on grass, he thought, fighting the impulse to scream what he thought of the kid's driving—as well as of the younger generation. The oppressive heat that blanketed the eastern seaboard did not help the matter. It was ten-thirty in the morning in Washington, D.C., and already it was eighty-seven degrees, with the humidity approaching eighty-five percent.

"I'm sorry, sir." The cabdriver looked in the rear-view mirror at Jonathan Rand seated in the backseat of the taxi. "These damn kids drive like there's no one else on the street. If I had my way, they wouldn't get a driver's license until they were twenty-one."

Not wanting to agree or to debate the issue, Jonathan politely smiled at the man. After all, he had enough to think about.

Jonathan's first effort at lobbying had been quite an education. Because he had donated to Congressman Radcliff's campaign and was one of his constituents, the Association of Trial Lawyers of America had asked him to speak to the congressman to present the trial lawyer's side on the issue of no-fault insurance. The Rheinhart bill had just cleared committee and was due for a vote on the floor of the House in two weeks.

Without much effort, Jonathan had managed to get a nine o'clock appointment with Radcliff that morning. Appearing at the congressman's Washington office promptly at nine o'clock, he unfortunately had to wait an agonizing forty minutes before he was finally shown in. Although he had now been practicing law for ten years, Jonathan had never gotten used to giving a formal argument to a judge sitting on the bench, or to any other dignitary holding a position of power. Thus, he had sat nervously for forty minutes, trying to remember each of the various points he wanted to make.

The meeting itself had been brief and frustrating. After only fifteen minutes, Jonathan was cut short. Radcliff had gone on to explain that he had gotten tied up on a call to the White House that morning, then had asked Jonathan to forward a letter to him setting forth his remaining arguments. Jonathan had been whisked out of the office with a smile, a handshake, and a pat on the back. Ten minutes later, he was in a taxi heading to Dulles Airport.

As he sat in the cab contemplating his exercise in futility, resentment began to build. He had taken his valuable time and spent his own money to come to Washington, only to be patronized like a child selling Girl Scout cookies. Dammit, if he'd gone in there with a five-thousand-dollar campaign contribution, he would have gotten a full hour, even if Radcliff had had an appointment with the *President*. A valuable lesson had been learned. Money talks in politics, just as in everything else—probably more.

For the next fifteen minutes, the cab slowly maneuvered through the heavy traffic; first, out Pennsylvania Avenue and then on to M Street into the Georgetown area. Sitting impatiently in the heat, Jonathan looked at his watch. Quarter to eleven; and his plane wasn't due to leave until two-eighteen. How was he going to kill the next three and a half hours?

*He looked more like he was frightened. . . . It's as if he knew he was going to die—like he foresaw it.*

Ruth's and Danielle's words leaped out at him as if they had been lying in wait on the edge of his subconscious, wanting to be pulled out and examined. Something didn't fit. By ignoring it, he was trying to force a square peg into a round hole. Compulsively, he had to have everything in its proper place; every last piece had to be explained, reconciled, and labeled. He had to have an answer.

When Ruth first saw the change, Aaron had just returned from the FDA. Maybe something had happened at the advisory committee meeting. Perhaps if he knew the reason for the meeting—the drug or drugs under consideration—he could finally put the matter to rest. In all likelihood there was a simple explanation for this mystery, and the FDA was probably where he would find it.

"How much time would it take to get to the Food and Drug Administration in Rockville?" he asked loudly. The windows had been rolled down and he could barely be heard over the noise of the traffic.

"Oh, thirty to forty minutes. Depends on how the traffic lets up," the driver shouted back.

Jonathan thought for a moment. "I've still got plenty of time. Why don't you go ahead and take me out there."

With that the cabdriver picked up the microphone, radioed in the new destination, then swung a right on Wisconsin Avenue and headed for Rockville, Maryland.

*Here we go again*, Jonathan thought as he leaned back in his seat. *Off on another imagined witch hunt.*

Behind the INFORMATION sign sat a prim, thin-lipped lady with large, round, hornrimmed glasses. Her dark blond hair was pulled straight back into a bun away from a blanched, narrow face. On the desk in front of her sat a phone, an interoffice directory, a Rolodex, and a stack of mimeographed memoranda that she was carefully reviewing.

"Excuse me, ma'am," Jonathan said as he stepped up to the counter. "I was wondering if you could provide me with some information."

Jonathan's deep voice immediately drew her away from her task.

"Yes, sir." She smiled, pleased at the sight of the handsome man standing in front of her.

"I'd like to get some information about one of your advisory committee meetings."

"I'll do what I can. How can I help?"

"I'd like to find out about the topics that were covered during the June first meeting of the Orthopedic Surgeons Advisory Committee."

"I'm sorry, sir," she said disappointedly, "but we don't carry that information at this desk. I'll have to direct you to the department that schedules those meetings."

Jonathan leaned against the counter and said, "I *am* in a tremendous hurry. I've got to catch a plane at Dulles in a little over two hours and would really appreciate your help. I also have a cab waiting outside, with the meter ticking."

Jonathan's pleading blue eyes flustered the woman as she nervously shuffled through the sheaf of memos. A long time ago he had learned that his engaging boyish charm could win favor among many of the opposite sex, and he never hesitated to use it when the need arose.

"I don't know, sir. It's a little irregular—"

"It really would mean a lot to me. Perhaps you could call someone."

"Well . . . let me see what I can do. I know I can't get the transcript of the hearing. You'll have to make a formal request under the Freedom of Information Act for that. But I might be able to get the agenda for you." Still looking at him, she lifted the phone receiver.

As she placed the call, Jonathan's thoughts strayed to the puzzling question of what could have taken place during the meeting to have created such anxiety. Could Aaron have been using Chymopapain himself?

"I'm sorry I can't help, sir," she said, hanging up the phone.

"You mean they won't give you the agenda over the phone?"

"No," she replied. "I mean that the Orthopedic Surgeons Advisory Committee did *not* meet on June first."

"What!" Jonathan's brow furrowed. "Maybe there's some mistake. Perhaps they met earlier that week."

"No, sir. I checked that. The last meeting was on March ninth."

Jonathan couldn't believe what he had heard. Aaron had lied to Ruth about his trip to Washington. But why? *An affair?* A distinct possibility, yet it was not easy to accept. The potential of the lawsuit would not *allow* him to accept it. After all, there certainly were other things that might have been going on in Washington that Aaron would have wanted to keep from Ruth; things that would not be injurious to the case. Maybe some secret government matter—some sort of research project.

"Were there any other meetings this year? Perhaps in January or February?"

"No. I checked that, too. There was only one meeting this year and one all of last year."

"There must be some mistake. I was told that the Orthopedic Surgeons Advisory Committee had met six or seven times over the past year."

"Sir, there is no mistake. The clerk I checked with is very competent. Maybe *your* source is in error."

"Look, I hate to question you on this, but is there someone else I could check with? Someone who could show me something in writing?"

The woman's patience was at an end. Her lips pressed tightly together and she began scribbling out a note on a scratch pad. "Here! Take this to room two forty-eight and ask for Doris. She will verify all the meetings for you."

As Jonathan pensively walked down the hall and out to his waiting cab, he tried to digest what was happening. Surprises were frequent in the active practice of a trial lawyer. Often a favorable witness would change his testimony on the witness stand or a client would lie. And years had taught him that although with preparation and thoroughness these obstacles could be kept to a minimum, they never could be eliminated. But never before had so much been at stake or the surprise so baffling.

Jonathan's mind began to sift and organize. There had been five, maybe six trips that Aaron had taken which he had lied to Ruth about. For two additional trips—one in March 1979 and one in October 1978—he was able to verify Aaron's attendance at advisory committee meetings. Possibly eight trips to Washington, six of them unexplained. If Aaron had been meeting someone, he could have seen him or her on the two days he was at the FDA. It was also possible that Aaron had been meeting someone in some place other than Washington, D.C. After the commuter flight from Sikorsky to Kennedy Airport, Aaron could easily have gotten onto another airplane to any other destination in the States—at least the eastern states—with the time available between his departures and arrivals. As a first step, he would have to verify that Aaron had in fact arrived in Washington on the seven or eight dates in question. This he could likely do by subpoenaing the airline records. But what then?

Why had Aaron been so terrified after the last trip, but not the others? And how did the alarming call from Dr. Lundgren tie in to this?

"Hi, Ma. It's Jon . . . Jonny." She was the only one who had ever called him Jonny—the only one he had ever *let* call him Jonny.

"Jonny! Is it really you? Where are you calling from?"

"I'm at home, Ma. Here in Stratford."

"It's been three months. I wish you wouldn't wait so long between calls. I always look forward to hearing from you."

Her aging voice was warm and comforting to him. She was his last link with anything resembling a family. A final, thin thread. Whenever his organized life was disrupted—financial trouble, the loss of a case, an illness—he would call and talk with her. It gave him the security he needed.

"I'm sorry it's been so long, but things have gotten out of hand around here, Ma. I've never been so busy. I wanted to call about a month ago, but I got involved in this case and it's taking almost all of my free time."

"What kind of case?"

"A malpractice suit."

"Malpractice. That means you're suing a doctor?"

Jonathan smiled to himself. How preciously innocent she was, isolated on a farm in Kansas for most of her life. "Yes . . . or a hospital. This case involves both."

"I don't know how you do it, Jonny. I could no more sue Dr. Krindle than I could sue your father."

"Dr. Krindle has been your family doctor for over thirty years, Ma. He's like one of the family. Believe me, *all* doctors are not like Dr. Krindle."

"I suppose you're right."

"Speaking of Pa, how is he doing? Last time we talked, you told me he wasn't feeling well. Something about high blood pressure."

"Your pa has really slowed down, Jonny. You'd never recognize him. He's nothing like he was when you were here. Dr. Krindle wants him to retire. Says the strain of work along with his high blood pressure could cause a heart attack."

"It's all those hard-working years on that *damn* farm. Is he going to do it?"

The thought that the farm was endangering his father

angered Jonathan. Even after seventeen years without contact, he still cared deeply for his father. Now the farm had its final hold and was pulling him away for good.

"You know your father. He's as stubborn as you are. I've begged him to stop, but he says he'd rather die with his hands on a plow than to wither away doing nothing."

"I wish I could help, Ma. Where is he now?"

"In the living room reading his *National Geographic*. Just like always."

"Do you think he would talk to me?"

"I ask him every time, Jonny. It's always the same answer. He says he doesn't know a Jonathan Rand and has no reason to speak to him."

"But last time you thought he weakened a little. Would you ask again?"

"I'll try, but I don't think he will."

At the other end he could hear her gently place the receiver on the kitchen table—the table on which he had eaten breakfast throughout his childhood and teens. He tried to imagine the appearance of the kitchen, but time had worn away his memory. Finally, he heard his mother pick up the phone.

"I'm sorry, Jonny. He's still the same." Jonathan heard his mother sniff. She frequently became emotional during his calls. "He's so darn obstinate . . . just like a mule."

"Ma, I wish . . . Would you like me to fly out? Maybe if I were there to talk to him—maybe he might listen."

"No, it would only upset him, Jonny. Just keep calling and asking about him. It may be doing some good. He said something . . . well, not much, but at least something. He said, 'Tell him I'm all right and there's no need to call about me.'"

"Really! He said that, Ma?" It was the first time his father had communicated a message of any kind to Jonathan since he had left.

"Yes, those were his words. 'Tell him I'm all right and there's no need to call about me,'" she repeated.

Jonathan's eyes became glazed with moisture. "Ma, do you realize this is the first time he's ever acknowledged that I even exist? Look," he said excitedly, "I'll call again next week. Next Wednesday. In fact, expect a call from me *every* Wednesday, around . . . oh, seven o'clock your time. Would that work out all right with you?"

"Oh, yes, Jonny. That would be wonderful. And who knows? Your father might just come around."

"I was wondering, Ma. Could you possibly describe the kitchen to me? I know you have before, but I was sitting here trying to remember and it's . . . it's just been too long."

"Is something wrong, Jonny?"

"No, Ma. Nothing's wrong. I was just trying to reminisce about how the kitchen looked."

"Jonny, this is your ma speaking. Maybe you've been gone for a while, but I still know you. There's something wrong, isn't there?"

"No. Really, Ma! What makes you think something's wrong?"

"Because every time you ask me to describe this old house, there's some little problem bothering you. Last year you lost that case where the elderly lady slipped on the grapes in the market. The time before that, some judge found you in contempt of court and you sat out a few days in jail. You're still my baby, Jonny. To me you're an open book."

His mother's perceptiveness leaped out and clutched him like an embrace. He really did belong to someone. He still had family.

"It's nothing big, Ma. Just a few unexpected developments in one of my cases."

"Would you like to talk about it?"

"Not now. Maybe some other time. Anyway, I'm sure they'll get straightened out. It's just a matter of time."

"You need a girl, Jonny. Someone to settle down with . . . to marry." The advice came out of nowhere. It was not like her to comment on his social life or his relationships with women. He was momentarily caught off guard.

"Why do you say that, Ma? I get along fine. I get lonely sometimes, it's true, but I'm just not cut out for settling down."

"Jonny, honey, you've got to be honest with yourself. You think that living alone is your way of life, but it's not. Deep down you want to share your life with someone and you're fighting it. You need someone. Don't waste these precious years hoping to find your father, when what you really need is a woman—maybe even children. Find a young lady, Jonny. It's time you started to build your own family."

"Ma, I'm sure you're right, as usual. But it's not that easy.

I've gotten so set in my way of doing things, I doubt that I could really change. But I'll give it some thought. I promise."

"Thank you, honey. Now, you wanted to know what the kitchen looked like. Well, on the west wall are all of my cabinets, just to the right of the walk-in pantry. They've been painted a couple of times since you left, of course. They're a very light green now. And then on the east wall is where . . ."

# Chapter XI

*Friday, August 10, 1979*

Jonathan sat restlessly in the Amtrak car as it clattered its way over the short distance to New Haven. His curiosity was now piqued. First the bothersome call from Dr. Lundgren on Wednesday and then the blockbusting disclosure in Washington the following day. Why had the doctor refused to discuss his findings over the telephone? And what was so damned mysterious about the slides?

The suspicious nature of the call would have been enough by itself to make Jonathan uncomfortable; but added to what he had learned at the FDA, it was causing him a great deal of anxiety. At first he tried to relax by reading a magazine, but he found himself incapable of concentrating on anything except his trip to Washington and the surprise Dr. Lundgren was saving for him. The minutes ticked slowly by; the train seemed to take an eternity to reach New Haven. Things were happening too fast, unexpectedly. Even his relationship with Danielle was unpredictable.

Was there any connection? It was an unsettling but realistic concern.

Finally he stepped off the train at the New Haven station. It felt good to move about again, as he hurried through the station to catch a taxi out in front. Luck was with him, and within a minute he was on his way to Yale University.

Jonathan stood examining a wall lined with electron

micrographs of an assortment of organisms enlarged several to thousand times their normal size. The creatures, grotesque and threatening in appearance, added to the uneasiness Jonathan was already experiencing. Intuitively, he knew he would shortly be hearing something upsetting, and now more than ever he wished he were anyplace else than where he was.

Wesley Lundgren entered the waiting room from his laboratory. Jonathan was surprised by his appearance. Although Lundgren had previously reviewed two or three cases for him, Jonathan had never seen him in person. Expecting a troll-like, wrinkled gray man suffering from fluorescent-light pallor and halitosis, he was astonished to see a six-foot-four-inch Swede smoking a fine antique meerschaum pipe and impeccably attired with a long white laboratory coat.

"I see you had no difficulty finding my workshop," said Lundgren.

"No. No problem at all. I'm not too excited about your friends, though," he said, motioning.

Lundgren laughed. "Keeps away unwanted visitors . . . But I'm glad you could make it out today," he added seriously. "This is one of the most complex cases I've reviewed in years. It also turns out to be one of the most mystifying. At first blush, it seemed like a straightforward septicemia, with a terminal shock-lung condition. The hip lesion seemed the likely portal of entry. On its face, almost open-and-shut."

"Portal of entry?"

"Yes, the way in which the bacteria migrated into the bloodstream."

Jonathan listened uneasily. He suspected he was being carefully led to a disclosure he did not want to hear. Still, he digested each word as Lundgren began slowly walking toward the lab.

"But as I reviewed the slides," Lundgren continued, "something didn't quite seem to fit. I wasn't sure why. There were definite streptococcal organisms identifiable in the pus from the abscess on the left hip. The petechial hemorrhages and sequestered white blood cells noted throughout the organs were also supportive of septicemia. I could find no evidence that the organisms entered the body through the surgical incision, and the lesion on the hip was certainly most suggestive of a contaminated medication site. Everything seemed to add up, except—"

"Except what, Doctor?"

"Well, I had spent a great deal of time reviewing the histologic sections from the lungs. The slides were very well prepared, but I can see how they initially would have resembled a viral pneumonia. However, there are an enormous number of things that can happen to the lungs from a wide variety of causes, all of which can produce similar changes both grossly and microscopically. A septicemia caused by streptococcus could *possibly* produce changes like those I found in the lungs. But without blood cultures, there was just no way I could step onto a witness stand and say the organisms throughout the cardiovascular system were the same as the ones in the hip lesion. That is, unless I had some special stains for bacteria." Lundgren showed Jonathan through the door and pointed the way to his lab, a short distance down the hall. "You weren't aware of this, but I sent to the hospital for preserved tissue samples from the lungs. From these samples, I did some stains for a more detailed study. These bacterial stains showed peculiar rod-shaped organisms circulating in the capillaries of the lungs."

Lundgren stopped at the entrance to the lab. He took a couple of contemplative puffs from his pipe, then pulled it from his mouth. He looked almost apologetically at Jonathan.

"The organisms, Mr. Rand, were *not* streptococci."

"What! But they've got to be! Are you sure about that?" Lundgren's words had just destroyed Jonathan's case against Rivergarden Hospital.

"Positive. Oh, there was a contaminated medication site on the hip—there's no question about that—*but it didn't kill him.*"

Jonathan didn't want to hear this. Why should Nicholas be wrong? He worked at the very hospital that was being sued. He had every motive to find nothing incriminating, yet he had.

"But the autopsy surgeon is convinced that death was due to a contaminated injection site. We even have a signed statement from him stating that."

"The autopsy surgeon is wrong. He never did the bacterial stains."

"But—"

"Mr. Rand, even if he *had* done them, he conceivably could have been misled. Postmortem contamination can occur from intestinal-type organisms when a person has been dead for a lengthy period before autopsy. But here the autopsy was performed only three or four hours after death. I also took it a step further—electron microscopy."

Lundgren motioned Jonathan through the door to the lab. "I presently have that microscope set up with a preparation from Dr. Feinerman's lungs. If you'll follow me into the 'scope room, I'll show you something rather astonishing."

Jonathan reacted promptly and without comment, although he desperately wanted to turn and leave. But if he excused himself and left, no one would ever learn of Lundgren's secret, the secret that was about to eliminate one of the defendants in his case of a lifetime—maybe even both of them. Yet, he *had* to know.

He passed through the laboratory and into a lightproof room. Above the door a red light served as a warning when the equipment inside was in use. As Lundgren closed the door, the hum of a generator could be heard, and a red glow from the darkroom lights engulfed the two men.

Lundgren flipped a switch and adjusted a couple of knobs. Immediately, a green fluorescence began to emanate from the screen. As their eyes adjusted to the darkness, peculiar configurations began to appear before them. Lundgren slowly moved them about, scanning the grid with the specimen of lung tissue. Gradually, delicately, they were brought into focus.

"What you are looking at, Mr. Rand, are a number of capillaries from Dr. Feinerman's left lung. These are the smallest vessels that transport blood into the lungs. Along with the septicemia, they also transported the bacterial organisms that ultimately killed him.

"Now we'll take a deeper look." Lundgren increased the magnification over a small capillary in the center of the field. "The strange creature that you see in this vessel is an organism that I can identify because of its ultrastructural features. It is the *Bacillus anthracis*, or anthrax bacillus, which causes animal and human anthrax. It also causes massive hemorrhagic pneumonitis, such as that which was found in Dr. Feinerman.

"Take a good look at it, Mr. Rand. There is your killer."

For a good thirty seconds Jonathan stared, paralyzed, absorbing the eerie-looking creature, the generator nagging its reminder that this was really happening.

"Anthrax!" he said to himself. More loudly he asked,

"You're actually saying that Dr. Feinerman died from *anthrax*?"

"That's right. He died as a result of an overwhelming septicemia from anthrax bacillus."

"But that's an *animal* disease! I had no idea that we . . . that humans could actually catch it."

"It's rare, but it happens. As a matter of fact, it's *extremely* rare. Which brings us to the reason why I didn't want to talk about this over the phone."

Lundgren switched on the lights and turned off the generator and electron microscope.

"Anthrax is not an organism that would normally be found in the lungs of a healthy individual, and it would be most unlikely to find it in someone such as a physician, who is generally confined to a hospital or office setting. In addition, we haven't had any human anthrax in this part of the state for years. To be sure, I also checked with Rivergarden. They haven't had a case in the seventeen years they have been a hospital."

"Are you sure that streptococcus wasn't involved in some way? If anthrax is so rare, maybe there's some other explanation that has to do with the injection site?" Jonathan was still fighting, clinging to his case.

"Make no mistake. There was some streptococcus infection present in the lungs. But not enough to kill him. His death was from an anthrax infection. Of that I am certain."

"Could anthrax have gotten into the injection needle in some way?"

"There were no anthrax bacilli in the hip lesion. The lesion could not have been involved in his death in any way. There were also none at the surgical site, nor, from the autopsy report and other slides, on any other surface area of the skin."

"But where does that leave us? How in the world would anthrax get into his bloodstream?"

Lundgren stared at Jonathan, then without a word opened the door and stepped through into the lab. He picked up his pipe and began sucking at it. Jonathan stood waiting impatiently.

"There's only one way that I can think of. From all the evidence available, it had to have come through the IV."

"The *IV*!"

Lundgren continued to work at his pipe; the tobacco

glowed with each inhalation of smoke. "That would leave us with only two possibilities. The first one is that there was a contaminated bottle. But if there was a batch of bottles infected with anthrax bacillus, there would have been reports of other cases of anthrax infection. When I called Rivergarden, they confirmed that they had not had any evidence of contaminated bottles of *any* organism, let alone anthrax. This is something that is closely monitored."

"And the second possibility?" Jonathan already suspected the answer but had to hear Lundgren say it.

"Mr. Rand, I spent twenty-two years with the county coroner's office before taking up the teaching side of this business. After a while you get kind of a sixth sense for these things. The rarity of the disease—everything about this case— leads to one very strong possibility. That possibility is that someone intentionally injected the organism into the IV tube. I feel that your doctored was *murdered*."

Murdered! The word had a chilling, almost nauseating effect on Jonathan. If Aaron had been murdered, then the infection had not resulted from any negligence by the hospital. Even if a nurse had intentionally given the lethal injection, by law it would not have been in the course of her employment, so Rivergarden would be relieved of any liability. *No, murder means that the hospital is out of the case. And Lundgren is right. One does not* accidentally *inject anthrax into an IV tube*.

"Doctor, I hope you can understand that this is a little difficult for me to adjust to. Murder is something you read about in the newspaper or see in the movies—something that happens to other people. To say that it happened to a friend of mine, that it's involved in one of my cases . . . well, it takes some getting used to."

"I can understand your reluctance to accept this, Mr. Rand, but believe me, the evidence is quite substantial. Not unequivocal, mind you, but still strong. In fact, if I were you, I would give very serious consideration to informing the authorities about this."

"I'm not sure I want to rush off and do that. There might be a logical explanation for all of this that we're both overlooking. Accidents can sometimes happen in very bizarre ways." Going to the police would mean an investigation and, likely, disclosure of Lundgren's opinions to the other side— something Jonathan could otherwise hide. No, he needed time to think this out, to analyze all the possible consequences of such an investigation.

Lundgren sucked at the meerschaum and let the smoke slowly escape into a small cloud. Pensively he looked at the immaculate floor of his laboratory. "You do what you have to, Mr. Rand. But remember, the longer you wait to go to the authorities, if that's your eventual decision, the more time you will have given to the killer to cover his or her tracks."

"Oh, I intend to take this to the police, but only after I'm satisfied that Dr. Feinerman was murdered. Just a little more time for some additional investigation. I owe it to my client." It was a lie, since for the moment Jonathan had serious doubts about *ever* going to the police. He would have to wrestle with his conscience later.

"This entire matter would bear further investigation," said Lundgren. "I can't deny that. But I seriously question that you should be the one doing it. I think the police would be better equipped to investigate a possible murder."

"I appreciate that. If I get in over my head, I'll go straight to the police. I just have to be sure about this before losing one of my two defendants."

"Suit yourself. But there is one further consideration you shouldn't overlook: Such an investigation would not be without *danger*. If I'm right, you're dealing with a very devious mind, not to mention one with a rather sophisticated knowledge of medicine. It doesn't take much imagination to figure out what the killer might do if you got close to disclosure."

A sobering thought, but one that was as difficult to appreciate as the fact that Aaron had been murdered. "I'll keep that in mind, Doctor. . . . Oh, one additional question—two questions, really. Can anthrax be effectively treated with antibiotics, and, if so, would there have been enough time to save Dr. Feinerman's life if they had been administered when Dr. Reed was first called at three A.M.?" Jonathan's stomach muscles tightened.

"The anthrax bacillus is an extremely virulent organism—much more so than streptococcus. But yes, it does respond to certain antibiotics. Your second question is a little more difficult, especially considering Dr. Feinerman's weakened condition because of the surgery." Lundgren again worked at his pipe, his mind deep in thought, weighing all the relevant data. "Well, it's a bit tenuous, and you might encounter some differing points of view, but yes, if they had dumped some heavy doses of a broad-spectrum antibiotic somewhere around three o'clock, Dr. Feinerman would probably be with us today. Mind you, anthrax is resistant to many drugs, but he would have had a chance."

"You'd be willing to testify to that?"

"Yes, I would."

"You say anthrax is more virulent than streptococcus. What exactly do you mean?"

"Virulent! It's a fast-working, aggressive bug and an excellent choice if you wanted to kill someone that way."

"Thank you for your help, Doctor. I'll keep in touch."

Jonathan hurriedly made his way out of Lundgren's offices and into a cab. Once in the taxi, he took a deep breath as if to cleanse away the oppressive news he had just heard. It felt good to be outside, away from the walls of the laboratory that had seemed to be closing in on him.

Decisions had to be made. Should he use Lundgren at all? Even without a murder, the case against Rivergarden was speculative at best. Lundgren had destroyed the theory that death was due to a contaminated needle injection. Anthrax was the cause of death and none of those organisms had been found in the infected injection site. No, the lethal germs had come through the IV tube. That was Lundgren's opinion and it was a convincing one. So how could Jonathan prove that the bacteria had entered the IV through some neglect or carelessness on the part of an employee of the hospital? It seemed an impossible task. There was no sense in ignoring it: Once Lundgren was disclosed, either as a witness in the lawsuit or through a murder investigation by the police, Rivergarden would be out of the case.

A further cause for alarm existed. Because anthrax was faster acting, Lundgren's testimony would also weaken the chances of ultimately prevailing against Reed. A good case of negligence, but had it caused Aaron's death? Anthrax was a more aggressive bacterium than the streptococcus organisms believed to be responsible by Nicholas.

"Virulent" Lundgren had called it. Jonathan could hear the defense experts now: "All the antibiotics in the world could not have saved Dr. Feinerman by three A.M. After all, he died only three hours and twenty minutes later. Everyone knows these drugs take time to work, and that, unfortunately, was something Dr. Feinerman did not have."

Anthrax was the key and Lundgren was the only person anywhere who knew it was involved—other than a possible murderer. As the case stood, Jonathan had the autopsy surgeon—one who had worked at the very hospital he was suing—implicating a contaminated needle, injected by a Rivergarden nurse, not to mention the bacteria that would more readily have responded to antibiotics.

How easy it would be to forget that Lundgren had seen the autopsy slides.

Jonathan sat back, weighing the alternatives, as his cab sped toward the New Haven train station. Why *should* he use Lundgren? After all, wasn't this really just one man's opinion against another's? Nicholas was a competent pathologist or he wouldn't have been on the staff at Rivergarden. He was also the one who had performed the autopsy. It was Nicholas, not Lundgren, who had had the very definite advantage of seeing and feeling all of Aaron's organs. Wasn't Lundgren relying in part on an autopsy report prepared by Nicholas? Sure he was. Maybe there were things that Nicholas had seen during the autopsy that were not accurately described in the report—or possibly not described at all.

And what about the client's interest? Disclosing Lundgren's opinions, by reporting them either to the police or to the defense attorneys in the lawsuit, would be damaging to the case. *Isn't it unethical for a lawyer to do something that might compromise a client's chance of winning? Of course it is. Rivergarden and Reed have expert witnesses at their disposal capable of reviewing slides and tissue samples in the same way Lundgren reviewed them, including electron microscopy. If they are not as thorough in their preparation of the case, that's their problem.*

Not reporting these new findings to the police, however, was a little more difficult for Jonathan to deal with. It would be very simple to discuss them with Ruth and let *her* make that decision. It was her husband who had been murdered—if indeed that was the case—and it might be more important to her to see his killer captured than to seek a large judgment or settlement.

But why alarm Ruth before he knew what had really happened? Hadn't she been through enough already? Such an accusation at this point would only add to her torment. She would know she hadn't detected the true cause of Aaron's fear, perhaps even condemn herself for not being able to help him. No, it wouldn't be right—at least not until he had satisfied himself, until he had clear and convincing proof to support Lundgren's opinion.

And who knew? Maybe he would never have to mention a word of this to her.

Jonathan reached into his brown attaché case beside him on the seat of the cab and pulled out a yellow legal tablet and a black ballpoint pen. It was time to start taking notes about this new discovery.

Jonathan pondered for a moment, chewing on the end of the pen, then began to write:

(1) RUTH: Following the last trip to Washington, Aaron appeared frightened. Had never seen him like it before. Lasted up until surgery.

(2) DANI: A few days before surgery, Aaron reacted as if he felt he was going to die. Possible intimate relationship between Aaron and medical assistant (Dani).

(3) FDA: Aaron had lied to Ruth about attending advisory committee meetings on five or six occasions, including last trip. Something happened on last trip that caused Aaron to fear for his life. Where was he going? Who was he seeing?

(4) LUNDGREN: Aaron probably murdered. Killed by intentional injection of anthrax into IV tube. Killer or accomplice had knowledge of medicine. Also had access to Aaron in hospital. Lundgren arrived at opinion without knowing of observations of Ruth and Dani—adds to credibility.

Shaking his head, Jonathan slowly returned the pen and pad to his attaché case. All the evidence pointed to murder, yet he would not willingly accept it. There *had* to be another explanation. Something was being overlooked, and he would just have to find it. His big break would not slip from his grasp without a fight. Damned if he'd turn his back on this without knowing every fact available, right down to the last detail. And if danger was involved, then so be it. Jonathan Rand would not be intimidated away from any goal, least of all from the lawsuit that could put him professionally and financially where he had dreamed of being throughout his career.

"Good afternoon. Dr. Jacobs's office."

"Hi! This is Jonathan Rand calling. Is Dani free? She asked me to give her a call this afternoon."

"Oh, I'm sorry, Mr. Rand. Dani called in sick today. She won't be in until Monday."

"Sick! Nothing serious, I hope. I was just talking to her on Wednesday." Jonathan's voice carried a trace of concern.

"No, no. Just flu or something. Said she had a slight temperature and an upset tummy. I'm sure she'll be back on Monday. Would you like me to have her call you?"

"Uh . . . no. Well, yeah. Maybe you'd better take a message. Just in case I miss her at home."

Jonathan gave her both his home and office numbers, wanting to ensure that Dani would not be reluctant to call him at work.

Jonathan then found Dani's home number in his small black address book and placed his call. She had reluctantly given it to him at the club on Saturday. "I never give out my home number to dates," she had said. "It can only lead to complications if I want to break it off." That she had given it to *him* seemed to add further intimacy to their relationship.

As the phone continued to ring, Jonathan tried to recall the sound of her voice and envision her sick in bed. But somehow the image would not come into focus. He had seen her only as vivacious and beautiful, not bedridden and sickly. By the seventh ring, his anticipation of speaking with, and perhaps seeing, her had faded into disappointment.

Jonathan let the phone ring three times more and hung up. Maybe she had given him the wrong number. After all, she had not wanted to give it out in the first place. Without hesitation he reached beneath the telephone stand, removed the directory, and began thumbing through it.

"Brendle . . . Brenemen . . . Brenkley . . . Brent. Dammit, she's unlisted," he said, slapping the book closed. "Dammit!" he said more loudly.

He looked at his watch: 3:18 P.M. If she was sick, why in the hell wasn't she home? Maybe she'd gone to a doctor. But then, she'd known he would be calling. Why hadn't she left a message for him with the receptionist at her office?

A thought! Perhaps she had called his office. Wanting solitude after leaving New Haven, Jonathan had gone straight to his apartment. Maybe that was it. She must have called him at the office. With dwindling hope he dialed the number.

"Hi, Sally. Any messages for me? I'm here at home."

"Yes, there are, Mr. Rand." A pause as she perused her message pad. "Mr. Hogan called; he'd like to change the date of his deposition. Mrs. Vaughn wants you to draw up a will for her. Mr. Epstein wants to know the status of his case—third time he called today. And Mr. Morris wants to confirm Dr. Reed's deposition on Tuesday."

"No one else?"

"No, that's it."

"Call the other side on the Hogan case, get some new dates, and reschedule the depo. Set up an appointment for next week with Mrs. Vaughn, and tell Morris I'll be ready to go on Tuesday. As for Epstein, tell him I'll give him a call on Monday. I'm about ready to have him come in and pick up his file. He's becoming a real pain in the ass. I'll be in early on Monday."

Jonathan hung up fuming. Not even the courtesy of a message. Again he had the feeling that she was making a fool of him—and he was being drawn to her in a way he could not understand.

"Why am I *taking* this shit?" he shouted to himself.

With that he picked up his coat with a swipe of his hand and went storming out the door. A few drinks at Hagan's were exactly what he needed.


# Chapter XII


*Tuesday, August 14, 1979*

At ten minutes after nine, Jonathan closed the front door to his office and walked through the reception room into the secretarial bay. Sally had already arrived and was busy at the keys of her IBM Selectric. A wire hung from a small earphone through which she was listening to Jonathan's dictation from the day before.

"Morning, Sally," Jonathan said as he continued toward the library.

Sally smiled and nodded while continuing to type.

Jonathan's office library had been professionally decorated and was a room in which he took considerable pride. In the center of the library was a heavy wooden table, purchased at an antique auction, surrounded by eight low-backed chairs. Above the table hung an antique lamp with alternating opaque glass panels of green and amber. A small, shallow closet in one corner housed a number of enlarged photographs, evidentiary exhibits, and a full-sized plastic replica of the human skeleton. Next to the closet was a built-in wet bar behind floor-to-ceiling cabinet doors. On the lone wall without library shelves hung several original oil paintings and lithographs depicting English barristers in courtroom scenes.

A feeling of tension hit Jonathan as he entered the library and began laying out the medical records and notes on the table in front of him. His highest verdict had been the $62,500 the jury had returned on the slip-and-fall case he had tried last year, and his largest settlement had been the $95,000 he received for a lady who had to undergo a fusion of her cervical spine due to a rear-end automobile collision. Never had he obtained for a client a financial recovery in the six-figure bracket, and now he was about to take the deposition of the primary defendant in a lawsuit that potentially could result in a judgment in excess of one million dollars.

With a strange uneasiness he sat down, picked up his notepad, and began to review the issues he wanted to cover, exactly as he had charted them the night before. With methodical care he had one by one laid out a series of questions, each strategically designed to lead Reed into a possible admission of fault. However, with each effort to read his notes, Jonathan's mind wandered back to the significance of the event that was about to take place that morning.

"Here's your coffee, Mr. Rand," said Sally, as she entered the library with a cup in one hand and a handful of mail in the other. "Would you like your mail here or in your office?"

The aroma of freshly brewed coffee offered a welcome relief as Jonathan extended his hand to take the cup.

"I'll take the mail in here, Sally. Thank you."

She deposited the mail in a neat stack on the table in front of Jonathan, who took a slurping sip of the hot coffee and then set it down to cool off.

"Oh, I almost forgot," Sally said, catching herself at the door and returning to Jonathan with a phone-message slip in her hand. "Received this a couple of minutes before you arrived."

Jonathan took the slip while Sally left for her typewriter. The name at the top precipitated immediate excitement: "Danielle Brennan." The phone number appeared to be the one he had dialed to reach Dr. Jacobs's office on Friday. Almost by reflex, Jonathan was out of his chair heading for the telephone in his office. Finally he would get to speak with her. Perhaps he would even see her that evening. Perhaps he would even . . .

*Wait a minute!* Just as quickly, Jonathan caught himself before taking a second step. *No! Not this time. Let her try to reach me for a change. Let her know she's not the only girl in Bridgeport.* After all, he had patiently waited for three long days to hear from her.

Jonathan returned to his chair and casually began to sort through his mail.

Finally, at ten minutes to ten, Sally appeared in the doorway and said, "Dr. Reed, Mr. Rabin, and the court reporter are here. We are only waiting now for Mr. Morris."

"Okay," Jonathan responded. "Let me know as soon as he arrives and we'll get started."

Again he looked at the phone message. Maybe he was being unfair to her. Was he going to deny her the chance to give him a reasonable explanation for not calling? To refuse to return her call was also a further indication of the effect she was having on him, and in Jonathan's mind that was probably the best reason to call her before starting what would likely turn out to be a day-long deposition.

"You called! How wonderful!" said the soft voice. "I wouldn't have blamed you one bit if you had never wanted to speak to me again."

The implied apology took him back momentarily, but his plan of indifference was not to be deterred. "Oh, no. I wasn't upset. Not at all. Figured something had just come up and you'd get in touch as soon as you could."

"I knew you'd understand." Her voice dropped to just

above a whisper. "It was totally unexpected. I had to leave town for a couple of days. Told them here I had a slight case of the flu. I would have called you Friday morning, but I was sure you'd be busy."

"You're quite the mystery lady."

A light chuckle. "Not really, although it must seem that way. I'll explain the whole thing to you later. Just as long as you forgive me for ducking out on you."

"Nothing to forgive. Believe me."

"Look, Jon, I've got to get back. Dr. Jacobs just called in another patient. Could I possibly see you tonight? I've really missed you."

Again the tickling sensation in the groin. "Sure, I'd love it. . . . Let me see. Why don't we do this: I'm taking Reed's deposition today and have a dinner reservation at the club for seven this evening. Why don't I swing by and pick you up at six-thirty?"

"No. That won't work out for me. I'll meet you there at seven."

"Okay. Seven it is. See you then."

Well, what the hell. Why *should* he be pissed? Hadn't she called and apologized? And was there really any doubt about her having a logical and reasonable explanation for the four-day absence?

Jonathan returned to his chair in the library. He was on a new high, ready to take on the world. Suddenly he was thinking with surprising clarity. He picked up his notes again and everything began falling into place.

He contemplated the verbal battles he expected to encounter. Unlike most depositions, which proceeded without much altercation and with all participants trying overtly to be congenial, it had been his experience that the defendant's deposition in a medical malpractice lawsuit was fraught with legal objections, frustrations, and, often, anger. Perhaps it was due to the personality of the physician, whose professional skill was under attack; or because the doctor's lawyer was trying to impress a more demanding client; or a combination of both. But, whatever the reason, invariably Jonathan concluded such depositions both exhausted and irritated.

However, it was not the *fear* of such an encounter that brought his past experience to mind. The anticipation of "locking horns" with formidable defense counsel served only to increase the excitement already built up by the size of the case.

Finally Sally leaned her head into the library. "Everybody's here now, Mr. Rand."

"Fine. Show them in, Sally, and bring in a fresh pot of coffee."

Within a minute, the assemblage began filing into the library. First, the court reporter, Miss Royster, carrying the case enclosing her stenotype machine; then Arnold Rabin, who was representing Rivergarden Community Hospital.

Rabin smiled as he set his briefcase next to a chair. "Morning, Jon."

"Morning, Arnie," replied Jonathan.

The two of them had been on opposite sides before, and Jonathan was well aware of the deceptive charm of Arnold Rabin. He was a rotund, mild-looking man in his late fifties, with gray hair and a receding hairline. His suits were always rumpled and on the end of his nose he wore small round glasses, which he looked through only to read. When talking with someone, he would tilt his head slightly forward and peer over the top of the glasses, with a smile that Jonathan would swear had been permanently molded into his pleasant-looking face. Rabin's demeanor was unexcitable, and he was softspoken, with a deliberate plodding style of asking questions. But beneath the misleading veil of cordiality, Arnold Rabin was as lethal as a viper. "Never turn your back on him," a friend had once told Jonathan, "because the next thing you'll feel will be something sharp trying to separate your shoulder blades from your spine."

A few steps behind Rabin walked Jason Reed, with Preston Morris trailing him through the door.

"Good morning," Jonathan said, extending his hand to Morris, whose briefcase helped to identify him as the other lawyer. "You must be Mr. Morris."

"Yes, I am," Morris replied sternly while shaking Jonathan's hand. "And this is Dr. Reed."

Jonathan turned toward Reed and reached to shake his hand. Mechanically, Reed forced his hand forward, shook twice, and dropped it to his side. "Good morning, Mr. Rand," he said. His eyes were cold and angry.

Jonathan stared back for a moment, then turned to reclaim his chair.

As the court reporter recited the oath, Jonathan took a

closer look at Morris. Preston J. Morris, III, was slight and short; not a fraction over five foot five. Attired in an expensive blue-vested tweed suit, his wavy blond hair was cut short and neatly parted on the left side. Beneath a narrow and slightly turned-up nose he sported a thin reddish-blond mustache. Although not an unattractive man, Jonathan would soon find out that Preston Morris had an abrasive personality rivaled only by that of his client, Jason Reed. Born into one of the wealthy old families of Greenwich, he had spent all of his thirty-nine years trying to prove that his size and wealth were not handicaps. Teased and taunted as a child, and even to a degree in college, Morris saw the courtroom as a forum to demonstrate not that he was *equal* to taller men but better. With conviction he had worked and polished his skills as a trial lawyer; and he soon had begun to earn a reputation as one of the outstanding defense attorneys in Connecticut. But his desire to achieve perfection, unfortunately, had brought with it an attitude of intolerance and contempt of those he did not consider his equal, which was just about everyone.

Finally Miss Royster concluded the oath and turned to her left to look at Jonathan, her hands poised over the keys of the stenotype, ready to record the first question.

"Doctor, would you please state your full name for the record," Jonathan began.

"Jason Bernard Reed."

"Have you ever had your deposition taken before?"

"Of course not," Reed snapped.

"Well, has your attorney, Mr. Morris, had the opportunity to explain the nature of this proceeding to you?"

"Objection, Counsel," Morris interjected smugly. "You're beginning to invade the area of attorney-client privilege. However, we'll stipulate that the doctor is aware of the general nature of a deposition."

Jonathan paused. It was a question usually asked without complaint. He then continued with the standard admonition given to a witness at the beginning of a deposition.

"Well, for the record, be advised that I'll be asking you a series of questions related to this lawsuit and the death of Dr. Aaron Feinerman. Be further advised that everything said in this room will be taken down by the certified shorthand reporter seated to my right, and at a later time it will be transcribed into booklet form. Once the deposition has been transcribed, you will be given the opportunity to read it over and, if you find it necessary, to make any changes, modifications, or deletions in your testimony that you see fit.

"However, please note that if you should change your testimony, that fact could be commented upon by myself, or any other attorney trying this case, and, depending upon what the change was, could be embarrassing. Do you understand that?"

"Yes, I do," Reed answered, his expression still scornful.

"Further understand that if you testify differently at trial as compared to what you state here today, that difference could also be commented upon and could be embarrassing. Do you understand that?"

"Yes, I do."

"For those reasons, I would ask you to listen carefully to all the questions and make sure you understand them before you give an answer. If you give an answer, it will be assumed that you heard and understood the question. Do you also understand that you are testifying under oath?"

"Yes, I do."

"And do you understand that the oath that you have taken has the same force and effect as if you were testifying in a court of law?"

"Yes."

"I would also ask you not to guess or speculate on any question, although you may give your best estimate or approximation where needed. Now, do you have any questions about the nature of this deposition?"

"No, I do not."

"Very well. Would you please state your current residential address."

"Objection," Morris again interposed. "Irrelevant to the subject matter of this lawsuit. I instruct the witness not to answer."

It was going to be a long day.

"Well, then, would you please state your current business address."

Without difficulty, Jonathan was able to elicit Reed's business address, how long he had been there, the names of his partners, and prior business addresses. Then, throughout the remainder of the morning, he meticulously probed and explored Reed's education, training, and experience through medical school, internship, residency, and, finally, that period of his active practice up until he first saw Aaron Feinerman professionally at his office.

By the time they broke for lunch, Jonathan was becoming cautiously optimistic that the day was not going to be as difficult as he had imagined.

Agreeing to be back by one o'clock, the five of them filed out of the office to head for the closest restaurant. Jonathan was the last to leave and found Rusty Murdoch waiting for him in the reception room.

"Go on without me," Jonathan said to the others. As the door closed, he looked down at the investigator, who had been sitting with a magazine, trying to look like a new client. "Ready for some more work?" he asked.

"Starving for it," said Rusty, struggling up from the chair. "I'm two months behind on my rent and my car needs a valve job. Yeah, ya might say I'm ready."

"Good. I'd like you to do a little nosing around the hospital. Be as inconspicuous as you can. I need some info about the bacteriology department."

"Name it, boss." Rusty referred to everyone he worked for as "boss," even though his sporadic assignments came from three or four different law firms and he was not a salaried employee.

"I want to know if there have been any thefts, if anyone has reported any strains of bacteria missing. In particular, anthrax."

"You've got to be kidding! Who'd want to steal germs?"

Jonathan looked at Sally busily typing in the secretarial bay. "I'd just as soon not go into that now. Let's just say that it's important. Talk to the orderlies, janitors, LVNs—the nonmanagement types."

Rusty pulled out a small notepad and jotted a few notes. "Okay, boss. Stolen bugs—in particular anthrax. If it happened, I'll find out." He spoke with the assurance of a man who has complete confidence in his skills. As long as he was off the bottle, Rusty Murdoch was as good an investigator as Jonathan had ever used; over the years he had turned several of Jonathan's tougher cases into winners.

"Give this top priority, Rusty. It might turn out to be critical."

"You got it."

Jonathan turned to leave, then stopped. "Oh, and, Rusty, no booze. Okay?"

Rusty raised his right hand. "I swear, boss. I've been off the stuff for six months and I'm not going back. Ask the boys over at AA."

Jonathan smiled. "I believe you. It just makes me feel good to hear you say it." After a moment's pause he added, "Tell you what. Tell Sally I authorized a five-hundred-dollar advance."

"That's not necessary, boss."

"I know. But I want to do it."

Rusty offered a big smile of gratitude, and Jonathan nodded good-bye and walked out the door. Out in the hallway, he paced anxiously toward the elevator. He had a lot to accomplish during the shortened lunch hour. Ahead of him stood Rabin, with his usual pleasant smile.

"Care to join me for lunch?" he asked.

"Well, I was thinking of just grabbing a sandwich and coming back to review my notes. Thanks anyway, Arnie." Jonathan had no desire to spend a tense lunch hour with Rabin, and preparation time was a justifiable excuse.

"I wish you'd reconsider, Jon. I've learned something from my people at the hospital that I'm *sure* you'll be very interested in hearing about."

For a moment, Jonathan stared inquisitively at Rabin. Was the snake beginning to coil?

"All right. I guess I can spare the time. Would the local cafeteria be all right?"

"Sure, Jon," Rabin said. "The cafeteria will do just fine."

Throughout lunch Rabin displayed no eagerness to broach the subject, talking only about courtroom "war stories" throughout the meal. Finally, Jonathan pressed the point.

"Okay, Arnie. I know you're dying to hit me over the head with your little news item. So go ahead. It's almost time to head back."

Rabin smiled at the younger lawyer. "Patience, my boy. You'll find it a rewarding virtue."

"Unfortunately, it's a luxury I can't afford right now. Too many things happening—including a deposition starting in about twelve minutes," he said, looking at his watch.

Rabin leaned his head forward and peered over the top of

his glasses. "You understand, Jon, that I have absolutely no desire to tarnish the image of such a fine doctor as Aaron Feinerman. Why, I've heard nothing but great things about him: his international reputation, the respect of his colleagues—a real pillar of society."

"Come on, Arnie. Cut the bullshit. You didn't pull me off in a corner to tell me what a great case I have."

Enjoying Jonathan's impatience, Rabin said, "This is a bit delicate. Not really my style at all."

"*Anything* is your style, Arnie, as long as it gets results. Spit it out. I've got to go." Jonathan put his napkin on his plate and slid his chair back.

"There's a strong rumor running around the hospital that Dr. Feinerman was having an affair."

"Bullshit!"

"Call it bullshit, but you've been talking to someone all morning who claims he can prove it."

"Reed?"

"That's what my people tell me."

"What else do your people tell you?"

"Just that it involved a staff nurse at Rivergarden."

"Which nurse?"

"Don't know. Apparently Reed doesn't want to get her in trouble."

"Doesn't sound like the Reed *I've* heard about. Why bring it up at all if he wanted to protect her?"

"My people overheard him blurt it out when he was served with your wonderful lawsuit. Kind of an impulsive thing. When he was asked to name the participant, he clammed up. Of course, in a deposition he'd *have* to answer the question."

"If he's not going to mention it, why should I bring it up at all?"

"Do you want to hear about it in trial for the first time? I seriously doubt that Morris is going to let this drop without working on Reed for the details. It's too devastating to the value of your case."

Rabin was right. If there was even a possibility of its coming out in trial, Jonathan would have to be prepared for it. And that meant learning of every piece of evidence that Reed and Morris might have to throw at him. "You keep talking about 'your people.' Who told you this little piece of news?"

"This was given to me in confidence, Jon. You know how that is." He smiled.

Jonathan nodded. "Sure. I understand. Anything you can do to help me out as long as your own client isn't involved in perpetrating a slander."

Again the smile. "Now, now, Jon. I'm just passing on a little information that might be of some use to you. The truth or falsity of it you'll have to get from Reed."

"Why are you doing me this great favor, Arnie? A little out of character to be helping a plaintiff's lawyer, isn't it?"

"I told you before, Jon. I have absolutely no desire to taint the memory of your fine doctor. Besides, sometimes these things have a way of backfiring, especially if the proof is weak. The last thing I need is an angry jury believing the hospital was implicated in trying to unjustifiably dirty the memory of a highly respected doctor—and in front of his bereaved widow no less. In short, I need to know what evidence Reed actually has, and I can't take the chance of alienating a codefendant by asking him myself."

Although the first reason given was unbelievable, the second had considerable merit. Still, Jonathan was certain that there was a deeper motive to Rabin's generous communication.

"I'll have to give it some thought on the way back to the office," Jonathan said as he rose from his chair.

"Do that, Jon. Give it *considerable* thought. Because I'm sure you'll agree that neither one of us can afford to leave this unexplored."

The afternoon session began exactly at one-ten and again involved little conflict as Jonathan questioned Reed about Aaron's initial examination. Referring to the medical chart, Jonathan had Reed explain in detail each medical term and description used in the notations both for the medical history and the physical examination. Nothing was left uncovered, as Jonathan elicited from Reed the significance of all findings and test results, both positive and negative.

He next turned his attention to the hospital admission and surgery. By three-thirty, all concerned were becoming tired, restless, and impatient.

"Come on, Mr. Rand," said Morris, trying to intimidate Jonathan. "We've been sitting here all day waiting for you to complete this ridiculous deposition. Dr. Reed's time is extremely valuable and it is quite absurd to waste it by exposing him to this continual barrage of insignificant and irrelevant questions."

Jonathan too was tired. His lower back was beginning to ache from tension and fatigue, and he felt the beginning of a headache just above his neck in the back of his head. The smoke that filled the room from Morris's cigarettes did little to help.

"If you don't like my questions, Counsel," Jonathan said angrily, "we can break this deposition right now and get a court ruling on their propriety."

"Just hurry it up," Morris replied, backing down. He knew Jonathan's questions were technically proper and, grudgingly, was even starting to respect his thoroughness. "It's getting late and we want to finish this deposition today."

"I'll do what I can, Counsel." Jonathan reached up and squeezed the back of his neck a couple of times to ease his headache. "I'm just as eager to conclude this deposition as you are."

Jonathan would soon be launching into the critical area of the phone calls from the hospital during the night of Aaron's death, and, according to plan, he suggested a ten-minute break. If he got Reed cornered, he didn't want Morris asking for a break under the guise of a restroom visit.

"Doctor, during the morning hours of June seventeenth, did you receive a telephone call from a nurse at Rivergarden Hospital?"

"I believe I did," he answered.

"Well, Doctor, I don't want there to be any question about this. Would you please look at the nurses' notes in the hospital records in front of you? As you can see, there is an entry for 3:10 A.M. that purports to document a call to you at that time. Does that refresh your recollection?"

Reed picked up the records and examined the entry referred to. "Yes," he said, putting the records back down. "I received the call."

"Were you sleeping at the time of the call?"

"Yes, I was."

"What time had you gone to bed that evening?"

"Oh, I don't know. It wasn't too late."

"Give us your best estimate, Doctor."

"Probably around midnight. Could have been as late as one or two, but I don't think so."

"Then you could have gone to bed as late as two A.M., is that correct?"

"It's possible."

"Where had you been that evening, prior to retiring?"

"My wife had gone to the West Coast to visit her mother, so I stayed home alone all evening."

Reed began nervously tapping his heel on the carpeted floor. Although any view of the foot was obstructed by the table, the up-and-down movement of his leg caused his torso to move, telegraphing his nervousness to Jonathan.

"Did you have anything to drink that evening?"

"I may have had something, maybe a little wine, but I'm not really sure. It's been over a couple of months now."

As Reed spoke, Jonathan noted an increase in the intensity of his foot tapping and sensed he was zeroing in on a vulnerable subject.

"Well, Doctor, I would just as soon avoid taking the deposition of the nurse who spoke with you that evening. If you would try to remember how much you had to drink, I would appreciate it."

Morris, who had just inhaled a puff of one of his numerous cigarettes, jumped up from his chair and at the same time forcefully blew the smoke from his mouth.

"Objection," he shouted. "You're trying to intimidate my client and I won't tolerate it. He said he wasn't sure about his drinking and you'll just have to accept it. If you want to take the nurse's deposition, go right ahead. But don't use it as a threat, or we're going to walk right out of here. I also object to the question on the grounds that it calls for speculation and is totally irrelevant to any issue in this lawsuit."

Jonathan had used his comment to push Reed into a more definite answer, but felt justified because he was convinced that Reed knew exactly how much he had consumed that evening.

"Sit down, Counsel," he barked. "No one is threatening your client, and I should be entitled to a little more effort to remember some things that occurred not that long ago."

Morris returned to his seat. "If he doesn't remember, he doesn't remember. Ask your next question."

Jonathan paused, staring at his notes.

"When you received the call at three-ten, Doctor, were you advised that Dr. Feinerman had a temperaturue of one hundred three point six degrees?"

"I assume so, since it's written there in the chart."

"Then you would have no reason to dispute that?"

"No, I wouldn't."

"Were you also advised that he had been perspiring profusely?"

"I would assume so, since it would normally go along with the temperature."

"You would have no reason to dispute that either?"

"No."

"Were you also advised that he had been experiencing shaking chills?"

"Mr. Rand, I would have no reason to dispute that I was told anything written in the chart, although I don't recall the exact conversation."

"Then you would have no reason to dispute that you were also advised of a respiration rate of thirty and a one-hundred-and-ten pulse rate, correct?"

"No, I wouldn't."

"Doctor, you are familiar with the condition known as septicemia, are you not?"

"Of course I am."

"And that condition is generally considered a bacterial infection of the blood, which produces a physiological reaction in the body, correct?"

"Some doctors would also include viral infections, but that is generally correct."

"Now, the autopsy report states that Dr. Feinerman died as a result of septicemia, true?"

"Yes."

"Did you diagnose his condition as septicemia at *any time* before he died?"

Reed again began tapping his foot. "He did not present a classic picture of septicemia," he answered nervously.

"Then your answer is no?"

"No, I did not make that diagnosis," Reed conceded.

"And is the use of antibiotics the primary means of treating bacterial septicemia?"

"There are other supplemental forms of treatment . . . but yes, it is the usual method of treating septicemia."

"Did you prescribe antibiotics at any time before Dr. Feinerman died?"

"No."

"Was Dr. Feinerman *given* any antibiotics at any time before he died?"

"Not to my knowledge."

"So Dr. Feinerman never received the accepted mode of treatment for the condition that killed him, is that correct?"

Reed did not immediately answer, but kept staring angrily at Jonathan. "Obviously," he growled, "if he was never diagnosed as having septicemia, he was never treated for it."

"Then your answer is no?" Jonathan persisted.

Reed exhaled loudly, signaling disgust at the question. "My answer is no," he conceded.

"Doctor, when you were advised of the vital signs at three-ten by Nurse Henderson, did you consider them abnormally high for a postsurgical patient such as Dr. Feinerman?"

"I considered them unusual, but not necessarily unexpected. Atelectasis produces the same symptoms and is seen frequently where there has been a general anesthetic."

"Well, unexpected or not, his vital signs suggested an abnormal condition that required some attention, did they not?"

"Yes, it required some attention and I ordered X-rays and suggested that the hospital staff have him blow up a rubber glove to expand his lungs."

"But that did *nothing* to treat his septicemia, did it, Doctor?" asked Jonathan, his voice slightly increasing in volume.

"Objection," Morris interjected. "Argumentative; and I instruct the witness not to answer. Ask your next question, Counsel."

Jonathan's tie was loosened now and he had already taken some aspirin, which somewhat helped his headache. However, the pain in his lower back was getting worse, and he rose from his chair in the hope of getting some relief.

"Doctor, you made a diagnosis of atelectasis," said Jonathan, "when in fact your patient was suffering from septicemia; is that correct?"

Reed dropped his hand on the table to further display his resentment. "Mr. Rand," he began slowly, gradually raising his voice, "medicine is not an exact science—not that I'd expect you or any other lay person to understand that."

Morris started to say something, but Reed stopped him by holding up his hand. "Let me say this," he directed at Morris. Then, turning his attention again to Jonathan, he stated, "A doctor does not see a patient with a sign on him saying 'I have septicemia.' He sees a multitude of signs and symptoms and then must exercise some kind of judgment in arriving at his diagnosis. It's a question of judgment, and that judgment is exercised by considering a number of conditions which can produce the same syndrome or set of symptoms. Septicemia produced by some exposure to bacteria during or following surgery normally does not begin so soon after the operation, and I felt that atelectasis was the most likely condition he was suffering from."

Jonathan folded his arms; he remained standing. "Then you were aware that septicemia could produce the same symptoms that Nurse Henderson related to you?"

"Yes, but as I told you before, one would not normally expect it that soon after surgery."

"Then you considered the *possibility* of septicemia?"

"Yes, I did."

"You were aware, were you not, that septicemia usually results in death when left untreated?"

Reed hesitated. "Yes, I have read statistics that have indicated that."

"And it was possible to treat atelectasis and septicemia at the same time, was it not?"

Reed again delayed giving his answer; his jittering leg was becoming more pronounced. "Yes, but you don't give drugs indiscriminately on a chance that a patient may have something. The chance of it being septicemia was too remote to give serious consideration to filling him with antibiotics—drugs, I might add, that are not without side effects themselves. As I've already said, septicemia generally does not develop this fast after surgery."

"Well, you *have* heard or read of instances where septicemia developed within hours after exposure to a bacteria, have you not?"

"I have heard of it happening, but only on extremely rare occasions."

"So you *knew* it was medically possible to have septicemia this early after surgery, correct?"

Reed's bald head began to radiate crimson, and his venemous eyes signaled the impending explosion.

"All right, Rand," he snapped. "I've taken just about all the crap from you that I'm going to take. You've been having your fun all day. Now *I've* got a few things to say."

Seeing that he had lost control over his client, Morris shouted at the court reporter, "Off the record!"

Needing his consent to stop recording, Miss Royster looked up at Jonathan. A quick shake of his head was the silent reply. There was no way he was going to forgo the chance of getting an impulsive or irrational statement on the record.

"For almost five hours I've had to sit here listening to your inane questions," Reed continued, his loud voice filling the room. "You have absolutely no comprehension of what's involved here. You know next to nothing about medicine, and I doubt you would have the intelligence required to use it if you had the education.

"How smug you are with your twenty-twenty hindsight, your . . . your Monday-morning quarterbacking. You expect perfection with absolutely no thought to the inexactness of medicine. Do you really believe that every patient reacts the same way to every illness and injury? We're not dealing with physics or mathematics—these are people. People with differing immunities, differing organs, differing weaknesses, differing . . . differing . . ." Reed hesitated, groping for words, panting with emotion.

"But what do *you* care," he said, poking a finger toward Jonathan, "as long as you can continue suing doctors? You and the rest of the blood-sucking lawyers in this society. As far as I'm concerned this whole system stinks. Any system that allows a money-hungry lawyer to take potshots at a physician of my caliber and then have him scrutinized by twelve imbecilic laymen has got to be something pulled right out of the Dark Ages."

Morris jumped to his feet. "All right! That's it!" he said. "There is to be no more recording. The doctor's comments have nothing to do with this lawsuit, and unless this is stopped immediately, we're going to walk right—"

"Sit down, Preston," said Reed. "My remarks have *everything* to do with this lawsuit. I know what I'm saying, and I wouldn't care if the *press* was here.

"I am one of the finest surgeons in this state. No, I am *the* finest surgeon in this state. And there isn't a doctor around who would disagree with that. I have saved hundreds, maybe even thousands of lives, and yet you stand there attacking my competence . . . my skill. And because of the death of *one* man, you . . . you try to wash away thirty-two years of that kind of work."

Trembling, Reed rose from his chair as he unleashed his fury. "Doctors should not be subject to suit," he screamed. "You hear me, Counselor! It's barbaric. It's ingratitude. A physician of my skill, my . . . esteem, should never be exposed to this ridicule. Dammit, I have earned the right not to be sued. *A man of my standing should be above the law.*"

Reed stopped, as his final words seemed to hang in the air. Had he actually said it? It was something he felt, something he had thought many times before. But to express it aloud was something he had fought, knowing the reaction it might bring. But yes, he had actually said it. Said it for the world to hear.

Slowly he eased into his seat, his eyes dropping to stare at the empty table in front of him.

Jonathan fought the urge to strike back. It was his natural instinct, and never had a witness been more deserving of being put in his place.

"Have you anything further to say, Doctor?" Jonathan's question was soft yet firm.

Reed shook his head, continuing his blank stare at the table. "No . . . no, that's all."

Throughout the remaining hours of the afternoon, Jonathan grilled Reed about his knowledge of the causes, symptoms, and treatment of septicemia, and his experiences with the disease; finally, he asked about the second telephone call from the hospital. By six-fifteen everyone was nagging at him to conclude the deposition. However, he still had one more subject to cover.

"Dr. Reed, prior to the time that you first saw Dr. Feinerman professionally, would you see each other frequently around the hospital?"

"Yes."

"Over the year before his death, had you ever seen him anywhere other than at the hospital?"

"Oh, maybe once or twice at the County Medical Association meeting; that's about all."

"Then you had occasionally observed Dr. Feinerman's relationships with other personnel at Rivergarden Community Hospital?"

Reed glanced suspiciously at Jonathan. "Yes . . . I have," he answered reluctantly

Jonathan's heart began beating faster. He wanted to frame carefully the question about a subject he felt uncomfortable dealing with. "Did you ever observe anything about those relationships that you feel might be relevant to this case— either about how Dr. Feinerman died, or regarding the value of his life to Mrs. Feinerman?"

Clasping his hands together, Reed stared at Jonathan and broke into a smile. "What you want to know, Counselor, is whether or not I have ever seen Dr. Feinerman get a little chummy with any of his nurses. Well, since you asked, the answer is yes. Dr. Feinerman was *quite* chummy with one nurse in particular, as I recall."

"Could you be more specific? Maybe what you saw was only an act of friendship."

"I'm not talking about a friendly hug or a little pat on the fanny. *That* you see a fair amount of around the hospital, but it's nothing that anyone takes seriously. No, what I'm talking about is an embrace—two people affectionately kissing each other."

From the end of the table, Jonathan detected an exchange of subtle smiles between Reed and Rabin and at once knew that the whole thing had been a plant from the beginning.

"And where did this little rendezvous take place?"

"In the hospital parking lot. No one else was around at the time."

"When?"

"Oh, about two months before his death. It was during the night shift, about ten o'clock in the evening."

"Anyone else see this?"

"No, just myself."

"Who was the young lady involved?"

"I'm not at liberty to say."

"I'm afraid you'll have to. If you refuse, I'll only get a court order and you'll have to come back and tell me anyway. So you'd save us both a lot of time if you'd tell me now."

"Is that true?" asked Reed, looking at his attorney.

"Yes, it is," Morris agreed.

Again the silent exchange between Reed and Rabin. "Her name is Jensen—Maureen Jensen. She's an RN at Rivergarden. Works the eleven-P.M.-to-seven shift now."

"Did Dr. Feinerman ever talk to you about this?"

"No. I guess he always felt I'd keep quiet about it."

Jonathan wanted to follow up with a few more questions, but could muster neither the energy nor the desire to proceed with the deposition. After a few short questions from Rabin and the usual stipulations between the attorneys, everyone except Jonathan quickly picked up what they had brought and left the room.

Rabin had set him up. The reason was not clear. However, whatever the motive, Rabin wanted Jonathan to believe that Aaron had been having an affair with this Maureen Jensen. Of course, this knowledge might well influence him to settle the case at a substantially lower amount. That seemed a likely reason for the disclosure and was something he would have to consider.

However, Jonathan was glad that he had asked the question, even if it had been prompted by the discussion with Rabin. If it were going to come out, it was just as well that it had come out now, when there was still time to investigate the facts. Clearly, he had a lot more to learn about the case. But with each day he was facing that prospect with more and more uncertainty.

Fifteen minutes later, Jonathan still sat staring across the conference table at the law books on the library shelves. The stench of cigarettes permeated the air. The ache in his back was more pronounced than ever.

Why would Reed lie about it? he wondered. Perhaps the reason was obvious, but perjury seemed an extreme action to take just to minimize the value of the case. The revelation about Aaron and Maureen Jensen was stunning for more reasons than one. It was as if Aaron were becoming a stranger. Jonathan arched his back and squeezed the nape of his neck but felt little relief.

Reassuring himself that the rumor had to be unfounded, Jonathan walked over to the credenza at the end of the room. He slid open the cabinet door, withdrew a glass and a bottle of Tanqueray, and poured it over a couple of ice cubes he had removed from the refrigerator.

"Will there be anything else, Mr. Rand?"

Jonathan had been so absorbed in his thoughts that he had forgotten that anyone else was in the office.

"No, Sally. Go on home. I'll see you in the morning."

"All right. Don't stay too late. Remember, you're supposed to meet Miss Brennan at the club at seven for dinner, and it's already six-forty."

As Jonathan heard the door close, he took a swallow of the Tanqueray. It felt warm trickling down his throat and into his empty stomach. He smiled at the prospect of seeing Danielle.

# Chapter XIII

Jonathan's brown Coupe de Ville pulled into the club parking lot and came to a stop facing the quiet waters of the marina. The sun was just settling on the western horizon and below he could see *Dreamboat* safely nestled in her slip. He smiled at his old friend, a toy boat compared to some of the larger sailing craft at the end of the dock. A quick glance in his rear-view mirror reminded him of his disheveled hair and loosened tie. A few strokes of his comb and a moment to straighten the tie improved his appearance, but did little to freshen him from the day-long battle. Recalling that he had some aftershave in the glove compartment, Jonathan pulled out the bottle and splashed a little on his cheeks. A definite improvement. At least he wouldn't *smell* tired.

He hesitated before opening the door. Would Danielle be there? He had reached the point where he expected disappointment—at least where she was concerned. Screw it! If she wasn't there, he would still enjoy a nice dinner and a good bottle of wine. He was bound to run into a few of the boaters he knew from the marina. Sure. If she wasn't there, he'd just take it in stride.

Jonathan eagerly walked to the club entrance. Maybe he'd be able to take it in stride, but he still couldn't hide his excitement to see if she was inside waiting for him.

ꞏThe club seemed alive with activity. At least a dozen people were sitting and standing in the foyer, waiting to be seated, the bar area was standing room only, and the waiters and bartenders were working at twice their usual pace. Tuesday afternoon was set aside for the club's weekly sailboat races and the last of the tail-enders would usually straggle in between six-thirty and seven. Rudy stood next to his desk giving a couple of waiters some instructions. As Jonathan approached, he sent the waiters on their way and smiled as he gave his standard greeting.

"Good evening, Mr. Rand. I hope you had a good day out on the Sound."

"Not today, Rudy. All work and no play. Only left the office about twenty-five minutes ago."

"Oh, I'm so sorry. Well, there's always next week. Your table's still ready. I held your reservations—although it wasn't easy."

"I appreciate your patience, Rudy," Jonathan said, anxiously looking up the stairs that led to his table. "Has my guest arrived yet?" Jonathan asked.

"No, sir. Not yet. But I'll seat her the minute she arrives."

Silently cursing, Jonathan followed Rudy to his usual table. If she wasn't interested, why didn't she just tell him?

Charlie Adams, his waiter, returned with the drink and Jonathan promptly consumed half of it in one swallow. His eyes drifted out the window to his small sloop, in which he and Danielle had shared that memorable day.

Why was he so drawn to her? She was beautiful and had a figure that men dreamed of, but it was something else. For the first time, he tried to analyze it. Danielle was impulsive and unpredictable. She did *what* she wanted *when* she wanted. And she did it seemingly with little or no thought.

It was not the way things should be done, thought Jonathan. Decisions should be made only after considering all the alternatives and the potential consequences of each. It was foolish to act without such deliberation. The world would be chaotic, disorganized, filled with one surprise after another. How disruptive not knowing at all times what was likely to happen. . . . Maybe that was it! The thing that was so fascinating, so intriguing about her. Danielle was Jonathan's exact opposite.

"Why is it that I always seem to be sneaking up on you?"

Danielle stood above him, displaying the teasing smile that had been haunting him over the past ten days. Her full auburn hair hung softly to her bare shoulders. She wore a light-blue cocktail dress that dropped to a plunging V between her breasts. In one hand she carried a small beaded matching purse. Her tan gave her an exotic appearance. Had he been looking, Jonathan would also have noticed a number of the other diners turning to stare at Danielle, as if she were a movie star.

Rising to his feet, Jonathan said, "Always deep in thought, I guess, but I can't think of a nicer surprise. You are absolutely stunning."

Danielle graciously accepted Jonathan's assistance and slid into the booth on the opposite side of the table. "Well, thank you! That's quite a compliment. And from a farm boy, no less."

Jonathan laughed, taking his own seat. "Will I ever live that down?"

"Nothing to live down," she said. "It only adds to your charm. In case you haven't noticed, I find you a very interesting man."

Jonathan almost blushed at the compliment. "Aw shucks, ma'am. I'm nothin' more than a simple homespun, straw-chewing country boy. Naw, nothin' special 'bout me—other than being the best lawyer in Connecticut."

"You joke. But I do find you a very fascinating man."

Jonathan looked into Danielle's sparkling hazel eyes. Was she setting him up for another barb?

"Like most farm boys, I'm also blessed with a slight streak of gullibility. So forgive me, but you *are* serious, aren't you?"

"Yes, I am." Her eyes unmistakably communicated her sincerity.

Just then Charlie arrived, was introduced, took Danielle's order for a Tom Collins and Jonathan's request for another Tanqueray, and left.

"You are a rarity," said Jonathan.

"How's that?"

"You're right up front with everything. You do what you want and say what you feel. No beating around the bush. So forgive my clumsiness, but I'm not quite sure how to deal with this. A thirty-five-year-old bachelor just doesn't run into that many young ladies who are so candid." Again she had him stumbling, trying to adjust, grasping to understand her actions. Could she really be so interested in him after such a short time? Or was there some hidden motive? But for now he didn't care. The infatuation—if that was her true feeling—was mutual, and Jonathan was uncharacteristically about to jump into something without any concern for the consequences.

"It just seems that so much time is wasted playing little games. I know because I've played them myself. I've played them and I'm sick of them. It also seems silly to pretend that I'm not interested after the day we spent on your boat. Can you imagine that? Why, I practically seduced you. We've already had some very intimate moments, and, quite frankly, I would like to be spending a lot more time with you."

"I'll do what I can to arrange it," said Jonathan, smiling.

Over the next hour, they ate and chatted about their childhood and earlier years and shared a bottle of cabernet sauvignon. Jonathan felt a deepening closeness between them. The barriers of unfamiliarity were gradually disappearing. The beautiful face with the unpredictable personality was becoming a real person with memories, problems, heartaches, and family ties like everyone else. Danielle's father had been killed during the Korean War, two months before she was born, and her mother had died in an auto accident only five years later. Unwanted by her stepfather, she and her elder sister had been raised by a maternal aunt and uncle. At eighteen, she left home, and had drifted through a number of jobs. Finally came the short-lived marriage. Jonathan could see that in many ways Danielle needed a family relationship as much as he did.

After dinner, Danielle sat sipping a glass of Amaretto and Jonathan some Hennessy Bras d'Or cognac.

"You were going to tell me about your weekend," Jonathan finally reminded her.

"Yes, I was," she said, her eyes reluctantly dropping to the table.

"If you feel uncomfortable about it, Dani, it's really unnecessary to say anything. What's happened in your past is unimportant to me. Honest!"

"No, I want to tell you. I . . . I've been seeing a man since my divorce from Barry. He's an executive with a large clothing company. The 'rag business' he calls it. His office is in Manhattan. He commutes from Long Island but maintains an apartment in the city. I've been seeing him there, usually on weekends—"

"Look, Dani, this is really unnecessary. I don't need to know this."

"No! I want you to know. It's one of the reasons I'm here tonight. I've got to say this—everything."

Danielle took another sip of her drink. "The relationship was already somewhat strained when I first met you. In fact, I broke a date with him that weekend to go boating with you. It's . . . the same story you've probably heard a thousand times before. Married man meets young lady, sweeps her off her feet, but refuses to get divorce." A sardonic smile. "I'd seen it so many times in the movies. I never imagined it would happen to me. But it did."

"And that's where you were last weekend?"

Danielle nodded. "Yes . . . but to say good-bye. And I had to do it in person. Not over the phone and not with a letter. It never would have satisfied him. I had to speak with him face-to-face to convince him I was serious. . . . I was to see him on Friday, but he couldn't get away until Sunday."

"Did he believe you?"

"He had to. I told him I was in love with someone else."

"I'm not sure I should ask who you're talking about," Jonathan said with some trepidation.

"You can't ignore this, Jon. Neither of us can."

"You're probably right. I *know* you're right, but I . . ." Jonathan wanted to tell her how he wasn't cut out to be tied down with one woman; how he was a loner with his own way of doing things. He wanted to tell her how he had spent his entire adulthood without commitment, even without love. He wanted to tell her why. He wanted to tell her how he was incapable of loving her and that she should be on guard not to get hurt. He wanted to tell her *all* of this, but he couldn't. He couldn't because he was uncertain if it was true anymore. Things were so different. *She* was so different. If he just had more time to think this through.

"I know I'm outspoken. I know I say things I probably shouldn't. But I've never been the one to keep my feelings bottled up inside." Danielle reached over and placed her hand on top of Jonathan's. "We've got to deal with this, Jon. At least I do."

Jonathan took her hand in both of his. It was delicate and soft and made him want to embrace her. "I've never been so confused about my feelings in my entire life. There's a change going on in me here, and I'm just trying to understand it."

"Don't fight them. Let them go."

"How ironic. Somebody else told me that once. But until now . . ." Jonathan's voice faded as he thought of Rachel's plea. It had been less than a month ago but seemed an eternity. "Well, I'm not fighting it anymore, Dani. I don't know if it's love. I'm not sure I would recognize love if it stepped up and slapped me in the face. But I know I feel an affection for you that I never thought myself capable of. And I know there isn't a day that goes by that I don't think of you. Whatever it is, Dani, I'm trying to understand it. And . . . yes, I guess I'm finally ready to deal with it." The words felt like they were coming out of the mouth of a stranger.

"There is a solution to all this, you know."

"Enlighten me. I'm badly in need of help."

"We could move in together. It's becoming quite stylish, I understand."

Jonathan looked at her with astonishment. Astonished not at her but at himself. He was tempted to accept her suggestion.

"This is not the kind of thing that I would treat lightly," Jonathan said. "To live with someone . . . I've never done anything like that before."

"Neither have I. Other than my marriage, of course."

"This is happening so fast. When do you suggest that this take place?"

"Now. Tonight. Why wait? I know what *I* want. And if you feel the same, why spend another night apart? I could follow you home and then pick up most of my things tomorrow. Anything heavy we could move on the weekend."

Jonathan examined her eyes, her nose, her hair. Two weeks ago she had been a complete stranger to him. And now he was about to make a decision that would have been totally alien to him before they had met. But what did he have to lose? If it didn't work out, all he had to do was ask her to leave. Jonathan inspected her hand within his palm, then again found her eyes.

"All right, let's do it. I can't really believe this, but I honestly want to live with you."

"How wonderful!" She smiled. "I just knew this evening would turn out to be something special. Let's order champagne. This is a night to celebrate."

They ordered a half-bottle and toasted their new allegiance. It was indeed a night to remember. A beginning.

"Now tell me," Danielle urged. "How did your deposition with Reed go? If you're going to be my lover, I'll want to know everything about you. And that also means your practice. You don't mind my asking, do you?"

"No, not in the least. But it was only routine. Just seven and a half hours of boring questions and answers. A deposition is nothing more than a fact-gathering mission. The real excitement won't come until trial."

"I guess, after a while, every case seems pretty much like another, doesn't it?"

"I wouldn't say that. Every case has its own unique challenges. But it's seldom that a deposition holds many surprises, and this one was no exception—other than a couple of temper tantrums by Reed, of course."

Although he was still shaken by this encounter with Danielle, Jonathan had the presence of mind not to disclose what he had learned about Maureen Jensen. That information might tie into a possible murder, and until he had it all sorted out, *no one* would be told anything. Danielle may have won his heart, but not yet his confidence. He would share with her Reed's egotistical display of contempt; it would make for good conversation and provide his first opportunity to express his feelings about the grueling ordeal. But caution and instinct for self-preservation would dictate when and if she would be told the facts that might well endanger his very life.

He also felt uncomfortable about the depth of her interest in the case. Was it just curiosity, or was there some hidden motive?

# Chapter XIV

Jonathan rolled over in his bed and stared at his clock. He knew what time it was even before looking, yet he followed the ritual of confirming the hour. As usual, he had beaten his alarm by almost thirty minutes.

The dinner, the conversation, the drive to his apartment, the tender romantic sex—all of it rushed into his mind. Then, almost as quickly, he sensed someone lying next to him, and at once appreciated the reality of the surprising decision he had made.

Jonathan eased onto his back and rotated his head on the pillow. Danielle lay on her side, facing him, her legs drawn up in a curled position. Her eyes were closed and her deep rhythmic breathing suggested she was still soundly asleep.

It was not an unfamiliar sight, seeing an attractive young lady sharing his bed. There had been so many faces before; too many even to recall their names. Faces that paraded across a span of more than fifteen years. Some, like Rachel, had earned a special place in his heart, while others were nothing more than one-night flings. Yet they all shared one common memory for Jonathan: the sight of them stretched out in his bed in the morning light had been repugnant to him. It was as if a net had been dropped over him, and he would anxiously rise early to jog, shower, and dress. Anything to reassert his independence.

Jonathan reached over and carefully pulled back a lock of hair that was masking most of Danielle's face. A faint smudge of tawny coral lipstick was rubbed over a corner of her mouth, and her hair wandered without direction over most of her pillow.

This time it was different—very different. She was there because he wanted her to be. It was her idea, but he had made the choice. Jonathan leaned closer, softly kissed her forehead, then rested his head again on his pillow. She belonged in bed

138

alongside him, and—at least for the moment—she belonged to him. Belonging. What a strange, alien word. Yet, it seemed to fit, and he used it over and over in his mind until it flowed as a natural description of their relationship.

The alarm went off, breaking the silence with a nagging buzz. Danielle's head shifted with a start and her eyes opened wide, while Jonathan's hand frantically patted at the clock for the plunger. Damn! He had forgotten to turn it off. He turned toward Danielle, who was propping herself up with her pillow.

"That has to be the most godawful noise I've heard in my entire life!" she exclaimed.

Jonathan chuckled. "I never hear it. I'm always awake before it goes off and hit the switch when I get up for my exercise."

"What happened this morning?"

"Forgot," he said sheepishly.

"Why set the alarm if you're going to wake up before it goes off?"

"It's my backup system . . . on the outside chance I oversleep. I've tried, but I can't go to sleep unless my alarm is set. I can't relax."

Danielle smiled. "My big masculine lover has a security blanket. I love it! What other habits do you have?"

"Habits? My whole *life* is a habit. When we have a couple of free hours I'll tell you about 'em."

"Well, this is one you'll have to break," she said, pointing at the clock. "I've got a clock radio, which I'll pick up tonight after work. You wouldn't mind a little soft music in the morning, would you?"

"Not in the least." Jonathan reached over and undraped the sheet from her bare breasts. "Music in the morning would be a perfect way to start the day. That and a little lovemaking."

Danielle looked down at herself, then back at Jonathan. "See anything you like?" she asked, smiling.

"Well, let me see," he said, inspecting. Softly he cupped one breast in his hand and touched her nipple with his tongue. "My favorite flavor. I'll take a pair."

His lips caressed her, then worked higher up to the nape of her neck. Responsively, Danielle sank back into the bed, her free hand searching its way over the taut muscles of his abdomen. Then she drove her hand lower until she reached the hardness she had enjoyed over a good part of the prior evening.

"Oh, yes." She sighed. Jonathan likewise began to work on her lower anatomy and eased himself over on top of her.

At times, the life of a trial lawyer is totally governed by the clock. Thus, it was more out of instinct than disinterest in his activities that Jonathan's eyes happened to catch a glimpse of the time. "Shit!" he said, pushing himself back. "It's six forty-eight. I've got to make a phone call."

"Oh, no!" she moaned. "Now? At this very moment?"

"Sorry," he said, rising from the bed. "I've got to make it before seven. My party will be gone after that."

"There are names for people like you," she said.

"I know. I'll make it up to you. I promise."

In less than a minute he found the hospital's number in his phone directory. Anxiously he placed the receiver to his ear, reached for the dial—and then hesitated. Suddenly he was confronted with a potential ethical problem he had subconsciously been shoving aside. The hospital was in litigation with him and was represented by attorneys. To speak with an employee of an opposing lawyer's client without the presence of the lawyer was in violation of the canons of ethics. However, he quickly rationalized, Jensen was not one of the treating nurses, and he would not be discussing any of Aaron's care and treatment at Rivergarden. And in Jonathan's mind there was an even stronger justification for the call: Reed and the hospital staff were attempting unjustly to impugn Aaron's fidelity. They were setting the ground rules. If they wanted to play dirty, Jonathan could roll in the dirt with the best of them. However, it was with some uncertainty that he dialed the number.

"Good morning! Rivergarden Community Hospital!" The voice was bright and cheerful.

"Good morning! I would like to speak with Maureen Jensen, please. She's a staff nurse on the eleven-to-seven shift, but I'm not sure where she's located."

"Thank you!" Silence while she checked the hospital directory. "You'll want orthopedics. Just a moment, I'll connect you."

"Orthopedics!"

"Nurse Jensen, please."

"Oh, I . . . Yes, she's still here. Just a moment." Apprehension.

How would she react to Mrs. Feinerman's lawyer calling her at the hospital? Was she loyal to her employer? If she knew who her caller was this morning, she might refuse to come to the phone and then notify Rabin. The thought was disconcerting, and the wait seemed to last an eternity.

"Hello, this is Maureen Jensen." The voice was guarded.

"Miss Jensen, you don't know me. My name is Jonathan Rand. I'm representing Ruth Feinerman in her lawsuit against Rivergarden Community Hospital."

For some reason, it seemed more expedient to be right up front. The silence that followed, however, appeared to signal what Jonathan had feared.

Finally she responded.

"I know who you are, Mr. Rand. What do you want?"

"I'd like to talk to you, if you have a few extra minutes."

"I doubt that we have anything to talk about. What could you possibly want with me?"

"I understand that you were acquainted with Dr. Feinerman. I was hoping you wouldn't mind answering a few questions about him. Shouldn't be more than five or ten minutes."

"Concerning what? Could you be a little more specific?"

"I'd prefer not—at least over the phone."

More silence.

Finally she asked, "Do you know where Stoneham Park is?"

"No, but I can find it."

"It's on the west side of town. I'll see you there at eleven A.M.," she said. "Please meet me at the fountain."

She hung up without further comment, and for a moment Jonathan stood listening to the dial tone. He had done it. Now, if she would only keep their meeting a secret.

Jonathan hung up the phone and returned to the bedroom. "Now, let me see. Weren't we in the middle of something a few moments ago?"

Stoneham Park extended a total of three blocks, cutting through a large complex of low-rise apartment buildings, each with its own exotic name, landscaping, and architectural design. Around town the area had become known as a haven for the free, the fast, and the young.

The park itself was honeycombed with acacias, eastern

maples, and willows, many of them extending over the bordering streets. Leaves, shuffled by occasional light gusts of wind, lay scattered over the pavement and the cars parked along the curb. Asphalt walkways ambled throughout the grounds, all ending up in the center of the park at the large circular fountain.

Jonathan eased his Cadillac to a stop at the curb behind another parked car. He could make out the fountain through the trees, almost a hundred yards away. Its dancing waters and white circular border gleamed like a beacon through the leaves. He pulled down his sunglasses and squinted, trying to get a better look. He saw no one even close to the fountain. He glanced at his wristwatch: it was seven minutes after eleven. She should have been there waiting for him.

Stepping into the sun, the heat hit him like a blast furnace. He loosened his tie, found the nearest pathway, and began walking toward the fountain. The playful staccato of chirping birds seemed to be the only sound on this quiet day. The fragrance of freshly cut grass brought on a feeling of exhilaration at being outdoors, away from stale law offices and stuffy courtrooms.

Something was bothering Jonathan. Something even more damaging than Feinerman's possible affair with Maureen Jensen. A jilted lover might well have had the motive to kill her paramour. The emotions of rejection, humiliation, anger, a blinding rage, an easy means at her disposal, opportunity . . . How many times had he read about it in the newspaper or heard it on the news? Jensen had a knowledge of medicine and worked the eleven-to-seven shift at Rivergarden. Motive, means, and opportunity—it would all be there. Like it or not, there was a distinct possibility that Jonathan might shortly be meeting Aaron's murderer.

Reaching the path that circled the fountain, Jonathan came to a stop and examined the immediate area.

"Mr. Rand?" The voice came from beneath the leafy awning of a large acacia tree. A woman in her late twenties wearing a white nurse's uniform stepped into the clearing.

"Yes—I'm Jonathan Rand. You must be Maureen Jensen."

She nodded, sizing him up with cold, pale blue eyes. "I waited for a while at the fountain, but the heat drove me to cover. Must be ninety degrees out here."

"It's a hot one. Seems that's all we're getting lately. Care to sit down?" He motioned to a convenient bench.

"No. I can't stay long. Perhaps you should get to the point of our meeting."

The voice was emotionless, displaying neither resentment nor cordiality, and her penetrating gaze made Jonathan fidget nervously with the knot of his tie.

"I . . . uh . . . mentioned over the phone that Ruth Feinerman had retained me to file a malpractice suit because of the death of her husband."

"I know who you are, Mr. Rand. The whole hospital knows. You've created quite a stir."

"Yes, I guess I have." Jonathan mopped at his brow and cheeks. "Would you have any objection to talking with me about Dr. Feinerman?"

"If I did, I wouldn't be here. Though I doubt that my employer would look favorably upon my chatting with the opposing lawyer."

The point was well taken. "I assume that's why you wanted to meet me at this end of town?"

"That, plus the fact that I only live about a block and a half from here."

So Jensen shared his feeling that Rivergarden should not know of their talk. The thought made him more at ease.

He began his appraisal of the mysterious stranger. Her hair, the color of a white Caribbean beach, was cut in a short shag and was a perfect complement to her peaches-and-cream complexion. Jensen's face, although pretty, had the lifeless look of a portrait. All her features were perfectly placed and manufactured to correct scale, but lacking personality or emotion. From all appearances, she lived her life through a series of well-considered and organized decisions, without guilt, conscience, worry, or regret. Beneath her perfect shell was possibly a live personality, thought Jonathan, but certainly not one easy to discover.

Jensen's figure, on the other hand, was totally obvious. Her most striking asset was a small waist that accentuated possibly the sexiest derriere that Jonathan had ever seen. Yes, maybe even sexier than Danielle's. If raw sex was what Aaron had been after, it was not hard to imagine that he would have quickly accepted the subtlest of Maureen Jensen's invitations.

Certainly Rabin and Morris would have little difficulty in convincing a jury of that possibility.

"I understand that you were well acquainted with Dr. Feinerman."

"Yes. I doubt that there were many at the hospital who weren't. Dr. Feinerman was a very gregarious person."

"You're in orthopedics. I suppose you had occasion to work with him—treating his patients, that is?"

"Yes. I was assigned to Dr. Feinerman's patients many times. As a doctor, he was quite in demand."

"Did you see him frequently at the hospital?"

"Yes."

"Several times a week?"

Jensen pondered the question, then said, "Let's say a couple of times a week." Not once had she taken her eyes off him.

Self-conscious, Jonathan tugged again at his tie. His heart was laboring at a more rapid rate as he closed in on the sensitive topic.

"Had you ever spent any time with Dr. Feinerman socially? Hospital parties, coffee in the cafeteria, anything?" Again he blotted perspiration from his forehead.

"Mr. Rand, you're putting yourself through a lot of unnecessary discomfort. If you have something to ask, why don't you come right out and ask it?"

Jonathan nodded. "You're right. Okay. Yesterday I took the deposition of Jason Reed, who is being sued along with Rivergarden. A deposition is—"

"I know what a deposition is. What was said that brings you all the way out to Stoneham Park in this damn heat?"

"Dr. Reed claims you were having an affair with Aaron Feinerman."

Jonathan had expected surprise or anger, but without reacting she said, "That's an interesting accusation. What else did he have to say?"

"Only that he saw you and Dr. Feinerman in some type of affectionate embrace in the hospital parking lot. This was supposed to have taken place about two months before his death."

"And you, of course, want to know if there is any truth in all of this?"

"It could turn out to be critical to the case. If you and Dr.

Feinerman were . . . lovers, it's essential that I know about it."

"Why? Would it change anything?"

"No, but I would know what I'm dealing with. My approach to this case might be entirely different."

"So knowing all about Dr. Feinerman and myself would help you with your lawsuit?"

"Would help Mrs. Feinerman," he corrected. "Oh, there was one other thing—although this didn't come from Dr. Reed."

"What's that?"

"I've also learned that Aaron Feinerman took five or six trips to Washington, D.C., the last one only two weeks before his death. . . . Look, I know how presumptuous this is of me, but I find myself with no alternative but to ask."

"You want to know if I was seeing Dr. Feinerman during his trips to Washington?"

Jonathan nodded. "Yes, I do."

For the first time, Jensen looked away, directing her attention toward the water spilling over into the lower pond of the fountain. She seemed to be searching her past, yet her face still betrayed no emotion.

"Aaron Feinerman and I were nothing more than very good friends," she said finally. "Anyone who tries to tell you otherwise is lying . . . You ask about Washington. I haven't been there in over five years, and two weeks before he died I was on my way to Miami for a Caribbean cruise.

"Dr. Feinerman—Aaron—and I met about a year ago. I was working in orthopedics and he was an orthopedic surgeon. It was inevitable that we'd meet and it was inevitable that we'd be working together. We were friends, but Aaron was friends with *everyone* he worked with. That's just the way he was."

Jensen directed her cold stare back up again at Jonathan. "I had a great deal of respect and admiration for Aaron, but I was never his lover. Not that I wouldn't have been interested. But he was always off limits and there was never any doubt of it."

"Then Reed was lying?"

"Figure it out for yourself. I have never had an affair with Aaron Feinerman."

"And the scene in the parking lot never happened?"

Jensen reached into her purse, pulled out a pair of

sunglasses, and put them on. "I recall the night," she said, straightening them on her nose. "I know the incident he was talking about." The dark glasses added another barrier to assessing her candor.

"Then it was true?"

"Only through Reed's eyes, which have always had a reputation for distorting things. I was in Aaron's arms that night, but I wasn't kissing him. It was actually quite innocent. I had received some bad news about my older sister, and it had finally gotten to me. Despite all the research in medicine, sometimes there's absolutely nothing that can be done. It gives you a feeling of helplessness that is rather hard to describe. As it happens, Aaron was walking to his car at the same time I was. He was a convenient shoulder to cry on. It was nothing more than that."

It was a reasonable explanation. The scene of the two of them in each other's arms in a dark parking lot could easily have been misinterpreted by anyone. Still, her credibility was suspect, to say the least. A woman is not likely to admit to an affair with a married man—especially if she has murdered him. What also was difficult for Jonathan to accept was that this distant and dispassionate woman standing before him would cry about *anyone*.

"You mentioned going on a cruise. What day did you leave?"

"My flight to Miami left Friday, June first. By noon the next day I was a hundred miles at sea."

"And you returned . . . ?"

"I disembarked back in Miami on Sunday, June seventeenth. It was a fifteen-day cruise."

"Can you prove this?" he asked. It was the first piece of verifiable evidence he had come upon since Reed's accusation.

"I don't know why I should have to. What does this have to do with your lawsuit?"

Jonathan detected a trace of anger. His mind raced, searching for an acceptable reason. Under no circumstances could he risk revealing his true motive.

"I'd simply like to verify that you were not in Washington on June first," he said. "I'd also feel more comfortable with proof that you were not at the hospital at the time of Aaron's surgery. With no personal knowledge of his admission, your employers could never criticize my ethics for talking to you without their lawyers being present." The quickness and credibility of his reply pleased Jonathan.

Jensen thought for a moment and said, "The SS *Barbados*. It belongs to the Caribbean Steamship Lines. Check their records if you want proof."

"I hope you understand. This morning has not been easy for me."

"It's your job. Why shouldn't it be easy? I thought lawyers delighted in digging into personal matters."

"I considered this meeting a rather sensitive subject. I didn't come out here to accuse, only to prepare for a client's case."

"Maybe so . . . Will there be anything else?"

"Just a couple more things." Jonathan pulled a small notepad out of his shirt pocket and entered the name of the cruise ship. "Just so my records will be complete, I could also use the name of your travel agent and your airline."

"Economy Travels in Bridgeport and National Airlines," she said without hesitation.

Jonathan scribbled down the information. Simultaneously, Jensen turned to leave, not seeking the consent of her interrogator. She had given all the information she intended to.

"You're a very persistent man," she said, stopping for a final word over her shoulder.

"I've been told that most of my life. There must be some truth in it," he said, looking up from his pad.

"People like you seldom listen to advice, but I'm going to give it anyway. You're in way over your head. This is one time in your life you should be backing off."

"I would find that very difficult. It goes against my nature. Once I take on a case, I commit myself."

"I would recommend making an exception with this one. You'll find the price of admission very expensive—and I'm not talking about money."

Jonathan returned the pad and pen to his pocket. Her words were sobering, even threatening. What little cordiality that had existed between them quickly vanished, like a sudden morning chill.

"You sound as if you know something," he said more firmly. "I think you should explain what you mean."

"I've said all I'm going to say. But you'd do well to listen to my advice."

Jensen then turned and began walking away. Jonathan watched for a moment as she disappeared into the shadows of the surrounding trees. He thought of following her, took a couple of uncertain steps in the same direction, then stopped. She had unexpectedly thrown a punch deep into his groin while his guard was down, and his impulse was to pursue and interrogate. Yet, from their brief encounter, he knew it would be useless.

*It doesn't take much imagination to figure out what the killer might do if you got close to disclosure.* Lundgren's words, which he had treated so lightly before, now began to look like an ominous message. Over five days, he had received two warnings to drop the case.

Feeling vulnerable in the bright sunlight, Jonathan stepped into the shadows and scanned the area. Fifty feet away, a malnourished mongrel sniffed the grass beneath a picnic table; to the north, he saw a bespectacled young man sitting on a blanket reading a book. Otherwise, the small park appeared deserted.

For the first time since taking on the Feinerman case, Jonathan was experiencing concern for his own safety. But he was not going to be intimidated by the thinly veiled threat of an attractive young lady. There was too much to gain—a multimillion-dollar lawsuit and the fame that would go with it.

Perhaps Aaron had been murdered. At least, Jonathan had reached the point where it seemed prudent to be more cautious. Nothing could be taken for granted.

The penetrating eyes of Maureen Jensen had made their mark.

# Chapter XV

*Monday, August 27, 1979*

"Where are *you* heading off to?"

Danielle, wearing a short negligee, stood in the doorway of their bedroom. She yawned once, softly rubbed an eye, and waited for her answer.

Jonathan released the knob to the front door and said, "Woke up early and couldn't get back to sleep. Thought I'd go for a short drive and take in some fresh air."

Danielle noted the unfamiliar dark burgundy jogging shorts.

"You're not jogging, are you?"

Jonathan shrugged. "Oh, I don't know. I'll see what I feel like when I get out there. If I do, it'll only be for a few blocks."

"Please don't! You know what Dr. Jacobs said."

"What do doctors know? I've lived with this knee for thirty-five years. Jacobs looks at it for ten minutes and is supposed to know everything."

"That's just plain stupid, Jon. He's an orthopedic surgeon—a specialist. And he examined your knee *twice*, not once, and reviewed all your X-rays. If you weren't going to follow his advice, why did you go to see him to begin with?"

Irritated at the questioning, Jonathan stared at the ceiling, then again at Danielle, exhaling in disgust. "Dani, I went to see him because I wanted to know exactly what was wrong with my knee. And I *do* intend to follow his advice, to a point. But I never signed an oath of blind obedience. Look," he said, softening his voice, "I just want to test it out myself. If it starts to swell or hurt even the slightest, I'll immediately stop running. I promise."

"But you could be damaging it without even knowing. Please come back to bed—as a favor to me?"

"I . . . can't."

"But why?"

"Don't ask me to explain, Dani. I'm not quite sure I understand, myself. I only know that I've got to go out there and find my own limitations; on my own, without restrictions from anyone else. I've *got* to have this freedom. I'll be back within an hour."

Abruptly he closed the door and headed for his car.

It felt good to stride along the near-desolate road of his old course. In the first ten minutes of jogging only one car passed Jonathan; one of those small Japanese economy cars he could never remember the name of. The air was motionless and he could smell the dampness that blanketed the countryside. The only sounds of the early morning were the repeated taps of

Jonathan's shoes on the asphalt roadway and the chirps of the awakening birds.

He cursed himself for the way he had talked to Danielle. After all, she was only interested in his health. If only she would understand that he still needed considerable freedom. It was essential that he be given a free rein to adapt to this new way of life.

At a distance too far behind Jonathan to be heard, a dark blue '78 Ford slowly inched closer to the unsuspecting jogger. The front and rear license plates had been removed, and in the center of the passenger side of the windshield was a sunburst-shaped crack, apparently caused by a stone thrown up by another vehicle. The driver's hands tightened on the steering wheel. His intense black eyes fixed on the target ahead of him. He had waited patiently over the past mile and a half for just the right opportunity.

When Jonathan returned, he would apologize to Danielle. She was getting to know him better and would certainly be understanding. Better, he would offer to take her out to dinner tonight as a peace offering.

The moment now was right. The man with the black eyes eased the accelerator to the floor, slowly, so as not to make the tires squeal. With a surge of power and a deep roar the dark blue Ford shot forward. The speedometer rapidly climbed to thirty, then forty . . . fifty . . . sixty miles per hour.

Deep in thought, Jonathan did not hear the initial charge of the Ford. His mind had drifted to the office and the lawsuit, which was demanding more and more of his time and attention. Today the records would be in on all of his subpoenas: Caribbean Steamship Lines, National Airlines, Economy Travels, and the employment records on Maureen Jensen from Rivergarden Hospital. Today, for the first time, he might get some idea whether Jensen was involved in the death of Aaron Feinerman. Today he would—

In an instant Jonathan knew that something was wrong.

The deep, guttural sound of a wide-open carburetor sucking air and the whine of an engine at high RPM were totally out-of-place on the quiet rural road. Instinct told him to move and move fast. Yet, the fear of imminent danger seemed to numb his body as, as if in slow motion, he stepped and then dived for the side of the road. No sooner had he begun his leap than he felt a painful blow shoot deep into his right thigh and throw him helplessly, rolling over and over into the roadside dirt and weeds.

For a moment Jonathan lay on his back, the sky above whirling and exploding miniature stars as he fought to retain consciousness. It was a dream! It *had* to be. Common sense told him that he was still lying next to Danielle in bed.

Had someone actually run him down *intentionally*?

Such things did not happen in real life. Not to him. But it took only a few seconds for the dream to become a reality. Suddenly the sky froze to a picture of a single billowy white cloud, his right leg began throbbing painfully, and in the distance he heard a car departing at high speed.

All the nagging doubts were gone. For the first time since he had been retained by Ruth Feinerman, he knew the truth about Aaron's death. Lundgren had been right. Aaron had been murdered, and *he* was to be the killer's next victim.

Jonathan pushed himself up to a sitting position and scanned the road. No sign of any vehicles in either direction. For the moment he was in no immediate danger—at least no apparent danger.

He looked down at his bare legs. Below the bottom of his jogging shorts he noted a number of small scrapes and lacerations. His legs were also covered with dirt, but he could see no discoloration or abnormal swelling. Running his hand over his right thigh, however, he grimaced with pain as he felt a hardening lump about six inches in diameter. Reluctantly taking a look, he observed a severe abrasion with shades of red and purple from the subcutaneous hemorrhaging. The impact of the car had apparently been a glancing blow. *This time he had been lucky*.

On trembling legs Jonathan stood and wiped the dirt from his sweatshirt and shorts. He had been careless. His legal mind, trained to organize, analyze, and prepare with logical precision, was failing him when he needed it most. He also knew why. He was subjectively involved, not sitting on the sidelines with detached coolness calling all the plays. Rather than Ruth or Aaron, Jonathan had become the center of attention in the case of *Feinerman v. Reed*.

Still, he had to think if he was to survive. . . . Had this been only a warning? There seemed to be sufficient room on the apron of the road for the car to have hit him more directly. If the driver had truly wanted to kill him, he had done a very poor job. Hopefully, he was right. . . . But then, would he heed the warning? Was he ready to drop his investigation into the mystery of Aaron's death—and maybe even the lawsuit itself?

To one who lived by persistence and stubbornness, the answer was not easy. The hit-and-run following Jensen's warning seemed more than just coincidence. If the records failed to support Jensen's story, Jonathan would have a possible suspect and something solid to take to the police. With the evidence developed by Dr. Lundgren, Reed's testimony, what Jonathan had gathered to date, and no alibi, the authorities might have enough to make an arrest; certainly enough to begin a very thorough investigation. It wouldn't surprise him one bit if Maureen Jensen had been sitting behind the wheel of that car.

The time had also come to tell Danielle, whatever his decision would be. Over the days that they had been living together their relationship had grown. He was growing to trust her, and if he decided to continue with his investigation, her life might be in danger. She had every right to know the whole story.

Jonathan was in his office reviewing the subpoenaed records. For over an hour he sat reading and taking notes, checking and rechecking each date and time against a time-table he had drawn up. As Maureen Jensen had claimed, the passenger lists, tickets, invoices, itinerary, and other documents confirmed that she had been on the SS *Barbados* for fifteen days, ending the morning of Sunday, June 17. Records from National Airlines disclosed that she had left Kennedy Airport in New York on June 1 and returned at 2:35 P.M. on the 18th. Copies of signed receipts on the ship for drinks and other items corroborated her presence on the *Barbados*: signatures from the receipts compared exactly with Jensen's signature in her employment records. Without question, Jensen could not have been at the hospital to kill Aaron, nor had she been in Washington, D.C., at the time of Aaron's last trip.

But if Jensen had not killed Aaron, who else would have had the motive and opportunity? What if Aaron had been having an affair with someone else? What if Aaron had never taken the other trips to Washington at all? Jonathan's scribbling began to slow down. What if Ruth had learned of the affair?

The ballpoint pen stopped and dropped from his hand. Stunned, he forced the next question: *What if Ruth in a blind fit of jealousy had killed Aaron?*

After all, she was a nurse and had complete access to Aaron in the hospital. What if she had planned the whole thing to look as though the death had occurred through the carelessness of Rivergarden and Jason Reed? She would receive not only Aaron's entire estate and life insurance, but perhaps several million dollars as the result of a successful malpractice suit.

At 11:00 A.M. sharp, Sally buzzed Jonathan over the intercom and informed him that Ruth Feinerman had arrived.

Her appointment! He had totally forgotten—or had he? Maybe that was why she was so much on his mind. "Tell her I'll be with her in just a few minutes," he said.

Jonathan began rehearsing what he was going to say to Ruth. Over and over he tried different lead-ins to explore any possibility that she had had even the slightest knowledge of an affair. However, no matter how he phrased the questions, each sounded like an accusation, something which he could not bring himself to make. Getting up from his desk, he decided the best approach would be to give Ruth the lead and let her open up. Perhaps a few innocuous questions might steer her into volunteering whether she had known if Aaron was seeing another woman.

Jonathan walked guardedly on his aching right leg through the secretarial bay and opened the door to the reception room. As usual, Ruth was beautifully groomed and dressed.

"Hi there," he said with his usual smile. "You're looking wonderful. Everything's going well, I hope?"

"Yes, it's getting better," she said, putting down a magazine. "But *you* don't look so hot. What happened to you?"

"Nothing serious," he said. "Pulled a muscle when I was out jogging today. Come on in. Sally mentioned you were eager to see me."

"Oh, I guess I sounded a bit eager," she said. "And I know I'm making a big deal out of nothing—"

"Not necessarily. I told you before, I want to know everything. You're just following instructions."

"Thanks, Jon. It's just sitting around that big lonely house. You get to thinking about so many things. I guess I really should get out of there."

"It might not be a bad idea, Ruth; at least for a couple of months. . . . But go ahead and tell me what's bothering you. It might be important."

Ruth looked down at the floor. "Oh, before I forget," she said, picking up an attaché case, "I want to give you some papers I picked up at the house yesterday. I was cleaning out the garage—just looking for something to do—and ran across this old box filled with business records. I rummaged through it myself. Nothing too important—canceled checks, invoices, copies of airline tickets. . . . Aaron never was that well organized. Don't know if there's anything of value, but felt you should make that decision."

*Airline tickets!* Maybe of the trips to D.C.—or to someplace else. "You did right. Never can tell when something important might turn up."

Jonathan took the attaché case from her and put it down next to his chair. It wouldn't leave his possession until he had gone through every document.

"Now, why don't you tell me the reason for your visit."

Ruth bit her bottom lip and shook her head. "I know you're going to think I'm crazy. Maybe I am. But I've just *got* to talk to someone about this. As more and more time passes, I keep thinking of more things. Things that might be important. And the more I think about it, the more I'm convinced that something wasn't right about Aaron's death—and I'm not talking about malpractice. Something different . . . something I can't quite put my finger on. Remember the day I first came to your office?"

Jonathan nodded.

"Remember, I told you how worried Aaron was after his last trip to D.C. I mean he was actually *afraid* of something. He claimed it was the surgery, but I just can't buy it. Anyway, one evening, just a couple of days after he got back, Aaron was acting rather odd. I mean really despondent; not talking; and a . . . a look of complete resignation in his eyes. I tried to get him to talk about it, but he just pushed me off, saying he had a lot on his mind." Ruth took a breath to maintain her control over her emotions. "Well, I decided to fix him a nice dinner to bring up his spirits. I was in the kitchen at the sink, and . . . and as I was standing there he walked up from behind, put his arms around me, and rested his head next to mine on my shoulder. For a couple of minutes he just held me tight, not saying a word. Then he slowly turned me around at arm's length and said, 'I love you, babe.' I looked up into his eyes and he . . . he had tears. . . . God, he was actually crying!" said Ruth, as a drop began to run down her own cheek. "He said he wanted me to go down to his insurance agent in the morning and increase his life-insurance policy from one hundred thousand dollars to half a million. He was busy and didn't have time to do it himself. He said it was going to be a simple operation and that there was nothing to be concerned about, but it always paid to be safe."

Jonathan felt a growing tightness in his throat.

"Jesus, Jon. Can't you see it? He knew what was going to happen. As sure as I'm sitting here, he *knew* it."

Seeing that she was about to break, Jonathan got up and offered his handkerchief.

"I'm sorry, Jon," she said, beginning to cry, "but I loved him so much." The dam holding back her emotions collapsed as Ruth broke into uncontrollable sobbing and thrust her face into the handkerchief.

In an effort to comfort her, Jonathan put his hand on the back of Ruth's shoulder. Instinctively, she rose and leaned her head against his chest. "Go ahead, Ruth. Just let it go."

As he stood looking at the wall, Jonathan tried to analyze what was happening. Ruth's emotions seemed so real, so genuinely spontaneous. Not at all contrived and fabricated. It was hard to imagine that she was not truly suffering.

*No!* He had to remain uninvolved. Nothing could be taken for granted. His very life might depend on it. But then it seemed inconsistent that a murderess would freely call attention to the mysterious nature of her victim's death. And why would she have retained him to begin with?

Ruth's crying gradually subsided. For a couple of minutes they stood silently holding on to each other. Finally, she sat down again and looked up at him.

"You're becoming a wonderful friend, Jon. I haven't cried that hard since Jason called and told me about Aaron. I wouldn't allow myself, though it hasn't been easy."

"Why not? It's only natural. Isn't it healthier than holding it inside?"

Ruth finished blotting her eyes with her handkerchief. "Depends on who you are, I guess. As a nurse, I had always tried to prepare myself to accept death—even of those who were close to me. After all, it's a reality we all must face. Everyone dies. Some just sooner than others. Since it's inevitable, it becomes easier to accept. It's only the occurrence of the *avoidable* that justifies remorse and regret."

"Sounds like a rather cold philosophy."

"Probably so. But with the suffering and death one sees in medicine, it's mandatory. Two years after I married Aaron, my father died. We were as close as a father and daughter could be. My mother had divorced him shortly after I was born and didn't want the burden of children. Every spare minute he had he spent with me. Yet, when he died, I was able to accept it. I didn't even cry at the funeral. I was sad, but I didn't cry."

Jonathan returned to his seat and leaned back, chewing on the end of a pen. "How old was your father when he died?"

"Seventy-two. I was a late-life accident. My mother never wanted children."

"That's why your philosophy fell apart when you lost Aaron."

Ruth looked at Jonathan with inquisitive, red eyes. "I'm not following you."

"Death is inevitable for all of us. But *when* it happens is not. Your father lived to a normal life expectancy. Aaron was entitled to another thirty years. There was nothing inevitable about dying at forty-three."

Ruth nodded. "And that's why I've been unable to accept it."

"Nor should you," he said, sharpening his voice. "And the time has come for the two of us to start working together on this case."

"I don't understand. I thought we had."

"Ruth, I'm talking about a total commitment to the lawsuit. I'm talking about having complete and absolute trust in each other, with total disclosure of all facts. Nothing, absolutely nothing, withheld."

Ruth's brow furrowed in confusion. Jonathan's mood had changed totally. "You sound angry. Has something happened?"

Jonathan dropped the pen on his desk and fixed his eyes sternly on Ruth. She was vulnerable now. "Yes, something *has* happened."

"But what? I'm still not following—"

"I took Reed's deposition about two weeks ago."

"Yes, you already told me about it. You thought it had gone very well."

"For the most part, it did. But I didn't tell you everything. I had a few facts I wanted to check out first."

"What facts?"

"Reed claims Aaron was having an affair with a nurse at Rivergarden." The words shot out of Jonathan's mouth with stunning coldness.

"It's . . . it's a lie. He's guessing. He's—"

"He said he saw them embracing in the hospital parking lot. He was testifying under penalty of perjury."

Ruth shook her head. "I don't believe it. I don't believe it. It's a goddamn lie, Jon. Surely you don't—" Suddenly Ruth detected his insinuation. "Wait a minute! Are you suggesting I *knew* about it?"

"I've never believed the adage that the wife is the last to know. There are always telltale signs: lipstick on his clothes; loss of affection; questionable late-night meetings; unexplained trips away from home."

"There's been none of that, Jon. I swear it. No lipstick. No loss of affection. Nothing."

"No unexplained trips away from home?"

"Absolutely not. His only trips were to the FDA. Outside of his business hours, Aaron spent virtually all his time with me."

"On six of his trips, Aaron did not go to the Food and Drug Administration. Twice he did. Six times he didn't. I verified it myself."

Ruth's mouth opened. She stared at Jonathan in disbelief. "I don't believe this. You're suggesting that Aaron was seeing another woman when he was in D.C.?"

"I don't even know if he *was* in Washington. Only that he wasn't where he was supposed to be."

"Jesus, Jon, you're describing a stranger—not . . . not my husband. I can't believe it. I *refuse* to believe it. I don't care what *anyone* says. Aaron was not having an affair. If he wasn't at the FDA meetings, he was at . . . at . . ." Ruth stopped, grasping for an explanation. "Well, wherever he was, it wasn't with a woman. You're right, Jon—if Aaron was seeing another woman, I would have known about it. We may not have had a perfect marriage, but I'm positive I was the only woman in his life."

Jonathan rubbed his hand over the stubble on his face. Because of the near-fatal encounter that morning, he had forgotten to shave. "I'm inclined to believe you, Ruth," he said pensively. "I doubt that Aaron was running around with Maureen Jensen—or anyone, for that matter. No, the more I think about it, the more I know that you're right."

"Jensen! Is that who Reed claims Aaron was seeing?"

"Yes. Do you know her?"

"I met her a couple of times. Seemed very quiet and withdrawn, always off to herself. A beautiful woman, but I somehow can't see her having an affair."

"Those are the kind you've got to watch out for. But I've spoken with her and have done some checking. I'm convinced she was never involved with Aaron. No, I don't believe she was the problem. . . ." Jonathan's voice tapered off as his mind drifted. It wasn't another woman. Ruth would have sensed it, and his intuition told him that she was telling the truth. It had to be something else. Aaron apparently had learned of something or crossed someone he shouldn't have.

Ruth looked at the eyes of her attorney. They were troubled eyes and seemed to be searching the far reaches of his brain for an elusive answer. "There's something else, isn't there?" she asked. "You're keeping something from me."

Jonathan looked at her but wouldn't answer.

"Dammit, Jon, you've got no right. I hired you as my attorney and you damn well better be telling me everything. Aaron was my husband—or did you forget?"

"Your husband was murdered, Ruth."

She stared in shock. "I want to know who did it," she said, her voice trembling. "Who was it, Jon? I want you to tell me."

"I wish I knew. I only know how it was done and that it was murder. Who it was, and why—I just don't know."

"Then tell me everything you do know."

"I will. Down to the smallest detail. But there's something you'll first have to understand."

"What's that?"

"Somebody tried to kill me today. Tried to run me down while I was out jogging this morning."

"Your leg?"

"Yes. I tried to jump out of the way, but the car caught me in the thigh. I haven't taken this to the police yet, either."

"Why not? My God, if Aaron was murdered and somebody just tried to kill you, why in the world would you want to wait?"

"A couple of reasons. First, we have nothing concrete. Everything that's happened might appear no more than an accident, or just coincidence. We also have no motive and no suspect—at least *now* we don't," he added, recalling his earlier suspicion of Maureen Jensen. "I doubt that the police would do much more than open a file and sit on it. *I'm* convinced, but I doubt that an overworked police department would be. Then there's the lawsuit to consider. If we disclose everything I know about Aaron's death, we lose Rivergarden as a defendant and substantially weaken the case against Reed."

"How does that happen?"

"My pathologist did a thorough workup on this, Ruth. Even electron microscopy. According to him, Aaron was intentionally injected with anthrax bacillus—"

"Anthrax! But how?"

"Probably through his IV. He didn't die from a contaminated needle injection into his hip like we first thought. Thus, his death was not the fault of a careless nurse working at Rivergarden. That lets the hospital off the hook. The next problem is the organism—anthrax—which is much more virulent and difficult to treat than the streptococcus that everyone believes Aaron died from. Once the other side learns of this, we might have a difficult time convincing a jury that an early visit by Reed would have made a difference."

"So you're telling me that there was nothing that Reed could have done anyway?"

"No, I'm telling you that it will only be more difficult to prove it to a jury. My doctor still believes that early treatment with antibiotics probably would have saved Aaron."

Ruth slowly shook her head and forced a sardonic laugh. "Kind of makes this lawsuit seem rather silly, doesn't it? I mean, here we've been going after Rivergarden and Reed when all along they've been nothing more than . . . pawns."

He should have seen it coming. Ruth's motivation for the lawsuit had never been financial. She had been a vindictive widow seeking revenge against those responsible for her husband's death. Now she was learning that her energies had been misdirected and the very reason for pursuing the lawsuit no longer existed. She would have to be dissuaded.

"I wouldn't go that far, Ruth. With Rivergarden you're

probably right, but not with Reed. He totally ignored Aaron's symptoms and didn't want to bother getting out of his nice warm bed. And my expert is convinced that if he had, Aaron would be with us today. We need the lawsuit if Reed is ever going to be held answerable for that conduct."

"Jon, at this point I don't really give a *damn* about the lawsuit. I want Aaron's killer, not the superficial victory of a malpractice judgment."

"All right. Let me put it this way, Ruth. We've got two choices. We can turn over all my evidence to the authorities; then drop the lawsuit, forget about Reed, and hope the killer forgets about us while the police stand around picking their noses wondering if this case is worthy of their time."

"And the second?"

"The police won't investigate Aaron's death, but *I* will. Continue with the lawsuit and I'll find Aaron's killer. When I find him—or her—we'll drop the suit against Rivergarden and proceed against Reed alone. . . . Ruth, I *need* this case. I've waited ten long years for this, and I'll take any risk necessary to keep it. You want Aaron's killer and I want your lawsuit. Work with me and we'll both get what we want."

# Chapter XVI

"Time for a break," said the soft voice over his shoulder. "Come on! Ten or fifteen minutes away from those silly medical records will not ordain the loss of the Feinerman case."

Jonathan yawned as he massaged his eyelids. "You're right," he said. "Anyway, I've been through these things five times tonight. Everything's starting to run together."

"Maybe this will help," said Danielle, as she placed a glass of cabernet in front of him. It looked enticing and Jonathan took a sip, let it trickle slowly down his throat, then turned in his chair to Danielle.

"It's frustrating," he said. "Every time I go through these records I find something I didn't see before. But I still can't find what I'm looking for."

"And just what is that?"

"I don't know."

"Yes, you do have a problem."

"What I mean is, I don't know the *specific* thing I'm looking for. It may be something out of sync: an entry out of order, or an inconsistent time between the nurse's notes and the medication record. Maybe the appearance that something's been erased. It could be anything that just doesn't fit. But after all the times I've been through this stack of headaches, I've not found one thing the least bit suspicious. Nothing. It's almost *too* perfect."

"Maybe the one you're after didn't make an entry in the chart."

It was a curious observation and drew Jonathan's attention to Danielle, who was wearing a short, sexy, terrycloth robe. In her hand she held a glass of wine.

"That's interesting," said Jonathan. "What made you think of that?"

"Oh, I don't know. It just seemed to logically follow. . . . Now you've got me thinking like a lawyer. My God, I've been contaminated."

Jonathan smiled, then thought about it again. "That wouldn't make sense. Anyone treating Aaron would have been making entries in the chart. What you're suggesting is that he was injected by someone not assigned to treat him." It *did* make sense, but how would Danielle have picked it up? He had not mentioned a word to her about it. He knew he would have to, but had procrastinated. For her safety, it would mean asking her to leave until it was over. And that might be never.

"You're right," she said reflectively. "It wouldn't make any sense at all. Do you always find errors in the records when there's malpractice?"

"No. But I frequently do when there's a coverup."

"Perhaps no one has tried to cover up the records."

"Perhaps not."

She was right on target. It was doubtful that the killer would be one of the treating nurses or doctors. That would certainly draw attention to his or her conduct. In terms of probability, Jonathan could eliminate the names of all those who appeared in the records. Maybe going over and over the chart had been a waste of time.

He would have to ascertain the name of every doctor,

nurse, aide, and orderly at the hospital that weekend; then, by process of elimination, narrow the list down to those who would have been there at the approximate time the IV had been injected. Every alibi would be checked. It would be tedious work, but he could do it.

Danielle sipped her Cabernet, a flirtatious gleam in her eyes. "What you really need is a little distraction." She smiled. "And I've got the perfect formula."

Jonathan surveyed the room. All the lights had been turned low, and soft music drifted subtly in the background. For the first time he also detected the fragrance of perfume.

"What do *you* have in mind—as if I didn't know?"

"You haven't touched me in almost a week. I thought tonight we might spend a little time together."

She was right. Every day for the past week he had taken the Feinerman file home, reading and researching until late at night. One night it was a text on bacteriology, the next a book on pathology, then back to the medical records. Each evening as midnight approached, Jonathan would collapse in bed. And each night Danielle's affection and advances would be placated by a promise of things to come the following evening. Finally, in despair, Danielle began going to bed early. Now she had drawn the line.

"So you want me to touch you tonight?" he asked teasingly.

"All over my body."

Jonathan looked at the stack of medical records and the black attaché case on the floor next to the desk. "I know you've been hearing this all week," he apologized, "but I still have a little more to do. Give me another hour—an hour and a half at the most."

"No, I won't!" she snapped, then caught herself.

She wasn't going to get angry. Not this time. Besides, anger never worked with Jonathan. It only drove him away. "I only want a little bit of your time," she pleaded more softly. "Just an hour; half an hour; anything. Only some time for a little affection." Danielle slowly dropped to her knees, sat back on her feet, and placed her hand on Jonathan's knee. "I promise. Give me thirty minutes and you'll sleep better tonight than you have in a month."

Danielle's voice was just above a whisper and her hazel eyes begged longingly for his submission. Loosened by design, the top of her robe bowed out, revealing two large mounds of flesh rising and falling in the faded shadows of the subdued lighting. Her skin looked like satin.

Jonathan swallowed. "You're making this very difficult for me."

"I never intended that it be easy."

"But I have a deposition tomorrow morning. An important one. Sarah Lawrence—the woman who gave Aaron the dirty hip injection."

"You know those records backwards. You already said it. It's all becoming senseless."

"I've finished going through the medical charts, but I wanted to spend a little time on the records in the attaché case. I might turn up something of critical importance."

Danielle sipped her wine, then ran her tongue along her upper lip. It glistened from the moisture. Casually, she began to slide her thumb along Jonathan's thigh. "Forget the records, Jonny . . . please. I want you . . . now . . . tonight."

Jonathan closed his eyes and took a breath. The spell had been broken. "Don't call me Jonny," he said abruptly.

"Why not?"

"Just don't."

"I didn't say it to upset you."

"I know."

"Then why are you upset?"

"I don't like to be called Jonny." That name had been reserved for use only by his mother. Danielle had intruded onto sacred ground.

"I only meant to be affectionate. You don't have to bite my head off."

"I know. I'm sorry," he said, shaking his head. "This work . . . this case . . . it must be getting to me."

Danielle took his hand. "Then stop. Right now. Let's go to bed and make love like we did that first day on the boat. Remember how reckless and wild it was?"

Jonathan smiled, then looked down at the attaché case. "I can't. This is too important. There may be something in that black case that I might want to ask Lawrence about."

"Please?" she asked with resignation.

"Dani, I just can't. There's too much at stake."

Suddenly she shot to her feet, her face flushed, one hand on her hip, the other gripping her wine. The volcano had erupted. "What's so goddamn important about a fucking lawsuit?" she cried. "That's all you think about anymore. Law and that fucking lawsuit."

"Dani, please," he said defensively. "It's more than a lawsuit. A lot more. There are things you don't know."

"What? All of that reputation crap? That's it, isn't it? You're on a big ego trip. You and your fucking lawsuit. Suing your way to stardom."

Jonathan stood and put his hand on her shoulder. "Dani, that's not it at all. You just don't know."

"Bullshit, I don't," she screamed, throwing his hand away. Her eyes were on fire. "The male and his macho ego. That's what it's all about. Just got to be the best. All the time. No matter what the cost." Danielle threw the rest of her wine down her throat. "Well, I'm not paying the price, buster. Not anymore. I need love and affection. I thrive on it—and you're not giving it. So if you want me to walk the streets, that's exactly where I'm going." Fuming, she spun around and went storming off to the bedroom.

*"Dani, somebody tried to kill me this morning."*

Danielle froze in the doorway. Jonathan's words lingered in the air. They were strange, alien words that didn't belong in her small, protected world, insulated from the dangers and tragedies outside. She turned slowly while digesting what he had just told her.

"What did you say?"

"I said somebody tried to kill me this morning." Silence fell over the room, except for a barely audible stringed version of the Beatles' "Norwegian Wood" floating from the stereo. Jonathan thought of the incongruity between what he had just said and the strings playing a Beatles' song. Quickly his mind returned to the reality of what he was about to tell Danielle.

"A car hit me when I was out jogging," he added. "I lied when I told you I had tripped over a rock."

"I don't believe this."

"It's true."

"It could have been an accident."

"I know it wasn't."

"But why would anyone want to kill you?"

"Something I learned," he said with a dead stare.

"What could you possibly know that someone would want to kill you for?" Danielle took a couple of steps toward him.

Jonathan's eyes drifted down to the carpeted floor; he was still reluctant to tell her. A disclosure might also endanger her, though the risk didn't seem high if she left.

"Well?" she urged.

"Just take my word. I've fallen into something that someone wanted kept a secret. It really doesn't concern you. But until I can get this straightened out, I want you—"

"What did you learn, goddammit?" Her voice was louder, sharper.

"I can't tell you, Dani. It might be dangerous if you knew."

"Danger! I *love* you, dammit. Do you think some danger is going to keep me uninvolved if someone is trying to kill you? Now *tell* me!"

Again he massaged his eyes, then stared at her while he gathered his thoughts. "Aaron Feinerman was murdered. Injected with a lethal dose of anthrax. Probably through his IV while he was recuperating from surgery."

Danielle took a couple more steps. Her hand went to her mouth. "Oh, my God!" she exclaimed.

"I'll tell you everything, Dani. But you're moving out tomorrow. I want you to call your sister. Tell her you want to visit for a few days. Give her some excuse. Tell her you lost your job. You want to see her kids. Anything. You're moving out, and there won't be any argument."

Stunned, Danielle only looked on while Jonathan explained in detail. He told her of the mysterious trips to Washington and about his discussion with Lundgren. He described Reed's accusation during the deposition and about the later meeting with Jensen. He even mentioned his suspicions about Ruth, though he carefully explained what she had said and how he was satisfied of her innocence. He described the records he had recently subpoenaed, pointing out the significance of each. Finally, he tried to explain his arrangement with Ruth.

"Ruth wants to drop the suit. She's made it quite clear. She's lost her interest now that she knows the truth."

"You don't agree with her? My God, we're talking about a murder."

Jonathan swallowed the rest of his wine in a single gulp. "I don't agree and I'm not dismissing the case. I've waited too long for this. Ten years. There's too much at stake."

"But it's only a lawsuit, Jon."

"That's where you're wrong. It's a career—*my* career—that we're talking about. It's the difference between being a famous trial lawyer and a life of routine and obscurity. Can't you see? Opportunity is knocking. And if I don't answer the call, I'll never hear it again. *Never.* I know it, Dani. I feel it."

"How can you be so sure? It happened once, it can happen again."

"It took ten years to happen this time. Major cases just don't come along that often in Bridgeport. And when they do—well, the client always seems to end up with a big name down in New York. I'm telling you, Dani, I'm a small-town lawyer without a big reputation. I have no draw. I need a major verdict . . . and I'm *not* going to wait another ten years to get it."

"You could be killed. Is your career worth getting killed over?"

"I can take care of myself. I always have."

"Dammit!" she shouted, her anger beginning to grow again. "Why are you so goddamned stubborn? Jesus, I'm sick of it. . . . Well, smart ass, this time you have no control over it. If Ruth wants to drop the suit, there's absolutely nothing you can do. Nothing but follow her instructions."

"Ruth isn't going to drop the suit. I made a deal with her."

"What kind of deal?"

"She continues with the case and I deliver Aaron's killer."

"You *what?*"

"I'm going to find his killer. Find him and deliver him in a nice neat package to the police."

"What do you think you are—a fucking cop? My God, you're insane. Your life won't be worth a dime. You've got no training, no experience."

"Investigative work is as much a part of my practice as standing in a courtroom. You're wrong. I'm a professional and I know my job well. If the killer can be found, I'll find him."

"If you're not killed first."

"As I said, I can take care of myself. Besides, I'm too far into this thing. I can't let go. I won't."

Frustrated by what she knew was a losing battle, Danielle began shaking with anger. Her eyes welled with tears and she tightened her hold on the stem of her wineglass. "You've got to. I'm . . . I'm not going to put up with this, Jon. Either drop the suit and forget this insanity or I'm walking right out of here."

"I don't want to lose you, Dani. But I can't be dictated to. Not about this. Not my career. I didn't want it to be this way, but I'd be asking you to leave for a while anyway."

"You *bastard!*" she screamed, as she fired the wineglass past Jonathan into the kitchen, where it fragmented against the sink into a hundred small slivers that fell across the floor.

Within five minutes she had dressed, thrown a couple of outfits, some underwear, and a toothbrush into a small suitcase, and departed for an unspecified hotel. As she left, she slammed the door so violently that a watercolor painting came crashing from the wall. Through it all, Jonathan stood watching, not uttering a word, listening to the slamming, the swearing, his jaw locked with defiant determination. No matter how much it hurt, it was for the best. She would understand later. Now she would be safe, and he would have the freedom to complete his investigation.

He listened for Danielle's car leaving the garage, wanting to cling to her presence. But it was fruitless. Even on the balcony he was unable to hear the familiar flutter of her VW Bug. Two doors down, a stereo bellowed out the Bee Gees' "Stayin' Alive." With resignation he turned his attention again to the small living room. It had never seemed so empty. A sense of finality overcame Jonathan. Breaking it off—even temporarily—had been much more difficult than he had anticipated.

Jonathan stepped into the kitchen, avoiding the pieces of broken glass on the floor, took a fifth of Tanqueray and a glass from a cabinet, then collapsed into a chair. He poured a couple of inches of the clear liquid into his glass, held it up to his nose to sample the bouquet, then took a swallow. The warmth in his throat had a sedating effect even before the alcohol reached his brain.

Why couldn't she understand? A man's vocation constitutes one-half of his entire life. At least of his waking hours. Why were women so blind to a man's need for achievement—for recognition? He had spent his entire adult life educating himself and honing his skills as a trial lawyer. The books he had read—hundreds of them—the hours in court, the trials, the unscrupulous lawyers, the belligerent and disrespectful judges, the capricious juries, the never-ending hours of research and review at night and on weekends. Why couldn't Danielle understand that every invested hour, every embarrassment, every heartache, every surprise, had all been in preparation for that one moment when Ruth Feinerman entered his office?

Jonathan examined the gin as he swirled his glass around in tight circular motions. He was alone again. Exactly as he had started. But this time there was a mark. An imprint indelibly etched in his heart. What would life be like without her? Again he scanned the empty room, tossed down his drink, and poured another.

Two drinks later, Jonathan attempted to note the time on his wristwatch. She had been gone just under an hour. His head felt weightless, and it seemed that a numbness had developed across his brow. He would have to retire now or he would be in no shape to do battle in the morning.

No sooner had he struggled to his feet than he heard a key jiggle into the lock of the front door. As the wheels of his mind rotated in slow motion, trying to identify the noise, the door swung open. In the entry stood Danielle, the small suitcase in her hand.

Jonathan squinted at her shadow. "Dani? Is it you?"

She did not answer; instead she dropped the suitcase, rushed to Jonathan, and clutched him in a tight embrace.

"Oh, God! Heaven help me," she said. "I can't leave you. I tried. But I can't."

"Dani, I don't want this. It's too dangerous."

"I can't help myself, Jon. I can't. I drove and I drove, but I couldn't bring myself to leave you. I just love you too much."

# Chapter XVII

At quarter after ten, Jonathan began to wonder if the subpoena had been properly served. It was now fifteen minutes after the time scheduled for the deposition, and Sarah Lawrence had yet to arrive. A quick review of his file, however, gave him some assurance. The process server had given her the subpoena five days earlier and additionally had paid her the standard witness fee.

Concerned about a further delay, Jonathan stepped into the reception room and noted that everyone else was there, including Arnold Rabin.

"Arnie, have you had a chance to speak with Lawrence yet?" Jonathan asked.

"No," he replied. "I was to meet her here at nine-thirty, but she hasn't shown up. Are you sure she was subpoenaed?"

"Yes, I just checked."

Just then Sarah Lawrence entered; and to a person, all were surprised at what they saw. She was a heavyset woman, of medium height, in her late forties. Her hair, light brown with a scattering of gray, was disheveled and uncombed. A wrinkled cotton dress hung loosely from her bustline in an unsuccessful attempt to hide her obese stomach. Her eyes had a look of confusion as she scanned the room. Nervously, she reached into her black patent-leather purse and pulled out a copy of her subpoena.

"Are you Mr. Rabin?" she asked, looking at Jonathan.

"No," said Jonathan, nodding toward Rabin. "That's your man over there. The one chewing on his nails."

"I'm sorry I'm late, Mr. Rabin," she said. "But I got lost. These office buildings always confuse me and I—"

"That's all right," Rabin interrupted. "Can you give me ten minutes, Jon?" His face was painted with worry.

"Sure," said Jonathan, trying not to smile. "Use the conference room and we'll start at ten-thirty."

Jonathan knew that it was essential to meet with a client a full day prior to a deposition and spend at least an hour preparing him for his testimony. He had learned that lesson in his first year of practice.

At ten-thirty Rabin stuck his head out of the conference room. "I'm ready—I guess."

After a few preliminary questions, Jonathan began to probe Sarah Lawrence's qualifications as a nurse.

"Are you a registered nurse?"

"Yes."

"Where did you receive your education?"

"I received my training at the University of California Medical Center in San Francisco."

"When did you finish your nurse's training?"

"In 1965."

"Have you taken any postgraduate courses or had any specialized training in nursing other than what you have already stated?"

"No, just my general nursing education."

"Then you became a registered nurse upon completion of your training in 1965, is that correct?"

"Yes."

"And you have had absolutely no further education in the field of nursing since that time, is that correct?"

"Yes, that is correct."

"Now, in June of this year did you work for Rivergarden Community Hospital?"

"I don't know."

"Well, do you recall working for Rivergarden Community Hospital at any time this year?"

"I'm not sure. I think I did."

"Do you have some uncertainty about working for Rivergarden this year?"

"I remember working for a hospital. I do nursing, you know. But usually I work with my flowers. They require a lot of nursing, too, you know. Because if you leave them unattended, they can get very sick."

"I'm sure you're right, Mrs. Lawrence," said Jonathan, looking confusedly at Rabin, who only shrugged his shoulders.

"But I'd just like to find out if you have any recollection of working for Rivergarden at any time this year."

"Why don't you let her look at the hospital records," Rabin interjected. "Maybe they will help refresh her recollection."

Jonathan handed Lawrence the subpoenaed copies of Aaron's hospital records and pointed out the entries under the nurses' notes. On the fourth page of the notes there were four entries over her signature, including one at 12:10 A.M. on June 17 for an injection of morphine sulfate into Aaron's left hip.

Jonathan pointed to the writing and asked, "Are those your signatures?"

"I don't know. It doesn't look like my signature. Well, it could be. Is somebody trying to accuse me of something here?"

"No, ma'am, I'm just trying to determine whether those are your signatures or if you can remember working at Rivergarden in June."

"I didn't do anything wrong and I'm sure that those are not my signatures. Somebody is trying to embarrass me. I bet I wasn't even working there then."

Lawrence's eyes were now rapidly darting around the room, suspiciously investigating the four strangers seated across from her. Nervously she would squeeze one clenched fist with the other hand and then alternate the procedure, first squeezing her left hand, then her right.

"Why are you all looking at me that way?" she said fearfully.

"Mrs. Lawrence," Jonathan responded, "please believe me, no one is trying to persecute you or take unfair advantage of you." It was readily apparent that she was emotionally unstable, and Jonathan knew that nothing would be accomplished until she was fully pacified. "If you feel uncomfortable at this deposition," he continued, "we could break now and reschedule it for a later time when you feel better or, for that matter, we could take it at your home, where you would have more familiar surroundings."

Lawrence stared at Jonathan, digesting his proposal. Finally she stated, "No, I want to go ahead and get this over with. Let me see those records again." Lawrence perused the records and then looked back again at Jonathan. "I don't remember the date that I treated him," she said, "but I do remember having Dr. Feinerman as one of my patients."

"What shift were you on at the time?"

"I was on the night shift, from eleven P.M. until seven A.M."

"What was your position at the hospital at that time?"

"I was a staff nurse, though I only worked on the weekends."

"Did you administer medication as part of your duties?"

"Yes, I did."

"Did you administer any medication to Dr. Feinerman after his surgery?"

"Yes, I believe I did."

"The medication records suggest that you gave him an injection of morphine sulfate into his left hip at twelve-ten A.M., the morning after his surgery. Would you have any reason to dispute that?"

"If the records say I did, I guess I did."

"Would you please explain how you prepared the syringe for the injection?"

"I prepared it very carefully, just like I prepare my flowers carefully. But it's very tiring. In fact, I'm quite tired right now from working with my plants and flowers. That's why I wish you wouldn't stare at me that way."

"Ma'am, if I appear to be staring at you, please accept my apology. I'm really only trying to find out how the injection was administered."

"Well, it wasn't me who left the vial on the table. You ought to talk to the nurse's aide. Maybe she left it there. I was very careful when I treated Dr. Feinerman. I didn't leave anything lying around."

"A what . . . ? You saw a vial?"

Lawrence scratched her head and blinked her eyes, appearing perplexed. "I . . . I'm sure I did."

"Now I want you to think. Was it empty or did it have something in it?"

"I'm really not . . . not sure. It's almost like a dream, a . . . vision."

"Mrs. Lawrence, this might be very important. Had you seen it before—that evening, the day before—at any time?"

She squinted her eyes, as if in pain, trying to remember. "It seems that I have. But I'm not sure. Maybe it was only similar to another one."

"Well, what did it look like? Can you describe it?"

"I really don't think I can."

"Try."

"I . . . I can't."

"You must!" he snapped. "Now think! Was it glass? Was it made out of glass?"

"Yes, it was made out of glass."

"Was it round—like a tube?"

"Yes."

"The glass—was it clear or colored?"

"I don't know."

"How long was it? An inch, three inches, six?"

Lawrence shook her head, her eyes staring blankly, her mouth slightly open.

"You're not trying. This may have been involved in Dr. Feinerman's death. You've got to *think*." He was positive he was onto something, but Lawrence's mind was too elusive.

"Counselor, you're badgering the witness," Rabin reminded. "I'd advise a little discretion in your manner of questioning."

"I'm sorry. You're right. Please accept my apology, Mrs. Lawrence. But a man has died, and this might be a vital piece of evidence. Perhaps you recall if it was open? Did it have a cap or a cork—a lid of some kind?"

Again a shake of the head. "I just don't remember. My . . . flowers take up so much of my time, it's difficult to recall these things."

"All right. You saw a glass vial on Dr. Feinerman's nightstand. Now think carefully. What time was that?"

"It was only last night about . . . No. No, it was last week or . . . a couple of months ago. I don't . . . Maybe I dreamed it. I've been having a lot of dreams lately. Do you think I'm responsible for Dr. Feinerman's death? You know, if I did something wrong, I want someone to tell me." Tears flushed her eyes and her lower lip quivered with emotion. "I . . . I don't think I can continue. I'm very tired . . . and I should get back to my flowers."

Sarah Lawrence was teetering on the brink of a nervous breakdown. Another question might be disastrous.

"That's all I have, Mrs. Lawrence. I see no reason to continue this any longer." Jonathan's voice was calm and soothing. "I'm also quite sure that these other gentlemen have nothing to ask either," he volunteered, looking at the willing faces of Rabin and Morris.

Perhaps the glass vial was a delusion fabricated by a guilt-ridden nurse. Lawrence had administered the intramuscular injection erroneously believed responsible for Aaron's death. If only he could tell her; if she could be spared the torment. She was only a pawn, but one that he needed. It was indeed unfortunate, but she would have to remain another victim of the tragedy until the killer was identified.

Jonathan doubted that the vial was in fact a delusion. If it could have been better identified, he might have been able to trace it. It certainly seemed a likely storage unit for the anthrax bacteria. Maybe he could locate someone who might have removed and discarded it. Yet, whatever the truth was, it was clear that nothing further could be learned from Lawrence. The extent of her participation in Aaron's death would have to be determined through other sources.

# Chapter XVIII

As the sun began its early-evening descent, the clouds over Stratford were aglow with bright yellows, oranges, and reds. For the past five days, rain had been falling intermittently. Now as the clouds that had blanketed the coast began to clear to the west, the departing sun illuminated them in a breathtaking sunset.

Jonathan sat in the cockpit of *Dreamboat* with his arm around Danielle watching the final traces of the sunset. The sloop sat motionless in the still waters which mirrored the lights beginning to blink on around the marina. Neither Jonathan nor Danielle said a word, choosing to sit quietly and contemplate.

Two New York steaks crackled over a portable barbecue. With each drip of fat into the glowing briquettes, a hiss of white smoke would ascend, then disappear into the fresh night air. Off in the distance, a single cabin cruiser could be heard with its engine growling at near-idle speed, gliding down the Housatonic.

Jonathan had left his office in the early afternoon. He needed a break. He was uneasy, sensing that something was wrong. He hadn't heard from Rusty since giving him the assignment two weeks ago. He had left three messages on Rusty's answering machine, which had gone unanswered, and last weekend he had stopped by Rusty's apartment, but no one was home. Maybe Rusty had fallen off the wagon again, but Jonathan didn't think so. It was only between assignments that he drank.

Jonathan needed some fresh air to think more clearly, and a relaxing time on the boat had always worked before. Yet, although he felt in no immediate danger, he found himself carefully scrutinizing every stranger who came within one hundred feet of *Dreamboat*. He could ill afford another careless lapse. Only after Dani had arrived at four-thirty was he finally able to loosen up and begin to contemplate his next move.

The answer was probably in the black attaché case that Ruth had given him. Maybe tonight he would finally have the time to peruse the records.

"I think the steaks are done," he said, turning to Danielle. "Would you like to run down below and grab a couple of plates?"

"Aye, aye, captain," she said, rising. She leaned over and gave Jonathan a peck on the cheek, turned, and disappeared down the steps to the galley.

For a brief moment Jonathan thought of a romantic interlude, then just as quickly dismissed the idea when he remembered the number of records that had to be reviewed later. Before the Feinerman case, nothing could have dissuaded him from such a sexual encounter. Not even if he was in the middle of a trial. But Jonathan Rand had become a man obsessed with finding a killer. Although he could not put his finger on it, he sensed that Aaron had tumbled into something of major importance. Whatever it was, Jonathan felt an urgency to complete the investigation, which had been progressing at an agonizingly slow pace.

Danielle climbed the stairs to the cockpit and confronted Jonathan.

"I've got a surprise for you." She grinned, holding a bottle behind her back.

"Let me guess," he said, furrowing his brow and feigning

a serious stare. After a long moment of contemplation he lifted his nose and took three strong sniffs of the air.

"Well, it's a little difficult because of the salt air," he remarked, "but I would definitely say Cabernet Sauvignon—probably a 1973 vintage."

Danielle's mouth dropped open. "You son of a bitch, you saw the bottle," she accused, holding the wine in a threatening manner over his head.

"No, I didn't," he defended, holding up his hand. "You know I haven't been down below since you got here."

Jonathan enjoyed teasing her, and it had been a good guess, since it was his favorite cabernet and he'd recently noticed a large supply of 1973 stock at the local liquor store.

"Really," he continued. "If you sniff hard enough, you can actually detect the aroma of the wine."

Danielle held the top of the bottle to her nose and took a big whiff.

Suddenly Jonathan broke into a laugh, doubling over in his seat. For a moment she felt foolish and angrily stared down at him.

"So you want to be funny," she said, putting down the wine and dishes. "Let's see how much you'll laugh while cooling off in the Housatonic." Grabbing Jonathan around the chest, she pretended to force him over the railing into the water.

"Wait a minute . . . wait a minute," he said, laughing, tears running down his face. "The steaks are burning."

Finally she let up, and Jonathan promptly pulled the steaks from the barbecue, managing to save them except for some charring on one side.

After Danielle had put the finishing touches to the tossed salad and baked potatoes, they sat outside and enjoyed their dinner and wine, marveling at the thousands of stars that sprinkled the night sky. A portable radio provided soft music.

Finally, as they finished the last few ounces of the cabernet, Jonathan pulled Danielle close, gave her a soft, caressing kiss, and said with a wink, "If you help me with these records, maybe we could go to bed a little early tonight."

"I'd be delighted. What are we looking for?"

"I really don't have any idea, except that we're looking for anything that might provide a motive for Aaron's death or, perhaps, explain the trips to Washington."

* * *

They had been reading and discussing the records for just over two hours. The job had taken a lot longer than they had anticipated. There were over three hundred pages of tickets, invoices, canceled checks, bills for business expenses, copies of statements for medical services, credit-card receipts, and a scattering of medical records. Danielle and Jonathan had tediously read everything, no matter how insignificant it seemed. It was baffling how such a successful man could keep his business records in such a disorganized mess.

Now Jonathan was getting tired and eager to fulfill his implied promise to Danielle. Looking across the dinette table at her as she intently read an invoice, he began to feel pangs of guilt. She had really put up with a lot lately. And he had responded selfishly. Jonathan looked at the small stack remaining, picked up another document, and assured himself that he would make it up to her.

Routinely he focused his tired eyes on the document. It was a medical chart, and the name and address of the patient at the top of the page immediately jolted him: "Senator Bradley Armstrong, Washington, D.C." Jonathan sat stunned. United States Senator Bradley Armstrong. Aaron had been treating a man rumored to be his party's leading candidate for the presidency in 1980. Feeling as though someone had just splashed cold water on his face, he read on:

> May 9, 1978. History: Patient is a forty-eight-year-old male who states he was born with a slight congenital scoliosis of the lumbar spine. He states that the problem had given him virtually no complaints until his middle thirties. He was able to serve as an army officer during the Korean conflict in the early 1950s. In 1967 he came under the care of Dr. Lawrence Bitner, an orthopedic surgeon in Washington, D.C. Over the past ten to twelve years, his condition has progressively gotten worse, in spite of receiving physical therapy and other forms of conservative treatment. He has been advised that there is presently no surgical procedure that can reasonably remedy his pain, which is becoming more unbearable. He presently has continuous low-back pain that is aggravated by any kind of physical activity and

necessitates his use of Empirin with codeine. He takes this medication three to four times per day.

Jonathan looked up at Danielle. "I think I've found something, Dani. It's a medical chart. It says that Senator Bradley Armstrong was seeing Aaron as a patient."

"Bradley Armstrong? *The* Bradley Armstrong?" Danielle was also now suddenly awakened. "What does it say?"

"Apparently he was treating Armstrong for a back problem. He had a scoliosis, a curvature of the spine. But let me finish," he said, holding up his hand and looking again at the chart.

The medical record continued to set forth the findings of Aaron's physical examination and the senator's response to the initial hypnotherapy. It also documented subsequent therapy sessions for July 13, 1978; September 20, 1978; November 8, 1978; January 12, 1979; and March 9, 1979. For each date it explained the method used during the session and the patient's physical complaints, which were progressively improving over the months. Finally Jonathan put the record back down and stared at Danielle.

"Well . . . what else does it say?" she asked anxiously.

Jonathan looked down at the table, as if in deep thought, then back at Danielle. "Apparently Aaron was giving hypnotherapy to the senator for about a year before he died."

Her face brightened. "That's it! There are your mysterious trips to Washington, D.C. Does it say where the therapy was taking place?"

"No, it doesn't. But that's got to be it. It would be more logical for Aaron to go to Washington than to have an important senator fly to Bridgeport."

"Wait a minute," said Danielle, digging back through some records. "I ran across some copies of airline tickets a few minutes ago. Let's compare the dates."

She found the passenger copies of the tickets and read them to Jonathan. Each one correlated exactly with a date on the medical chart. Inquisitively she looked across the table.

"What about the June-first flight? There's nothing for June first."

"I know. Maybe Aaron didn't have time to make the entry. Maybe he was worried about the surgery and forgot. Could be a dozen explanations."

"Maybe something happened at the last session that he didn't *want* to enter in his medical records," she suggested.

"I'm not following."

Danielle started shaking slightly, as she hugged herself to warm up. But it was more than the evening dampness. She could almost sense a message from the records, as if subconsciously something was telling her that they should be destroyed and forgotten.

"Would you please close the door, Jon? I'm getting a chill."

Jonathan got up, looked in both directions along the empty boat dock, closed the door, and returned to his seat. "You had a thought?"

"I really don't know," she said, shaking her head. "I just have this feeling that something may have happened that we shouldn't be getting involved with. Why was Aaron so damned secretive about this?"

"I think I can answer that. President Foster is in his second and last term of office and belongs to the same party as Armstrong. Apparently Armstrong has been building an extensive grass-roots base for next year's presidential election. You may recall when Foster ran in 1976. A lot of people tried to get Armstrong to run at that time, but he declined. Probably because he didn't want to run against his own party's incumbent, and possibly because of a deal with Foster to get his support in the next election. At any rate, at this time he is probably the odds-on favorite to be our next President. Any publicity about a serious back disability could conceivably damage those chances."

"Then you've given me another reason we should stay out of this," she stated adamantly. "Why can't you let it go? We know why Aaron was going to Washington and we also know why he wasn't *telling* anyone about it. And it doesn't tell us any more about why he died than we knew before. Let's just drop the whole thing. You really don't need it to prove your case against Reed anyway."

"I told you before. Without Aaron's killer, Ruth drops the lawsuit. Now—finally—we might find out what happened on that last trip."

"I don't *want* to know, Jon. I'm frightened."

"I'm sorry. I can't drop it. Not now. This may be the key to the whole goddamn mystery."

"And what do you intend to *do* with it?"

Jonathan examined the chart for a moment. "I'm going to take this to Armstrong."

"You're crazy! He's a senator. You think you can just waltz into his office and cross-examine him like a witness?"

"I'll get in. That's no problem. He's been trying to keep this a secret for a year. When he hears I've got the chart, he'll see me."

Danielle shook her head. "Do you know what you're saying? That's like blackmail."

"All I'm after is an audience—that and a couple of answers. It may sound like blackmail, but it's not."

"So you get your audience. And let's suppose he knows something about June first. Do you honestly believe he's going to chat openly about it?"

"I don't know. But I've got to try."

"Jon, it's a waste of time and it might get you into a lot of trouble. Please forget it."

"Dani, don't you understand? This is my only lead. Everything else has been a dead end. Ruth is not a patient woman. Not about this. If I don't turn up something soon, she's going to trash the case and go to the police. I've got to go after this. I *must!*"

Danielle took his hand. "Jon, Bradley Armstrong is one of the most powerful men in the country. If he's involved in this in some way . . ."

"Look," he said, "all I'll be doing is talking to Armstrong. What danger could there be? The man's probably going to be our next President."

"Presidents are capable of criminal conduct as anyone else."

"I know. I know. But *murder?* Maybe illegal wiretapping or even a little graft . . . but to kill someone in cold blood? It's just a little difficult to accept. Besides, all I'm going to do is ask him a couple of questions about Aaron and return his original medical records. He should be happy to get them."

"Let's face reality, Jon. There's been one attempt on your life already. Now, if Aaron was killed because of something he discovered on his last trip to Washington, what's going to happen if you learn the same thing? *Jesus!*" she cried. "Why are you being so damn stubborn about this? It's only a lawsuit."

Jonathan slammed his fist onto the table, rattling the lamp

and sending a couple of papers flying to the floor. *"Dammit!"* he shouted. "I told you last night. You've got to stop pulling at me. I'm a big boy and capable of making my own decisions. And, dammit, we're not married—or did you forget?"

Danielle squeezed her eyes tightly and bit her lower lip. "You're right," she said, slowly opening her eyes. "You're absolutely right. We're not married and I've got no right to tell you what you should do." She withdrew into her seat and began fishing in her purse for a Kleenex.

Jonathan reached across the table and grabbed Danielle's hand. "Jesus, Dani, I'm sorry. I don't know what's happening to me."

"No . . . Don't apologize. You've got your own life to live and I've got no right to interfere."

"You're wrong. I was way out of line. Your wishes and your feelings are very—"

"Take the trip, Jon," she said firmly. "Satisfy yourself, and I'll hope for the best. I can't ignore my feelings, but I'll hope for the best. This is obviously something you've got to do."

"Well, frankly," said Jonathan, "I really don't believe Aaron saw Armstrong on that last trip at all. I think he was someplace else—maybe in Washington—but not to see the senator. No, I'd be willing to bet the whole lawsuit that Aaron's death involved some kind of incident at the hospital."

"I hope you're right. But I have this feeling that you may be betting a lot more than that."

# Chapter XIX

*Wednesday, August 29, 1979*

"Hello. My name is Jonathan Rand. I'd like to schedule an appointment to see Senator Armstrong."

"Just a moment, Mr. Rand," said the courteous voice at the other end of the telephone line. "I'll connect you with the senator's personal secretary."

After a short interlude of recorded music, another

feminine, but more businesslike, voice came on the line. "Good morning. This is Ms. Schroeder. How may I help you?"

"I'd like to schedule an appointment to see Senator Armstrong—preferably within the next day or two."

"That's quite impossible. Senator Armstrong's time is committed for the next month and a half. What is the nature of your business with the senator?"

"This is somewhat personal," he said. "Let's just say it concerns some records. Medical records. The senator will be quite interested in seeing them, I'm sure."

"Medical records? I'm sorry, you'll have to be more specific."

"I can't. This is confidential."

"Sir," she said sharply. "You have no idea what you're asking. Senator Armstrong is a very busy man. I must know the exact nature of your business before I can schedule *anything*."

"The subject of my visit concerns Dr. Aaron Feinerman. Tell the senator. I'm sure he'll be quite eager to see me."

"Very well. I'll have to take your number and get back to you."

"When will that be?"

"Possibly tomorrow. But more likely on Friday."

"I can't wait that long."

"I'm afraid you'll have to. All of these requests are reviewed with the senator at the end of the day—or when he has the time. You'll simply have to wait your turn."

Jonathan's temper, which recently had been carrying a short fuse, began to boil. "Ma'am, I'll tell you this one more time: I have in my possession something of critical importance to the senator. They are medical records. And I have every reason to believe that he will be quite pleased—no, ecstatic— to get his hands on them. One thing I do not have is time. So if you want to gamble on these little pieces of paper getting lost while you play your little shuffle game, *you*, Ms. Schroeder, better be prepared to live with the consequences."

She was silent for what seemed an inordinate length of time, while Schroeder gathered control over her emotions, considered her next move, and selected the proper response.

"Senator Armstrong is not here at the moment. But hold the line for a few minutes. . . . I'll do what I can to see that he gets your message." Again the receiver filled with music.

Jonathan had anticipated some difficulty in getting in to see Armstrong, who, according to one article he had read, had been blazing an incredibly rigorous schedule across the country making speeches at fund raisers, college campuses, and civic meetings. Indeed, he would not have been the least bit surprised to learn that Armstrong was not in D.C. at all. But it was a time for desperate measures.

Finally the music stopped and Jonathan heard a throat being cleared.

"Ah . . . yes, Mr. Rand. Senator Armstrong will be glad to see you. Three o'clock this afternoon. He had to cancel an important meeting in Philadelphia and will be returning in his private jet within the hour. Please don't be late."

Jonathan stared for a moment at the heavy double doors to Bradley Armstrong's private suite of offices. Within a few minutes he would be meeting one of the most famous men in the country, a man he both admired and envied.

Bradley Armstrong had every ingredient needed to be the perfect trial lawyer. His looks were strikingly handsome, yet distinguished enough to give him a built-in air of credibility; he was always tastefully yet stylishly attired; his voice had the silver-toned resonance of a radio announcer; his personality exuded a certain flair that drew attention to him like a magnet.

Armstrong's wit and one-line jokes had become almost a national institution and had made him a highly prized subject for interviews among the news media. Hardly a week went by without his picture appearing in a newspaper or one of his quotes in a news release. He was single, which had led to a number of rumors linking him romantically with well-known and attractive actresses and models. These rumors, though, could not be confirmed by either photographs or by admissions by the principals involved. For Bradley Armstrong was extremely cautious about his public image, and whatever affairs he may have enjoyed in private, he took discreet measures to ensure that they would not become matters of public knowledge.

Jonathan walked awkwardly up to the attractive receptionist.

"Good afternoon, Mr. Rand," she said, smiling.

"You must be psychic."

"Not really. You are our only visitor this afternoon. Please have a seat. Someone will be out to see you within a few minutes."

Feeling out-of-place, Jonathan walked over to a couch and sat down. He scanned the elegantly appointed room, sighted a three-month-old copy of *Newsweek* with Armstrong's face on the cover, and picked it up. Out of curiosity he thumbed through the pages and found the cover article. It seemed a good idea to read it, on the outside chance that the topic of the senator's current activities surfaced during their talk.

The walls of the Senate heated up Tuesday as debate raged inside over the controversial military-cutback bill introduced last month by Senator Bradley Armstrong (Iowa). Opposition and support for the measure seemed to be evenly divided as tempers flared and accusations flew in both directions. Recognizing the need to "cool off" and cultivate uncommitted votes, both sides agreed to table further debate for a week.

"A few of us had to step into a heat wave to cool down," quipped a surprisingly calm and amused Armstrong. Then on a serious note he added, "It borders on insanity to pour millions of dollars into military installations in South America when our domestic needs are continuously found wanting. . . ."

Unnoticed by Jonathan, a dark-haired man emerged through a door to the left of the receptionist, leaned over and said a few words to her, then stared at Jonathan before walking over to him and extending his hand.

"Good afternoon, Mr. Rand. Thank you for being prompt. My name is Simon Crenshaw."

Jonathan looked up, then struggled to his feet and pumped the man's hand. "I wanted to inconvenience the senator as little as possible," he said. "This shouldn't take more than ten or fifteen minutes."

Crenshaw was slightly shorter than Jonathan, but heavier, almost to the point of obesity. His face was round, with a nose that began then abruptly dropped away, following a lumpy S to a heavy black mustache, giving him a pugilistic appearance. The top of his balding head was covered with thin strands of hair in a hopeless effort at camouflage. He wore a dark blue tweed suit with a matching vest and yellow dress shirt and would have looked neatly attired except for his loosened tie and his collar pulled away from his perspiring neck. His dark brown eyes stared intensely at Jonathan. Heavy, bushy eyebrows crowned his eyes and seemed to ramble like an untrimmed hedge. In his left hand he held a cigarette.

"Senator Armstrong will be tied up on the phone for a few minutes," Crenshaw said in a rough voice. "He asked that I speak with you while you're waiting. Just a few preliminary questions. So if you will follow me," he instructed.

"Certainly," Jonathan responded, feeling swept up into the machinery of a well-functioning operation. Without hesitation, he followed Crenshaw back through the door next to the receptionist.

In contrast to the quiet atmosphere of the reception room, the intermediate office was a hive of activity. To his left, as he entered the room, Jonathan saw four secretaries busily typing at their desks, while a young man sat at another desk talking on the telephone and at the same time checking off a list. On the right side of the office were two more desks, a long row of filing cabinets, and a photocopy machine. A hard-looking woman in her late forties sat at the front desk making entries into a ledger. Her graying hair was short and straight and parted on one side. When the men entered, she looked up from her work, stared at Jonathan for a moment, and then, without changing her stern expression, resumed her writing in the book. On the plate at the front of her desk was the name Hanna Schroeder. Jonathan followed Crenshaw past her desk and into a small interior office.

"Have a seat," Crenshaw directed, closing the door behind the younger man. "The senator will be on the phone for a few more minutes."

Jonathan sat down. But Crenshaw, rather than taking his usual seat, sat on the front corner of his desktop and looked down at Jonathan. The ashes of his cigarette having reached the filter, Crenshaw promptly crushed it in an already-filled ashtray. Without deliberation he pulled another one from a pack on his desk, stuck it into his mouth, and picked up a book of matches.

"Care for a cigarette?" he offered.

"No, thank you."

An offensive odor of stale cigarette smoke hung in the room. "You're a very persistent man," he said.

"Yes. I've heard that before."

"There are times, Mr. Rand, when such persistence can be quite rewarding." Crenshaw took a deep drag of the newly lighted cigarette. "On the other hand, one should be very selective about who he attempts to strong-arm. Senator Bradley Armstrong," he said, glaring, "is a very poor choice to attempt to intimidate. He does not like to be pushed, and *threats*, Mr. Rand, bring out the worst in him."

"I'm afraid there was a misunderstanding," Jonathan said apologetically. "Your Ms. Schroeder must have misinterpreted my words."

Without comment, Crenshaw reached over to a portable tape-recorder and pressed a button. "We know what was said, Mr. Rand. *Exactly* what was said."

From the beginning ring at Armstrong's office to Schroeder's parting comment, Jonathan heard the entire telephone conversation. Embarrassed at the sharpness of his own words, Jonathan uncomfortably shoved his chair back and crossed his legs, hoping at least to appear unaffected.

"Unauthorized telephone recordings are illegal," he said finally.

Crenshaw began to run his fingernail across the edge of a corner of the match cover. "If a court order is needed for such authority," he said, inspecting the match cover as if he were working over a prized piece of art, "we will obtain one— appropriately predated, of course."

"How are you going to accomplish that little trick?"

Crenshaw leaned over onto one knee, his face only two feet from Jonathan's. "You are very naïve, Mr. Rand. Such a trick—as you call it—is only a phone call away. In this town, whatever Bradley Armstrong needs, he gets." He continued sawing his nail into the laminations of the match cover, then tossed the book onto the table. "Now, tell me. How do these records involve Dr. Aaron Feinerman, and what are the consequences we better be prepared for?"

Jonathan rose from his chair, reciprocating Crenshaw's angry stare. "I must admit," he said, "my methods are at times quite crude—though usually effective. But I came here only to help the senator, not to hurt him. You'll just have to take my word for it. There was no threat intended."

For the first time Crenshaw allowed a slight smile. His demeanor, however, was not congenial but sinister. He sucked hard on the cigarette. "I believe you, Mr. Rand. I'm sure your intentions were nothing but honorable. A bit clumsy, but honorable. If I *didn't* . . . well, let's say you'd be talking to the FBI right now, not to me."

Recognizing his vulnerability, Jonathan nodded. "I'm sure you're right," he said.

"Now that we've got that out of the way, why don't you tell me about these records. In what way do they involve Dr. Feinerman?"

"I'm sorry. I came here to disclose that only to Senator Armstrong. This is of a very personal nature. If the senator wants you to know, he will have to make that decision himself."

"Mr. Rand, I'm the senator's legislative assistant and personal aide. I am with him almost every day of the week, and have been so since he arrived on Capitol Hill almost seven years ago. I assist him at everything from analyzing legislation to selecting what restaurant he will eat in. I know everything about his life, both political and personal. There are no secrets between us. If you feel compelled to tell the senator, you can feel free to disclose the same information to me."

"I'm sorry, Mr. Crenshaw. I will talk about this only with Senator Armstrong."

"I don't think you understand," said Crenshaw, poking his cigarette toward Jonathan. "No one gets in to see the senator without my approval. Either you talk to me or you don't go in."

Jonathan examined the overfilled ashtray on the desk. Resting on top of the mound of ashes and twisted cigarette butts were two other matchbooks, each with the same flared edge as the book on the desk. The mute evidence of a nervous habit eased his tension. "Then I've made a long trip for nothing," he said, turning toward the door. "If you should change your mind, please give me a call."

Crenshaw held up his hand. "Wait!" he barked.

Jonathan looked back. Crenshaw was seething, his face flushed. He was accustomed to getting his way and enjoyed seeing people submit to his demands. It came with the power of his position. Even men of importance would bend to his will, hoping to find favor with Bradley Armstrong. But this time it had not gone as intended, and he was having considerable difficulty coping with it.

"Before you go," said Crenshaw, "I'd better check with the senator. He may have his own reasons for seeing you."

Jonathan nodded his acquiescence, feeling confident about what the decision would be. After all, if the message had been accurately relayed to Armstrong, he no doubt had a very good idea about the records. And hadn't Schroeder told him that Armstrong was making a special trip from Philadelphia?

Crenshaw brushed by Jonathan, who had opened the door and stepped back. "I shouldn't be more than a couple of minutes," he offered over his shoulder. "Stay put until I get back."

"The word is 'please,'" Jonathan reminded, catching Crenshaw at the doorway.

Crenshaw stopped and turned. Jonathan's jaw was tightly set, communicating his intense determination. Crenshaw's eyes looked menacing as he drew a deep breath and said, "Would . . . you . . . please . . . wait, Mr. Rand? I should not be more than a couple of minutes."

Jonathan nodded and Crenshaw abruptly left. Within five minutes he returned.

"You are quite fortunate. The senator has agreed to see you. But he only has twenty minutes, so I would suggest getting right to the point." The abrasiveness in the voice had softened, but there was no mistaking the animosity communicated by the eyes. Jonathan had successfully challenged Crenshaw's authority, and it would not soon be forgotten. Uneasily, Jonathan followed him into Armstrong's office.

*Looks exactly like his pictures*, was the first thought that struck Jonathan. The smiling, deep blue eyes, the even bronzed tan, the straight nose, the gray hair peppered with brown that faded to a whitish gray over the ears and sideburns, all seemed to jump out of a living portrait. The only surprise was his height, as he stood eye to eye with Jonathan, extending his hand and displaying his familiar smile.

"Good afternoon, Mr. Rand. Pleased to meet you. I trust I didn't put you to too much trouble by rushing you here this afternoon." Armstrong's teeth were straight and ice-box white.

"No. No trouble at all," said Jonathan, accepting his firm handshake.

"I had a couple of other matters in town that needed some immediate attention, so it seemed a good idea to get you in today—assuming you had the time, of course."

"If I didn't, I would have made the time. This is quite an honor, Senator."

"Please have a seat." Armstrong directed Jonathan with his hand. Then he turned to Crenshaw. "Why don't you give us a few minutes, Simon? If I need anything, I'll give you a buzz."

"Yes, Senator." He nodded, then started for the door.

"And, Simon . . ."

"Yes, sir?"

"The cigarettes. You were going to watch the cigarettes. I cannot deal with that odor in this office."

"My apologies, Senator. It won't happen again." Following a quick, resentful glance at Jonathan, he closed the door.

Armstrong shook his head. "A good man. Devoted and as sharp as a whip. But sure as hell he's going to smoke himself right into an early grave. . . . Could I interest you in a drink? I was planning one myself. Been going since six this morning."

His first inclination was to decline, but after pondering for a moment, Jonathan said, "Yes. I think I will." A drink would cut the edge off his tension.

"Good!" said Armstrong, who stepped over to the far wall and pressed a section of paneling. A four-foot section opened up like a door and Armstrong folded it back. Inside, a light automatically went on over a fully equipped wet bar, including blender, ice bucket, and a variety of drinking glasses. He opened two eye-level cabinet doors, displaying numerous brands of bourbon, Scotch, gin, vodka, and liqueurs. "What is your pleasure?" he asked.

"Gin. Gin on the rocks. Tanqueray, if you have it."

"Oh, I think we have a little bit of everything. We try to please everyone who stops to water down here."

Armstrong found the Tanqueray and poured the drink while Jonathan gave the room a quick survey. The walls were paneled in a beautiful light walnut, decorated by original oils of Washington, Jefferson, Lincoln, and a number of other famous Presidents. The furnishings were antiques, with a lot of brass and wood, and distributed throughout was a generous array of plants. The room was exceptionally large for an office, and the floor, a highly polished parquet, was accented by an Oriental rug. In the middle of the rug sat Armstrong's heavy oak desk. It was curved like a half-moon, stained dark, in contrast to the lighter floor and walls, and polished to a glass finish. On top were two phones, one beige and one red, a pen set, and a single multipaged report sitting exactly in the middle. To the right of the desk was a standing pole with the American flag.

Armstrong poured himself a Chivas Regal straight up, tapped into the music playing in the reception room by hitting a switch at the bar, and brought Jonathan's drink over to him.

"One of the few vices I allow myself," said Armstrong, handing him the drink. "A good Scotch and a light dose of the classics does more to chase one's anxieties than a two-hundred-dollar-an-hour analyst."

"I fully agree," said Jonathan, smiling. "Only my version usually turns into the sweet smell of gin and a John Denver tape."

"Whatever relaxes the soul. If more of us would turn to a few minutes of relaxation and meditation each day, rather than drugs and a constant diet of television, we would rid ourselves of half the nation's ills. Even with my busy schedule I allow myself a minimum of one hour each day to sit, relax, and think. No interruptions. And no company. Nothing but music and this beautiful Scotch." He smiled, holding up his glass. Armstrong sipped, then stepped behind his desk.

"Sounds perfect for your presidential platform," Jonathan suggested.

Armstrong let out a hearty laugh. "No, you don't win elections by telling people what is best for them. You win by telling them what they want to hear. My supporters have spent hundreds of thousands just to find that out. Polls, surveys, psychologists, research—you name it. All of it just to find out what Mr. Average Citizen wants to hear from his future President. It's crazy, but that's what it takes to win elections." Armstrong eased into his chair and took another sip of his drink. "But of course you didn't come here to talk about how I might get elected next year."

"Nothing on that grand a scale, Senator. But still rather important."

"So I understand. I heard mention of Dr. Aaron Feinerman."

"Yes, sir." Jonathan hesitated, not knowing how he should approach the subject. "It's my understanding that you used to be acquainted with him."

"Yes. Aaron and I met at a Washington fund-raiser about a year ago."

"Were you aware that he had died?"

"Yes. A tragic loss. One of the finest orthopedic surgeons in the country. A mutual friend of ours called me about it a couple of months ago."

"Dr. Feinerman died shortly after a routine operation in one of our local hospitals. I've been retained to represent his widow in a malpractice suit against his doctor and the hospital."

"I know."

"You do?" Jonathan sat up straight in his chair.

"Yes, I do, Mr. Rand." Armstrong's voice was still casual, his eyes still smiling. "The suit was filed August first, 1979, naming Rivergarden Community Hospital and a Dr. Jason Reed. The autopsy was performed by a Dr. William Nicholas, who attributed the cause of death to septicemia due to an unsterile needle injection. And, let's see . . ." He turned a couple of pages of the report. "Your full name is Jonathan Lyman Rand. You were born on April fourth, 1944, in Lawrence, Kansas, and played defensive halfback in high school and college—Penn State it says here. You were admitted to practice law in Connecticut in 1969 and in New York in 1971. You presently live in a small apartment in Stratford with a young lady named Danielle Brennan, and—" Armstrong tossed the report in front of Jonathan. "Well, it's all here. I know everything about you and your lawsuit. *Everything*."

Without saying a word, Jonathan placed his drink on the desk, picked up the report marked "Personal and Confidential," and turned to the first page. Stunned by the detail, he turned a few more pages, found a section entitled "Biographical Sketch," briefly confirmed its accuracy, then looked up shaking his head.

Amused by the bewildered look on Jonathan's face, Armstrong sipped his drink, savoring the Scotch for a moment. "This is the age of computers, Mr. Rand. Computers, storage banks, and lightning-fast retrieval systems. Most of this information is a matter of public record. Even at that, this normally would have taken longer. But you're a lawyer and a registered member of the state bar. With staff members in every major city in the country, it only took a couple of phone calls to set the wheels in motion."

"But why? I'm also not too sure I like your invasion into my private life."

"I must admit, this wasn't my idea. I didn't know of the report until it was handed to me a half-hour before you arrived. Simon thought it might be advisable after your phone call this morning. As I said earlier, Mr. Crenshaw is very devoted. Devoted and protective."

"I know how all this must appear, Senator. But I assure you, I only came here out of a desire to help. I had to speak to you about something of relative urgency. My remarks were only intended—"

"You needn't explain," he said, smiling. "I never once considered you a threat. And I'm sure Simon overreacted. But you have to appreciate exactly what's at stake here." Armstrong's smile disappeared, and his eyes took on a distant appearance. "We've got a country that's teetering on the brink of financial disaster. Double-digit inflation has become so commonplace that people have come to accept it as readily as the common cold. While government spending is running virtually unbridled, people out there on fixed incomes are having a hell of a time just putting food on their tables. I mean actually *starving*."

Armstrong was now sitting forward over the desk. His hand tightly clenched his drink, which was otherwise being ignored, and his words were eloquently sharp as he rose to his cause. "You know, not long ago, I read a newspaper article about a congressional subcommittee that had just spent over two hundred thousand dollars to study the mating habits of the savannah sparrow. A couple of columns over—on the very same page—was a more tragic story. It was of a poor elderly lady living in a two-room flat. She had been trying to survive on her monthly Social Security checks. *Unsuccessfully* trying. She had frozen to death, unable to pay her monthly gas bill. I cut out those two stories, Mr. Rand. Cut them out and framed them over my desk at home. They are a reminder to me— should I ever dare to forget—that all is not well in this land of plenty. It is for these people that I am committing my career— my life. For every shivering old lady in every unheated two-room flat. It is for *these* people that I am determined to become President of the United States. Only then will I have the power to readjust the priorities in this country and, hopefully, establish some form of fiscal responsibility for those who run it; to once again make this a government *for* the people, not *over* them."

Armstrong's words still rang throughout the room as he stared deeply into his drink, then lifted it to his lips. He swallowed, found Jonathan's eyes, then added more calmly, "It is for this reason, Mr. Rand, that I cannot take even the slightest chance of having my candidacy jeopardized. Simon Crenshaw shares the same feeling. That is why this report was ordered. Needless to say, I was pleased at what I read. I may be in a minority, but I have always held the legal profession in very high esteem. I am fully satisfied that you are here only as a friend and have every intention of being completely open with me."

Jonathan sat awed. He was watching a master craftsman. Everything from intonation to delivery, to facial expressions, to knowing when to pause, was as polished as an Academy Award–winning performance. Yet, his words seemed spontaneous and sincere.

Jonathan cleared his throat, ran his fingers through his hair, and said, "It . . . uh . . . is my understanding, Senator, that you used to be a patient of Dr. Feinerman."

"You are seriously mistaken, sir. Dr. Feinerman and I were only social acquaintances. Nothing more."

"Please don't misunderstand me," he urged. "I am quite aware of the confidential nature of medical treatment and have every intention of honoring that confidence. I also have absolutely no desire to hurt you politically. But my information is unimpeachable. I *know* you were his patient."

"I'd be very interested in knowing how you arrived at that conclusion."

Without breaking his eye contact with Armstrong, Jonathan withdrew the original four-page medical chart from his coat pocket and handed it across the table. Armstrong carefully began to examine the documents.

"Where did you get these?" Armstrong demanded. For the first time his face conveyed a hint of concern.

"I found them stashed away in a box of Dr. Feinerman's business records. His widow gave them to me."

"Where did *she* get them?"

"In the garage of their home. Apparently Dr. Feinerman had left them there before he died."

"Who else has seen these?"

"No one other than my girl friend and I. Not even Mrs. Feinerman has the slightest idea of their existence."

Armstrong finished his drink and set the glass down loudly on the desk. "I guess the most important question, Mr. Rand, is what do you intend on doing with this?"

"Nothing. Absolutely nothing. I ran across them during the course of my investigation. Realizing you would not want them to fall into the wrong hands, I decided to deliver the records to you, for your own safekeeping."

"No strings attached?"

"No strings attached."

Armstrong walked to the bar, poured another drink, and turned to Jonathan, who took a long swallow of his own. "Do you have any idea what kind of impact something like this could have on my campaign?"

Jonathan shrugged. "Well, I would imagine some people might not want a President with a bum back. It might cost some votes, but I don't see it as a major obstacle. After all, Roosevelt ran this country from a wheelchair."

Armstrong shook his head. "No. You're missing it entirely. It's the hypnosis. The fact that I've recently undergone a series of hypnotherapy sessions. Somebody's been playing with my brain. *That's* what could be devastating. I dabbled in black magic. Maybe I'm mentally ill. Maybe through posthypnotic suggestion someone can make me push a button that would throw the world into a nuclear holocaust. I can see all kinds of outrageous charges by my opponent.

"The ironic reality of it, though, is that Aaron Feinerman lifted the torment of a pain-racked body and gave me a new life. I can think again. Think, and serve my country. But *not* if something like this," he said, holding up the chart, "got into the wrong hands."

Armstrong's eyes again began to radiate their typical warmth. "Can I count on you?"

"Without qualification. If I didn't feel that way, I wouldn't be sitting here."

"Wonderful. Are you aware of any other copies? I would feel quite uncomfortable to learn that other copies are floating around."

"To my knowledge, you have the only copy in existence."

"I will be eternally grateful," said Armstrong. "If there is ever anything I can do for you, please do not hesitate to call upon me."

"Well, there is one thing, Senator."

"Name it."

"We have a bit of a mystery back home. From your chart we can account for all of Dr. Feinerman's trips to Washington over the year before his death. All but one, that is. We know he flew to Washington on June first of this year, but we don't know where he went. It's not recorded on your chart, and we've verified that he wasn't at the FDA, which is where he told his wife he'd be going. I was somewhat curious. Is there any chance he came here and didn't record it in your records?"

"Is this important?"

"It might be, but probably not."

"I don't see how this could possibly be tied into your case. I'll be glad to help, though—if I can."

"I'm just trying to do my usual thorough job. There's been an allegation that Dr. Feinerman was developing some attractive interests away from his job and family—if you catch my meaning."

Armstrong nodded with a knowing smile, pulled open the top drawer of his desk, and withdrew a small black book.

"I can certainly understand. Still, I can't recall that he was here at that time. In fact, it seems that I was in Chicago about then. But why guess at it?" Armstrong began turning pages. "Let me see now. June first . . . Here it is." He abruptly stopped and folded back a page. "No, I was right. No appointment with Dr. Feinerman. I *was* in Chicago." Returning the book to the drawer, he added, "I'm sorry. Perhaps he saw another patient locally. Dr. Feinerman was a very well-known and sought-after physician."

Jonathan rose. "Perhaps you're right. Well, I don't want to keep you any longer and I have a plane to catch."

Armstrong responded politely and made his way around the desk to say his good-byes. "I want to thank you again, Mr. Rand. Believe me, I'll never forget you for this."

Jonathan stood in front of Armstrong's building, watching the stop-and-go traffic while waiting for his taxi to arrive. It was still hot and he felt beads of sweat trickling down his back and sides. He took off his coat and wiped his brow with his shirt sleeve. He was not looking forward to the long ride to the airport.

As he stood only a few feet from the curb, a bus drove by, throwing up a gust of air that seemed to turn his perspiration into tiny balls of ice. The accompanying chill caused him to tremble slightly and to back farther away from the curb, suddenly feeling quite vulnerable.

He still couldn't put his finger on it, but the encounter with Crenshaw and Armstrong had left him anxious. It was that same uncertainty he had when he impulsively argued something to a jury without first thinking it through. Maybe the trip had been a mistake. Maybe Danielle had been right. He was getting in far over his head. What in the hell was he doing investigating a murder? And what had possessed him to force his way into a meeting with a powerful United States senator?

Maybe he was really making more out of this than he should. But if that was true—if he really believed it—why had he made the extra photocopy of Armstrong's medical chart, and why had he lied to Armstrong about it?

# Chapter XX

*Thursday, August 30, 1979*

As Jonathan turned the corner, his pace quickened. At the end of the long terrazzo hallway he saw the door to his father's hospital room. There was the usual late-night activity—the janitor engaged in his nightly mopping, a couple of nurses making their rounds—but Jonathan saw only the large green door in the distance. He was on the final leg of a long journey. In a few moments he would come face to face with the memory that had haunted him since the day he had left home.

What would Pa look like? How much had he aged? Seventeen years was so long—so very long. Would Pa even talk to him? Look at him? Was he still alive? Or had the stroke taken him away forever?

Finally he stopped at the door. He stared down at the metal handle, not knowing if he wanted to see what was on the other side. Mechanically his hand reached forward.

The door opened with unexpected ease, unveiling the

vigil of an old woman clasping the hand of her critically ill husband. As Jonathan stepped into the room, his mother turned and for a moment gazed quizzically. Then her eyes, glassy and reddened, melted into her familiar smile.

In a moment they were clutching each other, openly crying, searching for the right words to express their feelings. Yet, for the moment, words seemed so inappropriate, unnecessary. So instead they only clung, their eyes closed, trying to forget the reason for their meeting; to wash away the years.

Finally Jonathan cradled her face, intently examining her delicate features as if to memorize every line. Time had taken its customary toll. Finally he spoke.

"Ma, I love you so much."

"I know, Jonny. I know."

"Oh, how I wish . . . If only I could relive that day."

Mildred reached up and covered his mouth. "No regrets, Jonny. I won't hear it. You had every right to the choice you made. Your father was wrong. He hasn't been often, God bless him. But this was one time he was totally wrong."

"But the pain it has caused—to *all* of us. Ma, it wasn't worth it. And now . . ." Jonathan looked over at his father. "Now he may be gone forever."

"That's your father down there, Jonny." The voice was soft yet firm. "I've never known a tougher man. He's a fighter. Been one since the day he was born. Dr. Krindle also says he's holding his own. He's . . . he's battled back before and he's going to do it again. I *know* it," she reassured, but more to herself. Mildred resecured her grip on Hiram's limp hand. Her lower lip quivered slightly. "My God, he's only sixty-three years old. He owes me another ten years. He *can't* leave me now. He *can't!*"

Jonathan reached forward, placing his free hand on Hiram's forearm. His skin felt ominously cold. "He's changed so much, Ma. I never would have believed . . . Seventeen years . . . What happened to him? It's a long time, I know, but how could he have changed so much in seventeen years?"

She shook her head in disbelief. "It seems now like it happened almost overnight. Really, though, it was over the last couple of years. Hiram seemed to be tiring more easily. He'd be up the same time every morning, but more and more he'd come walking in, right in the middle of the day, saying he'd had enough.

"And the headaches. How he would complain of the headaches. Every day he'd come in rubbing his forehead, his eyes tearing so bad he could hardly see, asking for some aspirin. And from your father—a man who would never take medicine. Finally he agreed to see Dr. Krindle."

"That's when you found out about his blood pressure?"

Mildred nodded. "Dr. Krindle said he had to cut back on the physical stress and gave him some pills to bring down the pressure. But you know your father. Never would listen to anyone. He took the pills—for a while—but refused to change his work habits. So stubborn . . ." She raised a damp handkerchief, clutched tightly, to her eyes. "Finally he even stopped taking the pills. Said they were making him light-headed and it just wasn't natural. I pleaded with him"—she sniffed—"but he just wouldn't listen."

Jonathan looked intently at Hiram's rugged and emotionless face. "Once Pa made up his mind, there wasn't a force on earth that could make him change it. It's the way he lived."

"Maybe that's why God stepped in," she said, looking up at her son, who towered well over a head above her. "Maybe this was the good Lord's way of bringing the two of you together."

"Maybe so, Ma . . . maybe so."

Suddenly a groan escaped Hiram's slightly parted lips. For a moment Jonathan and his mother just stared. Then the sound came again, this time louder. Mildred stepped closer, clutching Hiram's hand to her breast. "Hiram, honey, can you hear me? I'm here, honey. Right here by your side."

After what seemed an eternity, Hiram's eyes searched around his bed, then fixed on his wife standing over him with a reassuring smile. As his blank gaze came to life, his jaws moved as he tried to ask a question, but found his lungs lacking in strength, resulting in another groan.

"Don't try to speak, honey. Save your strength . . . You've had a stroke. You're in a hospital bed." Overcome with joy, Mildred's eyes flushed with tears. "You've been unconscious for the last sixteen hours, but Dr. Krindle says you're doing very well."

Again he tried to force a question and failed.

"Please, honey. You need rest. Save your energy. I want you to get a good night's sleep. Tomorrow morning we can have a nice long chat." Mildred turned to her son and pulled him next to the bed, saying, "You have a visitor. Someone you haven't seen in a very long time."

Jonathan leaned over, confronting his father face to face. It was a moment of truth. If ever they were to share again the relationship of father and son, it was to start now—or never.

"Hi, Pa. It's me, Jonathan."

Hiram's eyes were magnetized to Jonathan's face, yet betrayed no emotion.

"I came as soon as I heard. I . . . I wanted to be with you. I wanted . . Oh, God, Pa, I've missed you so much. We've missed so much together."

Without moving his eyes, Hiram's jaw rocked again, this time without uttering a sound, and his chest began to rise and fall excitedly. He was trying to communicate, but was being frustrated by his physical incapacity.

"No, Pa. Just relax . . . please. We'll have plenty of time to talk . . . if you want. If you want me to leave, I'll go. But please—"

Hiram shook his head, as he again tried to groan out a word. Then, as a final means of making known his wants, he motioned with a quivering hand toward his head, hooking his fingers.

Sensing his father's request, Jonathan leaned closer, placing his ear next to Hiram's mouth. Still no words came. But the embrace from his father told him what he had been wanting to hear for a very long time.

# Chapter XXI

*Sunday, September 2, 1979*

Ruth had been dreading this moment. She knew it wasn't going to be easy to return to *The Prescription* and had been putting it off. Of all the problems facing her, this was the worst. There had been too many happy days with Aaron there, too many memories, and she had kept pushing them back, avoiding the pain that would come with them.

He would be everywhere. For more than a year and a half, Aaron had put his heart and sweat into the boat. All the varnished panels, painted trim, brass, and chrome-plated fittings were his work. Even the labor that had been done by others he had closely supervised. No one had worked on *The Prescription* without Aaron standing right there, scrutinizing, supervising, asking questions. All materials that went into the boat were of the highest quality; all equipment the best on the market. As in his practice of medicine, Aaron had demanded perfection and would accept nothing less. Within ten months he had transformed *The Prescription* from a fifteen-year-old abused and weathered boat into an immaculate and majestic-looking yacht.

But the memories of their time together were what troubled Ruth the most. Memories of warm moments that had brought them so close together. Memories of long, open discussions that had contributed so much to their understanding of each other. And memories of countless good times and laughs.

She had always been emotionally strong, the stabilizing force in the marriage. When Aaron would impulsively suggest a trip to Europe or the purchase of some expensive "toy" for the boat, Ruth would immediately say, "Let's sit down and talk about it. We've got other commitments and responsibilities to worry about too." Aaron would respond, "Forget them, honey. Everything will take care of itself. It usually does." But it was Ruth who usually took care of it.

Now her emotions were being put to the supreme test, and Ruth was uncertain of her ability to meet it. Why put herself through this? There was plenty of time to go down to the yacht; no point in rushing it.

But it had to be done now, not next month or even next week. Enough time had passed for her to accept Aaron's death and to think about her future without him. However, time was also working against her. As the weeks passed, it would become increasingly easy to forget the boat and avoid going back for the painful reunion.

At a quarter to five, Ruth's silver Mercedes 450 SLC pulled into the club parking lot and eased into a space facing the marina. She could see *The Prescription* sitting in its usual slip at the end of the 150-foot-long dock.

She was a proud-looking boat and from a distance

appeared to have fared well after three months of neglect. From the stern, the white hull gracefully ascended the full eighty feet to a sharp, aggressive bow. Above deck, rather than the square lines of many yachts her size, the forward cabin windows were slanted back like the windshield of an automobile, giving her a sleek, racy appearance. "She looks more like an oversized speedboat than a yacht," Aaron had said. And indeed, her cruising speed of seventeen knots had cut quite a wake out in the Sound. Above was another sloping windshield that provided the visibility for the wheelhouse.

Taking a deep breath, as if drawing in the necessary courage, Ruth climbed out of her car and began her journey into the past. As she walked down the ramp and along the dock, the familiar sights—the boats she could call off by name sitting in their slips; the blue wheelbarrows used to transport supplies back and forth; the padlocked lockers; the smiles from the friendly faces; the open cans of paint—immediately brought her back, as if she had been gone only a week.

Slowly she walked up the portable steps and onto the deck of *The Prescription*. Over the past three months the weather had taken its toll. The fittings were tarnished and some even showed the first signs of corrosion. Dust had settled over everything.

"I've let you down, haven't I," Ruth said to herself. An old friend had been ignored.

She pulled out a key from her purse, unlocked the door to the main salon, and entered. Amazingly, other than the expected musty odor, the salon was exactly as it had been left that tragic Saturday when Aaron had injured himself. Everything was still in place and untouched—the throw pillows neatly placed on the couch, the clean ashtrays on the lamp stands, the teak cocktail table. The deep-pile beige carpet appeared freshly vacuumed.

On the paneled wet bar were the two cognac glasses in which Aaron and Ruth had shared their last drink together. Ruth walked over to the bar and picked up one of the glasses. Tears welled in her eyes as she recalled the two of them sitting on the couch, sipping their cognac and listening to one of Aaron's favorite pieces of music by Ravel. It wasn't going to be easy.

Then she saw it. At the end of the bar was the chrome-plated crescent wrench that Aaron had been using on the generator when he suffered the hernia. "The damn thing slipped on me," he had said. All her frustrations, her disappointments, her sorrow, her anger, suddenly became focused on the piece of metal sitting there where Aaron had left it. She walked to the end of the bar and picked it up in her hand. Anger continued to build as she held the wrench out at arm's length and stared out at it. The urge to strike back was overwhelming and she began to shake. She headed for the door to the aft deck, almost running. To her frustration, it was locked. Frantically she groped with the lock, shaking, fumbling. Tears rolled down her cheeks.

Finally she released the lock and flung the door open. Dashing to the stern railing, she reached back for all her strength and flung the wrench out into the river.

For a moment she stood there, holding on to the railing with both hands and sobbing. Then the anger began to dissipate. It was as though a thousand pounds had been lifted from her shoulders. She felt a sense of relief she hadn't known since Aaron had died. It was a physical sensation and it felt good.

She continued to gaze at the lazy waters of the Housatonic. The shadows were lengthening as the sun began to set, and the clean salt air blowing across the stern helped cleanse her sorrow. By five-thirty she was in control of her emotions and returned to the salon.

Behind the bar, Ruth poured some Martel Cordon Bleu into one of the two cognac glasses. She still felt in control and had selected the glass without the lipstick. To drink out of Aaron's glass would bring her as close to him as she could get. The cognac felt warm as it trickled down her throat.

Leaving the bottle on the bar, Ruth took her glass and walked over to a cassette player that had been installed in a specially constructed cabinet. The cassette tape they had listened to that last evening was on top of a stack of other cassettes. Ruth picked it up and hesitated a moment, then smiled. The thought that Aaron finally had her listening to some selections of classical music—and enjoying it—amused her. She had almost come full cycle. Not quite, but almost.

Although they had shared many common interests, when it came to music they had usually gone their own ways. Aaron had always been an ardent devotee of classical composers and would spend hours in his study listening to records and tapes.

Ruth, however, would spend her leisure time listening to popular music and occasionally light rock. Her real love, though, was show tunes.

Over the last two years of their marriage, Aaron had introduced Ruth to more and more music from the masters. And, although the metamorphosis had been slow, eventually she had begun to appreciate and learn about classical music. Saturday, May 26, 1979, was another one of those learning experiences. That was the day she had first been introduced to the music of the early-twentieth-century composer Maurice Ravel.

Ruth pushed in the cassette. Immediately, shimmering impressionistic music surged through the speakers and filled the cabin. She was really putting herself to the test now.

Outside, it was getting dark. The lights of the marina had been turned on and cast eerie-looking shadows among the masts. The muffled voices of boat owners could be heard on the dock, but otherwise it was unusually quiet for a Sunday night. The only other sounds were the groans of the rubber bumpers as the hull moved slowly up and down against the wooden dock.

Ruth poured herself another cognac and turned on a couple of lamps. She began to feel alone. One more test, then she could go home and make a decision about selling *The Prescription*.

Ruth removed the tape that had been playing and began sorting through the stack of cassettes. The fourth one down was what she had been looking for. A private tape filled with their favorite songs by Barbra Streisand. The tape contained some of the rare popular music that Aaron had enjoyed, including their favorite song, "The Way We Were." This was *their* song. Whenever they were out dancing, it was the song they requested. It was special to them and up to now Ruth had avoided listening to it. But now she was ready for the challenge. After this final test she could go home and begin building her future.

Methodically, as if performing a ritual, Ruth picked up the cassette and inserted it into the player. The lyrics of "Evergreen" filled the room. Ruth sat on the couch, slipped off her shoes, and curled her legs beneath her.

Finally, the haunting sounds of a solo piano, backed by the humming of Barbra Streisand, signaled the beginning of "their song." Through the high-quality sound system, Streisand had never sounded better. "Memories . . . light the corners of my mind . . . Misty watercolor memories . . . of the way we were . . . Can it be that it was all so simple then . . . or has time rewritten every line . . . If we had the chance to do it all again . . . tell me, would we . . . could we . . ."

"Hi, babe." The sudden, unexpected sound of Aaron's voice turned Ruth's face stone white. Her eyes became enlarged and her heart beat frantically. "I know how this is going to hit you, but I couldn't think of a better way to tell you about my secret—should the need arise." Ruth desperately looked around the room, expecting to see Aaron's spirit lingering in the background shadows of the salon. If he was there, she *had* to see him. Just one more time. "Unfortunately," he continued, "if you're listening to this tape, the need for this discussion already will have taken place."

Tape? For the first time, Ruth realized that the music had stopped and only the sound of Aaron's soft voice could be heard.

"Well, I guess it's more like a monologue than a discussion." He laughed; it was a forced, nervous laugh. "Anyway, I'm tape-recording this message on Friday, June fifteenth, the day before my surgery. You may recall, babe, that I told you I was going to run down here to make sure everything was turned off and locked up. Well, I hope you'll forgive me, but I told you a little white lie. I really came down here to tell you this story."

Ruth's lower lip was quivering. A single tear traversed her right cheek and dropped into her open mouth.

"I hope you don't mind my ruining our tape. I hate to do this, since I know how valuable it might be to you a couple of years from now. But I really couldn't think of a better way to tell you this, in the event of my . . . my death." The word came hard. "Anyway, babe, I figured you could always tape it again. What the hell, it's the memories that are important anyway.

"Where to start . . . I guess it all began when I was first contacted by Senator Bradley Armstrong about a year ago. That's right, Bradley Armstrong. I guess you never knew what a famous doctor your hubby was, did you? Anyway, he had a serious curvature of the spine a problem that had been getting progressively worse, and he had no surgical options available.

His only relief was through the use of analgesics, and he was getting dangerously close to drug addiction. His pain had gotten so bad, he couldn't live without medication. So he turned to me for help—lucky me. . . . Dammit, why me?"

Aaron's breath quivered as he took a deep breath.

"Anyway, he had heard about me and wanted to try some hypnotherapy. You know my giant ego. I was really impressed with myself: one of the most powerful men in the country as my patient. I had really arrived.

"But, you see, he had to insist on complete secrecy. As a politician, if this information had ever gone public, his career would have been over. So I swore never to divulge his history or treatment to anyone . . . even to my wife. Please forgive me, babe, but I really thought I was doing the right thing. I had always believed him to be a great man—someone who would be better than the typical politician and really do something good. . . . If I had only known. . . ."

Ruth held her handkerchief to her mouth. Her tears were flowing freely. She had almost forgotten what he had sounded like. Hearing him so clearly brought it all back.

"Anyway, every month or two I would fly to Washington and give him some hypnotherapy. Remember those times I told you I was attending FDA committee meetings? Well, that was another white lie. But not totally. I did work in some sessions with a couple of FDA meetings, but I was really seeing Senator Armstrong at his office in Washington.

"Then last March he approached me about using *The Prescription*. I guess that's when I really got myself involved. We had become quite friendly during previous treatments and I had told him about our boat and a couple of our vacations. He said he had his own experienced crew and that the boat he normally would use was in dry dock. He said it involved a top-security matter and that he couldn't disclose the purpose of the trip or where he was going. He also suggested that we treat it as a charter and paid me quite handsomely in cash. I should have been more suspicious, but at the time he sounded quite convincing. He said he needed the cover of a private yacht and could not use the traditional means of public transportation. . . . What do I know? He sounded legitimate, so I agreed.

"Because it was urgent, I had to decide immediately how to keep you away from the boat for a week. You may recall the day I showed up with two tickets for Hawaii. As it turns out, it's the best thing that came out of the whole mess. Without a doubt, the most wonderful week we ever spent with each other, especially those three days on the Hana Ranch on Maui."

After a long pause, Ruth heard Aaron sniff to clear his running nose. He was crying, and Ruth sat there helplessly, unable to comfort him.

"We *have* had some good times together, haven't we, babe? . . . Please remember them and never look back. No regrets. We've had a lot to be thankful for.

"Where was I? . . . Oh, yeah. He was gone about seven or eight days, and when I came down here after we got back from Hawaii, I was really amazed to see that he had left the boat spotless. You never would have known it had even been used. Everything had been cleaned and picked up . . . that is, all except one thing—a book of matches. I found it under the dinette table. It was dark blue with white lettering and had come from an inn on Grand Cayman Island.

"At first I was only slightly curious about why the senator had been so interested in going to the Cayman Islands. But as time passed, it began to eat at me. Maybe it was all the intrigue and secrecy . . . I don't know. But I was going crazy wondering about it. Then I finally got my chance to find out. . . . Dammit, babe, why was I given the chance? . . . It's almost as if fate pushed me into this whole thing. I've thought about it and thought about it, and it's the only consolation I can find for what I've gotten myself into.

"Anyway, on June first I gave my next and last hypnotherapy session to Armstrong. It was just like always except for one thing . . . one important thing. Simon Crenshaw, Armstrong's closest aide, had always been there. Every time I had given the therapy he had been right there, never leaving the room. But this time he was gone. Apparently he wasn't even in Washington. So Hanna Schroeder, Armstrong's secretary, sat in.

"The session had been going for about fifteen minutes when I got my opportunity. There was an argument out in the reception room between two lobbyists and Schroeder was called out to quiet them down. If Crenshaw had been there, he never would have left the room, but apparently Schroeder got all flustered. Whatever . . . The important thing is that I had been left there alone with Armstrong, who was in a state of deep hypnosis. It was too damn tempting, so I asked him why he had gone to the Cayman Islands. . . . What I heard made me shudder. . . . God, how I wish I'd kept my mouth shut." Another pause while Aaron sought the emotional strength to continue. "What he said was that . . . that . . . he maintained a large bank account on Grand Cayman and had to be present personally to make a substantial deposit into the account. I asked him how much he had put into the account and he said five million dollars—that's right, *five million dollars*. Well, my curiosity had been whetted, so I asked how much, total, he had in the account. His response was that over the past five years he had deposited a total of *twenty-seven . . . million . . . dollars*.

"Needless to say, babe, I was stunned. I wanted to find out where he was getting the money, but something deep inside kept telling me to drop it and get the hell out of there. Part of me wanted to find out everything and turn it over to the proper authorities, while the other part said to look out for number one and forget I had heard a word. For whatever it's worth, my animal instinct for self-preservation was winning me over when Schroeder entered the room again. I guess she hadn't been gone for more than three or four minutes. In a clumsy way I tried to act as if nothing had happened, but the senator kept answering my last question. . . . Dammit, he kept saying twenty-seven million . . . twenty-seven million . . . three or four times he said it. Jesus, I didn't know what to do. All I could think of was to shrug my shoulders and look like I didn't know what the hell he was talking about. But all she did was stare at me. That angry, piercing stare. She was almost shaking, she was so pissed. There I was, sitting there with my hand in the proverbial cookie jar. I had never felt at such a loss for words in my life. I thought of trying to talk her into forgetting it, but decided it would be fruitless and might make matters worse. So I brought Armstrong out of it and clumsily excused myself by saying I had some urgent matters I had to attend to back home. Really original, huh? . . . Schroeder didn't say anything while I was there, but I can imagine what was said after I left.

"I'm telling you, babe, I'm really scared. I thought you sensed it when I got off the plane that afternoon, but I didn't want to say anything to you until I had thought it all out. Over the past week I've had the distinct feeling that someone's been following me, though I'm sure it's probably a case of acute paranoia. And there's nowhere to run or hide. With his power and wealth, Armstrong could find us anyplace. He hasn't called me, either, which leads me to believe he doesn't want to talk about it. And that suggests to me that he's going to handle it in some other way.

"I really don't have anything I can take to anyone. It's only my word against his, not to mention the fact that it was a confidential statement from a patient to a physician. But this is really big—I just know it. Armstrong is being bought by someone and it's someone with power. I don't know who, but with that amount of money, it's got to be a crime syndicate or maybe some big industrial conglomerate.

"With this surgery coming up tomorrow, I feel especially vulnerable. . . . So I thought I'd come down here and put it all on tape for you. Believe me, I have serious misgivings about telling you. Your knowledge of this story could also endanger *you*. But we're talking about the possibility of our next President being controlled by some big power and—I know it sounds corny—but I feel a sense of obligation to pass this on to someone, and you're the most logical one to tell. I'm not sure what you should do with this. I guess that's something you'll have to decide on your own. . . . Oh, one other thing. Armstrong's medical chart is in that cardboard box in the garage where I keep a lot of my records. You won't find that last visit, though, since I never got around to making an entry. I guess I never really knew what I should put down."

Silence again, as Aaron searched for his final words.

"Words seem so inadequate now to express my love and affection for you. . . . We had something special, babe. Something most married couples never find. We had companionship and understanding along with our love, especially over the last year and a half. . . . Oh, God, I don't want to leave you, and please . . . *please* face the future with the strength of that knowledge."

Streisand was well into the opening lyrics of "Secondhand Rose" before Ruth realized that Aaron's message was over. She sat staring. Emotionally drained. Her tears had stopped and her hands were lying limp on her lap. One still held the tear-soaked handkerchief.

It was nine-thirty by the time Ruth began to organize her thoughts. Something had to be done and she knew she couldn't wait much longer to do it. She struggled up from the couch. Her legs shook weakly as she made her way down to the head of the master stateroom, where she splashed cold water on her face. After drying herself with a towel, she gave herself a quick once-over with some makeup, but without much improvement.

Five minutes later she made her way back upstairs and opened the salon door. She inhaled a deep breath of fresh air. For the first time, she understood what had happened to her husband. She didn't know *how* it had been done, but Aaron had indeed been murdered. She also knew who was responsible and was determined to do something about it.

Ruth took a quick look up the dock, then headed for the familiar green phone booth just beyond the entrance to the yacht club. The quiet shadows made her feel nervous, and to hear the sounds of activity inside the club gave her a needed sense of safety. Quickly she dialed Jonathan's number.

"Hello." Jonathan's voice sounded distant and impatient.

"Hello, Jon? This is Ruth Feinerman. I'm really sorry to bother you at this time of night."

"Oh, hi, Ruth. No bother at all. I just got in from Kansas. I was just . . . uh . . . just taking a shower. You got me standing here in the altogether."

"I'll be quick. I'm down here at the boat. A few minutes ago I came across something you've *got* to hear. It's of critical importance."

"Well . . . sure, Ruth. I'll drop by first thing in the morning."

"*No!* It's got to be *now!* This is urgent. I'm sorry. I would never ask this of you, except it's extremely urgent and I don't want to talk about it over the phone."

"All right, Ruth. I'll be down there in about thirty minutes."

Jonathan hung up the receiver and walked into the bedroom. The lights were out, but the open window cast enough light from outside that he could see Danielle's form outlined beneath the sheet.

"You awake, Dani?"

"Um-hmm."

"That was Ruth," Jonathan said, looking for his boxer shorts. "I've got to run down to *The Prescription* and listen to something . . . something or someone. I'm still not sure what. Anyway, she says it's urgent."

"Okay, honey," she replied sleepily. "See you when you get back."

To Ruth, the thirty-minute wait for Jonathan seemed like two hours. Upon returning to the boat she had immediately turned on every light and double-checked the lock on each door. With each noise her heart would race and she would nervously glance out the window. At first she wanted to turn on some music, but somehow she couldn't force herself to go near the cassette player again. She couldn't stand another shock, and if something was going on outside she wanted to hear it rather than be surprised later.

Ruth had already searched the boat for a weapon. The best she could find was a butcher knife in the galley.

She sat holding the knife in her lap and impatiently waiting, trying to think of how foolish she was being. After all, no one knew she had heard the tape—or even that one existed. And no one had even *attempted* to do anything over the three months since Aaron had died. But what if someone had been outside listening when the tape was going? *Dammit, why doesn't Jonathan get here?*

She looked down at the long, sharp knife she clutched tightly in her right hand. The thought of using it on someone made her shudder. Finally she heard a knock at the door. "Jon?" she asked anxiously.

"It's me, Ruth."

Ruth unlocked the door and swung it open. "Thank God you're here," she said. "I've been absolutely terrified since I called you."

Jonathan looked at Ruth's reddened eyes and down at the butcher knife, glistening from a light within the salon.

"What in the hell's going on?" he said.

"Come on in," she said. "I've got something I want you to hear. But first let me tell you how this all happened."

"What's this all about? And why the knife?"

Ruth joined Jonathan on the couch and proceeded to tell him everything that had happened up until she had played the Streisand tape. Then she got up and inserted the cassette into the slot. The sight of Jonathan sitting there gave her the strength to hear it again.

After Aaron's voice had concluded and the music again

filled the room, Jonathan slowly shook his head. Uneasily, he recalled his meeting and conversation with Armstrong.

"None of us are safe," he warned. "Armstrong is not aware of this tape, but he knows that Danielle and I have seen his medical chart and that I'm investigating Aaron's death. Don't ask how I know, but I know."

"Do you think that's enough to . . . kill us?"

"Aaron didn't know much more and he was killed. But more important, the man is desperate. He can't even take a *chance* that we might find out. This is too big. There's too much at stake. Millions . . . and possibly presidential control of this country. But I don't think he can take a chance on an overt attempt. He would probably want it to appear like an accident—just like Aaron."

Suddenly it struck Jonathan. "Oh, my God. Danielle's home alone." The possibilities started racing through his mind. "Look, Ruth, I want you to check into the Vista Hotel, under the name of . . . of . . . Judy . . . Judy Finn. I've got to get home. I'll call you tomorrow. And leave the boat the way it is. I'll have someone come down and lock it up tomorrow."

"Okay . . . Jon," she agreed hesitantly.

With a swipe of the hand, Jonathan grabbed the cassette and raced down the steps, then down the dock to his waiting car.

# Chapter XXII

Danielle stirred slightly. She was dreaming. That same dream she had had for the past two nights. She was running with every ounce of energy she could muster, but could move only in slow motion. She knew she could run faster, yet her legs would barely move. Behind her was a dark figure wearing a robe and a hood. There was no face; only green illuminated eyes. . . . The figure kept getting closer and closer. She tried to call out for help, but her voice was frozen. She was speechless and was about to be consumed and lost forever.

Behind her she could also hear barking. She couldn't see the dogs; she could only hear them. But they were there and getting closer. The barking was louder and more distinct. Gradually the haze began to disappear. The figure was gone and she could see the outline of a wineglass silhouetted on the nightstand. Still the barking continued. Danielle slowly began to separate the real from the unreal, the conscious world from the dream world.

*Goddamn those dogs. Mrs. Moffit and her goddamned miniature poodles.* They kept barking. And the longer they barked, the angrier she became. Dogs weren't allowed in the apartments; why should Mrs. Moffit be different from everyone else? First thing in the morning Danielle would go to the manager. She didn't give a shit if old lady Moffit *was* attached to them. A rule was a rule and this was the last time they'd ever keep *her* awake.

Finally the barking stopped and it was quiet again. *Now, where did Jonathan say he was going? Oh, yeah, Ruth wanted to see him about something.* . . . She thought about the time and wanted to look at the clock. But that would mean turning on the light and then she really *would* be awake. No, the sheets felt too comfortable, and Jonathan would wake her when he got back anyway. Gradually she began to drift off again.

Suddenly she heard something and was immediately jolted back to a fully conscious state. This was not a dream. At first she tried to reassure herself that it was nothing to be concerned about. One of those thousand and one night sounds that never evolve into anything. Anxiously she waited. One minute; two minutes; three minutes. Then she heard it again. It was a metallic sound and it seemed to be coming through the front door. She had heard Jonathan put his key in the door dozens of times before, and this . . . this was different. It *had* to be Jonathan . . . but she was hoping now.

She heard another sound, like something rolling; ever so softly, but definitely rolling. Suddenly it struck her. It was the sliding glass door. Somebody was opening the sliding glass door to the living room. Fear overcame her like a flash of light. Someone was coming through the sliding glass door—*her* sliding glass door—and it wasn't Jonathan. *Oh, God, let me be dreaming,* she pleaded. But she knew it wasn't a dream.

Danielle wanted to move, but she couldn't. Her breathing was short and quivering. Maybe if she called out, he'd run away. He had to be just as scared as she was. No. She couldn't. If he thought she was asleep, maybe he'd leave her alone.

She could hear the squeak of the wooden floor as a heavyset body stepped toward the bedroom door. It was only a few inches ajar; not enough to see, but wide enough to hear easily the sounds from the other room. She heard another squeak and another. Danielle began to shake uncontrollably. Why wasn't Jonathan home? Why now? *Why now?* And why did they have to have an apartment on the ground floor? A thousand questions raced through her mind. *Oh, please, God, don't let him come through the door.*

Danielle still couldn't move. She could only lie there waiting. Even if she could get up, where would she go? The bedroom windows had screens on them and she would never figure out how to get them off. *Please make him go away,* she again pleaded. Fighting for control, she bit into her pillow and squeezed her eyes shut.

Suddenly the door opened. Danielle looked up and saw him standing only fifteen feet away. He was tall and wore dark clothing. From the small amount of light that filtered through the window it seemed that he was wearing gloves. In his right hand he was holding something, but it was too dark to determine what it was. And then she saw his face. It was hideous. His features weren't clear, but his eyes were sunken and dark, his nose grotesquely flattened and distorted. Her breathing stopped and she began to feel faint.

The intruder took a step toward the bed. Danielle knew that her life was about to end. Right there in her own bed; unglamorously, with blood all over the sheets. All was hopeless now; but if it was going to happen, she wasn't going to let it happen easily. He was now only five feet away, and she could see for the first time that the man had a nylon stocking over his face.

With every ounce of courage she had, Danielle sucked in a deep breath, closed her eyes, and opened her mouth. Then, in final desperation, she let go with the loudest scream possible. She would continue screaming until it was over.

Jonathan was standing outside the glass security door searching for the right key when he heard the scream.

Frantically he tried one key, then another. Finally the third one fit. In one motion he turned the key, pushed open the door, and took a step into the lobby. Danielle was still screaming as his foot slipped on the tile floor and he began to fall. His left hand hit the floor with a slap as he caught his balance and managed to remain on his feet.

*No, not Danielle! Not her! Please, not her!* Taking two quick steps, Jonathan made it to the carpeting and began running the hundred feet to the door of his apartment.

Halfway down the hall the screaming stopped. The silence was something he did not welcome. As long as she was screaming, she was still alive. A feeling of hopelessness overcame him.

He was shaking, but this time the key went right into the lock. Jonathan threw open the door, flipped on the light switch, and darted for the open bedroom door. Out of the corner of his eye he saw that the sliding glass door was open, which confirmed his fears of what he would find in the bedroom.

"Danielle!" he shouted as he threw on the light and stopped in the open doorway. His eyes were wet and his chest was heaving.

On the bed, Danielle lay motionless, face down into the pillow. The sheet was draped just above her buttocks, revealing her naked back. Her long reddish brown hair was disheveled and covered the side of her face.

"Dani?" Jonathan asked quietly, without any hope of a reply. Reluctantly he took a step toward the bed.

Then he saw a movement, as Danielle drew a deep breath and slowly pulled her outstretched hand up to her face. Jonathan rushed to her side. She rolled over and tried to focus on the man sitting next to her on the bed.

Jonathan brushed the hair back from her face. "You all right, honey?" he asked, mopping his own eyes with his sleeve.

Danielle did not immediately react. Then Jonathan's familiar, strong features came into focus. At the very same moment, the realization of what had happened struck her. "Jonathan," she cried, sitting up and throwing her arms around him. "Thank God you're here! Thank God! Thank God!"

"Everything's all right," he assured. "No one's going to touch you. No one. Not as long as there's a breath in my body."

"Anything wrong in here?" Jonathan heard the voice of Jerry Grant from down the hall. Knowing he had to respond, Jonathan got up from the bed and walked to the bedroom door. Jerry was standing in the open front doorway wearing his robe and slippers. His hair looked like he had just gotten out of bed. Behind him stood other tenants in similar attire.

"Anything wrong, Jon?" he again asked.

"Not now," Jonathan replied. "We just had an attempted burglary, but everyone's all right."

"Would you like me to call the police?" Jerry offered.

"No. I'll do it myself in the morning. I'd prefer not to have them here tonight."

Jonathan closed and locked the door, then walked to the sliding glass door and rolled it shut. He set the lock and checked it. It still kept the door from opening, although he knew that it had not provided a significant obstacle for the intruder. With Danielle watching him, he walked to the bedroom closet and pulled out a shoebox.

"What are you doing, honey?"

Danielle was still sitting on the bed naked, but she had pulled the sheet up around her neck.

Jonathan removed a target pistol from the box. It was a Hi-Standard .22 long rifle semiautomatic, which he hadn't used in over a year. It looked like a toy German Luger. "I haven't had occasion to use this in quite some time," he said. "But if anyone else tries to come through this door tonight, they're going to gain about half a pound of lead in a span of about five seconds." Jonathan placed the box on the bed and began loading the clip.

"Where did that come from?" she asked. "I didn't know you owned a gun."

"I used to do a little target shooting," he replied. "Nothing serious. Just a small hobby." The muscles of his jaw tightened as he stared at the weapon in his hands. To Danielle his reaction was frightening.

"Honey, there's no need to get all uptight about this," she said. "It was only a burglar and he never touched me—I guess I fainted right after I started screaming. And we'll never see him again. So why don't you put the gun away and come to bed."

Jonathan put the cleaning equipment back into the box, picked up the clip, and snapped it into the bottom of the handle with the palm of his hand. "It wasn't a burglar," he said sharply, "and don't be surprised if we see him again."

"What do you mean? Who the hell else would it be?"

Jonathan pulled back the slide and let it go, which automatically loaded a cartridge into the chamber. "I mean it wasn't a burglar," he emphasized.

"What . . . what are you saying?"

"We've got problems. Serious problems. Whoever it was probably came here to kill us."

Danielle looked at him in shock.

"I'm sure he thought we were both in here sleeping," Jonathan explained. "Your screams probably scared the living shit out of him. Then he heard me running for the door and left before he had a chance to do anything."

Jonathan stood up, flipped on the safety to the gun, and stuck it into the front of his pants. The barrel pointed down between his trousers and his shorts.

"It's happening, isn't it? Aaron's killer. Now he's coming after us. . . . Oh, God, why didn't you listen to me?"

"I did what I had to do. Now . . . now we know too much," he explained, walking out of the bedroom. Within a minute he returned with a glass in his hand and began fishing through one of his dresser drawers.

"But what do we know that . . . that—" Then it all came to her, as her mind flashed back to that evening aboard *Dreamboat*. "This has something to do with Armstrong, doesn't it?"

Jonathan stopped but would not turn and look at her. His eyes remained fixed on the open dresser drawer. His feelings were a mixture of anger and guilt. If he hadn't insisted on seeing Armstrong, perhaps none of this would have happened.

"It involves the medical chart, doesn't it?" she persisted. "*Doesn't* it?"

He slowly turned and nodded. "Yes, it does."

"Well, for God's sake, tell me what's happened."

Pulling a ball of string out of the drawer, Jonathan proceeded with his task as calmly as if it were a nightly routine. "You already know about my returning the medical chart. . . . Well, when Armstrong asked me who else knew about it, I generously told him that we were the only ones that had seen the chart. So, at this very moment, he believes that we're the only two outsiders who know about his medical condition and the fact that he had been undergoing hyp-notherapy." Jonathan cut a four-foot length of string with a pocketknife and tied one end to the knob of the bedroom door. "He also knows that I'm continuing to investigate the circum-stances surrounding Aaron's death."

"My God! That's no reason to kill us. You're suggesting he wants us dead because we know of his *medical* history? There's . . . more, isn't there?"

"*Much* more," said Jonathan, as he tied the other end of the string to the glass and set it on the dresser next to the door. "Ruth just found a tape that Aaron recorded the night before his surgery." Jonathan pulled the cassette out of his pants pocket and held it up. He then reached into his other pocket, pulled out some change, and dropped it into the glass.

Danielle sat with her back against a pillow, not wanting to hear the story but knowing it was inevitable.

Jonathan tossed the cassette onto the sheet next to her and said, "It's all there. The whole ugly story in Aaron's own words. I'll let you listen to it later, but the bottom line is that Armstrong is on the take—and it's big. Apparently twenty-seven million in the last five years."

"This is insanity," she exclaimed, putting her hand over her eyes. "No, I don't believe it. I *won't* believe it! A United States senator just doesn't go around killing people."

Jonathan sat down on the bed and began removing his shoes and socks. "You'd *better* believe it. Our lives may depend on it. The money's being passed in the Cayman Islands and Aaron found out about it. That's why he was killed. He suspected that it was a crime syndicate or some big industrial conglomerate, but didn't know for sure."

"How did he find out?"

"During that last session when he had Armstrong under hypnosis. But, to Aaron's misfortune, one of Armstrong's staff members found out about it."

He pulled the gun out of his trousers, flipped off the safety, and laid it on the nightstand pointing at the door. He then took off his pants, tossed them onto a chair, and started to unbutton his shirt—but stopped. If someone broke in again, he didn't want to be caught in his shorts. Taking a last look around, he was satisfied that everything possible had been done. If the door opened while he was asleep, the glass with the coins in it could be pulled to the floor from his dresser, and the noise would wake him. Then he could grab the gun and fire. Something suddenly dawned on him.

"For God's sake, Dani, don't get up and go to the bathroom without telling me."

"Don't worry," she assured him. "I won't move without telling you about it."

He turned off the light and crawled into bed next to the gun. He propped the pillow against the headboard. Danielle snuggled up to him and he put his arm around her.

"What are we going to do, honey?" she asked. The warmth of his arm gave her security.

Jonathan stared at the door and shook his head. "I don't know. I just don't know. I've got to think this through."

"We've got to turn this over to the police," she insisted. "That's what they get paid for. Even United States senators are not allowed to kill people."

"You don't understand, Dani. We have no proof. We have absolutely no way of proving that this incident tonight was any more than what it appeared to be: an attempted burglary. And the copy of the medical chart only shows that Armstrong was being treated for a back condition. Nothing more."

"But the tape—"

"It's useless. It's a hearsay statement and a privileged communication on top of it. Besides, Armstrong could easily claim that Aaron had been upset because of some argument or an unpaid bill, and there would be no one to refute it. And who would you believe—a deceased doctor who was admittedly upset about an upcoming surgery, or one of the most popular men in our country?" Jonathan covered his eyes with his hand, agonizing over what he should do. "No—what we need is evidence. Strong, irrefutable evidence. Because of his office, his esteem, we'll need a hell of a lot more than if he were a transient farm worker. . . . Our problem now is how to survive until we find it. *If* we can find it."

"Can't we just go to another state and hide until this is all forgotten? We could change our names and—"

"It wouldn't do any good. This man has wealth, power, connections . . . he has everything he would need to find us, no matter where we went. Even to another country."

"We just can't sit here and wait to die."

"Don't worry. I'll get us out of this. I promise I'll lay out a plan tonight. I just need some time to think about it."

It was going to be a long night, and the decisions and plans he would make over the next few hours probably would determine whether they would both live out the week.

# Chapter XXIII

*Monday, September 3, 1979*

By the time Jonathan dozed off, a bird had begun to chirp the arrival of day. The sun had not yet risen and the sky was a dark blue, with a slight fluorescent glow. Everything was still, and a cool dampness came through the open window.

Jonathan had logically considered every option and its likely outcome. When he finally succumbed to the sanctuary of sleep, he had reached a decision. It was not foolproof, but he saw it as the only reasonable solution to their dilemma. Just before he drifted away, his last thought was of promptness. Indecision might cost them their lives. First thing in the morning they would move to a hotel under an assumed name. But for now he needed to sleep. Maybe only an hour . . .

At eight forty-five Jonathan woke with a start to the ringing of his telephone. Automatically he threw back the sheet and started for the door, staggering from sleepiness. His eyes were half-open and he yawned as he yanked open the bedroom door. At the moment that he realized his mistake, he saw the glass and its contents of coins descend from the edge of the dresser. Before his sluggish mind could transmit the command to catch them, the glass had slammed to the carpeting below.

Jonathan looked over at Danielle. She was sitting up in bed, her eyes wide open. "Sorry, Dani," he said. "I forgot about the glass." Again the phone rang in the other room.

"Shit, Jon! You just about gave me a heart attack."

"I'm sorry. The phone woke me out of a sound sleep and I just forgot about it."

It rang again, and he went to answer it.

"Hello," he answered cautiously, trying to concentrate on the circumstances of the morning. Quickly he glanced over at the kitchen clock and noted the time.

"Mr. Rand?" a female voice inquired. The voice was familiar, but he couldn't place it.

"Yes," he replied slowly.

"This is Maureen Jensen, Mr. Rand. I spoke with you about a month ago."

Jonathan furrowed his brow. "Yes, I remember our meeting. How can I help you?"

"I was wondering if I could possibly talk with you this morning?"

"Well, I . . . Sure. What did you want to talk about?"

"It concerns Dr. Feinerman's death, but I don't want to discuss it over the phone. Maybe we could meet at my apartment."

His immediate reaction was negative. To spend the morning talking to someone on the other side of town would mean leaving Danielle alone. He was also reluctant to bring her along, since it might be a setup.

"No, I'm sorry, but I have other plans today."

"I just learned of this yesterday at the hospital and it may explain what happened to Dr. Feinerman. Are you sure you can't see me?"

Now he was really pressed. He was suspicious, but could he afford to give up a chance to pick up some valuable evidence? This might be his only opportunity to nail Armstrong; he had seen damaging evidence lost before because of delays and procrastination. Then he remembered Ruth and knew where he could leave Danielle.

"All right. I'll meet you there at ten-thirty. What's your address?"

"Four thirty-five Cottage Avenue. Apartment three zero one. I'll see you in about an hour and a half. Good-bye."

Jonathan slowly hung up the receiver. He had been thrown off stride from his original plan and had to move with deliberation and caution. One mistake could be fatal.

"Who was that?" Danielle yelled from the bedroom.

"I'll tell you later," he replied. "Right now I want you to pack a suitcase and—"

"I want you to explain it to me *now*." Danielle was standing at the door wearing a bathrobe. "I'm tired of being kept in the dark. Dammit, it was *me* they almost carried out of here last night."

"I'm sorry, Dani. I just don't want to waste any time. The longer we stay here, the longer our lives are in danger. . . . It was Maureen Jensen. She wants to see me at her apartment."

"What about?"

"She claims she knows something about Aaron's death."

"You don't believe her, do you?"

"I don't know. Can we afford not to? This may be our only chance out of this nightmare."

"I don't trust that woman. I've never met her, but I don't trust her."

"I don't either," Jonathan said, putting his arm around Danielle's waist and kissing her forehead. "But we've got to take some chances. There's no safe way out of this mess." Jonathan slapped her on the rear and gently pushed her toward the bedroom door. "So please pack a suitcase—but only one. We've got to travel light. Pack only the barest essentials."

Mellowed by Jonathan's affection, Danielle proceeded to the bedroom. She knew he was right, but she couldn't resign herself to taking *any* risk. As far as she was concerned, their immediate safety should be given priority. But she also recognized that she had to have faith in him. Jonathan was her only hope. "There's just one thing," she said, stopping and turning in the doorway.

"Name it."

"I don't want you to withhold *anything* from me. I want your absolute promise that we share everything. If we've come to the end, I want you to tell me. I want to know."

Jonathan thought for a moment. "You have my promise."

Danielle disappeared into the bedroom and Jonathan picked up the telephone. A quick call to Ruth and then he could pack and be on his way. He dialed the information operator. In the middle of the fourth ring, a voice answered, "Information. What city, please?"

Jonathan started to say, "Bridgeport. Vista Hotel," but couldn't get the words out. He just stood there holding the receiver in his hand.

"Information. What city, please?" he heard again.

He was becoming paranoid. He was sure of it as he pressed the button to terminate the call. Maybe he *should* be paranoid. No surprises that way. Then he looked at the mouthpiece of the receiver and a terrifying thought crossed his mind. He unscrewed the plastic cover and lifted it off. Beneath the perforated cap sat a round metal disc, about two and a half inches in diameter, which he also removed.

What he saw inside almost made his heart stop. Nestled between the coated wires was a miniature transmitter, no larger than his thumbnail. Jonathan immediately tried to remember his recent calls. What had he talked about over the phone? Jesus, they knew about the meeting with Jensen. He had to reach her and change the meeting—and he'd better use a public telephone.

Jonathan quickly replaced the pieces to the phone and rushed to the bedroom. Danielle was loading her bag on the bed.

"Where are we going to go?" she casually asked, looking up.

Jonathan held his index finger up to his lip, signaling to be quiet. If the phone was tapped, there might be other bugs in the apartment.

"But why should I—"

Jonathan waved his hand frantically back and forth with a grimace on his face. Danielle immediately understood and stopped.

He motioned to her, beckoning her to follow him into the living room and over to his desk. He quickly scribbled a message onto one of his legal pads:

"Our telephone is bugged and possibly our apartment. So don't say anything other than to agree with me. Then finish packing as quickly as you can."

Danielle nodded her understanding and agreement, then followed Jonathan back into the bedroom. He pulled a suitcase out of the closet, threw it onto the bed next to Danielle's, and began throwing in clothes.

"Dani, I think it would be a good idea if we forgot about the meeting with Jensen and get the hell out of this state. I don't think we should stick around here a minute longer than we have to."

"Okay. But where should we go?"

"Florida! Maybe the Everglades. People get lost there by accident. Think of what we could do with a little bit of effort."

"You're the boss. I'm with you all the way." The look on

Danielle's face conveyed a sincerity beyond anything intended for their possible eavesdroppers.

They quickly finished packing and dressing. Their urgency to leave the apartment was overwhelming. They felt as if they had been undressing in front of a picture window. Ears had been listening. Evil, uninvited ears that had heard every intimate moment and conversation. They felt naked, dirty, and vulnerable.

With Danielle holding her bag at the front door, Jonathan took a last look around the bedroom, then picked up his gun. Danielle saw him flip the safety on and stick it back into the front of his pants. To camouflage the weapon, he pulled out his shirt. The sight of the gun, although an awesome reminder of the seriousness of their plight, gave Danielle a feeling of security.

In the garage, Jonathan looked at his Cadillac with some misgivings. Although it was parked in a locked security garage, he knew the place was not impregnable. The iron gate had to be opened with a plastic key, but someone could easily walk in with anyone who had a key.

Jonathan instructed Danielle to stand at the rear of the garage and not to move until he called for her.

Danielle started to inquire why, but before she could ask, Jonathan was gone. When she saw him looking under the wheel wells and bumpers, she knew immediately what he was looking for. Dynamite. A bomb. *My God, would they actually try something like that?*

Satisfied that there were no bombs or transmitters under the car, Jonathan opened the driver's door and carefully looked over the interior and under the dash. Clean. Apparently. One more place and then they could leave. Jonathan reached down to the side panel just to the left of the emergency brake pedal and pulled the lever to release the hood. Hearing the thud of the release, he walked around to the front of the car. If dynamite had been planted, this would be the most likely location.

Perspiration started beading on Jonathan's forehead and palms. With the one-and-a-half-inch gap between the bottom of the hood and the grille, it looked like the jaws of a shark. Maybe it was set to be tripped by the opening of the hood.

Jonathan squatted and looked into the gap for wires, but it was too dark and the opening too small to know for sure.

Jesus, why hadn't he locked the car? *If the car's locked, no one can open the hood without breaking a window*. Every night he parked the car and locked it. Every fucking night except last night.

Jonathan slowly reached his shaking hand into the jaws and found the second lever. As he pushed it up, some drops of perspiration found their way through his right eyebrow and down into his eye. The burning sensation caused him to release the lever and wipe his eye with the sleeve of his shirt.

"Are you all right, honey?" shouted Danielle. Even from fifty feet away she could feel the tension.

Jonathan didn't answer, choosing only to nod his head. Again he reached down and squeezed the lever. This was it. A slight lift and he would know for sure. Grimacing in anticipation of the worst, he pulled the hood.

But it caught on something. He looked back into the gap, which was now about three inches wide. Still he couldn't see anything. Probably the hook of the latch hadn't cleared. One more tug and he should have it.

Gathering more strength, Jonathan pulled up again on the hood. This time his perspiring hands slipped and rose uselessly in the air as the hood came crashing down. Defensively he threw himself back and crouched into a fetal position, waiting for the explosion. But all he heard was the echo of the closing hood rebounding off the walls of the garage.

"What happened?" Danielle yelled, starting to come toward the car.

"Nothing, Dani," he replied. "The hood just slipped. . . . Stay right where you are."

"Are you all right?" she again asked, taking another step.

"I'm fine. I'm fine," he snapped, standing. "Now get back behind that car."

Danielle turned and walked behind a blue Ford, peering over the top of its roof.

Angry at himself, Jonathan again pulled the release inside the car and walked to the front. "If it's going to happen, it's going to happen," he said under his breath. And reached into the gap, squeezed the lever, closed his eyes, and yanked the hood to its full upright position.

To his relief, he heard nothing. No click; no buzz; no

explosion—nothing. Only wonderful silence. Then he opened his eyes and carefully examined the engine. Nothing. Jonathan drew a deep breath and exhaled. "Jesus, I can't take much more of this," he said to himself.

"Let's go, Dani. Everything's fine," he shouted as the hood dropped shut. Danielle rushed over and threw her arms around him.

Two blocks from the apartment Jonathan swung into a gas station and pulled up to the phone booth.

"What are we doing here?" Danielle asked.

"I've got to call Jensen. If she's legitimate, her life isn't worth a penny, and they also know I'm going to be at her apartment at ten-thirty. I've got to reschedule our meeting. . . . I also want to call Ruth. I've got to tell her what's happened and let her know I'll be dropping you off at her hotel room."

"What! Oh, no, you don't. I'm not leaving you for one minute. If you've got a meeting with Jensen, we're going to see her together."

"I can't take you with me, Dani. I've got to know that you're at least relatively safe. I don't have any idea what's going to happen. If I have to worry about you, too, I might get both of us killed. By myself, I've got a chance."

Danielle stared at him, not wanting to agree but knowing he was right.

"You've got to understand," he urged. "Trust my decisions. I'll let you in on everything, but I've got to have your full cooperation and commitment to follow my directions without question. I've thought it all out and I have a plan. But hesitation on your part could make a difference between life and death."

"All right . . . I understand. And I agree, but I . . . I . . ." Danielle looked into Jonathan's deep blue eyes. He had a strong, determined look about him and she had never before felt such pride. "If anything happened to you," she said, grabbing his hand, "I'd just want to die." Danielle fought to swallow the lump in her throat.

"Nothing's going to happen to me, nor is anything going to happen to you. Trust me, Dani. Trust me!" Jonathan leaned over and kissed her on the forehead, then opened the door and walked to the phone booth.

The call to Jensen didn't take more than two minutes. He told her that he couldn't explain why over the phone but her life might be in danger, and that she should leave her apartment immediately. He asked her to meet him at Hagan's at eleven o'clock, to which she agreed without hesitation.

Jonathan next called the Vista Hotel. As the phone rang, he began to worry that Ruth had disregarded his instructions and gone home. Armstrong probably knew about the tape; he would know that Ruth had heard it along with Jonathan. Finally, the hotel operator answered.

"Judy Finn, please. She should have registered last night."

Silence followed, as Jonathan nervously tapped his foot.

"Yes, sir," she responded finally. "I'll put you through."

Ruth answered the phone in the middle of the first ring.

"Ruth, this is Jon."

"Thank God it's you! I've been going crazy sitting here. I've got no idea what I should be doing—if I can leave my room; if I can call out. . . . I'm about ready to climb the walls."

"Look, Ruth. I'm going to be fast, so just listen. Armstong has had my phone tapped and probably knows all about the tape. And if he knows that, he also knows that you and I have heard it. So don't leave your room or make any calls. Sit tight and I'll be there with Danielle in ten minutes. What room are you in?"

"Fourteen fifty-six. On the fourteenth floor. Please hurry, Jon."

"I'll be right there."

Jonathan hung up the phone, jumped into his car, and was on his way before Danielle could ask a question. As they sped down the street she looked over at him. She still wasn't certain that they shouldn't at least *try* the police. Maybe they didn't have evidence that could be introduced in a courtroom, but if Armstrong knew that the police were involved, maybe he wouldn't be so quick to make an attempt on their lives. And maybe the police would take Jonathan seriously: after all, he was an attorney and wouldn't make spurious accusations.

"Just one more question," she ventured.

"What's that?" he replied, glancing in his rear-view mirror to see if they were being followed.

"It seems that we would have nothing to lose by going to

the police, and, who knows, they might be able to help us. Why don't we just go in and give them the whole story?"

"I'll tell you why. I've given this a lot of thought. There is one area where Armstrong is vulnerable—his reputation. His entire political career hinges on his clean all-American image. If a story was released implicating him in a murder, all his presidential hopes would be destroyed. That twenty-seven-million-dollar investment would go right down the drain. He'll go to great lengths to preserve that image, which is something we'll use to our advantage."

"I still don't understand. You said this tape and our other evidence wasn't admissible."

"Newspapers print stories all the time that are based on inadmissible evidence. And they love to tear into politicians. If we sent our story to a few major newspapers like the *Washington Post* and the—"

Jonathan stopped as he looked again in the rear-view mirror.

"What's wrong, honey?"

"There's a brown Chevy that has made the last two turns with me."

Danielle started to turn.

"Don't look! I can see him in my mirror. It's a man and he seems to be alone."

Jonathan went three more blocks, then made a quick left turn without signaling. The Chevy went straight.

"I guess it was nothing," he said. *Continue being a paranoid,* he reminded himself. *The only way to survive.*

"You were mentioning the newspapers," Danielle said.

"Yes. If we sent them our story and maybe a duplicate of the tape and medical chart, they might print it. At the very least they would probably start an investigation."

"Are you suggesting that we send these things out to some newspapers?"

"No. Not right now. But if we had a neat package with notarized signatures, duplicate tapes, and medical records—all ready to be mailed—and put them into a safe-deposit box, to be mailed in the event of either one of our deaths, it might be our life-insurance policy. The only other thing we would have to do would be to notify Armstrong."

Jonathan spent an extra five minutes making random turns in a direction away from the hotel. After he was satisfied that he was not being followed, he proceeded to the Vista and parked in its garage.

In the hotel room, Jonathan's instructions were concise and unequivocal. No leaving the room. No phone calls out. All meals brought in by room service, and when they were delivered, either Ruth or Danielle would remain in the bathroom with Jonathan's gun. The drapes were to be drawn at all times and there was to be no standing in front of the windows. And, other than when they called room service, *no one* was to be admitted unless they heard three quick raps and then another on the door.

Just before leaving, Jonathan handed the Hi-Standard .22 to Danielle. Terrified of guns, she declined to take it. "Give it to Ruth," she said. "I couldn't use it on a snake, let alone a human being."

Jonathan again reminded her of her promise to follow his instructions without reservation. "If your life is on the line, you'll use it," he said. He also gave her the tape and told her to find a good hiding place for it. After a good-luck kiss from Ruth and an embrace from Danielle, he was on his way.

Before meeting Jensen, Jonathan had one quick stop to make. Armstrong—or whoever was working with him— appeared to be coming out in the open. Perhaps he was desperate now. Why else the attempt on Danielle? He also must know about the tape and would no doubt go to any length to get it. For the first time, Jonathan experienced a sickening uneasiness about the lengthy silence from Rusty.

Jonathan parked his Cadillac in front of the rundown apartment building. On the sidewalk a trash can had been overturned and its contents scattered over a large area of the pavement. The same container had met a similar fate when Jonathan had made his last visit, over a week earlier. He wondered if it was the same debris.

He felt a tightness in the pit of his stomach as he climbed out of his car and entered the four-story building. His intuition told him that something was wrong, but he fought it off. No doubt Rusty had gone on another binge. At the top of the first flight of stairs he turned and faced apartment 23. The same green paint was peeling off the door. He wondered why someone as aggressive as Rusty would accept living under these conditions.

Jonathan knocked on the door. Then again and a third time. Could he still be gone? Maybe he was inside in a drunken stupor. Maybe he needed help.

"Rusty, it's me," he shouted, this time pounding hard on the wooden door. "Jonathan! Jonathan Rand!"

Dammit, he was going in if he had to go *through* the door. He turned the knob and pushed. It was unlocked; the door swung open. Jonathan entered.

The living room looked as it always did: badly in need of cleaning, clothes scattered around, and a pile of books next to Rusty's easy chair.

"Rusty! It's Jonathan! You here?"

Then for the first time he detected a sharp odor. The knot in his stomach began to tighten. He walked to the partially open bedroom door and pushed.

On the bed Rusty lay partially propped up against the headboard. He was wearing trousers, a sports shirt, and white socks, one with a large hole in it. His eyes, half-open, appeared to be staring blankly down at his feet. His face had a pasty appearance. He was not breathing.

Jonathan took a step forward, but the odor stopped him and brought on a wave of nausea. Tears flooded his eyes as he looked down at the almost empty quart of liquor clutched in Rusty's hand.

"Oh, why, Rusty? Why? You were doing so well."

Fighting the urge to vomit, he stepped over to the bed and sat. He reached out and felt Rusty's ice-cold hand that clung to the bottle.

Then he noticed it. The one thing that was out-of-place, that didn't fit into the total picture. He pulled hard at Rusty's fingers, enough to get a glimpse of the label.

*Bourbon!* Rusty never drank bourbon. It had always made him sick. The result of a very bad drunk many years before. "I'd rather battle the little varmints than pour that stuff down my throat," he had once told Jonathan.

Suddenly Jonathan felt a surge of guilt and screamed out in pain. His persistence in pushing the lawsuit had cost the life of a friend.

Hagan's Restaurant was located in the heart of the financial district of Bridgeport. On any given day, one could walk into Hagan's and retain stockholders, bankers, lawyers, doctors, accountants, or any other professional or business-man. Because it also served a breakfast menu from eight o'clock in the morning until midnight, there was a continual flow of business. During the lunch hour it was not unusual to wait as long as thirty minutes for a table. On Saturdays there was a large draw from the weekend shoppers who would wander over from the shopping mall two blocks away. It was because of the crowds that Jonathan had selected Hagan's for his rendezvous with Jensen.

Jonathan entered the foyer and approached the maître d', who was taking a reservation over the phone. It was eleven-fifteen and he was nervous about being late. Maybe she hadn't waited.

As the maître d' continued with the phone call, Jonathan squinted to look over at the large dining area, but it was too dark to locate Jensen. Eagerly he hung up the phone and walked over to Jonathan. "I'm sorry to keep you waiting, sir. Did you have a reservation?"

"No. But I'm meeting someone who is probably already seated. A Miss Jensen. My name is Jonathan Rand."

"Miss Jensen? Oh, yes, sir. This way, please."

Jonathan followed the maître d' to a small alcove that accommodated two medium-sized booths. One of them was empty and had a reserved sign on the table. In the other sat an attractive blonde whose features Jonathan could barely make out behind the flickering candle.

Jonathan leaned over to get a better look. "Miss Jensen?" he inquired.

"Good morning. I didn't think you were coming."

"I'm sorry I'm late," he said, sliding over in the seat. "I had a personal matter to tend to."

Jensen looked different. In fact, Jonathan probably would not have recognized her if he had seen her on the street. She was out of uniform and wearing baby-blue slacks with a matching polyester blouse. But it was more than the clothes she was wearing. It was *how* she was wearing them. She looked as if she had been poured into her slacks. Her blouse was sheer, revealing two dark circles where the nipples of her bare breasts gently tugged at the buttons over her bustline. Above them, the blouse was unbuttoned, exposing just enough cleavage to catch his attention. Although they were seated three feet apart, he detected an enticing fragrance of perfume. For a moment, it seemed to Jonathan that he was sitting there as a prelude to some wild, exotic affair. He thought of Danielle and squirmed a little in his seat, looking suspiciously at the nearby tables.

"Did you want to go someplace else?" she asked. "You seemed quite nervous over the phone."

"No. No, this is fine." Suddenly he was brought back to his reason for being there.

"Why don't you go first?" she suggested. "Your matter seemed somewhat more important than mine. What makes you think my life is in danger?" Her face again showed no emotion.

"I'm sorry, but I can't be too specific. Probably the less you know, the better off you'll be. Let's just say that there's someone out there who brought about Aaron's death and will stop at nothing to hide his involvement."

"Are you suggesting *murder*?" Jensen stared coldly at Jonathan and started fishing in her purse for her cigarettes. Calmly she pulled one out of a gold cigarette case, put it in her mouth, and started flicking at her lighter.

"Yes, I guess I am," he said. Jonathan reached over, took the lighter, and flicked it once.

"Thank you," she said, blowing the smoke out of her mouth. "What makes you think he was murdered?"

"I'd prefer not to say."

"Well, then, would you tell me why you think my life's in danger? I think you at least owe me that."

Jonathan hesitated. He was reluctant to reveal anything he had learned, especially to Jensen, whose involvement was questionable at best. "I *will* say this," he began cautiously. "Last night someone made an attempt on my girl friend's life while she was at our apartment. And it would have been successful, except that I happened to arrive home just in time to stop him."

"Is she all right?"

"Yes, she's fine. Still a little upset, but physically she's fine. . . . But right after your call this morning, I checked the phone and found that it had been bugged—I found a small transmitter inserted into the mouthpiece of the receiver. Then I remembered what you had told me over the same phone. If the murderer heard us through the phone tap—and I have no reason to believe he didn't—he may have some ideas about whether or not you should be talking to me. Of course, if you don't know anything that might implicate the murderer, perhaps there's no danger. Maybe if you told me what you know, we could determine whether you have something to worry about."

Jensen took another puff on her cigarette and started to say something, but stopped when the waiter arrived at their table.

"Would you care for a cocktail, sir, or would you prefer to order?" he asked, filling their water glasses.

Jonathan looked over at Jensen. "I'd like a drink," she said. "A Bloody Mary . . . and hold the Tabasco sauce."

"I'll have the same," Jonathan said, "but *with* the Tabasco."

When the waiter left, Jonathan directed his attention again to Jensen.

"You might as well tell me what you know. It might be our only protection."

Jensen took another drag on her cigarette and forcefully blew the smoke. Her eyes darted around the darkened room.

"You're sure about this?"

Jonathan nodded.

"It's probably nothing at all," she began, "but I heard from an RN who works Recovery that Dr. Feinerman had gotten into a violent argument with another nurse at the hospital only three weeks before he died."

"Who did you hear this from?"

"In view of everything that's happened, I'd rather not say. I've given you the lead. Why can't you take it from there?"

"Well, what was the argument about? If it was violent, it must have been over something quite serious."

"Yes, it was. This nurse had apparently misread some written orders on a patient and had injected him with penicillin for a minor infection at an incision site. The patient, who was noted to be allergic to penicillin, went into anaphylactic shock and almost died. When Dr. Feinerman found out what had happened, he exploded. Within an hour he had the nurse on the carpet, and she was almost fired. As it was, she was put on a three-month probation."

"Who was the nurse? Do you know her name?"

Jensen looked around the room again and then back at Jonathan. "I'd really prefer that *you* find that out. I've said enough already."

"Look, goddammit! I'm tired of playing these fucking games. There's a killer running around out there, and he's probably looking for *you*. Now, do you think we've got time for guessing games?"

A pause, then she said, "Lawrence. Sarah Lawrence."

Jonathan stared at her with a confused and unsettled look. "Are you sure?" he said, narrowing his eyes. This added a new twist to the pattern of facts, and it didn't fit. It *had* to be someone Armstrong hired, not an emotionally weak nurse who killed him in a fit of vengeance. And what about Jensen's earlier threat in the park?

"All I can tell you is that the person who told me overheard the argument. And I doubt that it's a lie. She has no motive for it."

Mentally trying to place this new piece into the puzzle, Jonathan reached over and took a sip of his ice water.

"Yes, I guess you're right," he said, looking at the dancing candlelight in front of him.

As the ice chips melted in his mouth, Jonathan tasted a slight residual bitterness. The thought that such a fine restaurant would use rusty ice water angered him.

"Mary without . . . and with," the waiter said as he arrived with their drinks. Jonathan grabbed his glass, took a big swallow, and waited for the bite of the Tabasco to erase the bitterness.

"Just a minute," Jonathan said before the waiter had a chance to leave. "This water is awful. Could you get us another glass? Maybe you should check it out before you serve anyone else."

"I'm sorry, sir. I'll check into it right away."

*Sure*, he thought, as the waiter left hastily. *He'll take both glasses, pour them into the sink, and forget it was ever mentioned.*

Within a minute, the bitterness had disappeared and Jonathan had taken another sip of his Bloody Mary.

Jensen leaned forward in her seat and said, "You've got to tell me more. This isn't fair. I must protect myself. Who told you Dr. Feinerman was murdered?"

Jonathan examined her eyes. "I can't say."

"Well, do you think it's Sarah Lawrence?"

"Could be, but I doubt it." Jonathan still would not open up. The experience with Rusty had hardened him to his plight.

"Mr. Rand, won't you *please* help me? I have no way to protect myself."

"Something tells me you are *quite* capable of protecting yourself," he said. "Stay with a friend for a week if you feel uneasy. But I doubt that you have anything to worry about."

Jonathan finished his drink, excused himself, and got up to leave. To stay in one spot for more than fifteen minutes made him nervous. A moving target is more difficult to hit, and he still had a number of things to do. "If you need to reach me for any reason," he said, putting his napkin on the table, "leave a message and phone number at my office or with my answering service. I won't be in for the next few days, but I'll be calling in. Good-bye, Miss Jensen."

# Chapter XXIV

Jonathan slammed the cabinet door shut and stood up from behind the bar. "Dammit! They've got to be here someplace." For the past hour he had meticulously searched *The Prescription* for the book of matches from the Cayman Islands. Aaron must have hidden it someplace. He would not have left it just lying around, and he certainly wouldn't have thrown it away. It was too damn important. It was evidence.

Wiping the perspiration from his forehead with his sleeve, he slowly looked around the salon. Where in the hell would he put it? Then his eye focused on the cassette-player cabinet at the opposite end of the room. "Do you suppose?" he said to himself.

Jonathan took a step toward the player and his leg almost collapsed beneath his weight. Instinctively he grabbed the corner of the bar for support. He felt a quivering in his legs, and a wave of lightheadedness overcame him. He looked down at the floor and blinked. Then, just as quickly, the dizziness disappeared. *Must be the heat,* he rationalized.

Inside the open cabinet door, at eye level, sat the small

cardboard box that held the cassette tapes. Jonathan reached up and carefully brought down the box. Just behind the tapes sat the elusive book of matches.

The cover was midnight blue with white Old English lettering: TURTLE SHELL INN. At the bottom in smaller lettering was added: GRAND CAYMAN.

Jonathan immediately noted a familiar trademark. At each corner the laminated paper had been separated, leaving the ends curled. Crenshaw had used these matches, just as he had used the ones last Wednesday at Armstrong's office. It was the same damn habit and it couldn't have been better if he had personally signed the book.

Jonathan dropped the matches into his shirt pocket and started for the door. As he walked across the room he felt weak. His upper abdomen was tight, as if he had just forced himself through a hundred sit-ups. Jonathan closed and locked the door, then cautiously descended the steps to the dock, bewildered by his instability.

He was normally quite healthy. He hadn't been sick since influenza had hit him three and a half years ago. Why now? Maybe he pulled something while crawling around that stupid galley.

At the base of the ramp to the parking lot he looked up, steadying himself with one hand on the railing. The ramp was only twenty feet long and ascended at a thirty-degree angle, but to Jonathan it looked like the side of a mountain.

He began to struggle up the ramp. After three short steps, he stopped to rest and a wave of dizziness hit him again. What was happening to him? He held up his hand and watched it quiver uncontrollably. Perspiration broke out all over his body. He looked up at the top of the ramp again and thought of sitting down. It was too far; he'd never make it. Then with determination he bit his lower lip and forced himself up the remaining fifteen feet.

At the top he stopped and rested, as another attack of lightheadedness came and quickly disappeared. The tightness in his stomach felt like a fist trying to force its way to his back. He looked out at the marina and the river beyond, but the horizon started tilting and he looked back down at the ground to regain his balance.

"Are you all right, sir?"

Jonathan looked up and saw an overweight, bald man

wearing Bermuda shorts and carrying a bag of groceries standing in front of him.

"Yes . . . yes, I'm fine. Thank you. Just a little dizzy spell."

The man walked on.

Jonathan's car was only another seventy-five feet away. Maybe if he sat down and rested he would feel better. And the air-conditioning—the cool air on his face. He *had* to feel better.

Finally he reached the car, opened the door, and dropped onto the seat. For a moment he thought of checking under the hood again, but it was broad daylight, and if he exerted himself any more, he would probably pass out. With difficulty he pulled the heavy door shut, then turned on the ignition. Soon the cool, refreshing air from his air-conditioner was gently massaging his face.

For the next few minutes Jonathan just sat there gaining strength and trying to grasp what was happening. He couldn't remember being exposed to anyone who had been sick; and although he had had little sleep last night, it shouldn't have made him ill. Maybe a little tired, but nothing like this. He thought of his search through the boat, but couldn't remember injuring himself. Maybe it was something he ate or . . . drank. *The water at Hagan's—Jesus, it was bad. But Jensen drank it too. Maybe she's also . . . Oh, my God! No! No, he couldn't be* that *stupid*.

The thought stupid that Jensen had slipped something into his water didn't come easy. He'd thought he was being so careful. Every move had been planned, weighed, and evaluated, and his carelessness made him angry. But it also demonstrated his vulnerability. Jonathan's hands began to shake again. My God, what had she given him?

He had to move—and fast. Jonathan threw the car into reverse, shot back out of the parking lot, then slammed the transmission into drive; the tires screeched as he accelerated. At the exit, he suddenly realized he was traveling too fast and slammed on his brakes while sharply jerking the steering wheel to his left. Like an out-of-control stock car, the rear of the Cadillac began to swing out. He felt the right rear fender bounce off the fence with a jolt.

He knew he had damaged his car, but it didn't mean anything. His head was numb, and he now had only one goal:

to get help—fast. Regaining control, Jonathan shoved his foot onto the accelerator and sped off down the street.

Now he had to make a decision. Was he going to a hospital first—Rivergarden was the closest—or was he going to pick up Danielle? The choice was surprisingly easy. If he entered a hospital alone, he would never walk out. He had to reach Danielle before he went under. Jonathan weakly forced a smile and shook his head. He had never thought he would see the day he had to rely on a woman for his personal safety.

Jonathan fought to keep his eyes open. He wanted to curl up in a ball in the backseat and fall asleep. Every couple of blocks he would try to force his eyes open wide. *I've got to make it, I've got to make it,* he kept telling himself. He directed the vents of the air-conditioner directly into his face, but it was of little help. His whole body was starting to shake. The dull tightness in his abdomen had now advanced to a sharp, piercing pain that was spreading to his back.

Every stoplight, every turn, every block seemed to take an eternity. Then mercifully he screeched to a stop in the garage of the Vista and staggered over to the elevator. Luck was with him and the door opened immediately. He stumbled into the car, pushed the button for the fourteenth floor, leaned against the wall, and waited. Slowly each floor number blinked on above the doors as the elevator climbed. Then the doors opened.

His stomach was churning and saliva was beginning to accumulate in his mouth. Something deep inside felt like it was forcing its way up through him, and his throat started to burn. Jonathan sensed what was about to happen and gave three quick raps on the door, then another.

"Jonathan?" he heard from inside.

"Yes," he said weakly.

The door opened three inches, straining at the lock chain on the door. Through the opening, Jonathan saw Ruth's inquisitive eyes. Then the door shut and immediately opened wide.

"Jonathan, my God, what happened?" Ruth shouted.

Jonathan's face was white and his perspiration-soaked hair hung down over his forehead. Under each arm and on his chest his yellow sport shirt was darkened with sweat. His whole body trembled.

He started to say something, but as he opened his mouth

a surge of nausea hit and he threw his hand up as a dam, and darted through the door. With Danielle and Ruth watching in shock, he dropped to his hands and began to purge his stomach. Again and again he spewed the yellowish green substance from within. Vomit was dripping from his lips and nose as he retched out the remaining bile that filled his mouth.

Within seconds, Danielle and Ruth had thrown a towel over the mess on the floor and were wiping Jonathan's face with a cold washcloth. His head rested in Danielle's lap as she knelt on the floor.

Jonathan looked up at his two rescuers. His eyelids were heavy, but he fought to maintain consciousness.

"I . . . I think . . . I think I've been drugged . . . or something." His eyes closed and then opened again. His voice was barely audible. "Got to get to . . . a . . . hospital. Something I drank at . . . Hagan's."

Ruth looked down at Jonathan's abdomen; it appeared bloated. She gently pressed just below his beltline. Jonathan winced.

"Come on," Ruth said to Danielle. "Give me a hand. We've got to get him to a hospital right away. We don't have a moment to lose."

"Please . . ." said Jonathan, as Danielle helped him to his feet. "Don't . . . leave me."

"Don't worry, honey," Danielle replied. "I won't leave the hospital until you do."

Jonathan tried to open his eyes, but his lids were too heavy. Complete rest; that's what he needed. A complete escape from reality. But what had happened? Where was he? He couldn't understand why, but something deep inside would not let him drift back into total darkness. He had to fight back to a conscious state and he again strained to open his eyes.

This time he was successful. At first he could only perceive some light, then he made out a couple of blurry images beside his bed. Again his eyes closed and opened; the images were a little clearer now. He wanted to talk, but his mouth felt like cotton and his throat was sore.

"Dani?" he whispered hoarsely.

He felt someone grab his right hand. "I'm right here, honey. You're doing fine—just fine."

Now the indistinct figures came into focus. Danielle's eyes

were red and her hair was unkempt. Jonathan started to move his left hand over to Danielle, then felt a sharp jab in his forearm. He looked over and saw a plastic tube taped to the inside of his forearm and leading up to a bottle hanging a couple of feet above him.

"It's an IV," Danielle said. "They've been shooting you full of antibiotics for a few hours."

"When your white count dropped from twenty-two thousand to fourteen thousand, they decided to continue the drugs and hold off on the surgery," Ruth volunteered.

"They also said that if you had come in an hour later, you probably would not have made it. . . . We've been here all the time. They wanted us to leave, but Ruth talked them into allowing us to stay with you. Oh—something else: look at your wristband."

Jonathan weakly held up his right arm and focused on the white band snapped to his wrist. Across the back it said, RAND, JONATHAN L.—NO. 26891—DR. REED. Reed? Jason Reed? No, it must be someone else. Jonathan made no effort to speak but looked inquisitively at his two companions.

"What can I say?" Danielle shrugged. "He was standing right there when the orderly brought you into the emergency room on the stretcher. He must have recognized you, because within seconds he started an examination. Listening . . . looking . . . tapping . . . feeling. Before we knew it, he was shouting orders, drawing blood. People were running all over everywhere—nurses, orderlies, everyone. Of course, I didn't know who he was, and Ruth was too busy helping to say anything. I bet within five minutes you were on your way to intensive care, with that IV sticking in your arm." Danielle hesitated, then added, "He probably saved your life."

Bewildered, Jonathan stared at the two tents formed by his feet at the end of the bed. Why did it have to be Reed? He had enjoyed disliking him—it had made his job easier.

"They brought you out of ICU about an hour ago," said Ruth. "Your white count had already dropped and your vitals were continuing to improve."

"Is Reed still here?" Jonathan asked, sounding a little better.

Danielle brushed back his hair with her hand. "No," she answered, "but he said he would be in first thing in the morning."

"Dani, I have some bad news," he said with torment in his eyes. "It's Rusty. I found him dead in his bedroom."

"Oh, no!"

"The bastards killed him. Shoved a quart of bourbon down his throat and God knows what else."

"Rusty?" Ruth inquired.

"Rusty Murdoch, my investigator. He must have been getting warm. . . . I should have told him what this was all about. Damn! I'll never forgive myself."

"How can you be so sure he was murdered?" Ruth asked.

"I know," Jonathan said. "It was an efficient job—not even a hint of violence. But I know."

"All right, you two," came an authoritative voice from behind them. "Visiting hours are now over. Our patient needs some rest."

Nurse Montgomery walked to the foot of the bed and lowered the opposite end, while Danielle and Ruth kissed Jonathan good-night.

"We'll be downstairs in the lobby, honey. Ruth and I have decided to stay here all night, and if anything happens we've left orders to be notified immediately. We'll also be checking in on you every hour. So don't worry, and get some rest."

Jonathan weakly waved good-night and watched them disappear through the doorway, then directed his attention to Montgomery, who was fluffing up his pillow and straightening his sheets. For the first time he reached down to his groin. Through the sheets and blanket he could feel the plastic tubing, as well as the heavy tape that held it in.

"You be careful with that, Mr. Rand. Too much moving around will irritate it."

Jonathan nodded his understanding.

Finally she held out to him two tablets and a small white cup of water. "Go ahead," she said. "They'll give you some sleep."

"I'll pass," he said, holding up his hand. No one could be trusted. He was as vulnerable as Aaron had been, and every precaution had to be taken.

"Suit yourself. I doubt you'll make it another ten minutes anyway." Montgomery turned out the lights, with the exception of a small night-light on the wall between the beds, and closed the door. Silence followed in the dimly lit room and Jonathan took his first look around.

To his left was the other bed. It was unoccupied and neatly folded down, with clean sheets and a fresh-looking pillow. The blanket, like Jonathan's, was a soft yellow and was neatly tucked under the mattress. Between the beds, just below the night-light, was a small table. On it sat an ashtray, a plastic pitcher full of cold water, and two clear plastic glasses, one half-filled with water and holding a flex straw bent over the edge of the glass. At the end of the room were drapes, which appeared to be drawn over a window.

Jonathan looked at the wall opposite his bed. High up on it was a small television set on a shelf. Below and to the right of the TV was another shelf, which supported a beautiful bouquet of red roses that Jonathan could see just above his feet. He smiled. It made him feel warm inside that something from Danielle was there with him. A personal touch in the otherwise cold and sterile room.

The side railings were up on both sides of the bed, and clipped to one of the vertical rails was a small control box containing a buzzer for the nurses and some buttons for the TV.

Jonathan glanced back at the flowers; they were the last thing he saw before closing his eyes again.


# Chapter XXV


*Tuesday, September 4, 1979*

He awoke trembling. His first thought was that someone had left the window open, but the drapes were still closed. He also noted that it was dark and that the small light over the nightstand was still on. He pulled the blanket up to his neck. His teeth were chattering and his breathing was labored. He tried to take a deep breath, but it was impossible. He couldn't understand it; he had been feeling so much better. Maybe it was a slight relapse. If he waited, it would probably go away. He was sure of it.

As Jonathan lay waiting, his thoughts flashed back to Aaron. He recalled his medical chart, which he now had almost committed to memory. First came the elevated temperature, then the perspiration and shaking chills. Finally, in his waning minutes, his pulse and respiration had shot sky high; then the overwhelming weakness and cardiac arrest.

Again he tried to inhale deeply—but no sooner would he breathe in than his lungs would spontaneously exhale. The similarity in the patterns added to his anxiety. He could now hear his already rapid pulse thumping in his ears. It got louder and louder until it consumed his every conscious thought. A drop of perspiration ran down his forehead to his cheek and he automatically reached up with his left hand to wipe it off.

What he saw threw him into panic. Where the life-supporting IV had been inserted into the vein in his forearm, there was nothing more than a tiny hole and a spot of dried blood. He looked up at the IV bottle hanging from the metal stand. From the bottom of the bottle, he followed the four feet of hanging tube to a point where the needle was dripping antibiotics uselessly onto the floor. The adhesive tape was still attached to the needle and tube.

He grabbed the control box and pushed the button to summon the RN at the nurses' station. A red light would blink on and someone would be there within a minute.

How had it happened? Had he inadvertently pulled it out during his sleep? He had heard of such things happening, but it didn't seem likely. He had awakened in virtually the same position as he was in when he had fallen asleep. Besides, if he had been tossing and turning, his bed would have been a mess. The alternative, of course, was that *someone else* had pulled it out.

Where the hell was the damn nurse? With a mixture of fear and anger he again pressed the button. This time he pushed harder, four times. Subconsciously he knew it wouldn't make a difference.

Still she didn't come. Five minutes had now passed and Jonathan was getting weaker. Again he pressed the button. This wasn't really happening. He *had* to be dreaming.

Then a thought that had been nagging at him exploded into a startling realization: *no one was going to come.* He was dying and there was no one to help him.

Jonathan rolled onto his left side and grabbed the top of the bed rail with his right hand. In a brief second, before falling back onto his bed, he saw something that confirmed his deepest fear: the plug at the other end of the control box had been disconnected and was lying on the floor. Nothing had happened by accident. He was being murdered.

Jonathan tried to call out for help, but his rapid breathing and weakness made it a futile act.

He had to get to the door. It was his only chance. Whatever it took, he had to get there. He looked at the side rails and realized that he might as well have been in a jail. He could never climb them. Then he noted that the railing at the foot of his bed was significantly lower. That was it—his only avenue of escape.

For a moment Jonathan lost consciousness. When he regained his senses, he used his left hand to pull himself up to a sitting position. He felt like he weighed five hundred pounds.

As he sat up, the room began to spin and a wave of nausea hit him. Jonathan hooked his arm over the rail to support himself. He tried closing his eyes, but that only made him dizzier, so he opened them and stared at the bed. To keep from vomiting, he attempted to swallow, but he had become too dehydrated. He merely gagged. Nothing came up. Only some bile, which sent a burning sensation searing up his throat.

Jonathan curled his legs beneath him and slowly crawled to the end of the bed. The floor looked as if it were ten feet below. With considerable difficulty, he pulled his right leg over the railing, straddling it and balancing himself on his chest.

Then as Jonathan's right leg began to drop, his grip weakened and slipped from the railing, and he fell to the floor, rolling like a log on his way down. With a stunning thud, he struck the floor. His right cheek slammed into the wheel of the bed, throwing his head back and leaving him flat on his back. Again he lost consciousness.

As he came to, Jonathan groaned and reached up to feel his face. A welt was rising just below his cheekbone. Everything was spinning, and the sound of his heartbeat had been replaced by a deafening buzz. He could not think clearly. Every move, every reaction, wary instinct.

Rolling over and rising to his hands and knees, he began crawling toward the door. Every inch of his body seemed racked with pain. After a couple of feet, his shaking left arm collapsed and he fell to the floor, flat onto his face. From his stomach he peered toward the door. At the bottom, about ten feet away, he could see a fuzzy line of light. "I've got to make it," he whispered to himself, and continued crawling.

Finally he reached the door and looked up. Above him was the metal handle. Jonathan reached up but was too weak to grasp it. Then in final desperation, with every ounce of his remaining strength, he stretched back his arm and threw his fist into the door. And again . . . and again.

Jake Thurman was half-asleep when he heard the first thud. After all, there wasn't much for an orderly to do at three-fifteen in the morning. The night was quiet, and other than an occasional bed check by the nursing assistant, there was no activity. So there he stood, sleepily mopping a small section of the hallway, waiting for the early morning hours to pass.

But as the third tap echoed down the hallway, he knew something was wrong and was on his way. Initially he tried to open the door to Jonathan's room—but it was blocked. He shoved and felt something heavy give on the other side of the door. Having forced a gap wide enough for his head, he leaned in and saw Jonathan on the floor.

"What the hell! . . . Nurse!" he yelled to the nurses' station seventy-five feet down the hall. "Call ER, we have a patient on the floor."

# Chapter XXVI

"All right, young man," said Montgomery, firmly gripping Jonathan's wrist. "Time for vitals." She looked down at her watch, silently mouthing the numbers.

"Come on, Mr. Rand. Time to wake up. Seems all you patients want to do anymore is *sleep*. It's a conspiracy. Clear and simple. All designed to dump the workload on the poor nursing staff." She spoke kiddingly, but with a professional smoothness.

Jonathan opened his eyes and blinked twice.

"There we are. And how do we feel this morning?"

Jonathan looked at her inquisitively, then up at the IV

bottle. There it was. Hanging just like before, the intravenous medication coursing its way down the plastic tube and through the needle inserted into his forearm. The adhesive tape still covered the needle.

Had it been a nightmare?

He looked at his sheets and blanket neatly folded and tucked in.

"What time is it?" he softly asked.

"Six A.M. . . . Open up. You gave us all a scare last night," she continued. "Of all things. Taking a walk in the middle of the night—and without even telling us, mind you." Montgomery picked up the armband to record Jonathan's blood pressure. "Next time the need arises, though, I want you to buzz me. No heroic ventures over the end of your bed."

Jonathan tried to say something, but it came out as a mumble.

"I know. I know. It was unplugged last night. But that won't happen again. We just had the maintenance man secure the plug with another set of screws. I guess the old ones must have fallen out."

She removed the thermometer and held it up to the light.

"Where's Dani?" he asked. "Danielle Brennan . . . my girl."

"Don't you worry about her," she said, smiling warmly. "She's doing fine. Miss Brennan and Mrs. Feinerman are both down in the lobby . . . probably still sound asleep. There," she noted with a final swirl of the pen on the chart. "I would say you're doing quite well—*amazingly* well," she emphasized. "In a couple more days you should be good as new."

Jonathan looked down at his fingernails and the skin of his forearms, noting the small red-brown flecks of capillary hemorrhage, the only stigma left from the bizarre febrile attack that had almost cost him his life. *Petechial hemorrhaging*, Jonathan thought. *Just like Aaron.*

"What happened to me last night?" he asked suspiciously.

"I really don't know, Mr. Rand. It seems the orderly found you on the floor. You had apparently crawled out over the end of your bed. You also took a pretty good wallop on your cheek last night. Probably from falling out of the bed."

Jonathan reached up and felt the tender lump under his right eye. "Did you know that I woke up during the night without my IV? In fact, it was hanging from the bottle alongside my bed."

Montgomery looked at him, startled. "You . . . you must be mistaken. I'm sure it was a dream."

"It wasn't a dream. I was as wide awake as I am right now."

"Well, I'm sure you must have pulled it out during your sleep. It's rare, but it's been known to happen before."

"No. There is no way I pulled it out myself—accidentally or otherwise. I'm normally a sound sleeper and I never toss and turn. Besides, I was so weak I could hardly lift my hand, let alone pull off the adhesive and take out the needle in my sleep. And my bed—when I awoke, there wasn't a sheet or blanket out of place."

"I'm sure there's *some* reasonable explanation," said a bewildered Montgomery.

"There is. Someone came in here last night and removed the IV while I was asleep."

"What!"

"That's right. Someone tried to kill me last night. And I bet everything I own it was the same person who killed Aaron Feinerman."

Montgomery shook her head, her eyes wide with astonishment. "I don't believe I'm hearing this. You're talking about *murder?*"

"I am. There have also been two attempts on *my* life."

Montgomery looked at Jonathan as if he were a psychiatric patient. "I . . . I think I had better report this, Mr. Rand," she said, backing up. "If we have murderers running around our hospital, the police should be notified—and the sooner the better."

"Please don't leave. I'm not crazy and I haven't been hallucinating. I know how this must seem to you, but . . . I know you find this difficult to believe, Mrs. Montgomery. But let me ask you this. Have you seen Maureen Jensen tonight?" Jonathan helped himself higher in the bed.

"No, she never showed up for work. I guess she must be ill."

"Did anyone call her?"

"Yes, but there was no . . . I'm not sure I should be talking to you about this, Mr. Rand. I might be getting myself into a lot of trouble."

"Please, Mrs. Montgomery. Nobody will ever hear it from *me*. But I've got to know. Did she answer the phone?"

Montgomery hesitated. "No. There was no answer. She's probably staying with a friend. Maybe a boyfriend. Who knows? It's not my business anyway."

"Doesn't it strike you as a little strange that Miss Jensen would fail to report without even calling in?"

Montgomery didn't answer, wanting to leave but too stunned from the implied accusation to react. Something had always bothered her about Maureen Jensen.

"I seem to recall you were on duty the night of Dr. Feinerman's death. Am I correct?"

Montgomery nodded, staring hard into Jonathan's eyes. "Yes. I was subbing as floor supervisor that night."

"I only want you to think about this for a second. Do you recall seeing Maureen Jensen at the hospital at any time that night?"

Montgomery opened her mouth as if to say something, shaking her head back and forth. "I've got to go," she said slowly.

As she reached the door, Jonathan yelled, "For God's sake, she tried to kill me yesterday . . . and probably this morning too. *Please!*"

Montgomery froze in her tracks, holding the door partially open, not looking back.

"Did you *see* her?" Jonathan asked again. "Did you see her at all, that night?"

Montgomery nodded, still staring at the door.

"*Please*, Mrs. Montgomery. If you know something—*anything*—you've got to tell me. My life may depend on it."

Slowly she turned and looked at Jonathan, letting the door ease shut again. "Yes . . . yes, I saw her that night."

Jonathan pulled himself even higher in the bed, squinting from the pain. "Where? What time? Please tell me whatever you remember."

Montgomery took a step toward the bed. Her head felt almost numb as she began to realize that she had been carrying incriminating knowledge for the past three months. "I *did* see her," she said. "I had just started my rounds. Must have been around eleven-thirty. I was carrying my tray of medications when I noticed Maureen walk out of Dr. Feinerman's room. She . . . seemed to be in a bit of a hurry and never saw me.

At first I was a little surprised, since I knew she was still on vacation. But I figured she was visiting after his surgery. They always did seem to be a little friendly. But . . . but there had always been something that bothered me about it, and I never could quite put my finger on it until . . . now."

"What was it? What was bothering you?"

Montgomery's brow furrowed. "She was wearing her *uniform*. If she was only visiting, why would she put on her uniform? She certainly didn't need it to go into his room. . . . Isn't that funny, it's been nagging at me all this time and it didn't really hit me until right now."

"Well, *I* know why she wore a uniform," said Jonathan. "So she wouldn't be conspicuous. With a nurse's uniform on, she would have blended right in with the rest of the staff. At *that* hour, if she had worn her street clothes, she would have drawn attention. Something she didn't want."

"What should I do?" Montgomery asked.

Jonathan thought for a moment. "Don't mention this to anyone. Not yet. I've got to have a chance to talk with her."

"I don't know. It seems that this should be reported to the police right away."

"Give me just two days. Then go ahead and tell them what you know. All I want is a little more time. They would never arrest her on the basis of this information anyway. Believe me, there's something of vital importance that I *must* find out before she's tipped off."

"Okay. Two days, then I go to the police." After one last glance at Jonathan, she disappeared through the door.

The brilliance of the early-morning sun filtering through the lush green plants in front of the bay windows in the lobby foretold of a warm, sparkling late-summer day. Inside, wrapped like cocoons in lightweight blankets, Danielle and Ruth slept soundly in a corner of the room.

The all-night housekeeping crew finished their work with great quiet and care, trying to avoid waking the two women. But the usual hustle and bustle of the seven-o'clock shift was just now getting under way. Early arrivals for the day shift were pulling into the parking lot, the team leaders for both shifts were exchanging reports on the activities of the patients over the night, and new admissions were beginning to trickle in. The hospital was starting to come alive.

* * *

At 7:10 A.M. a much-subdued Jason Reed entered Jonathan's room. His usual egocentricity was not evident and the look on his face betrayed genuine concern.

"Good morning, Mr. Rand," he stated, still maintaining a professional atmosphere. The tone, however, was not hostile as it had been in the past. "And how are *you* doing this morning? Considering what you've been through, I'm amazed to see you sitting up in bed."

Jonathan felt uncomfortable and began to fidget with his wristband. "I . . . guess I'm doing fine," he said, with some uncertainty. "What happened to me yesterday—and last night?"

"Well . . . it seems you had a cecal perforation, apparently due to pasteurella pseudotuberculosis. Then, just when we thought we had you out of it, you developed an acute septicemia that was leading to a disseminated intravascular coagulation process. Fortunately, the emergency-room crew, under my direction, managed to control it with massive intravenous antibiotics and heparin."

"Come again?"

"When you were first brought in, a hole was beginning to form in your large intestine, apparently caused by a highly virulent bug called pasteurella pseudotuberculosis. This later relapsed into a severe infection of the blood, which was tending to coagulate throughout your body. We treated it with antibiotics and an anticoagulant called heparin."

Reed walked over, inserted his stethoscope into his ears, and began listening at various locations on Jonathan's chest. He next checked the pulse rate against his watch.

"Almost down to normal," Reed said while pulling the stethoscope from his ears.

"You mentioned that you were directing the emergency-room crew last night?"

"Uh-huh," he answered, not looking up from the chart.

"Does that mean you were actually down here at the hospital?" Jonathan felt uneasy about the question.

Reed looked up and stared for a moment. "Yes, it does," he said without expression. Reed set the medical chart down on the bed, crossed his arms, and looked down at the floor for a moment. "Mr. Rand, I know you don't believe this, but I *am* a good doctor. I realize that I might come off a little cocky at times, but that is often a byproduct of being highly skilled at one's profession."

Feeling embarrassed, Jonathan said, "I'm sorry, Doctor. I was just a little surprised. . . . I should be thanking you for saving my life."

"Surprised?" Reed nodded knowingly. "I can understand. All too well, I can." He looked over at the window, where the drapes had been opened. "Sometimes circumstances do not lend themselves to doing certain things that you later wish you had done. . . . You may not know this, but Aaron Feinerman was a friend of mine. A good friend. I wish things had happened differently, but . . ." His voice trailed off sadly.

Jonathan cleared his throat and said, "Look, Dr. Reed, about that lawsuit. I hope you understand that this in no way attacks your professional competence. It only charges that on this one occasion you got a little careless . . . you made a mistake . . . something we *all* do from time to time."

Reed still stared, deep in thought. "Careless . . ." He shook his head. "I only wish it were that simple."

"Sometimes it helps to talk about things like this. If you're worried about the lawsuit, you have my complete assurance that I will never repeat one word mentioned in this room."

Reed smiled, but still continued his blank stare out the window. "Mr. Rand, by now I should think you would know I don't give a damn *who* quotes me."

"I guess I should. I . . . I just feel it's about time that you and I had a straight talk about Aaron's death. You're carrying around a false burden."

Reed took a deep, purging breath and exhaled. "You're going to have to be more explicit," he said distantly. "I've had very little sleep over the past twenty-four hours and am not too sharp right now."

"Someone used you—used your surgery, anyway. You were a pawn."

"What are you talking about?" Reed seemed to be getting irritated.

"I'm telling you, Dr. Reed, that someone wanted Aaron dead and used your surgery to do it—that and a lethal organism called anthrax."

Reed suddenly became pale and eased himself into a chair. "You're . . . you're talking about—"

"I'm talking about *murder*."

"That's crazy. Why would anyone want to kill Aaron?"

"He knew too much about something—I'm not sure what. But he was silenced."

"But who . . . ?" Reed was visibly shaken.

"Let me put it this way," offered Jonathan, who at the moment was intent on baring his soul; he had always found it to be the best way to get at the truth. "Four hours before Aaron broke into severe shaking chills, Maureen Jensen was seen coming out of his room. This was at a time when she was allegedly out of town on vacation. But, more incriminating than that, she was wearing a uniform. A *uniform*, mind you, when she wasn't even working."

"That's impossible," snapped Reed. "She was . . . she was . . ."

"She was what?"

Reed closed his eyes in anguish. "She was with me that night."

Jonathan nodded his understanding. It was all beginning to make sense now. "But at what time? At ten forty-five the evening before he died, she was at this hospital. It must have been later."

"It was. She met me at my home somewhere around midnight."

"A prearranged time?"

"Yes."

"It fits. According to my pathologist, someone injected a vial of anthrax bacillus into Aaron's IV. Jensen probably did it late in the evening after the surgery, then went to see you to ensure you would never do anything about it. Since you were married, she figured you would never mention the visit to anyone. As I said, you were a pawn."

Reed's head dropped, his face twisting in anguish.

"God, no! Jesus, don't do this to me!" His head trembled. "You're lying, aren't you? For God's sake, please tell me you're lying!"

Jonathan looked at him sympathetically. "No," he said, shaking his head. "No, I'm not."

Reed raised his hand to his forehead. "God, why am I being punished? Haven't I had enough?" Slowly he rose and walked to the window. Three floors below he could see several of his colleagues parking their cars and walking toward the hospital. At that moment he was envious of them all. "I can't believe this has happened."

Jonathan's eyes were fixed on Reed. "It might help to talk about it. I'm not taking this too well myself."

"You don't understand. What's happened has happened. It's my destiny . . . my fate."

"You're being too hard on yourself."

"Don't you understand? I was used. The night Aaron lay dying in this hospital, I was sharing a bed with his killer. Jesus . . . I was being fucked and . . ." Reed began an insane laugh. "Oh, how I was being fucked. Me and my life." Again laughter.

Jonathan began to grasp the complete story. He looked at Reed with pity. Reed had been used and now had to live with the knowledge that he had been instrumental in the murder of a friend.

"She had the whole thing planned," he continued, wiping his tearing eyes. "Only a couple of weeks earlier, we had talked in the hospital cafeteria. Just by chance we happened to be sitting near each other . . . well, maybe not by chance. Anyway, she started coming on strong—how she had always admired me, how she was turned on by famous surgeons. I had never had such a beautiful woman throw herself at me and . . . I guess I wanted to believe it."

Jonathan listened, unable to say anything.

"Then she suggested that we get together some night. She said she was going on a vacation but would like to see me the Saturday after she got back. Of course, I never dreamed of associating the meeting with Aaron's surgery . . . and it *did* give me the chance to convince my wife to visit her mother over that weekend.

"Then, about midnight she showed up, a bottle of Canadian Club in hand, wearing a tight dress with a plunging neckline and doused in a perfume that was . . . hypnotizing. By the time I got the call on Aaron, I was half-drunk and totally occupied. I guess her timing was absolutely perfect. She had already done her thing at the hospital. Then, in the most effective way that she could, she ensured that I would be of no help. . . . How am I ever going to live with this?" Reed's glassy eyes again gazed down at the floor. "But I don't understand. Why would she want to kill Aaron? What could he possibly know about her that she would want to kill him over?"

"She was a hired killer," said Jonathan. "Probably planted here over a year ago. The information involved someone else."

"Who?"

"I can't say."

"You *won't* say."

"You're right," said Jonathan. His plan was contingent upon Armstrong's involvement being unknown by anyone. Only then would Jonathan's threat of disclosure have value. "It's best that you not know. For your own safety if for no other reason."

Reed laughed again. "At this moment my safety doesn't seem too important to me. I was unfaithful and it cost my dearest friend his life. And that's something I don't know if I can ever come to grips with."

Finally Reed straightened up. "I'll be in again this afternoon to remove the drain. You'll have to excuse me now." Composing himself for his walk down the hallway, he added, "I've got a lot of thinking to do . . . some important decisions to make."

Jonathan closed his eyes, cursing his big mouth. A fatal flaw for a lawyer and one he had worked hard to eliminate. But his disclosure had produced a vital piece of evidence, and he was fighting for survival. Reed would have to deal with his own problems in his own way.

Jonathan pondered Reed's feelings of guilt, wondering what impact they might have on the lawsuit. Would he go so far as to concede his neglect? But then again, he now knew about the anthrax.

The *lawsuit!* For the first time the word seemed out-of-place. At the moment, the fact that he had a case pending against Reed and the hospital seemed almost silly; certainly small and insignificant compared to the nightmare he had uncovered.

Suddenly the door burst open, revealing a breakfast cart pushed by the day-shift orderly. "*Good* morning," he said, his manner cheerful and exuberant. "Food man is here. Serving delectable morsels of cuisine from that world-famous haven of the culinary arts, locally known as the cafeteria of Rivergarden Community Hospital. Caterer to the sick, the lame, and the aged. Restaurant for the rich and poor alike. *Everyone* stays and enjoys the food at Rivergarden."

Jonathan smiled as the orderly served him.

"Oh, just one thing," said the orderly. "Don't touch a morsel until I get my butt out of here."

Jonathan laughed and lifted the cover from the first dish, as the orderly scooted out of the room.

However, his grin changed to a snarl as he discovered a bowl of gruel that Oliver Twist would have rejected. Hoping for better, he lifted the second cover. What he saw made his stomach turn. There, sitting loosely in the middle of the dish, were two barely coddled soft-boiled eggs. *Soft-boiled eggs*: he hated them.

With some reservation, Jonathan picked up the toast and started poking at the eggs. He swallowed hard and began mopping up the yolks with the toast. Some of the vitamins and protein must have survived the cook's assault on the breakfast, and one thing he needed badly was energy and strength. Even if it made him sick, he *had* to eat the breakfast—all of it. He must have the strength to leave the hospital today.

No sooner had he forced down the last bit of toast than Danielle and Ruth came in. Both looked somewhat haggard, but smiled as if they had just arisen from a twelve-hour sleep.

"Morning, honey," Danielle said as she walked over to the bed. Her hair was unkempt and dark shadows hung beneath her eyes. Ruth looked no better. Danielle leaned over and kissed Jonathan on the cheek.

"Morning," replied Jonathan. He smiled and added, "You two look more like patients than I do."

"I *feel* like a patient," said Ruth, yawning and rubbing the back of her neck. "One night on that concrete bench they call a couch is enough to put *anyone* into a hospital."

"You spent the whole night in the lobby?"

"Only about five or six hours," Danielle answered. "They woke us up at three when they found you out of your bed. After that I spent the next couple of hours up here, trying to sleep in a chair. But about five I gave up and hit the couch in the lobby." Still perplexed about the events of the night, she asked, "What in the world *happened*? They said you pulled out your IV and crawled over the end of your bed."

"All I can remember is waking up feeling like I was being suffocated. At first I couldn't understand why. I had been doing so well. But then I saw my IV tube hanging next to the bed, dripping onto the floor. I couldn't believe it. It was like a dream. Then I tried to buzz the nurse. That's when I really began to panic. I found the cord to my buzzer had been disconnected from the wall."

Ruth looked at him in astonishment. "My God, Jon. Do you know what you're suggesting?"

"You're damn right I do. Somebody pulled them out. It sure as hell wasn't an accident. There's a killer running loose in this hospital, and I'm sitting here in this goddamn bed like a target in a penny arcade."

"Then it's time we went to the police," Ruth demanded. "I'm fed up with this lawsuit, and I'm not going to let you die trying to pursue it."

"She's right," Danielle added.

"I don't think you two understand," Jonathan snapped. "There isn't a place in this country where we're safe. A hospital, a restaurant, your home; and even the goddamn police department. Any place can be infiltrated, and no place is a sanctuary."

Motioning to the two visitor's chairs, Jonathan continued, "I want you to sit down a moment. I've got a few things to tell you. I've had quite an education this morning."

Jonathan revealed everything he had learned from Montgomery and Reed. When he finished, the two women sat speechless, trying to grasp what was happening to their lives.

For a moment Jonathan looked at them. "Things are happening pretty fast, but I know we can get out of this. I'm sure of it. But I've got to get out of here and find Jensen. And I mean this morning. She's *got* to be the key to getting to Armstrong."

"What!" Ruth exclaimed. "You've got to be crazy! You can't leave here now! You're still on intravenous antibiotics."

"Well, I'll not spend another night in this hospital. I'm like a steer waiting for the slaughter. I'm hooked up like a machine, flat on my back, not knowing whom to trust, what to eat. Reed said he would be in this afternoon. So I'll wait until then. But not a minute later."

"Okay," Ruth said. "Then it's agreed. You stay until this afternoon. In the meantime, let me see if I can help. You mentioned a nurse seeing a vial in Aaron's room. Let me check with the bug ranch, as we used to call it. If you're right about what happened, microbiology may have a record of a theft around the time of Aaron's surgery."

"Good idea," Jonathan observed. "You'll be looking for

something on anthrax. Remember, Lundgren believes Aaron was injected in some way with anthrax bacillus."

"Something else I'll never forget," Ruth responded.

Jonathan nodded to Danielle. "Why don't you go with her, Dani? There's nothing to do around here, and you might be able to help her."

"Not on your life," she snapped. "Not after what happened last night. They'll have to carry me out of here before I leave you alone again. I don't leave this room until *you* do."

"She's right," Ruth agreed. "Why take a chance on something else happening? Besides, I know the staff in microbiology and shouldn't have any problem."

# Chapter XXVII

Reed sat in his Silver Cloud, his hands gripping the steering wheel, unwilling to relinquish their hold on life, success, and prosperity. His face was ashen and lifeless. His eyes had the sadness of a man who has given up, resigned to the inevitable.

Finally he dropped his hands, pulled himself from the car, and stood looking at the front door to his house. He had tentatively made his decision as to what was going to happen inside. Something he had always thought himself incapable of. Still, the decision had been surprisingly easy. His home was merely a place to stop, a respite between the long hours at the hospital and his office. His whole life was geared to his reputation as a surgeon. All his energies, goals, and ambitions were focused on being the best.

Now his professional reputation was on the verge of being destroyed. The police would soon learn the facts surrounding Aaron's death. And that would mean questions. Questions he would have to answer.

He indulged himself in a last look at the parklike grounds in front of his home. Some of the leaves were beginning to turn brown, shadows were longer, and autumn was around the corner. Inside, he looked for Patricia, but she wasn't around. Probably she was upstairs sewing. He opened the double doors to his study, then quietly closed them behind himself. His shoulders hung heavy; his eyes were glassy and distant. He looked at his desk. Inside the top right-hand drawer was a .38 revolver. Loaded.

The rumor of his affair with Jensen would be flowing through the hospital grapevine. They had always been against him before, but at least he had had their respect and envy as a surgeon. Now he wouldn't have that.

Nostalgically he gazed at the medical textbooks that covered one wall. Thousands of hours had gone into reading them. He had actually calculated it out one time. The equivalent of three years and two months of solid reading. No one had ever believed that he had actually read *all* the books. But he had.

Now it seemed a meaningless and useless waste of time.

Reed hesitated, then pulled open the top right drawer. The polished black gun gave him a feeling of finality. His shaking hand reached down, then stopped. Fighting for courage, he closed his eyes and tried to swallow the tightness in his throat.

Patricia! As usual, he had almost forgotten Patricia. He had to tell her why. He owed her at least that. His affection for her had dwindled over the years, but he still respected her and cherished her companionship. And in his own distorted way he knew he still loved her.

After a few moments of pondering, he began to write.

> Dearest Patricia,
> I am sitting here trying to think of the words that would best describe to you the set of circumstances and pressures that have led me to what I am about to do. It isn't easy. Up until Aaron died in June, I was on top of my world. I had reached the pinnacle of success professionally. Then it all changed.
> It is the events of that night last June that make it impossible for me to go on living. Not since the day we lost Randy, eighteen years ago, have I failed a patient like I did Aaron.

Reed paused, recalling Patricia screaming for him from the backyard of their home. Their son had fallen from the large oak tree behind the garage. Upon reaching him, he had quickly diagnosed a punctured and collapsed lung. Short of time, he had tried an emergency operation in his home, but he had been unsuccessful in stopping the internal bleeding. Randy had died of shock in the ambulance on the way to the hospital. Painfully Reed relived the tragic sequence, just as he had many times over the years.

Two times I received calls that night, but I ignored them. I knew the staff was panicking, but I just felt they were overreacting. That's what I have been telling myself. But deep inside I know that if I had done what was right, I would have gone down to the hospital, and Aaron would be alive today.

That's what keeps tearing at me. That, plus my reason for staying home. In truth, Aaron was not the only person I failed that night. I also failed you. The reason I never answered those calls from the nursing staff was because I was sharing our bed with another woman.

I only hope you will believe me now, when I tell you that it was the only time that I was unfaithful to you during the entire twenty-nine years of our marriage. Still, I know I have let you down in many other ways. I know our marriage had degenerated to the point

With a loud click the door to the study opened and Patricia stood staring at Reed.

"What are you doing home? I thought you were making rounds this morning."

Reed nervously tried to compose himself.

"I . . . I only stopped in on Rand. He's doing . . . fine." Reed stroked his bald head, trying to think of an explanation. His scalp gleamed with perspiration. "Russ Simpson is covering for the rest of my patients. I wanted to get home to . . . uh . . . work on my lecture at Yale next week." Reed's trembling hands covered the letter in front of him. "I shouldn't be much longer."

Patricia took a few steps toward the desk. "Is there anything wrong? You don't look well."

"No," he said, closing the top right drawer as inconspicuously as possible. "No, I'm just fine. Just a little tired from last night. All I need is a quick nap and I'll be as good as new. Maybe I can catch forty winks this afternoon."

"Did you have anything to eat before you went in this morning?"

"No, just a quick cup of coffee."

"Why don't I fix you some bacon and eggs. A little food in your stomach might help."

Reed started to decline, then caught himself. Fixing breakfast would keep her occupied. "Sure. Bacon and eggs would be fine. Maybe a short stack of hotcakes on the side, too. You know how I love hotcakes."

"Okay. The works. I shouldn't be over twenty minutes or half an hour, so try to finish up if you can."

Patricia turned to leave; then it dawned on Reed that this would be the last time he would ever see her.

"*Patty!*" he called out.

She stopped and turned back, looking curiously at Reed's troubled face. "'Patty'? You haven't called me that in years. Are you sure there's nothing wrong?"

"No," he replied, forcing a smile. "Nothing's wrong. Just wanted to . . ." Reed hesitated, the words seeming clumsy to him. "You *do* know I love you, don't you, Patty?"

Patricia nodded, trying to understand the unusual behavior. "I guess I'm . . . *Sure* I do. I'm just not used to hearing you say it. . . . If there's something bothering you, I really wish you'd tell me about it."

"Nothing to tell," he assured her.

Reed waited a few moments, then hastily continued his letter. He wrote of his conversation with Jonathan and attempted to explain why he couldn't live knowing his weakness had been a useful and necessary factor in Aaron's killing. Finally, he professed his love, then dropped his pencil to the desk.

He couldn't delay now. She would be back shortly.

Reed pulled open the drawer and reached inside. Unable to look at the instrument of his own death, he began feeling around until he touched the smooth, hard metal of the gun. It felt cold as he closed his hand around the handle. For the first time, the ominous reality of what he was about to do overcame him. He swallowed hard, his hands shook, and his ears filled with a numbing buzz.

It would be quick. He knew exactly where to place the barrel, if only he could steady his hands. Reed pulled back the hammer until he heard it click into place. A slight squeeze and he would retire to oblivion, total blackness . . . peace. Still he couldn't look at the gun, as he continued to squeeze his eyes shut. If he saw it, he might lose his nerve.

Reed leaned forward, supporting his arms on the desk, both hands holding the gun pointing back at his face, his right thumb over the trigger. *Please forgive me, Patty*. His mind whirled as a parade of images flashed through. Reed leaned forward, swallowing the barrel of the .38.

At that moment, the door swung open and Patricia stood at the entrance to the study, a glass of orange juice in her hand.

"Jason, I thought you might be interested in a glass of—"

For a moment Patricia stood frozen, her face changing first into a perplexed frown and then to a pale expression of horror.

"Jason, *nooooo!*" she screamed, as the glass dropped from her hand and shattered on the hardwood floor.

For what seemed an eternity, Patricia's whole world turned in slow motion. Helplessly she waited to see the back of Reed's head fragment and pepper the wall behind his desk.

Reed opened his eyes and for a breathless moment stared pleadingly at Patricia. His thumb still rested on the trigger.

Patricia mouthed the word *please*. She stood motionless, fearful that any movement might provoke a reflex that would fire the gun. "Please," she said, in a very soft whisper.

Reed continued to hold his position, a man teetering between destruction and retreat.

Then he slowly pulled the barrel from his mouth and laid the .38 down on his desk. "Why, Jason? Why?" she asked.

Reed briefly looked up at her with saddened eyes, then slowly back down at the desk top.

"My God, what's happened to us?" she cried, throwing her hands up to her face and sobbing.

Reed pulled his heavy frame from the chair, walked over to Patricia, and handed her the letter.

Intently, Patricia reviewed the three-page letter. Upon

concluding, she dropped her hands to her lap and despondently stared down at the floor.

"Now you know," said Reed, with a note of finality.

Patricia finally looked up at him. "Why . . . why couldn't we have talked about this?"

"I didn't want to hurt you."

"*Hurt me!* What did you think your suicide would do?"

"Suicide is a selfish act. This was something that was decided without thinking of anyone . . . that is, anyone but me."

"But why couldn't we have talked about this? I know we could have worked it out. At least we could have tried."

"I didn't want to burden you with it. I made the mistakes. Why should you have to carry around the same problems? This was something I had to work out by myself."

Patricia looked at Reed through reddened eyes. Tears had stained a path through her makeup. "In all the years we've been married, you've never shared anything with me. Not once. If only you could have trusted me to sit down and discuss this, you would have seen how understanding I really am."

Reed stared at her apologetically. "I never thought you could handle this. Not another woman."

"I know what our life has been like together, the emptiness, the routine. . . . I would have understood."

Taking a deep breath, Reed said, "Do you think . . . maybe . . . maybe we could spend some time talking this morning?"

Patricia nodded her agreement.


Jonathan stood in a phone booth outside the entrance to Rivergarden Hospital. He had just been discharged, and a brief check with Sally at the office had left him perplexed. Someone had left a message. Someone he had not thought of in weeks.

"I'll just be a minute," he said to Danielle, who stood nearby holding a small suitcase. "Bill Nicholas called me. Apparently something urgent. Sally said he seemed upset."

He dialed the number given to him by Sally.

"I thought he didn't want anything to do with you," Danielle said.

"Not since he talked to Rusty. Claims he was blackballed in this town because he gave us a statement. I guess he's living down in Westport now. . . . Oh, yes, operator! One minute." Jonathan pulled some coins out of his pocket and dumped them down the slot. Fifteen minutes earlier he had signed himself out "against advice of physician." He was weak, lightheaded, and had a burning pain in his groin, but he was determined not to delay his investigation another hour. Things were happening fast—too fast. It was as if he were being swept up in a big wave. If he didn't start swimming now, he would be sucked under. Finally the phone at the other end started ringing. It was promptly picked up.

"Dr. Nicholas here," said a trembling voice.

"Dr. Nicholas, this is Jonathan Rand. You wanted to talk to me?"

"You're damn right I do! What's going on up there? What kind of people are you involved with?"

Jonathan was taken aback by Nicholas's anger. "What the hell are you talking about?"

"Your *fucking* lawsuit! *That's* what I'm talking about! I don't know what's going on, but it's gonna stop—and now!"

"What's going to stop? What in the hell happened?"

A momentary silence as Nicholas strained for control. "Things have not been easy for me this past month. First I lost my job. Then I had to move out of my home. Now this!"

"For Christ's sake, would you tell me what's wrong?"

"My *lab!* That's what's wrong. It ain't much. It's small and needs some equipment. But it's a start. It *was*, anyway. I walked in here this morning and found everything a shambles. Almost every piece of equipment I own. Destroyed."

Nicholas was near tears, and Jonathan felt immediate sorrow. The young doctor had been through a lot. "Look, I'm sorry, Dr. Nicholas. But you've got to believe me. Neither I nor anyone I work with had anything to do with it. I'd have no reason to."

"You misunderstand," said Nicholas, now more subdued. "It's not *you*. It's someone touched by your lawsuit."

"But why the lawsuit? Why not a vandal—a burglar?"

Nicholas was again silent, as if surveying the wreckage. "It's the paint, Mr. Rand. It's sprayed all over the place. Every place you look. 'Rat fink.' The words. They're sprayed all over the room. There's not much doubt in *my* mind what it means. There's also something else."

Jonathan was almost afraid to ask. The cancer was spreading. The attempt on Dani's life; his own; Rusty.

"My pictures are gone," Nicholas continued.

"Pictures?"

"The photos I took of the pathology slides. My insurance. My proof. They're gone. The only thing stolen."

"I'm sure they can be replaced—"

"No, they can't!" Nicholas snapped. "I checked with Ray Hoefsteader. The original slides are missing too. Completely vanished. And no one has the foggiest idea who would have taken them."

Jonathan suddenly went pale. The major piece of evidence in the case was gone. The only solid proof of septicemia. Someone had ripped the heart right out of his lawsuit.

But there was still Dr. Lundgren. Maybe he had made duplicates before returning the slides to Rivergarden. There was a chance.

"Look, I'm sure you've seen the end of this," Jonathan said. "The only thing you had to hurt them is gone."

"Mr. Rand, the only way this is going to end for me is if the lawsuit is over. This is a small hospital and there'll be some questions. But I can handle that. At least *this* time. I also had everything insured. But a repetition of this will destroy me. I . . . I'm begging you. For my wife and kids. Please drop the lawsuit."

Jonathan thought for a moment. The thief had nothing to do with the malpractice case. He knew it immediately. The graffiti was a cover. It was evidence of a *murder* that had been stolen, not evidence of a wrongful-death case. But Nicholas could not be told.

"You have to trust me, Dr. Nicholas. You have seen the last of this. I won't drop the lawsuit, but there'll be no more repercussions because of it."

He next called Lundgren's office and got no answer. He would have to call back later. For the moment, though, he would have to learn more about the Cayman Islands. Whether the slides existed or not—whether a *lawsuit* existed or not—he had to push forward with his plan.

# Chapter XXVIII

"My God, man, you look like death warmed over. What the hell have you been doing to yourself?" Ralph Garrett stood up from behind his desk, startled at the sight of his law-school roommate.

"Ralph, you wouldn't believe it if I told you. Two days ago I wasn't even warmed over. The grim reaper and I almost became eternal companions." Jonathan stood weakly in the doorway to Ralph's office. His face was blanched the color of chalk, his cheeks drawn. Danielle clung tightly to his arm, providing him with support.

"Well, sit, sit," he urged. "You look like you should be in a wheelchair."

"Almost," Jonathan agreed. Then he introduced Danielle, and eased into one of Ralph's client chairs.

"I still don't understand," Ralph persisted. "What happened to you? Two weeks ago you looked like you were ready for a tryout with the Patriots."

"That was two weeks ago. Yesterday afternoon I checked myself out of Rivergarden after a near-fatal infection. Some kind of intestinal thing."

Ralph resumed his seat. He was a true intellectual and looked every bit the part. A gray wool vested suit, metal-rimmed glasses, slender build, with a narrow face and a long nose as straight as a ruler.

Ralph stared at Jonathan for a few quiet moments. "Well, I know you didn't crawl out of your deathbed to come here and listen to my wit and charm. Why don't you tell me what's wrong?"

"Oh, nothing . . . at least, nothing I could lay on you right now." Jonathan ran his hand through his hair. "But you *could* do me a favor."

"Name it."

"About six months ago I read an article—I think in one of our local papers. Something about laundering money in the Cayman Islands. You're the great tax expert in town. I was wondering if you could fill me in on what's going on down there."

"Well! At least I'll give you credit for knowing how to pick your lawyers."

"Sure I do. I'm no dummy. Anyone else would charge me a hundred dollars an hour."

Ralph laughed. "Don't forget the old adage, 'You get what you pay for.'" But his smile faded quickly and he pondered Jonathan's question for a moment. "Laundering money, huh?" He looked intently at Jonathan, serious for the first time. "I hope you're not getting into something, Jon. This is heavy stuff. If you're caught in the cookie jar, you're looking at a federal rap."

Jonathan held up a hand. "This is only informative. Believe me, I don't know the first thing about it."

"Well, it's not just the Cayman Islands. It's also Bermuda, the Bahamas, Costa Rica, any number of other places. Most of them in the Caribbean. The common denominator is that they all have little or no income taxes and strict laws that prohibit disclosure of the names of investors in their local banks. So someone could go to—let's say the Cayman Islands—with a large sum of money and open an account under the name of a fictitious corporation or a specified serial number—a numbered account, as they say. The money could then be invested in any number of ventures or even lent back to the original depositor. He could charge himself a high interest rate, write the interest off as an expense against his U.S. income, and avoid reporting the income from the Cayman Islands deposit. And, of course, there would be little or no income taxes paid in the Caymans."

"That's tax evasion. You mean to tell me that people are actually getting away with this?"

"The IRS has been investigating this problem for years, but with only a few exceptions they've been totally unsuccessful. The local confidentiality laws are too tight."

Jonathan pondered the possibilities for a moment. "Let's assume I had a lot of money and wanted to buy someone in a high position—totally hypothetical, you understand—and this someone wanted the exchange to take place in the Cayman

Islands in a way that would never be detected. How could it be done?"

"Relatively simple," Ralph replied. "Mr. Big would merely open an account in the name of ABC Trust Corporation—or some such name—and you would deposit your enormous life savings in his account. Then, whenever he needed to tap the money, he would merely make a loan to himself through ABC Trust Corporation or the bank. In the same way, he could also use the funds to buy and sell various properties and otherwise to make any number of investments."

"But what's to prevent Uncle Sam from finding out about this?" Danielle interjected. "It seems to me that Big Brother can get into *any* bank account it pretty well wants to."

"Not outside the United States. At least not in one of these tax havens. Their secrecy laws are virtually ironclad. In fact, the IRS and the Justice Department have been investigating this problem for the past ten years and only have a handful of arrests to show for their troubles."

"Why won't the foreign country cooperate with our government?" Jonathan asked.

"Because they want all that money running through their own banks. If they started releasing names of the depositors, everyone would pull their funds and go somewhere else."

"Then you're saying it might be a little difficult if I wanted to find out who was passing money to someone through such an account?"

"I'd say impossible. If the feds can't turn anything, I don't know how the hell you'd be able to."

"You sure about this, Ralph? There's got to be a hole there someplace."

"If there is, I don't know where it could be." Ralph scrutinized the couple sitting across the desk from him. They looked tired, discouraged, and unkempt. "I have this feeling that you two are into something way over your heads. I wish you'd confide in me. I might be able to help."

Jonathan struggled up weakly from the chair and Danielle followed his lead. "No, this is something we've got to face alone," he said. "Someday I might be able to tell you about it, but not now. . . . Oh, one other thing," he added. "How does the money get out of our country and into the bank?"

"Simple. It's usually just carried out in a briefcase by some kind of a courier. 'Bagman,' 'dropman'—they have all kinds of names for them. The easiest way, of course, is by boat. Less chance of running into someone from customs."

Jonathan started for the door with Danielle arm in arm. But as he reached for the doorknob, Ralph shouted out, "Dammit, Jon. If you need help, you should tell me. I'm sure there's *something* I could do."

Jonathan looked warmly at his good friend of eleven years. "Maybe you already have," he said. "But, believe me, Ralph, the less you know about this mess, the better for all of us."

Jonathan said good-bye, and continued through the door. At the end of the hall, Danielle pressed the elevator button and turned to Jonathan.

"What are we going to do now? It sounds like a trip to the Caymans would be a waste of time."

"You may be right. But I've got this gut feeling that the key to this whole thing is down there in the Caribbean. That's where the money is changing hands and that's where our evidence is. Look, we know that Armstrong has made at least one visit down there—and probably a number of others. You just can't spend any length of time down there without leaving tracks. The islands are too small."

"Where would we start?"

"We've got a lead with the book of matches. That's as good a place as any."

"Well, we're set for tomorrow morning at nine-fifteen, with a connecting flight in Miami. What now?" Danielle asked, hanging up the phone in the lobby.

"Now," he said, taking her hand. "Now we go see Jensen. She's got a lot of explaining to do. Right down to being seen in microbiology only thirty minutes before the theft of some anthrax. Ruth has the intuition of a Sherlock Holmes."

Danielle frowned. "I don't know, Jon. I wish we'd take this to the police. She almost killed you once—maybe twice. I'm petrified of even being near that woman."

Tapping the weapon under his shirt, Jonathan said, "Don't worry. I've got protection this time, and we also know what we're up against. Besides, if we go to the police, what will we have to hold over Armstrong's head? If the police know the whole plot, why should we be kept alive?"

Danielle bit her lower lip. "I suppose you're right, but let's not be too long. I don't like leaving Ruth alone."

Jonathan looked at his watch. "It's quarter after five, and we shouldn't be longer than another three or four hours. If we haven't found her by then, we'll go back to the hotel." Jonathan patted Danielle on the arm reassuringly. "Ruth will be fine, honey. All she has to do is stay in her room."

# Chapter XXIX

Ruth tossed in her bed. She was trapped in a dream. That last vivid dream that lingers on even after awakening. That last dream that is compressed into a few seconds, but seems to last an eternity.

As she fought her way up through the clinging shrouds of the vision, she could still see Aaron. He was close and trying to speak, trying to tell her something—a warning. She could see his face so clearly, the concerned eyes, the moving lips. His hand reached for hers, only inches away. He was beckoning, urging her to follow. Aaron had come back to take her away. It was as if he had never been gone. The surgery, the telephone call from Reed, the funeral—none of it had really happened. Ruth fought back reality. She wanted to follow, to reach out and grab Aaron's hand, to feel his warm touch one more time. If only she could move.

Aaron turned to leave and again gestured for her to follow. He was standing in the middle of a long hallway. At the distant end a door was open, the light on the other side radiating a brilliant glow. Ruth wanted to follow but still couldn't react. Slowly Aaron walked away, continuously waving at her to join him. If only she could reach him, they would be together forever.

Abruptly, with a shake of her head, Ruth opened her eyes and stared at the naked ceiling above the bed. Just as quickly the image was gone and for a few moments she groped for the realization of what had happened. As she began to reconcile with reality, her eyes moistened. It had all really happened. Aaron was dead. And she was lying alone in a small hotel room with musty fifteen-year-old furniture.

It had been the same dream again, identical every night since she had heard the tape. But clearer this time, incredibly vivid—almost real.

Ruth raised herself to her elbows and looked around. She felt the warmth of her tears as they migrated down her cheeks. The room was dark, a streetlamp just outside her hotel window casting a dim light onto her bed.

Where had the time gone? She had only snuggled up at five for a quick doze. She held her wrist up toward the window to note the time on her watch: 8:50 P.M.

Ruth rolled over, put her feet on the floor, and reached over and turned on the lamp next to the bed. In the silence of the room she felt totally alone. Maybe she was the only one left in the hotel, maybe even the city. What had gone on while she had been asleep?

As Ruth sat patiently waiting for the energy to rise, she suddenly became aware of a cramping ache in her abdomen. It had been there most of the day in a nagging but almost imperceptible way. She now recognized the familiar pattern. It had been four months, but there was no mistaking it. At the same moment, she felt something wet.

"Shit," she said aloud. "Why now? Jesus, why does this have to happen today?"

She dismissed it as having something to do with the emotional trauma of the past couple of days and reached for her purse. Maybe she had some tampons that hadn't been used the last time around. *Fat chance,* she thought as she rummaged through the purse. *When I flow it's like Niagara Falls, and always at the wrong time.*

She sat down on the toilet seat and checked herself. Yes, she hadn't been mistaken. It was there and heavy. With a sigh of disgust, she rolled some toilet tissue around her hand and pressed it up inside. Temporary sandbags for the flood. Pulling up her slacks, she opened the door to the medicine cabinet, then looked at the shelves below the sink.

Still no luck.

Again she looked at her watch: 9:07. Maybe the gift shop downstairs was open, she thought, as she glanced at the phone on the nightstand in the other room. She'd give them a call.

Maybe for a nice tip someone in the gift shop would bring them up.

The calm evening produced a stillness to the water of Long Island Sound. Those still on board their boats were scarcely aware of any motion, other than a gentle lapping of the water and an occasional creak or two in the older vessels. Ron and Shirley Birnbaum were spending their second consecutive night on their thirty-four-foot sloop during the move from their apartment to their first home. Because the termination of the lease and the closing of escrow had not coincided, they had decided to spend a few days aboard the boat. A second honeymoon, they had called it, even though the first one had been only four years earlier.

Shirley, a slight, petite woman with a pixie face and closely cut hair, snuggled romantically up to her husband. A stack of dirty dishes sat on the sink in the galley and an open, half-empty bottle of Chablis was conveniently positioned on the end of the dining table, a few feet across from the couch. "Why don't we forget buying the house," she said half-jokingly, while massaging the top of his thigh. "We could take the down payment, invest in a larger boat—maybe a ketch—and give the yacht club as our address. Wouldn't that be dreamy? Then, whenever we wanted a change of scenery, all we'd have to do is cast off and hoist sail."

"You and your romantic ideas." Ron smiled. "You're not exactly the Tugboat Annie type."

Shirley raised her chin pridefully. "I don't know about that. You just might be surprised at what I can do when I make my mind up to it."

Ron continued to smile, as he smoothly began unbuttoning her blouse. With his boyish face and curly black hair, he looked five years younger than his twenty-eight years. "I know you like the back of my hand, Shirl. You are an incurable romantic, straight out of the thirteenth century. And I, my dear," he said while plunging his hand under the cup of her bra, "I am your great white knight, come to rescue you from your pangs of horniness."

"Oh, yes, yes," she cried. "Take me, O magnificent knight."

* * *

Ruth waited impatiently, telephone to her ear, hip cocked to the side, slouching, her foot tapping nervously on the floor. The gift shop had closed at nine o'clock. She was now trying room service, hoping that one of the staff might be carrying a couple of extra tampons with her, or that maybe there was a dispenser somewhere in the hotel—anything. Finally, a sleepy, uninspired voice answered; it had taken nine rings.

"Good evening, room service."

Thank heavens, the voice was female.

"This is Mrs. . . . Mrs. Finn in room fourteen fifty-six. I . . . I'm in need of some tampons. Would it be possible to have someone bring a package up to my room?"

"I'm sorry, ma'am. You'll have to get those at the gift shop. Room service doesn't carry tampons."

"But they're closed. They closed at nine. Can't you help me out? Maybe there's a dispenser someplace . . . or one of the girls on the staff may have a couple of extras. Anything to get me through till morning. I'm somewhat desperate right now."

"Well, I don't know of a dispenser in the building, but let me check with a couple of the girls. I'll call you back."

"Thank you. Please hurry."

Patience had always been Ruth's hallmark. Throughout her marriage she had persevered through one thing after another: the long hours at home, waiting for Aaron's career to blossom; the wait for children, first until Aaron could spend the needed time with his family, then all the maddening months trying to conceive. Even in the beginning, Ruth had spent a full four months working with Aaron at the hospital before he asked her out on their first date. All of those months admiring, loving, yearning.

But on this particular day, at this particular time, everything was different. She had been confined in the small room for most of three days, fighting solitude and fear—and, worse, not knowing what was happening outside.

Now she began to pace like a trapped animal. Three or four times she walked to the window and back to the phone. How long should it take the room-service girl to ask a couple of the other girls if they had any stupid tampons? Ruth dropped onto the bed, crossed her legs, and began gnawing at a fingernail, cradling her elbow with her left hand. Unpacified, she picked up a copy of Vogue that she had thumbed through three times before. No good. She couldn't concentrate; nothing caught her interest.

"Shit!" she exclaimed.

Anxiously she picked up the phone and dialed room service. The same lazy voice answered.

"Good evening, room service."

"Hello. This is Mrs. Finn again. You said you'd ask around about some tampons?"

"Tampons? Oh . . . yeah. No, I wasn't able to find any. Sorry I forgot to call back."

*Bitch*, Ruth thought. *She never even tried.* "Look, are you sure? I've *got* to get something."

"Why don't you try the drugstore across the street. It's down about a block. But it closes at ten, so I wouldn't wait too long."

Ruth pondered the dark, lonely street outside. "Could I get someone to run down there for me? I'd be more than happy to pay."

"I'm sorry, ma'am. We're not allowed to leave the hotel."

"Look! I'll give twenty dollars if someone will run down and pick me up a pack." Ruth's voice was strained, desperate.

Nervously the voice at the other end said, "I'm sorry, Mrs. Finn. We can't leave our jobs. We'd be fired. The drugstore is only across the street. I'm sure it wouldn't take you more than ten minutes."

"But you don't understand. I—" Ruth stopped and slammed down the phone. "Shit!"

She got up from the bed, stepped to the window, pulled back the drapes, and peered out at the desolate street. All the stores appeared closed, lights out, protective gratings pulled across the front. Looking a little farther down the street, she saw a red tubular neon sign: DRUGS. It was at the corner next to a streetlight and a crosswalk.

Ten minutes, the girl had said. The thought of crossing the street was frightening, but . . . only ten minutes and she'd be back inside her sanctuary. Ruth felt the moisture again. She'd never make it through the night.

Where was Jonathan? He should have been back by now. Maybe something happened. It was 9:28. What if the drugstore closed early? No, she couldn't wait for him. A change of toilet tissue and she'd have to leave.

* * *

Tranquility and silence again prevailed, as Ron relaxed with his head on a pillow in the forward stateroom. Equally drained, Shirley lay diagonally over Ron's chest, her eyes closed, a lingering smile on her face. She was nude, while Ron sported only a pair of socks.

In the distance they heard a powerboat coming closer. As the sound grew louder, Ron opened his eyes, waiting for the vessel to pass and the inevitable swells from the wake that would follow.

Finally it went gurgling by, followed a few seconds later by a large swell that lurched the sloop up on its starboard side. Simultaneously a muted thump could be heard against the side of the hull.

"Damn powerboats," said Ron, almost under his breath.

Shirley opened her eyes, startled. "What the hell was that?" she asked.

"Probably a stray four-by-four. Don't worry about it," he added. "It'll float away." Ron again closed his eyes.

As the boat continued rocking with the gradually dissipating swells, a strange rubbing sound came from the hull. Shirley shivered and reached for the blanket folded at the foot of the bunk and pulled it over her shoulders.

"Cold, sweetie?" Ron asked.

"No . . . Yes . . . I don't know. I guess I feel naked. Almost like someone was watching me."

Ron chuckled. "And here I had always thought you were an exhibitionist."

Shirley didn't reply, but instead snuggled tighter against Ron's chest.

"Yeah, I guess it was that . . . that rubbing; it seemed eerie." Shirley trembled again.

Ron listened. The rocking had stopped and so had the sound. "Well, it's gone now."

Five minutes later, another boat cruised within twenty-five feet of the sloop, this one faster than the last. The bothersome noise started up again.

Shirley looked up at Ron. "Honey?"

"Yes, sweetie?" His eyes remained closed.

"If it's a piece of wood, don't you think it could be scratching the paint on the hull? It *has* been only two months since we pulled her out in dry dock."

Ron yawned, then slowly opened his eyes, blinking

himself awake. "I guess you're right," he said. He yawned again, rubbed his eyes, then struggled up from the bunk.

"Hurry back," Shirley urged. "I'll keep your spot warm."

Ron nodded, sleepily picked up his trousers, found the front, and clumsily threaded his feet into the pant legs.

Ruth closed the door to her hotel room. The snapping shut of the latch had a certain permanency about it. She started to fish for her key in her purse, then dismissed the idea as silly. She had used the key in the lock a number of times before; it worked.

With some uncertainty she looked at the elevator a hundred feet up the hall, and took a deep breath to relieve her tension. The air had a musty smell, and the plastic plants along the corridor were covered with a fine layer of dust. The fourth overhead light down, immediately adjacent to the elevator, had a bulb that was out. The area looked dark and forbidding.

*The cleaning crew hasn't been up here in a month,* she thought angrily. She began walking toward the elevator, looking for anything that might be suspicious. Pressing the elevator call button, she stepped back. If she was going to be surprised, she didn't want to be standing too close when the door opened.

Across the hall she heard a man and woman arguing loudly. The voices were muffled, but it seemed to have something to do with the man's drinking.

Finally the door opened, and to Ruth's relief the elevator was empty. Quickly she stepped inside and pushed the button for the lobby. The electric motor above began to whine and the elevator started its descent with a jar. Ruth looked up, following the lights blinking on with each floor that she passed. When the door rolled open, Ruth stepped out. Still there was no one around, except an elderly white-haired man propped on a high stool behind the registration desk, his face buried in a newspaper. He wore round bifocals on the end of his nose.

Ruth walked by the desk, hoping for some kind of recognition: a smile, a "good evening," anything. At least she would know that someone in the hotel knew she was alive, maybe even concerned about her well-being. He gave no reaction other than a short, hacking cough.

Outside, she began to appreciate for the first time what it meant to be alone. The streets were shrouded in darkness.

The area where she was standing gathered its only light from the doorway and the blue neon sign that said VISTA HOTEL. She could see the drugstore sign and the streetlamp on the corner at the end of the block. All other lights were out. Along either side of the street were a number of parked cars; each seemed deserted. No life was immediately discernible, except a dark-colored cat that jumped from a trash can next to the curb fifty feet away. Ruth trembled and pulled her sweater up higher on her neck. She wasn't really cold; the night was somewhat humid. But it made her feel slightly more secure.

Anxiously she began walking. The heels of her shoes clattered loudly on the concrete sidewalk. As she neared the end of the block, she suddenly heard a crash. She froze, unwilling to look. It was to her left. Momentarily she stopped breathing, then slowly directed her gaze up a short flight of steps to a stoop in front of an apartment building. There in the shadows sat a man leaning against the wall. He was wearing rumpled clothes, a soiled hat pulled low on his forehead. His left arm was extended toward the street. Three steps below was a paper bag, probably containing a broken liquor bottle. Ruth waited for some form of movement; then, seeing none, she continued her journey.

At the corner she stopped and looked both ways. It was an uncontrolled intersection with four white-line crosswalks. She began to step down onto the street, but hesitated when she heard a siren. Quickly she noted that it was several blocks away and traveling in the opposite direction. Again she looked for traffic. Nothing.

As she took her first step, she stared over at the drugstore and noted the OPEN sign hanging on the door. Inside, she saw a man standing behind a counter. For the first time she relaxed, and began walking.

Suddenly she heard a starter kick an engine over several times, then the growl of a powerful exhaust. She looked as she continued walking, but couldn't see anything. The streetlamp above blinded her. In the distance, a man with black eyes sat behind a sunburst-cracked windshield, and dropped a gear lever into drive. A second later there was a short squeal of tires on pavement, followed by the high-pitched whine of an engine. A sense of immediate danger overwhelmed Ruth and she began to run. She was halfway across the street. Closer and closer the sound screamed at her from out of the darkness.

The curb on the other side of the street looked five hundred feet away. Her heart began pounding, her mind numbed with fear.

Then out of the corner of her eye she caught the flash of metal as it hurled at her through the intersection. She was still fifteen feet from safety, and in a fraction of a second she knew that she would never make it. The headlights of the automobile finally flashed on, momentarily blinding her.

The impact was mercifully fast. The sickening thud of bones breaking, flesh tearing, the shattering of glass, the twisting of metal, were never to be part of her conscious thoughts. Only the distant, almost metaphysical sense of soaring through space like a rag doll, the breathtaking slam onto the asphalt, and then the abrupt stop in the gutter up against the curbing.

For a few moments Ruth lay gasping for air, a searing pain stabbing into her chest. She looked down to see a large depression on the left side of her torso. Her brown wool sweater was soaked with blood, which began to collect in a pool next to her. Her mind buzzed. Gradually her brain responded with a comforting anesthesia and she began to lose consciousness. An elderly couple, holding on to each other, walked over and stared down at her. They neither ran for help nor tried to assist her, temporarily paralyzed by the tragedy before them. Finally their faces became unrecognizable blurs.

Ruth looked out into darkness. Death was about to take her away. Suddenly a brilliant light appeared, silhouetting an image that stood before her. It was like nothing she had ever seen before, awesome, consuming. The image came closer and reached for her, but she had no fear. She felt only tenderness and warmth. It was Aaron and this time it was real. Aaron's hand reached, closed around hers, and began to lead her away through a doorway to eternal peace.

Ron Birnbaum struggled up the steep ladder-type stairway and stood for a moment, fumbling with the last couple of buttons on his sport shirt. He yawned, scratched his head, then took a deep breath of the clean, refreshing salt air. It was exactly the tonic he needed and helped to clean away the cobwebs.

Perusing the starboard side, Ron realized that he would need some portable lighting. The closest funnel-shaped dockside light was to the port side and three slips over, leaving in shadow the area from which the noise came. The water seemed a dark blue ink.

Ron yelled below, "Shirley, would you look under the seat in the—" then caught himself. To hell with it. She'd never find the flashlight anyway.

"What, honey?" she responded.

"Never mind."

Ron stepped out of the cockpit area onto the topside decking and began making his way forward, next to the gunnels. If he could get close enough, he wouldn't need a flashlight, he assured himself. He bent over and squinted. Maybe he could even reach it. Ten feet from the point of the bow, he dropped to his knees and leaned over as far as he could, hanging on to the cable railing with his left hand.

Then, from below, a white, chalklike face broke the surface of the water, preceded by an open hand, reaching for help. The eyes were open and begging.

Ron's mouth dropped open, his startled eyes widened.

"My God! Someone's in the water," he screamed. Instinctively he grabbed the bone-white hand and pulled. The skin was cold as ice and wrinkled. Higher he pulled until the face broke into the light from behind him.

What he saw forced a deep, bloodcurdling scream that carried for a mile over the water.

The face was bloated and beginning to decompose, the lips swollen, the tongue protruding from the mouth. The eyes bulged as if they were about to fall from their sockets. A few strands of washed-out blond hair clung to the scalp.

In spite of Ron's frozen grip, the corpse began to slide back into the deep, leaving a large sheath of slimy skin hanging from his hand. Ron fell back onto his haunches, holding the dripping epidermis, stunned, gasping, unable to move. As he sat trying to regain his senses, something hard fell from his clutching fingers to his lap, then rolled onto the deck. Reacting as if in a trance, Ron dropped the skin back into the water and slowly picked up the object. It was a small signet ring, bearing the Gothic initials MJ.

As Ron held the ring into the light, his dinner surged back up through his throat and spouted out onto his lap. Ron only sat staring at the ring, mouth open, lips dripping.

\* \* \*

Jonathan eased his Cadillac to a stop in front of the Vista Hotel, preparing to make a left turn into the hotel garage. He and Danielle looked curiously at the crowd gathering a few hundred feet ahead of them. It was 9:56 P.M.

"What do you think happened?" Danielle asked.

"I don't know. But I don't like it. . . . I just don't like it." Jonathan flipped off the turn signal, straightened out his steering wheel, and proceeded slowly down the street. In the distance, he heard the siren of an emergency vehicle fast approaching. He pulled up behind a parked car at the curb. Sixty feet ahead, the crowd gathered in a circle.

Jonathan turned to Danielle. "I'm not so sure I want to see this." Ruth had been alone most of the day, and this was too close to the hotel.

"Do you think it could be—" Danielle couldn't say it.

"I'm sure it's not. Why would she leave the room?" Jonathan got out and closed the car door. "But I've got to know for sure."

Danielle leaned out the window and said, "Please hurry, honey. I want to get out of here—and quickly."

"I'll be right back," he said, still looking at the crowd.

Danielle watched Jonathan hurry over to the crowd, move a few people aside, crouch, and then stand up again. As he returned, his head was dropped, his eyes staring at the ground. Danielle turned away while Jonathan opened the door and climbed in beside her. When the heavy door slammed shut, she turned slowly and found Jonathan's eyes.

His eyes communicated without words what had been her worst fear.

# Chapter XXX

*Thursday, September 6, 1979*

The sedating hum of the jet engines had long since blended into the other background sounds of the flight. The quiet chatter, the clinking of bottles as the stewardess rolled the refreshment cart up and down the aisle, the occasional low monotone announcements by the captain, were all beyond the point of being noticed or listened to.

The events of the past few days, as well as the flight from New York to Miami and the one-and-a-half-hour layover before boarding the Caribbean Airlines 727, had taken their toll on Dani and Jonathan. They were tired and emotionally spent. And, in contrast to the vacationers and businessmen anticipating their jaunt on Grand Cayman, they looked at their trip with serious misgivings, and a considerable amount of uncertainty about what they were going to do and what they might encounter.

Jonathan blinked open his bloodshot eyes and looked at Danielle. Like Jonathan's, her seat was in its reclining position. Her head faced Jonathan and she appeared in deep sleep. With his fingers, he brushed back his hair, then let his hand slide down over his face. The stubble of his two-day beard was quite prominent now. He turned his head and focused on the panorama below. Through patches of white billowy clouds he could see the beautiful turquoise Caribbean, with dark blotches of coral beneath the water so clearly defined that they seemed only a few feet below the surface.

"The captain advises me that we are approaching Owen Roberts International on Grand Cayman," came the announcement over the PA system. The 480 miles south from Miami had been traveled in just under an hour and it seemed to Jonathan that he had just closed his eyes. As the voice requested the passengers to prepare for landing, Jonathan gently shook Danielle's shoulder.

She opened her eyes wide. "Are we there already?" she asked, yawning.

"We're about to make our descent. How was your sleep?"

"I slept like a baby. I had no idea how tired I was. How about you?"

"Couldn't have slept better. Oh—I never asked: were you able to get room reservations?"

"Yes. At the Tortuga Inn. I booked us in as Mr. and Mrs. John Fuller. You said not to use our own names."

Within thirty minutes of landing, Jonathan and Danielle had gathered their luggage, rented a well-used English Ford, and were on their way to Seven Mile Beach, at the west end of the island.

With the fragrance of bougainvillea, the colorful sights, and the gentle warm breeze buffeting their faces through the open windows, it was easy to forget the purpose of their visit. For the moment, they were vacationers enjoying the relaxing tropical atmosphere of a small Caribbean paradise. The terrain was almost flat, with low, green hills sprinkled with cacti, coconut palms, tropical plants, and tall Australian pines. Along the coast, the wide and desolate beaches seemed to stretch for miles, their powdery white sand forming a border around the twenty-two-by-four-mile island.

Danielle looked at Jonathan, whose mind seemed a thousand miles away. "Penny for your thoughts," she said.

Jonathan smiled. "Just pretending. It's easy to do down here. How nice it would be just to fade into the countryside and never be seen again."

"It's nice to dream."

"But unrealistic," Jonathan added, reminding himself of their plight. "We can't afford to drop our guard for one minute. Not even down here. I have this uneasy feeling that Armstrong knows exactly where we are—at least that we're on this island."

Danielle turned and looked at the road behind them. It was clear, and for a moment she again took in the scenery. Along the road were a number of small, quaint cottages, with paned windows, and an abundance of brilliant, colorful flowers. The mood was warm and hospitable—and, from the left side of the road, very British. It was difficult for her to appreciate their danger.

"You don't really think someone's on this island, do you?" she asked.

"They're down here all right. Probably waiting to see what we dig up. Need I remind you about Rusty and Ruth? They're running desperate, Dani. I mean *desperate!*" He paused. "Something else I haven't told you about."

"I don't want to hear it, Jon. You've made your point."

"Well, you're going to hear it." This was not the time for delicacy. Fear would help give her the extra edge of caution they needed. "Lundgren is also dead. I called his secretary when you were making our reservations. She told me it appeared to be a coronary. But I've got my doubts. It's too much of a coincidence. She also can't find a number of his slides—including Feinerman's. She thinks the doctor may have misplaced them, but I doubt it."

"Everything is gone," she said with a note of emptiness. "Ruth; your evidence . . . everything. Seems like you don't have much of a lawsuit anymore."

"The lawsuit died with Ruth, Dani. But the slides—they were our strongest evidence of murder."

Jonathan pulled into the gravel parking area in front of the Tortuga Inn. Like many of the hotels along that stretch of beach, it faced the ocean and offered guests an unsurpassed view of the blue Caribbean. Although small compared to the enormous hotels of New York and Miami, the Tortuga appeared no older than five or six years and seemed clean and well maintained.

Jonathan crawled out of the small car, grabbed the two suitcases in the backseat, and started for the lobby, with Danielle on his arm.

"Remember, we're Mr. and Mrs. Fuller," she reminded. More and more the thought of marriage was occupying her thoughts.

"I had almost forgotten," he said, almost to himself.

Danielle looked at him. "I haven't. I kinda *like* the idea."

"Welcome to the Turtle Shell, sir," came the warm and enthusiastic greeting. The *r* had a guttural trill, straight out of Scotland. "Woo'd ya prefer a table or woo'd ya rather sit at the bar?" The man was short, not an inch over five-foot-four, and as round as a ball. His cherubic face with rosy cheeks sported a pleasant, engaging smile. His head was cleanly bald, almost polished.

"A table would be fine," Jonathan responded. "Thank you."

They followed the man toward the rear of the tavern. As they walked, Jonathan discreetly examined the room. The floor was hardwood and gleamed like polished marble. The walls reached up to a twelve-foot-high beamed ceiling, and one-third of the way into the room was a white pillared arch, which separated the bar from the dining areas.

A bartender smiled at the new customers as he twisted a towel into a Collins glass. He wore a red-and-black-plaid vest with matching tie and a white shirt.

At the bar, an older couple sat sipping English ale, while a few other customers occupied scattered tables. At three o'clock in the afternoon, there was an obvious ebb in the business. Too late for the lunch crowd, and a couple of hours before the early-evening sightseers would be wandering into the authentic Cayman tavern to partake of the island's famous turtle steak.

The bald man seated them at a table in the rear of the room, next to a window. Outside was a view of North Sound, a harbor that cuts almost through the island at its western end. "A waiter will be right with ya, folks," he said, still wearing his smile. He handed Jonathan a menu and left for the kitchen. Soon a Cuban waiter approached their table, his pencil poised over an order pad. Unlike his predecessor, he had no smile.

"Have you decided yet?" he asked tersely. He stared at Jonathan with dark, challenging eyes.

"Bring us a couple of ales," Jonathan replied uneasily. "What's with *him*?" he wondered out loud, as the waiter left for the bar.

Danielle shrugged. "I don't know. But whatever it is, I don't like it. He gives me the creeps."

"Well, I doubt we'll get much cooperation from him, but no harm in trying." Jonathan reached into his shirt pocket and began unfolding a newspaper clipping.

Jonathan handed the piece of paper to Danielle. She immediately recognized the familiar face of Bradley Armstrong. A young, attractive woman was on his arm. Behind the couple, but equally visible, was a man she had never seen before. At the bottom of the picture was a brief story about the senator arriving in New York for a charity fund-raiser.

"What are you going to do with this?" she asked.

"See the balding man standing behind Armstrong? That's Simon Crenshaw. I told you about our altercation at Armstrong's office. I *know* he was on *The Prescription* when Armstrong was down here. The book of matches I found on board had his trademark on it. Maybe our waiter will remember seeing him, or possibly even Armstrong."

"Are you sure you really want to go through—" Danielle stopped as the Cuban returned with their ale. The fear she had tried to leave behind in Connecticut was beginning to swallow her again. The waiter set their mugs down and abruptly turned to leave.

"Excuse me," Jonathan interceded.

"Yes, señor," he snapped, turning back to look at Jonathan. His black eyes stared coldly.

Jonathan picked up the clipping and handed it to him. "Maybe you could help me. I'm trying to find out if either of these two men have ever been in this tavern, possibly about five or six months ago. If you would look closely at the balding man, you might recall him."

The Cuban inspected the picture. At once his eyes widened, almost imperceptibly, but the recognition was immediately apparent. Now interested in the two Americans, he stared at Jonathan, then at Danielle. She shuddered. He seemed to be memorizing her features.

"No, señor," he said, shaking his head. "Never see . . . never see them."

Before Jonathan could ask another question, the Cuban had tossed the clipping onto the table and disappeared into the kitchen.

"I think we ought to go," Danielle said. "He recognized *someone* in that picture, and I almost wish he hadn't."

Jonathan shared her eagerness to leave, but there was one more person he had to try. The bald man had been very pleasant and might be more cooperative. "Let me just talk to the man who seated us and then we'll go," he said.

For the next fifteen minutes, they sat staring out the window, nervously sipping their ale. Below them in the sound the fishing boats were beginning to return for the day—the sport fishers and commercial trawlers with their collections of wahoo, marlin, bonito, amberjack, and barracuda; the smaller skiffs with the grouper and yellow-tailed snapper.

Minute after minute they anxiously waited. With each additional minute came the feeling of increasing vulnerability. Jonathan's eyes nervously searched the room, looking at the strangers quietly talking to one another. For the fifth time he looked down at his watch: 3:17. Why had the waiter reacted that way to Armstrong's picture? He sensed an impending danger.

"Let's leave!" Danielle pleaded.

"Just three more minutes, Dani. This was our reason for being here. We've got to find out what went on in this tavern."

Jonathan thought of asking the bartender, but saw that he too was gone, which made him even more fearful of his suspicions. He also noticed that the couple at the bar had left. Only three other customers remained in the tavern.

Sitting there pondering his dilemma, Jonathan remembered a dream he had once had. He was sitting in his car on a desolate set of railroad tracks. There was nothing but desert for miles around. A train was getting closer and closer to his car, and he was unable to get the engine started. Over and over the ignition would turn the engine, but still it wouldn't start. In the distance he could see the train. The train came closer. He could even make out the face of the engineer. The engineer tooted his whistle, desperately trying to get Jonathan to move. He tried the engine again and it started, then died. He still had time to get out and run, but then the car would be destroyed. And he had to save his car. He needed it to survive. Did he still have time? The train was so close that he could almost feel the rumble of the ground as the tons of metal came careening toward his car.

Finally, the bald man came walking out of the kitchen and Jonathan motioned him over to their table. Maybe they still had time to get some answers and leave before they were crushed by the train.

"Yes, sir. How can Ah help ya?" He smiled.

"About five months ago a friend of mine met someone in your tavern, and I was wondering whether you might recall seeing him."

"Ah don' know, sir," he responded, stroking his chin with his hand. "That was a very long time ago. Ah doo't Ah coo'd remember now."

"Well, if you possibly could," said Jonathan, handing him the piece of newspaper, "I would appreciate it. I've been trying to find the man he met here. This is a picture of my friend."

The bald man pulled some spectacles out of his pocket and put them on. For a few moments he looked seriously at the photo, shaking his head. Then he stopped. "Wait a moment," he said. "Maybe Ah do." The man turned sideways and held the clipping up so that he could catch more light from the window. "Yes . . . it's him. Yes, Ah do. Matter a fact, he was sittin' right at your table."

"Which one did you see?"

"This'n right hur," he said, pointing at Crenshaw. "Ah remember the bushy eyebrows. Like a ramblin' boosh, they wur. An di' he smoke. Like a chimney he smoked. One right after another."

Jonathan was encouraged. "Yes. That was him. Do you remember who he was with? Maybe an old customer or someone you had seen before?"

"No. Ah had newer seen either of thum before. Although Ah doo recall the other man was dark complected. Probably a Latin."

"Do you remember anything about their meeting? Something they said? Something they did? *Anything?*"

"Ah do remember that they wur arguin'. Got quite loud, as a matter of fact. Ah guess that's why Ah recall thum. But Ah don' remember what was said."

"And that was the only time you saw them, either before or since?"

"The only time."

Jonathan sighed. "Thank you for your help."

"Ma pleasure, sir." The bald man turned to leave, took a step, then stopped. Again he stroked his chin. "Just thought o' one more thin'. Ah remember him talkin' to Alejandro, one o' ma waiters . . . in Spanish. Ah think he may have been Cuban too. Anyway, they were carryin' on quite a conversation, Alejandro and the other man."

"Does Alejandro still work for you?"

"Shoor does. It was him that gave ya your ale."

He knew it. The bastard had been lying all along. "Could you possibly have Alejandro step out so I might ask what he recalls?"

"Ah'd be glad ta help ya, sir, but Ah can't find the bugger. He's vanished. Ah've been lookin' fur him fur the las' ten or fift'n minootes."

Now they *knew* the time was short. Alejandro had recognized Crenshaw and had gone to tell whoever Crenshaw had been talking to in the tavern. Now Jonathan was desperate to leave. His time might be shorter than he had hoped. He had stayed too long.

"Thank you again," he said, rising from the table. The bald man smiled and again left for the kitchen. As Jonathan stood upright he felt the hard nose of his Hi-Standard against his abdomen.

"Let's go down to the waterfront and talk to some

fishermen. Most of them should be in by now. Maybe someone will remember seeing *The Prescription*," he suggested.

"Do you really think so? There are hundreds of boats around here, and it *has* been almost half a year."

"Well, it was a big yacht and might have attracted someone's attention. Anyway, it's the only thing I can think of. And we have to do something."

Five minutes later Jonathan parked the Ford next to a dock in old Georgetown, the capital of the Cayman Islands.

The sun in the Caribbean falls fast over the sea. One moment it is radiating warmth to its temperamental waters; the next it is submerging on the distant horizon, painting layers of pink, orange, and blue clouds. Within minutes the sky turns from a light blue, backdropping white and gray fluffy clouds, to a deep navy blue and then to blackness.

In the last few hours, Jonathan and Danielle had struck it rich. They had walked close to two miles, asking questions, listening to small talk, taking pictures, acting like tourists. Danielle had wanted to split up, but Jonathan refused. Maybe they could have covered more ground, but it would have meant leaving her alone, unprotected.

Then at a quarter to six they had met him. His face was weathered—baked by the ever-present sun, aged by the ruthless salt air. His complexion made him look in his seventies, but he probably wasn't more than fifty. He smelled of fish, and a chaw of tobacco formed a prominent lump in his cheek.

When the young couple had asked him about *The Prescription* he had smiled, displaying a gap in his stained, uneven teeth. His life had always been a simple one. But here someone was coming to him for information. He held knowledge that appeared of value and for one moment his life was important to someone other than himself.

Wanting to savor the feeling, he had teased them. "Oh, I might recall somethin'," he had said. The anxious young eyes gave him pleasure. Finally he had relented and told them. Yes, he had seen the boat. He recalled how he had been amused at the name. He had seen it while bonefishing off Cayman Brac, eighty-nine miles to the east by northeast. It had dropped hook about a half-mile offshore near North East Point. No one could be seen on board; the boat had seemed deserted. The old man had smiled when Jonathan and Danielle had thanked him, then winked and bade them good luck.

Not wanting to linger in one place for any length of time, they had picked up sandwiches to go and had returned to their room, taking care that they were not followed. After a quick meal, they had phoned for plane reservations to Cayman Brac the following morning, then collapsed on their bed.

The night was still young and they pondered how to pass the time until they would drift off to sleep. Outside, through the screens over their windows, the Caribbean could be heard lapping at the shore. The lights were out and they lay looking at the ceiling, not wanting to talk, listening for anything unusual outside.

"Why don't I look over the cruise-ship records?" Danielle finally suggested. "Maybe I might pick up something you overlooked. At least it would help kill some time."

"Sure. Why not?" Jonathan agreed.

Danielle flicked on the lamp on the nightstand. The records were in Jonathan's suitcase, near the door to the patio. She rolled uneasily out of bed and picked them up. A slight breeze was blowing through the screen next to the door, causing a haunting, barely audible whistle. Danielle started for the bed, then hesitated. She thought she had heard something. She stood and listened, but it stopped. Probably nothing. A second time she started for the bed, then heard it again. The tapping was rhythmic, beginning slow and working to a more rapid pace, then slow again.

"Did you hear that?" she whispered, quickly crawling back onto the bed.

"Hear what?"

"That sound. It's coming from the patio."

"Are you sure?"

*"Listen!"*

Jonathan rose and picked up his Hi-Standard. He listened, couldn't hear anything, and walked to the screened window. The louvered shutters were closed from outside and prevented him from looking onto the patio. Slowly he flipped off the safety to the weapon and unlocked the door. The barrel pointed at the floor, his hand shaking. The muscles of Danielle's jaw tightened as she sat on the bed, not wanting to breathe. As the door opened, a twisting squeal pierced through the room. The door was ajar by a foot, but Jonathan still could not see what was causing the noise. He motioned for Danielle to turn off the light and she obliged. The tapping was louder. Jonathan pointed the gun into the opening and bit his lip. His heart was pounding hard against his chest. Then in the same moment he threw back the door and darted onto the patio, gun leveled in the direction of the tapping.

What he saw brought a smile to his face. There, waving in the wind, were the two cords that controlled the roll of rattan slats fixed to the roof of the patio. As the wind gusted, the plastic knobs at the end of the cords rapped against a patio chair. Jonathan covered his eyes with his hand and shook his head.

"It's all right, Dani," he yelled. "You can turn the light back on."

After a relieved laugh, Danielle proceeded with her review of the records, which were not extensive. It did not take her long to find something of value. Of *real* value. It was in the roster of passengers. Immediately her face brightened.

"Jonathan! Look at this!" Danielle underlined two names with a pencil and handed him the sheet.

"I don't see what you're . . . Jesus, you're right. How did I miss it?"

The list of passengers, in alphabetical order, itemized the last, first, and middle names of each traveler and then in a corresponding column gave the number of his or her stateroom. As he had before, Jonathan went directly to the Js and found "Jensen, Maureen L.—B47." This time, however, he went backward to where Danielle had underlined another name. There it was. He had read it before—two weeks ago. But it had had no meaning then. It jumped out at him: *Crenshaw, Simon—B49.* Simon Crenshaw not only had been on the cruise with Jensen, just before she had killed Aaron, but he had occupied an adjoining stateroom. This was the tie he had been searching for. The link between Armstrong and Jensen. With the other facts, it would defy coincidence. During the week before Aaron's death, Jensen had been involved in conferences with Bradley Armstrong's number-one assistant.

The following morning, before leaving for Cayman Brac, Jonathan would mail the records to his banker with a sealed letter explaining their importance and requesting that they be placed in his safe-deposit box.

Jonathan put the records aside and kissed Danielle on the

forehead. "We're going to make it out of this, Dani. Trust me. With the both of us working together, we can't miss. My brawn and your brains." Danielle smiled.

Before turning out the light, Jonathan checked both doors that opened to their room from outside. Next to each of them was a glass filled with coins and tied by a string to the doorknob.

# Chapter XXXI

*Friday, September 7, 1979*

Cayman Brac, with its immense bluff that runs the length of the island and rises from sea level to a height of 140 feet, sits almost ninety miles closer to the eastern end of Cuba than does Grand Cayman. Its limestone cliffs are honeycombed with caverns, many carrying legends of buccaneer treasures buried in the distant past. Buffeted by the winds, green pastures and coconut palms are found on its level plateau above. Dairy and beef cattle are raised on the small one-by-twelve-mile island. With a population of fewer than two thousand, it is known as the island for those who want to escape. Only one inn is found on Brac, at its western end near the airport. Five miles farther west sits the third island, Little Cayman.

Their flight arrived at midmorning. Without wasting a minute, Jonathan and Danielle picked up a map, rented bikes, and began their trip to North East Point, at the opposite end of the island. They knew exactly where they wanted to go. Once they got there, they would look, take pictures, and ask questions, just as they had back in Georgetown. Maybe they would get lucky again. After all, the people were friendly, and perhaps they had seen something unusual. Some strange activity, unusual behavior, or possibly even *The Prescription*.

Time was getting short. Armstrong no doubt was aware that they were in the Caymans and most certainly had someone looking for them. The islands were small, with not many places to get lost. The message was clear: the time had come for taking chances. They would *have* to come out into the open.

They had ridden their bicycles for two hours, stopping three times to rest. Each time they had stopped, he had asked questions of the local residents, but to no avail. He had handed around the newspaper clipping and described *The Prescription*. The reply had always been the same: a smile, an apology, but no information.

Jonathan looked ahead at Danielle leaning over the handlebars, her trim tan legs straining as they pressed on the pedals. Beyond her he could see a sharp break in the terrain, with a view of the peaceful blue Caribbean.

"This is it," he yelled. "Pull your bike off the road. This is North East Point."

Danielle braked to a stop and turned to look back at Jonathan.

They pulled their bikes off to the side of the road and placed them down in the tall grass. No one was around, and all that could be heard were the rustling leaves. Jonathan grabbed Danielle's hand and led her to the edge of a cliff. The wind was even stronger there, gusting from below over the top of the bluff. Danielle strained on Jonathan's hand and said, "Be careful! I don't like this."

Jonathan stopped and leaned slightly forward. He was only five feet from the edge. "Just a minute, Dani. I've got to see something." Their arms were still extended and Danielle pulled back, using her weight as a ballast. The wind felt good, drying the perspiration that covered their faces. Jonathan squinted. A half-mile out he could see where *The Prescription* had anchored, and he followed the expanse of water up to the shoreline, 140 feet below. He leaned forward even more.

"Jon! For God's sake!" Danielle yelled.

Below, Jonathan saw a small sandy beach. An ideal place for beaching a shore boat. A few hundred yards to his left, the beach opened to a narrow pathway that seemed to lead up the side of the cliff. He leaned out even farther to get a better look. Three feet ahead of him, the rock ledge dropped away to nothing.

Then all at once it happened. A sudden gust of wind hit Jonathan and he lost his balance. He felt his body begin to roll forward, but there was nothing he could do. He felt himself going and closed his eyes, his right hand grasping helplessly at the empty air.

Danielle screamed and her grip tightened like a vise; adrenaline surged through her body. In a horrible flash she envisioned Jonathan plummeting to his death below. Desperately she pulled and at the same time tried to fall backward. But his 180 pounds offset her weight, causing her instead to fall on her side. Still she hung on. Jonathan's legs were hanging over the edge from the waist down. His eyes held a look of horror as he pleaded, "Pull!"

Danielle looked around for something to hold on to. Her right arm burned from the strain. Behind her she saw a crag in the rock and grabbed it with her free hand. Seeing that she was secure, Jonathan began pulling himself up. Slowly, like a lizard, he inched forward on his chest until he was able to get a knee over the ledge. Unsteadily he crawled over and embraced her.

He wanted to express his thanks for saving his life, but the thought made him uncomfortable. He wanted to tell her how sorry he was that he had persisted in the lawsuit and how deeply he cared for her. Yet, words would not come.

"Come on," he said finally, pulling her up and away from the cliff. "Let's get away from here."

Midway back to the road, Danielle pulled her hand from his and stopped. Jonathan turned and looked at her. She was standing there, arms hanging at her sides, blankly gazing at the ground. Slowly she started shaking her head back and forth, then looked up at Jonathan.

"I . . . I can't take this anymore," she said. "This hiding, this running—it's too much. I'm ready to crack."

Jonathan tried to put his arms around her, but she held him back. "*No*," she screamed. "I'm serious. I want to go back." Her shorts and blouse were dirty, and tears were running down her cheeks.

"Dani, we can't. We go back home and we're dead. Have you forgotten what happened in the apartment?"

"I know . . . I know. But we could go to the police. I know what you said before, but maybe we could be put into protective custody. Anything. My God, if they *killed* us, it couldn't be as bad as this. Please let's go back."

"Dani, we're too close—just inches away from that one solid piece of evidence we need. I just know it. I can feel it."

"How can you *know* it? You're just guessing. The only solid thing we've found was in the cruise-ship records . . . and we could have found that back home. I want to go back."

"You're wrong, Dani. We know that Armstrong and Crenshaw were anchored here only a half-mile offshore. Which means that they probably came on shore. And they weren't on the island sightseeing. You can bet your last dollar on that."

"How can you be so damn sure they came onto the island? Maybe someone just met them on the boat and then left."

Danielle was standing firm. For the first time, her faith in Jonathan had been shaken.

"Because the old man had been fishing here all day and never once saw a sign of life on board. With these temperatures, even in March, someone certainly would have gone topside to get some fresh air. There's also a beach where they could easily have come ashore."

"Even assuming they came on shore, how would you know where they went? They could have gone anyplace on this island."

"There appears to be a path that leads up from the beach. I saw it when I almost fell. They must have met somewhere close to here. Close to the top of the path. Why else come to this specific location? Most of the tourist trade is at the other end of the island. But even if I'm wrong, why not take a look? We've come all this way—thousands of miles. It would be foolish to turn around now without at least taking a look. My God, Dani, look what's at stake—our lives. This is our only chance."

"Then promise me we'll go home if we don't find what we're after."

"I promise we'll leave, but not to go home. It's too dangerous. We'll find someplace to hide, someplace far away— a place to be forgotten."

Danielle took his hand and said, "Okay. Where do we go?"

Jonathan pointed a short distance up the street. "It should be no more than two or three hundred yards from here, so let's walk the rest of the way and stay off the road. I would prefer that no one saw us right now."

Suddenly they heard an automobile growling its way up the street. It sounded not more than a quarter of a mile away. Automobiles were unusual on Cayman Brac; most travelers used bicycles or motorbikes. Instinctively Jonathan pulled Danielle back behind some foliage. While squatting behind the plants waiting for the car to pass, she managed a smile. "Do you feel as foolish as I do?"

"Yeah. Kinda like a kid playing hide and seek."

As the small vehicle sped by, Jonathan tried to catch a glimpse of its occupants, but all he could see was the rear end of a rust-colored Cortina. A moment later it was gone, and again they heard only the sound of the wind whistling in the trees.

"Come on," Jonathan urged. "Let's go take a look."

Danielle reached down to her bike, unstrapped her purse, and said, "Okay, I'm ready."

They found the pathway without much difficulty. It was a couple of feet wide, and it zigzagged treacherously down the cliff. Every couple of feet there were handholds chiseled into the limestone. At the top of the bluff, a trail led from the edge back to the roadway. It seemed seldom used, with grass covering most of the sand that marked the center of the path. Shoulder-high vegetation had grown almost across it, allowing only a narrow opening just wide enough for one person to squeeze through.

Back at the road, Jonathan looked down the desolate stretch of asphalt in either direction. Still no traffic. Between the palm trees and junglelike vegetation that bordered the other side of the street, it was impossible to see any structures or even animal life. Jonathan looked farther up the street and saw a mailbox about two hundred feet away. No other sign of life was even close. Next to the mailbox was a dirt driveway. It was barely visible and disappeared into the brush only a few feet from the blacktop.

"This way," Jonathan directed as he started across the street. Without comment Dani followed him. Carefully he made his way toward the mailbox, looking in every direction as he walked. Danielle started to say something, but he put a finger to his pursed lips.

Cautiously they continued walking until Jonathan had reached the edge of the driveway and stopped, gesturing for Danielle to do the same. In front of him was the mailbox. It was a square wooden box with an open front. It was dirty, weathered, and its sides were warped, baring the nails that held it together. On the side in faded white paint was the number 93 and the name C. THORNTON. He leaned over and looked inside. A lone spider, nestled in its white silky web, was the only occupant.

"Did you bring my microcassette recorder?" Jonathan whispered.

"It's here in my purse." Danielle pulled out the black Sony tape-recorder and handed it to him.

Jonathan held it up to his mouth and recorded the name and address on the box, as well as the location of the driveway in relation to the path down the cliff. Then he motioned to Danielle to follow him down the driveway. Sixty feet ahead, it curved to the right and disappeared. Protected by the heavy growth on either side of the driveway, the wind only toyed with the tops of the trees, leaving quietness below. Birds were chirping and the air was filled with the aroma of the bright red bougainvillea that bordered the path. It was warmer now, and Jonathan wiped the perspiration from his brow. Danielle slapped at her leg just as a mosquito was beginning its feast.

"Shh," Jonathan hissed, holding his finger to his lips. Jonathan crouched ahead of her as he neared the curve and peered over some leaves.

Then for the first time he saw something. Set back another 150 feet was a cottage. It was old, with wood siding, but appeared well kept and lived in. It was only one story, although it was larger than most of the cottages he had seen on the island. Across the front of the building was a porch, covered by an extension of the red roof. The walls were painted light cream, the trim chocolate brown. In front, the dirt driveway opened to an asphalt parking area wide enough to accommodate at least eight vehicles. Neatly parked on the asphalt were three automobiles, including the rust-colored Cortina that had passed them only minutes earlier.

Jonathan grabbed Danielle's hand and pushed his way into the heavy vegetation.

"Stay here," he said. "I'm going to get a closer look."

Danielle squatted. She was tired and resigned; if it was going to happen, it would happen.

Jonathan kissed her on the forehead and began his trek through the green underbrush. It was thick, although he could occasionally see the cottage through openings in the leaves. Like a World War II guerrilla, he crouched, pushing aside the vegetation. There was probably no one in the house, except some old couple. And he would probably end up scaring the living hell out of them. Still, a fear spread through him and he found it difficult to breathe. Twigs were scratching his legs and arms, leaving long white lines. Mosquitoes began to bite him. It was hot and he was soaked with sweat.

Then he could hear voices through the open windows. They were indistinct, but there were people inside talking, perhaps even arguing. Jonathan pushed his way closer, taking care to minimize his noise. Now he was only fifteen feet from a window, and for the first time he heard something that excited him. It was a man's voice and it was familiar. There was no mistaking that low gravelly sound. It was the voice of Simon Crenshaw.

Jonathan dropped to his hands and knees and began to crawl until he reached a clearing. It was a stretch of grass about ten feet wide and ran right up to the wall of the house. He pulled aside some foliage and looked at the window. If he stood up, he would be looking directly inside. His heart pounded loudly in his ears. He was petrified and beyond feeling any physical discomfort. He looked in both directions. It was clear. If he was going to do it, he had to move now. *Don't think about it, just do it,* he thought. Against the wall and next to the window were some tall bushes. They would provide some cover. He looked down at his right hand; he was still holding the small black cassette recorder. Pressing the record button, he went over to the window.

With his back to the wall he nervously scanned the area, blinking away the sweat, trembling. Why did the sun have to be so damn bright? He felt exposed. The voices were clear now. He held the recorder up to the edge of the screen.

"We told you about this problem as soon as we knew about it," said the raspy voice of Simon Crenshaw. "We tried to handle it at our own end, but we've had a few bad breaks."

"I don't give a damn about your bad breaks. You've been paid enough to solve it on your own. Millions. Or need I remind you?" The other voice had a heavy Latin accent and it was angry. "This whole affair has been a fuckup since your nurse killed that doctor."

"You've got to understand. We had no idea there'd be a lawsuit over this. Everything had been carefully planned, right down to Jensen sleeping with Feinerman's surgeon. Who would have believed a nurse—the wife of a doctor—would file a malpractice suit? If Rand hadn't gotten involved, we—"

"But Rand *did* get involved," he snapped back. "And now he's about to blow Operation Spiderweb to pieces. Twenty-seven million dollars . . . years of planning . . . and you blow it all with incompetent personnel."

"You wanted it to look like an accident. Every death was to appear as an accident. Not an easy task with today's technology."

"I expected better. You came very highly recommended. A mercenary with a brain."

"I'm only as good as the tools I use. I needed a nurse and Jensen seemed the answer. She did well on the doctor, but failed with Rand—and she's paid for her incompetence."

"I know. We received your coded message. But killing Jensen doesn't take care of Rand." A hand slapped hard on a table. "And, *dammit*, Cuba has worked on this too long to have some incapable Americano fuck it up. We have twenty-seven seats in Congress, but it won't mean a damn without Armstrong in the White House. With Armstrong we control the country. Without him, we face a ten-year setback."

Jonathan sat on his heels, a stunned look on his face. Operation Spiderweb. Cuba. Armstrong was involved with Cuba. He sat unbelieving. No. This was something you read about in spy novels. But he had heard it, and the danger he and Dani were facing was real enough.

Suddenly, he heard other voices in front of the cottage. *Jesus, someone's outside.* The voices got closer. *God, no. Please, no.* Instinctively Jonathan pushed away from the wall and darted back into the vegetation, leaning over, his hands touching the ground. For a moment he glanced over his shoulder, just in time to see three dark-complected Latins round the corner. Apparently they hadn't seen him.

He had no time to waste now. He had all he needed. If only he could get back to Grand Cayman alive. Quickly he moved through the undergrowth, pushing aside limbs and leaves. He should be quieter, he knew, but all he could think of was to reach Danielle safely and run. If only they could reach their bikes without anyone seeing them. He looked back again. Still no one could be seen. Finally he reached Danielle.

"I've got it. I've got it," he whispered excitedly. "I've got the whole story. Everything." His chest heaved and he found it hard to breathe. "I know what it's all about. Armstrong. Crenshaw. Jensen. All of them. It was a master plan. They were all involved with Cuba to—"

Suddenly Danielle's face was transformed by a look of sheer terror. Her eyes widened and her mouth opened as she tried to scream out a warning.

But she was too late.

At the same moment, a severe pain exploded from the top of Jonathan's skull, radiating into his temples and eyes. His head seemed to bury itself into his shoulders. Before he could comprehend what was happening, everything whirled in front of him and the ground came up to greet his face. The light of day immediately turned into darkness. Silence followed.

# Chapter XXXII

The first thing he felt was the excruciating headache. It gripped his head like a vise, throbbing with each beat of his heart. The pain enveloped his skull. He felt a radiating pressure: it was his brain, trying to force its way out. He knew it. His eyes watered even though they were still closed.

Semiconscious, Jonathan yearned for relief. The pain was unbearable. He was aware of nothing else. If only someone would do something, give him something. Maybe if he could reach up to rub his head . . .

He attempted to bend his arm up to his neck, but it wouldn't move. He could wiggle his fingers slightly, but his arm, even his hand, was incapable of motion. Slowly he was coming to. He could even hear a noise, although it made no sense to him. He had to be lying on his arm. Maybe if he rolled off it, he could rub his head. He made an effort to twist his back, but with the same result. Now he was almost awake. Desperately he tried to raise his legs, bend his knees, twist his ankles. *Oh, Jesus . . . God. I can't move. Oh, my God, I'm paralyzed.* A flash of scenes raced through his tormented mind. Being pushed in a wheelchair, carried into cars, into beds, catheters for urination . . . *Please let me be dreaming. Oh, God, please don't let it be true. Jesus . . . please.* His eyes blinked open and he tried to focus on some light in front of him. Maybe if he screamed, someone would come and help him. He tried to take a deep breath, to expand his lungs. It was impossible. A heavy weight pressed against his chest. *Oh, God, what's happening to me?*

The sound he had heard earlier was clearer now. It was crashing, pounding the ground, and it was close. He could even feel the vibration. It sounded like water. Then he knew what it was. He had heard it before, thousands of times. It was the sound of waves crashing onto a beach. He was close to a beach. He smelled the familiar salt air of the ocean.

Again he tried moving and again was jolted by the same frustration and fears. This time, however, he could sense a sharp prickling sensation, as if his whole body were asleep. If he were paralyzed, he wouldn't feel *anything*. He knew it wasn't true. It was all a dream.

Then his eyes saw it for the first time and a new horror struck him. Now he knew what had happened and where he was.

He was in a shallow cave on a beach, its dark jagged mouth opening to a view of the sand and ocean. He had seen this view before when he had explored caves and tide pools along the eastern coast. But never from this perspective.

His chin was resting on soft sand. But his head was without a body. It sat there, like a recent decapitation, neatly placed in the center of the chamber. He had been buried in sand up to the top of his neck and apparently left to die.

In front of him a wave would rise for a moment against the darkening blue sky, then come cascading down, transforming into a frothy foam that would gracefully cruise to a stop, then slither back to sea. The water was only fifteen feet away. Above the hard wet beach, the mounds of sand reached deep into the cave, abutting the damp limestone walls. The late-afternoon shadows reached out to sea. The tide was coming in.

Jonathan twisted his head to the right, trying to inspect the walls. His view was partially obstructed by a large rock jutting out from the side of the cave. It was slightly ahead of him, with a ledge that extended about two feet above his head. Barnacles covered the rock like a cloak. The wall itself was pitted, with a sharp craggy surface. Five feet up from the smooth sand floor, the wall gradually began to change from a dark greenish brown to a light beige impregnated by bits of shell and coral. Surrounding him were strings of seaweed. Jonathan's initial fear was confirmed. The high-tide line was well above his head.

Danielle! What had happened to her? She had been with him when everything went dark. For a moment he thought of her last, terrified look. *Oh, please let her be all right.*

Outside, another thundering wave crashed onto the beach, the sound resonating inside the cave. The noise was deafening, and a sharp pain pierced his eardrums. This time the water ran even higher, up into the dry sand, where it was quickly absorbed as if by a sponge. The water wasn't more than ten feet away now.

Maybe he could dig his way out. After all, he was strong. Much stronger than most men, he reassured himself. He tried again to move his arms. They were behind him, crossed at his beltline. Why couldn't he move them? Even the heavy sand shouldn't prevent him from moving his hands and arms. Not totally. Another wave crashed ashore, then another. They seemed to be coming at intervals of about ten seconds. Jonathan closed his eyes, clenched his teeth, and pulled his right arm with every ounce of strength in his body. His head trembled with the strain, and his face grew red. Immediately a sharp pain cut into his crotch and wrist, causing him to abandon his effort. Now he knew why he was unable to move . . . and why all was hopeless. His hands had been tightly bound to his lower torso, right at the junction of his thigh and groin.

No, it couldn't be hopeless. There had to be some way out. This time he turned his head to the left, looking at the sand, the wall, anything that might help. It was all the same ominous-looking enclosure. No openings, no help, nothing. He was in a tomb.

Then he saw something that tore at his heart. It was Danielle. She was only five feet away. *Oh, God, no.* Out of the corner of his eye he saw that her head too was hideously nestled in a dish of sand. She appeared unconscious—maybe even dead—her head tilted slightly forward, her eyes closed. A trickle of blood ran down her forehead into an eyebrow.

"Dani?" he called out weakly. "Dani, honey?"

She neither answered nor moved.

The sight of Danielle, her head resting like it had just been severed, brought an anguish that was almost unbearable. He squeezed his eyes shut, forcing tears to run down his cheeks, but the image remained. "You rotten bastards," he screamed. Again he opened his eyes. She had to be alive. If she was gone, he would not want to live. He continued to strain his neck, looking, hoping for some sign of life.

Then he saw it. Only a couple of inches beneath her nose, he saw a slight movement in the sand. It was only a few grains, almost imperceptible, but they had definitely moved. He waited and saw it again, and again. *She's alive. Thank you, God. Thank you.*

This time he took in as much air as he could gather and yelled, "Danielle!" Still she did not respond. He continued to shout her name, over and over, but without success. She was unconscious. Maybe it was just as well, he thought, as the waves continued to pound near the mouth of the cave.

As Jonathan continued looking at her, he felt something cold and wet crawl up his neck. Instinctively he snapped his head forward, just in time to see the water sliding back to the opening. Small sand crabs, carried in by the sea, were burrowing into the newly saturated floor. It had been a half-hour since he had first awakened.

Now Jonathan tried calling out for help, but each time the thundering waves drowned out his weak voice. Besides, it was a weekday, it was late, and they were at the remote eastern end of Cayman Brac. The chances of a tourist, or even a resident, hearing him would be a thousand to one. Maybe more. Still, he tried.

Again the ocean flowed in and splashed onto his face. His voice was now hoarse, and the salt water burned his eyes. Time was getting short. He began thinking of the events that had dramatically altered his life over the past three months: Aaron's death; the interview with Ruth; the discovery at the FDA; the meeting with the pathologist; the encounter with Maureen Jensen; the visit with Senator Armstrong; the cassette tape; the attempt on Danielle's life; his own brush with death; the loss of Rusty and Ruth; the flight to the Caymans.

Another wave pounded his face, this time harder than before. As it receded, he heard Danielle for the first time. She was gagging and coughing. He turned and saw her face, her eyes closed, her mouth open, her tongue extended.

"Jon—" Again she coughed. "My God, what's happening?"

"Dani, honey, just listen and don't talk. When the next wave comes, I want you to hold your breath. Just until it recedes."

Just then more water surged over them and in a few seconds shrank back down to nothing. Danielle's hair was soaked. She blinked her eyes, trying to clear away the water.

"Jon. For God's sake, where are we?" she cried, gasping.

"Crenshaw apparently had us buried in this cave, hoping we'd drown before high tide. I think we're still at North East Point."

"Oh God, we're going to die," she screamed. "We're going to—"

Another wave flowed over them, completely covering their heads. Danielle began coughing as the water departed.

"Dani, you've got to *listen* to me. No more talking. Just hold your breath every time the wave comes in. However long it takes, just hold it. You can do it. You've got to." He stopped abruptly as another wave washed in.

"I can get loose from this binding, but it's going to take some time. You've *got* to keep holding your breath until I can dig myself out." Jonathan had little hope of getting out, but he wanted to give Danielle some encouragement. "Can you do it?"

"All . . . all right. I'll try."

"Good girl. Are you okay?"

Danielle nodded slightly, just before they were hit by another wave. As it departed, they both saw only a faint light through the mouth of the cave. Night was falling fast and with it all hope of being found.

For the next hour they somehow managed to survive. With each minute, with each successive wave, it became more difficult. They were forced to hold their breaths for almost a full sixty seconds. Even when the water had fully receded, it still covered their mouths.

Still another surge of water crashed over their heads. The sea seemed to cover them for an eternity. Deprived of air, they were plunged into a dizzy euphoria. Their lungs burned as if on fire.

Danielle knew she was beginning to drift away. Her strength, her consciousness, even her will to live had almost abandoned her. What good did it do to fight? All she was doing was prolonging her agony. If only she could tell Jonathan she loved him. Just one more time.

As Danielle fought the nearly overwhelming temptation to swallow the next wave, Jonathan realized his clothes had become soaked as the water had seeped into the sand around him. And if his clothes had absorbed the water, so had his bindings. He tilted his head back and sucked air through his nostrils. His nose burned from the foam and spray of the surf. Still, he inhaled deeply until his lungs felt as if they would burst. Then he fixed his mind on Simon Crenshaw and pulled. The sweaty round face, the bushy eyebrows, the dark evil eyes, the face he had grown to hate. With every ounce of his dwindling strength he pulled. The pain ripped through his wrist and groin, but he didn't care. His hand felt as if it were being pulled from his arm.

Then he felt it give. It was only a small amount of slack, but it was all he needed. The flicker of hope pumped added strength through his body. As his face again cleared the water, his hand broke free. A searing pain covered the back of his wrist where it had been stripped of skin. The sand that surrounded him had turned to a mush and he quickly untwisted his arm and thrust it up, like a weightlifter pushing a dumbbell. Just before another wave struck, his hand broke through the surface, pointing toward the roof of the cave. The warm air engulfed his hand, while the sea again buried him.

Silhouetted by the reflected moonlight, Jonathan's outstretched arm served as a beacon of hope for Danielle. It was vague, and she saw it for only a moment before she was consumed by the wall of water. But she had seen it and now fought to see it again. No, she would not die. She would not quit.

Even before his head bobbed back up through the water, Jonathan was frantically scooping up the sand like a bulldozer. But as fast as he forced it out, the sea slid it right back. It was useless. He might as well have been standing in quicksand.

Then he looked up at the jutting rock just above his head. His only hope. With one desperate swing, he threw his right hand over the ledge and grabbed it. The barnacles cut into his fingers, but still he held. He would not let go. Never. He would die like this first.

With his shoulder out of the sand, Jonathan's body

writhed. The suction from below was tremendous, and he tried pumping his legs. But still it continued to hold him down. Jonathan's forearm ached, and he grimaced from the pain. His hand was on fire as the salt water soaked the cuts. But he would not let go.

Desperately, he began to flail more violently, throwing himself back and forth. Finally the sand began to fill beneath his shoes and gradually he began to rise. Slowly he got higher and higher above the water. Now he was waist-deep in the sea. He looked back to where Danielle had been buried. It was too dark; he couldn't see her face.

"Dani?" he called out. "Hang on, honey. I'm almost out. I'm almost there, honey."

No answer. Only the voice of the angry sea.

Then with one final yank he pulled his left foot free, leaving his shoe behind. Without hesitation he threw himself toward Danielle, landing on his knees. His left hand was still strapped to his buttocks. As the water flowed back to the entrance of the cave, he could see the upper part of her face. Her nose was barely clear.

With his free hand he began digging into the sand and pushing it away. But it would take too long. He needed both hands.

"Hold on, honey," he pleaded.

He couldn't see her eyes but prayed that they were open. If she fell into unconsciousness, she would drown. With his right hand, Jonathan pulled at the rope around the top of his thigh. He was finally able to stretch it enough to twist his left hand free. Now he fell back to his knees and feverishly began digging.

Down and down he dug, until he was able to slip his arms under her shoulders. Then he pulled, every muscle in his back hardening like a rock. But she weighed a thousand pounds.

"Dani. Help me, honey," he pleaded, almost crying.

The water flowed back on top of them and then out again. Now her head was clear of the water and she began to cough.

"Pedal, honey . . . Kick. Twist. Anything."

Danielle began wiggling her body back and forth as she continued to gag. Slowly she squirmed, inch by inch, out of her watery grave. Mercilessly the waves kept pounding at them. Time after time Jonathan was knocked down, only to scramble back and grab her again. Finally, she too was free.

With her legs quivering from weakness, Danielle climbed to her feet and threw her arms around Jonathan. Silently they stood there, clutching each other tightly, not moving, not kissing. Only holding on to each other.

*They had survived.*

"I love you," she softly said in his ear. "I love you, I love you. . . . How many times I wanted to say it when I was down there, under the water." Jonathan kissed her cheek. "At one point, if I could have told you, I . . . I would willingly have died. Isn't that funny, I didn't die because I couldn't tell you I loved you."

Jonathan held her face between his hands. He could barely see her features in the dim moonlight.

"I don't know what's going to happen to us, Dani," he said. "But if two people can survive after what we've been through, it just seems that they deserve to live. Know what I mean?"

Danielle nodded.

"Let's get out of here," he said, taking her hand.

Carefully they waded through the surf, which climbed only to their knees. How ironic. They had almost drowned in water that was no deeper than a bathtub.

Jonathan reached down, pulled off his remaining shoe, and tossed it back into the cave.

At the mouth of the shallow cave, Jonathan leaned out and looked down the stretch of narrow beach. He recognized it. It was the small white beach he had seen at the base of the bluff. This gave him a feeling of confidence. The pathway had to be near. Cautiously he ventured out farther, inspecting the side of the cliff. At the top he could see only the palm trees waving back and forth in the wind.

"Come on, Dani," he said. "I think I know the way back to the road."

Fifty yards up the beach they found the steep zigzagging path. It looked treacherous, especially at night. But compared to what they had just been through it seemed no more than a climb up a long flight of stairs. Ten minutes later they were standing next to their bikes.

Danielle leaned over to pick up her bicycle, eager to begin pedaling back to the airport. It was a long ride, but with every mile she would be farther away from the nightmare.

"Just a second," Jonathan whispered. "I've got to get something. At least see if it's gone."

"What?"

"I was wondering—did you notice what happened to my recorder when I was hit from behind?"

"Well, I thought I saw it drop. . . . Oh, no. Oh, *no*. We're not going back there. Never. You've got to be *crazy*."

"I have to get it. It's our only ticket back to a normal life in Bridgeport. . . . I didn't have a chance to tell you, Dani. While I was at the cottage, I recorded the whole story. Do you understand what I'm telling you? I got everything down on tape. Armstrong's connection with Cuba, the murderers—everything."

"Cuba? You mean all that money was coming from Cuba?"

"Yes. And that's exactly why I have to go back and find it. If it's there, I have Crenshaw on tape—openly discussing the killing of Aaron, the funding from Cuba. They're even bankrolling other politicians. My God, do you know what we've fallen into? Cuba is on the brink of controlling our government. And I got it all on tape. They would never *touch* us if they knew this tape would get into the right hands."

"But . . . but . . ." She wanted to argue but knew he was right. Instead she embraced him and said, "Okay, let's see if we can find it."

"No. I want you to stay here. And no argument. If I'm not back in fifteen minutes, ride back to the airport as fast as you can. If you hear a car coming, pull off the road and hide. Don't take any chances. Our plane leaves at seven-thirty A.M. and I want you on it. Then, when you get back to Grand Cayman, go directly to the police and tell them the whole story."

Danielle hugged him tight, then kissed him. It was as if she would never see him again, as if this was their final moment together.

"I love you, honey," she whispered softly, almost to herself.

"I'll be all right. Don't worry. It happened right near the bend in the driveway, only a few feet in. They'll never hear me." Firmly he cradled her chin with his right hand and pointed her face up to his. His hand was wrapped in a torn piece of his shirt, and his gaze had a look of determination. His hair ruffled in the wind. "I'll be back and that's a promise."

He turned and vanished into the darkness.

Danielle had no watch, which seemed to lengthen the minutes. What did it matter anyway? She would wait for an hour, two hours, maybe more. She had not persuaded herself to leave even if he failed to return. How could she? Maybe she could help him. She had done it before. And maybe she would rather die trying to help him than go on living. Somehow, their ordeal had created a bond beyond her comprehension. She would willingly die for him, and the thought made her warm inside.

Slowly the minutes crept by. If only she knew how long it had been. She looked down the empty dark road but could see nothing. She started pacing back and forth. *Why doesn't he come? It's been over a half-hour now. Should I go after him?*

Just as she was about to start walking, she heard something. At first she wondered if it had been the wind. No. It was too rhythmic and it seemed to get louder. It sounded like grass being crushed. That was it. Someone was walking toward her in the grass. Her heart began pounding and her breathing quickened.

*Please, God, make it be Jonathan.*

Then a face gleamed out of the darkness. The face of Jonathan Rand, smiling. He held up his hand. In it was the black microcassette tape-recorder.

# Chapter XXXIII

*Saturday, September 8, 1979*

Danielle stood before the mirror, pulling a comb through her damp, tangled hair. It looked horrible. It was frizzy, and the sheen was gone after soaking for almost two hours in the salt water.

"Are you going to call?" she yelled to Jonathan in the other room. He was sitting on the bed, addressing a brown manila envelope.

"Yes, in just a minute. I want this envelope stamped, addressed, and ready to go as soon as I hang up. There's no telling who they have around here."

Danielle drew the comb down a length of her hair until it

hit a snag. *"Dammit!"* she said, wincing. She threw down the comb. To hell with it. She should be happy she was still alive.

She wandered to the doorway, peered across the room at Jonathan, and added, "Really, Jon. The sooner he hears that tape, the sooner we can start living again."

"I know. I just want to make sure that everything is ready. The moment I hang up, I'm flying out of here to the closest post office and dropping this cassette in the box. I'm not wasting a minute."

Jonathan picked up his Hi-Standard, which had been next to him on the bed. Like a hit man ready for an execution, he pulled out the clip, checked the bullets, slammed it back in, and loaded a shell by pulling and releasing the slide.

"It's lucky we left this behind," he said while pushing on the safety. Jonathan had not wanted to stow it in his luggage as he had on the first flight to Grand Cayman. "If we had taken it along, either the airline would have confiscated it or it would have been taken by Crenshaw at North East Point. At least we still have *some* protection."

He glanced at his watch. It was 9:10 A.M. Satisfied that all was ready, he reached over and dialed the number for C. Thornton on Cayman Brac.

"Mr. Thornton?"

"Yes, this is Charles Thornton." The voice sounded polite and very British.

"Mr. Thornton, this is Jonathan Rand. May I speak with Simon Crenshaw? I believe he's a houseguest of yours."

A brief pause, then he responded, "I'm afraid you're mistaken, sir. There is no one by that name here."

"I know he's there. Just tell him that Mr. Rand enjoyed his swim and would like to talk to him about Project Spiderweb." For the first time Jonathan was dealing from a position of strength, and he was beginning to enjoy it.

An even longer pause followed.

"Hello, Mr. Rand," came the gruff reply. "You are in the Caymans. How pleasant! You must come and join us if you have a chance."

"I really hate to beg off, but I think this can be disposed of over the phone. Anyway, the conditions at Cayman Brac seem to disagree with my health."

"Well, I'm sure you can be persuaded. As a matter of fact,

I would bet before the day's over you will be sitting right here in front of me."

Jonathan picked up his gun as if he were about to use it. His hatred of Crenshaw flushed his face, and he imagined firing several rounds point-blank into his chest. "I'll tell you what, Crenshaw. Why don't you listen to something, then think of who I may be talking to later today." The threat gave him pleasure.

"I doubt that you'll have the time to be talking to—"

Jonathan clicked on the small recorder and held it to the phone. As the miniature wheels of the cassette slowly turned, there was silence at the other end of the line. Only the vague whine of the small motor and the fuzzy but clear voices from the tape could be heard. Jonathan grinned as the incriminating dialogue continued to unravel. Finally it was over and he snapped it off.

"Before you open your offensive mouth again, I want to tell you something," Jonathan barked. "A duplicate of this tape has already been mailed to a certain bank in the United States." A lie, but it might buy him the time to reach the post office. "Three days ago, at the same bank, a trust was set up in which I deposited a copy of Armstrong's medical chart, a frayed book of matches from the Turtle Shell Inn—which I'm sure has your fingerprints all over it—a cassette tape that was recorded by Aaron Feinerman relating what he learned in a hypnotherapy session with the senator, and two affidavits from myself and my girl about everything we have learned up to the present. . . . Oh, and a certified copy of the passenger list from the SS *Barbados* showing you and Maureen Jensen with adjoining staterooms a few days before the death of Aaron Feinerman. In the event of my death or the death of Danielle Brennan, or thirty days after my last communication with the bank, all the contents of that trust—everything, including the tape you just heard—will be mailed to the CIA, FBI, Justice Department, and the three major newspapers in Washington, D.C., New York, and Los Angeles. I would thus suggest that you *immediately* call off your thugs. And I mean *immediately*. If there is one more attempt on our lives, I will make a call to that bank and your game will be blown wide open."

"I doubt you're that much of a fool, Mr. Rand. Assuming you were telling the truth, there'd be no further reason to keep you alive."

"Try me," Jonathan snapped. "I get rather foolish when someone tries to kill me. And I get especially irrational when the same thing happens to my girl."

"Look," he said in a patronizing tone, "don't get all uptight. No one will be trying to kill you—or your girl. I think the best thing for you and I to do would be to sit down and talk this out."

Jonathan had not given thought to them meeting face to face, but the idea did not sit well with him. "I'm quite sure that anything we have to say to each other can be taken care of over the phone."

"Well, I have a proposal to make to you, one that would be in the best interests of all concerned. But it *cannot* be discussed over the phone. It's too delicate. I'm sure a sophisticated lawyer like yourself can understand that. Phones have too many ears."

"Your point is well taken," he replied, recalling the phone tap at his apartment. "But you've given me no reason to trust you, and the less I see of you the better I like it. Besides, any proposals you wish to make would have to come straight from Armstrong."

"Still hung up on that, are you. . . . Very well, that's no problem. Senator Armstrong flew in with me yesterday and is staying on a local yacht. If you're agreeable, we could meet there."

"I don't know."

"What in the hell are you worrying about? You're holding all the cards," Crenshaw growled.

Jonathan pondered the alternatives. There were too many loose ends and it made him uneasy. Could Armstrong be allowed to continue in office? His and Dani's safety was important, but could it be put over that of their country? And there was also the problem of Crenshaw—there would be no sleep, no relaxation, until Jonathan knew what he was up to. Too much was at stake for Crenshaw just to ignore the threat of disclosure.

Jonathan watched Danielle brushing her hair. Could he expose her to any more danger? Maybe it would be a greater risk *not* to listen to Crenshaw's offer.

"All right, but this meeting will be on *my* terms, not yours. We'll meet on your boat. However, it'll be just the four of us. You, Armstrong, myself, and my girl. No goons. The first sign of anyone else and I'll abort the meeting and go straight to the police—that's a promise. And no weapons, or the same result. And one more thing: the meeting will have to be at Grand Cayman, close to Georgetown." Jonathan hesitated, waiting for an argument.

Silence followed, then a muffled voice as if someone was talking with his hand over the phone.

"Okay," came the reply. "We'll meet you at three o'clock this afternoon . . . at Grand Cayman. But the boat will be anchored one-half mile off the Great Bluff, not near George-town. Armstrong and I are in the islands without papers. For obvious reasons, we cannot take a chance on company. That's the only place we can risk seeing you."

"Okay," said Jonathan, with some uncertainty. "What's the name of your yacht?"

"*Santiago*."

"We'll be there at three."

Jonathan hung up the receiver, popped up from the bed, stuck the Hi-Standard into the waistband of his pants under his shirt, and shot toward the door, envelope in hand. As he passed Danielle, he gave her a slap on the rear.

"See ya in ten minutes," he said without breaking stride.

"Oh, no, you don't," she said, putting on her sandals. "You're not going *anyplace* without me."

Jonathan stopped at the door and turned toward her. "But you're not even dressed. You haven't got a *stitch* on under that robe."

"You told me to dress casual, didn't you?" She looked up at him with a devilish grin.

Jonathan returned her smile and shook his head. "Look at you! Stringy hair, eyes like a road map, and still I can't keep my hands off you. You'd still look delicious after crossing the Gobi Desert." Jonathan then dropped the envelope on a chair, took her face in his hands, and kissed her softly on the lips. "All right, Lady Godiva, let's get out of here before you get me sidetracked. But you stay in the car while I'm inside."

# Chapter XXXIV

The twelve-foot skiff slapped across the choppy waters stirred up by the afternoon wind. Occasionally a spray would break over the bow and over its two occupants. The sky was blue, but in the distance to the east were some dark, ominous-looking clouds. Below the clouds was a vague hazy blanket, suggesting rain.

"Looks like we have a storm coming," Jonathan shouted, barely audible above the mosquitolike buzz of the small outboard. His eyes squinted in the wind.

Danielle, who had her back to the bow, turned to look over her shoulder. The sky seemed angry and violent. Another omen, she thought.

Feeling a chill, she reached behind her, picked up a towel, and pulled it over her shoulders. Between her legs on the floor sat a new basket purse. She had just picked it up in a small tourist shop, shortly before they had rented the skiff. It was large and deep, with flowers woven into the sides.

"You cold?"

"Just a little," she replied loudly, nodding.

"We don't have much farther. I think that's it straight ahead."

Navigating from west to east along the north side of the island, he saw a large boat anchored less than a mile away. No other vessels could be seen for miles.

In another five minutes they were idling up to the starboard side, lee of the wind, near a stairway and boarding ramp. The yacht was at least a hundred feet in length. It was stately, with classic lines. From bow to stern, everything was finished with varnished mahogany and chrome. The decks were deserted and no one could be seen through any of the windows.

"Is anybody aboard?" Jonathan yelled.

The skiff coasted to a stop against the boarding ramp and

311

Jonathan grabbed the railing. All he could hear was the gurgling of his own engine.

"Is anybody aboard?" he repeated.

Still no reply.

Jonathan killed the engine and scanned the length of the yacht, listening for any activity. All was quiet, except for the wind racing over the cabin and decks.

"Hello!" he shouted.

Again the buffeting of the wind was his reply. Jonathan glanced at his watch. It was 3:10.

"Maybe this is the wrong boat," Danielle volunteered.

"No. This is it. I saw the name on the stern: *Santiago*."

"Hello! Is anybody aboard?" This time he was louder.

"Come on," he said, tying the bow line to the railing. "Let's go up and take a look."

Danielle wrinkled her nose and said, "I don't know. Why don't we wait. I'm sure someone will be out in a minute or two. Let's give them a little more time."

"I want to get this over with. They probably can't hear us because of the wind." Jonathan stepped onto the boarding ramp and reached down to pull her up. Reluctantly she took his hand and joined him on the ramp.

"What are we going to do?" she asked.

"Go knock on some doors. Come on."

They cautiously climbed the boarding ladder. Preceding Danielle, Jonathan reached the top, stepped onto the deck, and looked in either direction down the long passageway. The boat was immaculate, the varnish and hardware gleaming as the sun peeked through patches of dark-gray clouds. To the east the sky was almost black.

Jonathan pulled Danielle aboard and headed toward the stern. Ahead of him he heard a ruffling sound. It reminded him of a sail fluttering loose in the wind. As he approached each window, he attempted to look inside, but to no avail. All the drapes were drawn.

Finally they turned the corner and were confronted with a lanai area just to the rear of the salon. Around the deck were a number of rattan chaise-longues and patio chairs covered with bright-colored cushions. Something caught Jonathan's eye; curious, he walked over to a small cocktail table. In the middle was a black ashtray containing a half-smoked cigarette.

From its flattened end a wavy line of smoke rose into the air. Next to the ashtray was a book of matches with frayed corners.

Jonathan reached over and held up the cigarette to show Danielle.

"See this?" he said. She was standing apprehensively at his side. "Crenshaw is around. I can almost smell him."

From behind came a loud voice: "Haven't you heard that it's impolite to talk about people behind their backs?"

They spun around. There, not ten feet away, was Crenshaw, with one arm folded across his chest, the other up, bent at the elbow, casually holding a burning cigarette between his thumb and index finger.

"I knew I smelled something," Jonathan snarled.

"Mr. Rand, let us dispense with the name-calling. Whether an effort to display bravado in front of your girl, or an infantile attempt to provoke me, it serves no purpose. As you'll soon find out, I'm a professional, and not easily angered. By the same token, I can *kill without emotion*. And I need little reason to do so. I would suggest we get on with our business. For if we have no business, you might well get a firsthand view of my unique talent."

"Maybe you might—"

"Please, Jon!" Danielle pleaded, tugging at his arm.

Jonathan said grudgingly, "All right. Where's Armstrong? Let's get on with this."

"Senator Armstrong is on board. But you're going to be searched before any meeting. We don't want any weapons."

Jonathan held up his arms like he was under arrest. "Go ahead and search me. I'm not carrying a thing."

Crenshaw quickly obliged, patting him down from his chest to his ankles.

"Okay. Now let's see about your girl friend." Crenshaw stepped toward Danielle, his eyes roving up and down her hourglass figure.

Jonathan grabbed Crenshaw's bicep and whirled him around. "Lay a hand on her and I'll tear you to pieces." The muscles of Jonathan's jaw tightened and his eyes glared in anger. "She's as clean as I am and you'll have to take my word for it."

Crenshaw began breathing heavily. Even the professional had his limit. "You've got quite a temper, Rand. But I'll promise you this. If she's not searched, you don't go inside.

And if we don't reach some kind of an agreement today, your life is valueless. You hear me, mister? You're *dead* . . . you *and* your girl."

Jonathan clenched his fist, fighting a near-impossible urge to throw it into Crenshaw's face. "You're not only an animal, Crenshaw, you're a fool. You're in a corner—I know it and you know it. And you're not going to blow Operation Spiderweb to satisfy your homicidal thirst."

"It would cause problems—or I wouldn't be standing here talking to you. But don't delude yourself into believing you're indispensable. No problem is insurmountable. And if forced to, I'd kill you as quickly as I'd step on an ant."

"Let him do it," Danielle interceded. "This is no time for modesty. I just want to get out of here—as fast as I can."

Danielle's offer momentarily stunned Jonathan, but he knew she was right. For a few seconds they stared at each other, communicating silently.

"All right," Jonathan said with resignation. "But make it fast."

Crenshaw dropped his cigarette onto the deck, crushed it with his shoe, then stepped in front of Danielle. His face glistened with perspiration, his beady eyes swimming up and down, inspecting, enjoying.

Crenshaw smirked as he squatted down to begin at the bottom. First, her ankles; then he inched his way up her slacks, methodically fondling the curves of her calves and thighs.

Jonathan stood still, biting his lower lip, his eyes closed.

Tears rolled down Danielle's face as Crenshaw began a caressing pat of her buttocks. Her lip quivered. He then worked his way forward to her abdomen and up to her waist. Crenshaw continued palpating her back, then moved his hands under her arms and in toward her bust. Slowly he drew his hands forward until they cupped her breasts, rolling his hands over the tops to a point where his thumbs almost touched each other.

It was at this point that Jonathan opened his eyes. Like a catapult, his hand shot out and pulled at Crenshaw, whose grin disappeared as he stumbled backward.

"That's enough," Jonathan shouted.

Crenshaw glared at Jonathan. "All right," he said, then broke into a smile.

"Are you through?" Jonathan snapped.

Crenshaw looked down at Danielle's purse on the deck. "No. Not until I've been through that purse," he said, pointing.

Danielle picked it up by the two long straps and held it open in front of her for Crenshaw to look inside. He stuck his arm in and began foraging. Finding nothing more deadly than the handle of a plastic comb, he said, "Okay. Let's go inside."

Danielle preceded Jonathan and Crenshaw into the salon. As the door closed, a crack of thunder could be heard echoing over the water.

"Sounds like we're in store for some rain," came a polished and courteous voice from across the room.

Danielle stood only a few feet inside, gawking at the silver-haired man who had just spoken. He had an engaging smile, and his eyes sparkled with friendliness. She had seen pictures of Bradley Armstrong before, hundreds of times; magazine and newspaper photos, television interviews, and even once in a bit part for a movie. But never in person.

Armstrong was seated at a finely crafted French provincial desk, hands clasped in front of him, looking up at Danielle and the two men who followed her through the door.

"Come in and sit down," he invited.

Around the room the chairs and other furnishings were artistically coordinated, showing a professional's touch. The carpeting was an eggshell-white deep pile. The overall effect was light, elegant, and expensive.

Without speaking, Danielle and Jonathan moved forward to the two chairs in front of the desk and sat down, their eyes riveted on Armstrong. Crenshaw followed and stepped off to the side.

"Don't just stand there, Simon. Why don't you get our young guests a drink?"

Jonathan looked curiously at Armstrong, then over at Crenshaw, who was walking toward a built-in bar.

"No, thank you, Senator. We'd prefer to keep this a business meeting."

"Certainly, Mr. Rand. I'm just trying to make you comfortable."

Armstrong's politeness was becoming contagious.

"Well, you've got to understand, sir, what we've been

through for the past . . . *Sir!*" Jonathan exploded. "*Fuck* this politeness shit. *You* know what we've been through and you know what I'm holding over your head. So tell me what your proposal is—straight up front. I'm in no mood for games."

Armstrong's smile faded into a scowl. A truer picture, Jonathan thought.

"Very well, Mr. Rand. I'll tell you what I have in mind."

At that moment the room brightened with a flash from outside, followed closely by a deafening roar of thunder.

"I understand that you're holding a number of incriminating documents and tapes in a bank," he continued. "And supposedly they will all be mailed to—well, let's say the authorities—in the event of your deaths. Let me suggest this: You first go to a bank in the Cayman Islands, or the Bahamas, or Bermuda, or Switzerland—any bank. Anywhere you choose. And you'll find two and a half million dollars in both of your names. You then draw it out and do whatever you want. Then, within seven days, you turn over every single original and copy of everything, in a manner that will be designated later. Upon completion of that transaction you will return to the original bank and find *another* two and a half million, which will be your final payment. That's it. Five million dollars for all your evidence. You hand over the tapes and other documents and you become instant millionaires—tax free."

Jonathan said nothing, overwhelmed by the enormous amount of money so quickly within reach. He looked over at Danielle, who had a similar look of astonishment.

Again a bright flash and roar from outside, this time accompanied by a heavy rain pelting the water and boat. From inside it sounded like someone had opened a hose onto the roof.

Finally Jonathan said, "I appreciate your generous offer, Senator. But I'm not a fool. You want to buy my only insurance. Once that's gone, we're both dead. I know it and you know it."

"You're not thinking, Mr. Rand. Once you turn over the tapes, you are no longer a threat. All you have is your own uncorroborated statements. You'd never get a prosecution against a United States senator with evidence like that, let alone a conviction. But, more important, once you've accepted the first deposit of money, you're implicated. You can't implicate us without implicating yourselves." Armstrong stared at Danielle. "And I rather doubt that you'd enjoy seeing this beautiful girl wasting away in some prison. Under these circumstances, *why* would I want to involve myself in a murder . . . two of them," he reminded. "There'd be no need."

"I don't know," Jonathan responded, shaking his head.

"Let me run through the alternative with you. Every week, every month, every year for the rest of your lives, I'll be using every resource at my disposal to get hold of those tapes and documents. Every connection will be used . . . and there will be a virtually unlimited supply of funds. There will not be a day that goes by when I won't be doing something to eliminate your threat. And every one of those days you'll be living with that thought. The two of you won't know a minute's peace. And once they're found—well, I guess I don't have to spell it out. You *have* made a number of enemies," he emphasized, looking at Crenshaw.

Jonathan glanced at Crenshaw and back at the senator. He was in a quandary and had to buy some time. This decision was too important. Too many things had to be considered. "I need to think about this," he said. "Is there someplace I can go and talk with Danielle?"

"Sure. Go through that door and down the stairs," he said, pointing. "Take any room you want. You'll have complete privacy. No one else is on board."

Jonathan took Danielle's hand and began instead to walk *up* a stairway next to the door. "Thanks anyway, Senator," he said over his shoulder. "We'll just go up to the helm. You get a better view of things from up there."

At the top of the stairs he and Danielle entered the small room and closed the door behind them. As the latch snapped shut, they felt a release of tension. For the first time, they truly felt alone and could relax somewhat. Danielle sat down on a cushioned bench seat along the back wall of the room.

"What do you think?" she asked. "It's not so easy, is it?"

Jonathan only shook his head while stepping over to the large varnished steering wheel. Casually he examined the panel of instruments and gauges in front of him. At either end was a key inserted into an ignition switch.

"I think . . . I think I'd like to start this boat and head out for some forgotten island," he said dreamily. "Just get lost someplace where nobody could find us . . . nobody."

Through the water-beaded windshield he could see the churning sea, whitecaps spraying in the gusting wind. A bolt of lightning arced against the backdrop of the dark gray sky. Thunder cracked at almost the same moment. The large yacht gracefully swayed with the swells.

Jonathan caressingly gripped one of the spoked handles of the wheel, still gazing into the distance. "There's no simple solution, Dani. There are risks in both directions. . . . Anyway, what do *you* think? You've got a stake in this too," he said, turning around to face her.

"That's a lot of money," she said. "And if we wanted to get lost, it would be much easier to do it with five million dollars." Danielle found a gold compact in her purse, opened it, and began inspecting her face and hair in the small mirror. "And maybe he *will* let us go. Anyway, he sounded pretty convincing to me." Dissatisfied with what she saw, Danielle began dabbing at her tear-stained cheeks with a powder puff. "I'll tell you this," she said, looking up at him. "I'm not too excited about the other choice."

Jonathan shook his head and smiled. "You amaze me. Over a thousand miles away from home, the world exploding into the day of reckoning outside, two men in the other room probably flipping a quarter to see who gets to kill us, and you sit there primping like you were getting ready for the senior prom." Jonathan laughed as he stepped over and sat next to her. "You give me renewed hope. All is not crazy out there after all. The world is still rotating and women are still putting on their makeup, no matter *what* happens. You're wonderful." He put his arms around her.

Danielle returned his smile. "Well, you wouldn't want them to believe that all this has upset me, would you?"

They laughed, until Jonathan's grin faded to a stare at the floor.

"Don't like my preference, do you?" she asked rhetorically.

Jonathan continued to stare. "It's not that," he said. "There's something bothering me about *either* choice. Something that's more important than even our own lives."

"You mean Armstrong becoming President, don't you?"

Jonathan nodded. "And it's more of a certainty than in any election since Roosevelt."

"So an evil man becomes President. We've had criminal politicians in office before and have managed to survive."

"It's more than having a ruthless criminal in the White House, Dani. Much more. Armstrong is a puppet for Cuba. That means Cuba pulls a string and Armstrong's right arm moves. *They* push a button and he picks up a telephone. Cuba would end up dictating all our foreign policy, not to mention domestic matters that could indirectly affect Cuba. . . . The possibilities are frightening."

"For instance?"

"For instance, return of Guantanamo Naval Base to Cuba. For instance, providing them with nuclear arms and other advanced weapon systems. For instance, giving them all our scientific and technological secrets . . . And what would happen if Cuba had an inside track on our entire intelligence system or knew our exact military strengths and weaknesses. What if Cuba knew where every one of our missiles was located and its exact capability. We would be totally vulnerable to nuclear attack. Even now he's introduced a bill to cut back on military aid in South America."

Danielle's question had triggered open the floodgates. Jonathan had been mulling over the contingencies since he had overheard the conversation back at the cottage on Cayman Brac, and now he couldn't hold himself back.

He looked at Danielle almost apologetically, then covered his eyes with his hand. "I'm sorry, Dani, but this had been eating at me. We've got to do something to stop him. We just can't let it happen. We can't." Jonathan dropped his hand into his lap, continuing to gaze out the window. "Think about it. Look what Castro did in Angola. The man is ambitious. He has troops and advisers all over the world. If he wanted to focus world opinion against the United States, he would only have to order some action or statement out of Armstrong." Again he shook his head. "They have *got* to be stopped."

Danielle threaded her hand through his arm. "I know," she said with conviction. "I want you to do what you think is right, honey. I'll stand with you all the way. Please believe that."

He stared into her eyes. "I believe you, Dani. And I think I know what I'm going to do. But, whatever happens, remember I love you. That's important to me. I haven't said it too often in the past, but I have never been more serious about anything in my life."

Danielle clutched him tightly and kissed his cheek. A fear began to engulf her. A fear that their time together was drawing to a close.

Jonathan started to get up, but she would not let go. Reluctantly he pulled her arms away from his neck.

"Come on, honey," he said. "Let's go in there and set them straight."

"Well, have you reached a decision?" Armstrong inquired as they again stepped into the salon. His face had the same glare. Crenshaw stood near him beside the desk.

"Yes, we have," Jonathan replied. This time they remained standing.

"Which way is it?"

"Neither."

Armstrong looked surprised. "What do you mean?"

"I mean we don't like the options. I mean we're going to give *you* a choice."

"Don't be funny, Rand. You won't like the way I laugh."

"Nothing funny about it. As a matter of fact, it's quite simple—we're giving you the choice of stepping down from public office within two weeks. If your public announcement has not reached the press by that time, everything gets mailed and I go straight to the newspapers, then to the FBI."

"You're bluffing," Armstrong said, standing up behind his desk. His voice was sharp and angry. "If you no longer have your evidence and I'm prosecuted, your deaths are a *certainty*."

"I know," Jonathan replied. He was dead serious and Armstrong could see it. "But I see no difference between dying over this and losing my life on Iwo Jima or on a beach in Normandy. I would willingly have given my life to defeat Hitler then, and would do the same now to defeat you."

"And your girl? Are you willing to give away *her* life, too?" Armstrong's face was red with rage.

"Women die in war, too, Senator," Danielle said.

Jonathan looked at her with pride, then stared back at Armstrong. "There *is* another choice, you know. You step down and go *your* way and we fly home and go *our* way. You forget about public office and we forget about the tapes."

"You're overlooking something, Counselor," Crenshaw

interjected. Until now he had remained in the background. "If the senator leaves Washington, Cuba has no reason to keep you alive."

"If we die," Jonathan said, "you go to prison. I rather doubt that you'll have any difficulty convincing them to forget us."

"They'll never listen to us," Crenshaw snarled. "In Cuba's eyes we are as expendable as you are. Don't be a fool." Crenshaw sounded desperate. "If you force Armstrong to retire, the two of you are dead and we're in prison. *Think*, dammit."

"Our decision has been made. And if we pay the price, you can *rot* in prison for all I care. . . . Come on. Let's get out of here, Dani." Jonathan motioned to Danielle to leave. As he continued to scowl at Crenshaw, Danielle took a couple of steps toward the aft door. Crenshaw was livid, his venomous eyes piercing through Jonathan.

Jonathan began to follow, then he heard Crenshaw shout, "*Stop!*" His deep voice boomed through the room.

Jonathan looked back over his shoulder. Crenshaw was fuming, his lower lip quivering with emotion. Jonathan's eyes slowly dropped to what he held in his left hand. It was a snub-nosed .38 revolver and it was leveled directly at Jonathan's chest.

"Now *you* are being a fool, Crenshaw. Killing me won't save Armstrong's career." Jonathan's voice was weak. The realization of imminent death flushed his face, and his head began to spin. He swallowed hard as he stared at the large bore at the mouth of the barrel. "If I die, Armstrong not only loses the presidency, he gets prosecuted for treason and murder. You stand to gain nothing." Jonathan's voice quivered as he tried to catch his breath.

Danielle turned sideways. A look of concern gripped her face, her right hand dropping inconspicuously into her purse.

Armstrong held up a calming hand. "Easy, Simon. He's right. There's no sense in killing him now. I have no desire to go to jail and I doubt that you do either."

Crenshaw and Armstrong were standing six feet apart, facing Jonathan, who was ten feet ahead of them.

"Think about what you're doing," Jonathan urged. "I die and you go to jail."

"This is what I think of your threat, Mr. Rand."

Suddenly, like an explosion, the deafening report of a gunshot rang out.

For a moment all was frozen. A small cloud of smoke settled between the threesome near the table. Danielle stood between the desk and the door, her mouth open, her eyes searching for a clue that the worst had not happened.

Jonathan momentarily stopped breathing as he waited for the pain to spread through his chest.

But it didn't come.

His mind raced wildly, searching for an answer to what was happening. Then in an instant he knew. Armstrong's face began to transform from startled shock to a grimace of twisted anguish. His eyes squinted from the pain. His teeth clenched. Reflexively he clutched at his chest. Blood began to flow through his fingers and down the backs of his hands. In another instant his legs buckled and he fell forward, his arms momentarily holding him up on the desk. With questioning eyes he stared up at Crenshaw. He tried to speak, but his mouth only moved.

"Sorry, Senator," Crenshaw answered. "But you just lost your value . . . and I had my instructions."

Armstrong's legs went limp, causing his head to drop and bounce off the desk. As his body crumpled to the floor, he struck a chair, knocking it over.

Jonathan looked down at Armstrong on the other side of the desk. Only his head was visible. His lifeless eyes stared at the ceiling. Blood trickled out of his mouth.

"So much for the value of your tapes," Crenshaw said smugly. A smile of satisfaction creased his face. "You thought you knew so much, but you only saw the tip of the iceberg. You didn't know how much of a puppet Armstrong *really* was."

"What are you talking about?" asked a bewildered Jonathan. His heart still pounded rapidly against his chest, his legs near collapse from fear. He was facing a madman.

"I'm talking about the *real* brains behind Bradley Armstrong. I'm talking about myself," he said with a note of pride.

Unnoticed, Danielle frantically fumbled through her purse, while the two men faced each other.

"Who did you think made all the decisions for Armstrong? *Him?*" he said, motioning the gun toward the body on the floor. "He was nothing more than a glamour boy with the right personality. *I* made the decisions . . . from the very beginning. Every political move, even every vote in Congress, was mine." Crenshaw's suppressed ego was now bursting free. "He was nothing more than the shell of a politician . . . no more than a lot of others. But he had something different going for him: my brains, and millions of dollars. And it won't be long before I replace him. With the amount of money at my disposal, I can put anyone with the right image into the Oval Office. I almost did it once, and I'll pull it off yet."

"That may be rather difficult from prison," Jonathan rebutted.

"I still have thirty days to get hold of your tapes and other evidence. And it won't be as difficult to get as you might believe. Not with the connections at my disposal. But even if I don't, I'll just disappear and someone else will take my place. The machinery for this has been set up for a long time. So you can see," he said, raising the gun to Jonathan's head, "there's *really* no reason to keep you alive."

The muscles of Crenshaw's forearm tightened and his finger began to squeeze the trigger. From her vantage point twelve feet away, Danielle saw the cylinder begin to rotate, aligning the next bullet to be propelled into Jonathan's brain.

Jonathan was frozen. In a moment it would be over, useless . . . unless she could do it.

Initially the thought had repelled her. She was not a violent woman, and to kill someone violated everything she believed in. Even after the terror she had experienced at Cayman Brac.

But now she saw it all in a different light. Revenge, anger, hate, even fear—every violent emotion stored inside—grabbed at her. She stared at the fat, repulsive, perspiring face in front of her. A face that smiled. Finally she broke.

As if she had practiced it a thousand times, Danielle shoved the straps from her shoulder, letting the purse drop to the floor, uncovering her right hand. Clutched tightly in her grip was Jonathan's Hi-Standard .22. Her arm swung up as she faced Crenshaw. By the time her purse hit the floor, the gun was aimed at his head.

Hearing the thud, Crenshaw glanced toward Danielle, a startled look on his face. She cracked off a shot.

Glass shattered behind Crenshaw as the first bullet missed its mark and slammed into a cabinet door. Reacting to the crash, Crenshaw stumbled backward while trying to squeeze off a shot at his surprise assailant. Losing his balance, the round went wild, hitting the ceiling.

Again the .22 cracked, Danielle's hand kicking from the recoil. This time the bullet tore into Crenshaw's neck; a ruby stream of blood fountained from the wound. Stunned, he dropped to one knee, the .38 pointing at the floor.

Danielle took a couple of steps toward Crenshaw, now crying as she continued to point the gun at him.

Still Crenshaw would not quit, as he weakly tried to point his gun at her. Again she fired at him. She was only seven feet away. This time he was struck in the mouth. Particles of skin, bone, and blood sprayed out the back of his neck as his head snapped back, causing him to collapse to the floor. His mouth immediately filled with blood, which cascaded over his quivering lips. His left hand twitched, the .38 resting loosely in his palm.

Danielle was near hysteria now as she took another step and began emptying the clip into Crenshaw's chest, her left hand steadying her right wrist, eyes closed, tears flowing, openly sobbing. Again and again she squeezed the trigger, until the bullets finally stopped. She tried to squeeze again, but the trigger would not move. So she tried it again, and again.

The sight of Danielle continuing to "fire" the empty .22 finally penetrated Jonathan's consciousness. He lurched forward, throwing his arms around her. The whole sequence had taken only seconds.

"It's over, Dani. It's over," he said, trying to calm her.

"I killed him," she screamed. "I killed him!" Her arms hung limply at her sides, her right hand barely clinging to the gun. Jonathan still held her close. "I killed him," she said again, this time only a whisper. Jonathan softly stroked her hair with his hand.

Everything was quiet now. Other than the light, persistent patter of the rain, all was still. Despite the apparent serenity, around the room was scattered mute evidence of the violence that had erupted only minutes earlier. Glass was strewn over one corner of the salon near an overturned chair. On either side of the desk was a body resting in a pool of dark red blood that soaked into the white carpeting.

Jonathan held Danielle back at arm's length. "We've got to get out of here, Dani. Are you all right?"

Danielle nodded, while staring blankly at his chest.

"Are you sure?"

"Yes, I'm fine. I just . . ." Her voice faded away.

Jonathan took the .22 from her hand and stuck it into his belt. "Come on, Dani. You've got to snap out of it," he said, gently shaking her by the shoulders. Danielle shook her head, as if clearing her mind.

"I'm fine . . . I'm okay," she said, this time more firmly. She looked up at Jonathan.

"We've got to move fast. Do you have a handkerchief in your purse?"

"Yes . . . I think I do."

"Well, take it out and start wiping off everything that we may have touched. And I mean *everything*. I'm going up to the helm."

Danielle was feverishly rubbing the arms of the two chairs they had been sitting in, when she suddenly looked down at Crenshaw. For a moment she shuddered and closed her eyes. But still she could see the hideous reminder of what she had done. The right side of his face and neck was coated with blood. His mouth was gaping, his frozen eyelids partially revealing the stare of death. She squeezed her eyes tighter, but it was of no use. For years to come she would relive the experience.

Danielle looked up with a start as she heard the two engines turn over. A few seconds later, Jonthan raced down the stairs.

"I've got an idea," he said. "Have you finished?"

"Yes," she replied, examining the remainder of the room. "I'm sure I got it all."

"Good. I cleaned everything upstairs. Do you remember when I showed you how to start the skiff?"

"Yes. What do you have in mind?"

"I'm going to send this boat back to Cuba. I've got the autopilot set for due north. It'll be there in five or six hours. Let *them* decide how they want to report this . . . this mess. Anyway, I want you to go down and start the engine on the skiff. When you get it going, give me the sign at the helm and I'll start the boat on its way. Then follow close to the ramp so I can jump on board. Understand?"

Danielle nodded.

"Oh, and be careful about what you touch. Use your handkerchief. We don't want to leave any prints."

Jonathan darted back up to the helm, while Danielle exited through the aft door and scurried to the boarding steps. As she broke into the open, the fresh, cool rain caught her by surprise, sprinkling her face and immediately saturating her clothing. Still, it felt good.

Her first effort at starting the outboard motor almost sent her into the water. After three fruitless efforts, the outboard finally started. She stepped forward and unfastened the line, then returned to her seat. She then gunned the skiff away and waved at Jonathan as she circled to come about along the starboard side of the yacht.

The engines of the big boat revved, water churning a white bubbly foam at its stern, the aft end settling deeper in the water. Slowly it moved forward, picking up speed. A wake began cresting from its bow. The pilotless yacht was on its way.

Jonathan emerged from above and raced down the stairs to the boarding platform. Like a seasoned sea captain, Danielle pulled alongside and he jumped aboard. After they exchanged positions, the skiff veered away and headed west to North Sound Harbor.

For the next ten minutes they sat quietly, huddled near the rear of the boat. The sea was calmer and the rain only a gentle sprinkle. The continuous buzz of the small outboard had a mesmerizing effect. Jonathan looked to his right at the *Santiago* getting smaller in the distance. He reached under his shirt and pulled out the .22.

"I guess this is as good a place as any," he said, tossing it overboard. "If anyone should ever find it, the barrel will be so corroded that they could never match up the bullets."

Danielle silently stared at him, crossing her arms in an effort to keep warm. Her teeth chattered. They still had a major task ahead of them. They would turn the evidence over to the authorities. But to whom? Who could be trusted? How deeply had the government been infiltrated? A lot of thought and planning would have to go into their course of action. But for now they didn't want to think about it.

"Are you all right?" Jonathan asked.

Danielle shook her head. "I don't know. I killed some-one."

Jonathan reached over and put his hand on her wet cheek. "You did it to save my life, Dani. You killed a vicious, sick animal that needed to be destroyed."

"I know, but I wish—"

"Think about it. If we hadn't put that false bottom into your purse, we'd both be dead right now. And Cuba would be putting a puppet into the White House. You're a *hero*, Dani."

"*Heroine*," she corrected, beginning to feel better. "Look, Jon. If we're going to be spending more time together, there's something I think we'd better get straight. If you're going to be taking me on these Caribbean vacations, I must insist on a little more peace and quiet."

Jonathan smiled and gently stroked her cheek with his hand. "Do me a favor," he asked. "Please call me Jonny."

*Monday, September 10, 1979*

Banner headlines across the United States:

### NATION MOURNS TRAGIC DEATH OF UNITED STATES SENATOR BRADLEY ARMSTRONG

In a prepared statement from State Department officials, it was reported today that presidential hopeful United States Senator Bradley Armstrong and his chief legislative assistant, Simon Crenshaw, were killed during a tragic explosion while vacationing on a friend's yacht some forty miles off the southern coast of Cuba. Identity of both victims was made with the use of dental charts. Diplomatic sources have disclosed that arrangements are presently being made with Cuban officials for the transfer of the remains of both bodies, which were found at the explosion site.

The President has declared today a national day of mourning and ordered all flags lowered to halfmast. The President has also . . .

## ABOUT THE AUTHORS

Terence Mix practices law in California and is a former President of the Los Angeles Trial Lawyers Association.

Victor Rosen is an MD who was medical advisor for the hit show "Quincy."

# FATAL DOSAGE

## By Gary Provost

**She claimed she was only following orders.**

Anne Capute had wanted to be a nurse since she was a little girl. But an early marriage and the arrival of a family postponed her dream until she was well into middle age. After achieving her degree as a licensed practical nurse, Anne found nursing as wonderful as she had dreamed. But then one incident turned her dream into a nightmare.

She thought she was only following orders when she injected Norma Leanues with what turned out to be a fatal dose of morphine. Before she knew what was happening, Nurse Capute found herself indicted for First Degree Murder. She was on trial for her very life.

## FATAL DOSAGE
**A true life medical/legal drama**

# Special Offer
# Buy a Bantam Book
## *for only 50¢.*

*Now you can have an up-to-date listing of Bantam's hundreds of titles plus take advantage of our unique and exciting bonus book offer. A special offer which gives you the opportunity to purchase a Bantam book for only 50¢. Here's how!*

*By ordering any five books at the regular price per order, you can also choose any other single book listed (up to a $4.95 value) for just 50¢. Some restrictions do apply, but for further details why not send for Bantam's listing of titles today!*

*Just send us your name and address and we will send you a catalog!*